DEFIANT

P. J. O'DWYER

Black Siren Books

New York

PRAISE FOR THE AUTHOR . . .

"P. J. O'Dwyer's got talent, in spades."

"P.J. O'Dwyer's writing is charged with authenticity and filled with humanity, passion, and high adventure. Hers is a fresh voice that takes you on a riveting journey of intertwining relationships, pain, and love, leaving you with a lasting picture of emotional truth and beauty."

*"*DEFIANT *. . . entertaining characters and a great story."*

"O'Dwyer's research for her subject matter is exceptional . . ."

"From the first page DEFIANT *had me hooked. Non-stop suspense and twists and turns left me baffled . . . [but] those detours are well worth the ride. This second installment of the Fallon Sisters series features a strong determined heroine struggling to overcome obstacles and dealing with personal issues, which may lead to her untimely death. I absolutely loved this story and cannot wait for book three."*

"Well Done. O'Dwyer's pacing is excellent . . ."

Novels written by P. J. O'Dwyer

THE FALLON SISTERS TRILOGY

Relentless

Defiant

Forsaken

Black Siren Books

331 West 57th Street
Suite 510
New York, NY 10019
www.blacksirenbooks.com
inquiries@blacksirenbooks.com

Printed in the United States of America

"Creede" from *Songs of Cy Warman*, second edition, published by Rand Avery Company, Boston, and McLeod & Allen Toronto.

Library of Congress Control Number: 2012921966

ISBN 978-0-9848997-4-6 (hardcover)

ISBN 978-0-9848997-5-3 (ebook)

Cover design by Duncan Long, www.duncanlong.com

Interior layout and design by Ronda Taylor, www.taylorbydesign.com

To my beautiful, intelligent daughter Katie, whose name inspired my heroine's in *Defiant*. Live your dreams, share your life, but never lose yourself.

DEDICATION

In keeping with my writer's platform of writing stories that educate as well as entertain, *Defiant*, the second book in the Fallon Sisters Trilogy, confronts the issue of domestic violence. Domestic violence and abuse can happen to anyone. It does not discriminate between women and men, rich or poor, young or old, or ethnicity.

For the victims who suffer unimaginable physical and emotional trauma at the hands of a loved one and those who dedicate their lives to offering shelter, education, and the promise of a new life, I dedicate *Defiant*.

Acknowledgments

To my brilliant editors Amy Harke-Moore, Ally Peltier, and Carolyn Haley, thank you, again, for an enjoyable and rewarding journey. Your insight has given *Defiant* that extra bit of sparkle that comes from years of experience in publishing. I'm truly blessed to have found an editing team that heightens my awareness and abilities as a wordsmith. Because of you, I never tire of the editing process.

To my talented illustrator Duncan Long, you've captured Kate beautifully, and the backdrop is breathtaking. Thank you for your creativity and humor.

Thank you, as always, to Ronda Taylor. The layout is exceptional and a testament to your talent as a graphic designer.

A special thanks to attorney Lorraine Lawrence-Whittaker for her knowledge of law and trial procedure and to retired FBI Special Agent Jackie Dalrymple who, other than my husband on the local law enforcement side, patiently answered my law enforcement questions pertaining to the FBI. As always, any and all mistakes are my own.

To the helpful folks from Creede, Colorado: Jack Morris, Owner and Operator of the Last Chance Mine; The Mineral County Sheriff's Department; Jan Jacobs, Photo Director, and Johanna Gray, Librarian, Creede Historical Society; Della Brown, Director, Creede & Mineral County Chamber of Commerce; Shane Birdsey, Owner and Operator of Ramble House Sporting Goods; and Brian Brittain, Owner and Operator of Creede's local watering hole, Tommyknocker Tavern—thank you for answering all my myriad questions on the colorful past and present-day charm of your historic, Western mining town, set in the picturesque San Juan Mountains and the headwaters of the Rio Grande.

To the "Fabulous Four"—my father, Turk Divver; his wife, Pat Moran; my brother, Joe Divver; and my favorite cousin, Danny Divver. Thank you, again, for believing in me and making this journey a continued reality. *xoxoxo*

And to all my fans who have offered wonderful reviews of *Relentless*, the first book in the Fallon Sisters Trilogy, and have waited patiently for the second installment, I thank you for your continued support.

Prologue

"P-thirty-six, Glen Burnie, I'll be out with a dark blue minivan, inoperable taillights." Trooper Jenna McGuinn clicked off the radio, leaned into the dash, and tried to read the tag number of the late-model Dodge Caravan parked thirty feet ahead of her on the shoulder of the highway. "P-thirty-six, Glen Burnie, there's rear damage . . . can't make out the plate." Grabbing the flashlight from her cruiser's side door pocket, she exited her vehicle and hustled forward to get a better look. She squinted against the glare of oncoming traffic, the rush of air hitting her back as vehicles whizzed past.

She kept her body tucked tight inside the shoulder, a ribbon of white paint separating her from the roadway. As she stood at the rear of the van, her flashlight lit the area and the twisted piece of metal no longer resembling a license plate. She groaned. There was no way to run the tag before she approached the passengers.

"Ten-four, Glen Burnie, P-thirty-six. What's your ten-twenty?"

Trooper McGuinn placed her flashlight into the metal ring of her gun belt and keyed her mike. "P-thirty-six, Glen Burnie, Interstate 97 South, mile marker 3."

"Ten-four, Glen Burnie, P-thirty-six. Standing by."

She stepped around the rear of the van and pressed her palm and all five fingers against the left rear quarter panel of the vehicle, using her fingerprints to link the van to her traffic stop. Grabbing her flashlight again, she slowly approached the driver's side door with her right hand placed on her gun. From the rear corner of the van, she glanced sideways into the cargo and back seat area, looking for any overt movement. She relaxed. In a child safety seat, the silhouette of curls bobbed while a child's chunky arms flailed in the second-row bench seat of the van.

Now parallel with the rear passenger window, she tensed at the suction-cupped sun visor in its extended position, which obscured the back seat and floor. Reaching the open driver's side window, she stood at an angle, the doorframe a buffer between herself and the driver, her eyes a constant bead on his movements.

"Good evening, may I see your driver's license and registration?"

A shot rang out. The impact of the bullet forced her backward. The jolt struck her left shoulder like a sledgehammer, stealing her breath. Tightening her grip on her service weapon, she yanked it from its holster. She needed cover in the worst way. Everything around her intensified—sounds, lights. As she staggered into the interstate, an SUV swerved, its horn a blast against her ears. No one stopped. She found her balance, turned on her heels, but her arm hung to her side, immobile, the ache now a slow burn. She stumbled past the van and kept moving until she could touch the hood of her cruiser to steady herself. She glanced back toward the van. The doors remained closed. She pushed off the hood, slid past the driver's and passenger doors, rounded the rear, and collapsed onto the gravel, her back resting up against the bumper.

The bulletproof vest, meant to save her life, was now a huge burden, tight against her chest. Struggling for breath, she keyed the mike. "P-thirty-six, Glen Burnie. I've been . . . shot . . . need . . . backup."

The dispatcher's words were like a slow drum beating in her ear. "Signal thirteen. Officer in trouble."

Leaning her back into the bumper, she pushed up with her thighs and angled her body to face the suspect's vehicle. Her eyes banked left, then right. Thankful for her cruiser's protection but frustrated she only had a partial view of the van, she cursed under her breath. Unable to ignore the constant pulse of her shoulder, she glanced down—no pain, now only a rich, dark stain of warm blood.

The crunch of gravel alerted her to the right rear of her cruiser. The shooter stood on the soft shoulder, the full weight of his body resting evenly on the soles of his leather dress shoes. Peering up from her crouched position, she could only meet his stare—dark-eyed, emotionless—her finger frozen on the trigger.

He held the child tight against his chest, the baby content and quiet, eyes wide awake, cheeks rosy from sleep, and lips glistening under the highway lights. With his right hand extended, the shooter drew down on her, the barrel pointed at her head.

Chapter One

October 25, five years later . . .

KATE REYNOLDS KEPT HER FOOT ON THE ACCELERATOR. A COLD uneasiness settled in as she drove. The heated seats of her BMW offered little in the way of warmth to rid the chill riding along her spine. Glancing down into the darkened interior of her car, she grabbed her iPhone from the cup holder, punched in her sister's cell phone number, and then frowned at the green glow of the clock in the dash—twelve forty-two in the morning. Too early to call. She'd only worry Bren. Kate shoved the phone into the front pocket of her sweatshirt and concentrated on the road. If she cleared this side of the Chesapeake Bay Bridge, he'd be less likely to catch up to her. She'd fill Bren in once she made it to the family farm.

With the island of Tilghman in her rearview mirror, she concentrated on the double-yellow centerline and putting miles behind her. The side street came up fast. She swiveled her head to check for oncoming traffic and caught her reflection in the rearview mirror. She groaned and grudgingly transferred her eyes back to the road and continued through the intersection. Unable to ignore the sensation, she ran her tongue along her swollen bottom lip; the bitter taste of blood filled her mouth.

Damn him!

This had been a horrendous week. She'd gotten her final answer from the U. S. Supreme Court—appeal denied. She had eight months to find new evidence that could turn over a death penalty conviction, and it started with her husband's desk.

The light changed from yellow to red when she approached the intersection of Routes 33 and 322. The stop allowed her another visual of her face. She pressed back a shaft of blonde hair behind her right ear and gingerly touched the purple haze of her eyelid. The swollen skin, plump like a marshmallow, made her grit her teeth. She grabbed for the steering wheel and held it tight. The light turned green, and with her eyes on the road she let off the brake, easing back up to forty.

Her muscles bunched. Unexpected bright lights filled her rearview mirror, and she sucked air through her teeth. Kate reached to adjust her mirror and flew forward from a sudden impact. Her seatbelt pressed against her chest and hips like a vise.

Oh God! He found me!

She punched the accelerator and kept up the pressure. But the lights in her rearview mirror never wavered. The force of the second collision sent her vehicle into a tailspin. The car slid off the road and struck the guardrail.

Everything stopped.

Kate's forehead rested against the cushion of the airbag. The powder that had exploded upon impact filled the air, making everything seem muzzy, her head a boulder too heavy to move. A stab of pain radiated down her back when she tried to turn her neck. She reached for the door handle, but before she could grasp it, a rush of frosty, late October air hit her body. Strong fingers dug into her shoulders. She moaned, and her eyelids fluttered open. The interior light, a halo of brightness, illuminated steel-blue eyes, glassed over and bloodshot, spearing into her.

"Where the fuck were you going, Kate?"

A blast of bourbon singed her face, and she recoiled into the opening of her sweatshirt—not good. Making her mind up tonight had weighed heavily. She and Jack had a love-hate relationship. But tonight, she hated him, and the decision was easy.

Jack dragged her from the driver's seat, fumbled with something on the interior of her driver's door before slamming it, and sprawled her across the side of the car. Her breath caught, and her heart dove straight for her stomach.

"Look at me." He grabbed her face. "You're the most ungrateful bitch. I've given you everything."

His fingers bit into her flesh, and she shook. The darkness frightened her, but his expression frightened her more. Kate pulled wildly at his hands. She brought her knee up in between his legs. He yelped. The pain along her jawline disappeared. His quick release had her staggering, desperate to find her equilibrium. Her eyes shifted. Her trembling fingers reached for the car, only to find he'd locked it. Cursing under her breath, she ran up the embankment into the woods.

Darkness enveloped her. She dodged tree stumps and vines but kept moving. Branches slapped her face, and her lungs burned as she gulped for air. She stopped to catch her breath, placed her hands on her knees, and hung there a moment. Her eyes scanned the area—nothing.

But her heart quickened. In the distance leaves and underbrush crunched and snapped, so she ran even harder, her tennis shoes sinking into the soft matting of leaves. She stumbled into a ravine and fell on her bottom, letting herself slide down the rest of the way, the ride like a pothole-laden street; her butt took most of the shock. A thin sapling whipped across her cheek. She placed her hands out front to shield her face and pushed away spindly, outstretched limbs until she hit bottom. She spied a tangle of underbrush several yards away and started toward it. Kate shoved her body deep into the entanglement of vines, ignoring their sharp points as she nestled down among the decaying leaves. Her breath mingled with the autumn air, causing bursts of white steam. Afraid he'd see it, she cupped her mouth with her hands and breathed into her palms, the warmth damp against her skin.

A single beam of light shimmered in the distance. It moved closer and then veered off in a different direction.

"Kate, I know you're here," he called out.

She squatted lower to the ground and pressed her head to her knees.

"I'm not leaving until I find you."

His voice grew closer; the white haze from his flashlight became brighter. She had to move. But her hands stung. Pushing through vines and thorns had her weighing her options. They weren't good. She yanked her sweatshirt sleeves over her hands, placed her arm in front of her face, and propelled forward.

She ran from the light, refusing to glance backward, hoping she could outrun him. Those thoughts slipped away when the woodland floor crunched behind her. A blinding force collided with her back, sending her sprawling onto the unforgiving earth. Her eyes popped wide, her mouth agape with her desperate attempt to take a breath—no air. She struggled for oxygen while clawing, trying to wriggle free. He tossed the flashlight next to them. It rolled away, but the brightness from the bulb fanned out, illuminating them while his strong hands rolled her on her back. He straddled her torso, clenched her arms above her head, and pinned them to the ground, his knee knocking into the cell phone tucked in her sweatshirt pocket.

"What's this?" With one hand pressing painfully into her wrists, he took his other and shoved it inside the pocket and took her phone.

She pulled against his grip. "Give it to me." The last word took all her breath, and she struggled against his weight.

"Like hell." He pressed the button. Light poured up. Angry lines formed around his mouth. "You call your sister?" he snapped.

He couldn't prove she'd thought about it. He didn't know the pattern to unlock the passcode.

"Not talking, huh?" He sat the phone on the ground next to her and slid his finger down until it opened to the nine-button lock screen. "You know why I'm successful at my job?" He eyed her speculatively.

She didn't answer. She looked away from him, keeping her eyes trained on his finger and her phone. He swiped the familiar pattern on her iPhone's screen.

The last bit of warmth left her. How long had he been monitoring her phone, e-mails, browsing history?

His expression stiffened at the most recent name and number she had dialed. "I hope you're not spreading rumors, Kate." He leaned into her face. His breathing had slowed. "It's none of Bren's business." For a moment, he only stared at her, his dark brows furrowed together. "Don't look at me with those damn brown eyes."

His hand flinched, and she jerked her head to the side. "Relax. I'm not going to hurt you." Gentle outstretched fingers examined her eyelid, and he winced. "I'm sorry. It won't happen again. But you make me so damn angry sometimes."

Same old Jack—blameless.

Rotting branches and twigs pressed into her back. She struggled against his weight and began to hyperventilate. He readjusted his weight, and his expression softened. He moved his hand toward her cheek and gently caressed her skin. "Kate," he whispered. "Stop fighting me. You're going to make this worse."

"Let go of me." She tried to rise up against him, but her body only made an upper thrust before coming back to rest on the hard ground.

"Not on your life, sweetheart."

"You tried to kill me."

"I tapped your car."

"You sent me into a ravine."

"You lost control."

The treetops rustled. A fleeting thread of moonlight fell across Jack's face, and his steel-blue eyes hardened—her cue to tone it down. "You hit me, Jack." Her voice cracked. Tears burned the backs of her eyes. She had loved him once—forgiven him when he'd hurt her feelings with his cutting words. But tonight he'd actually struck her, and forgiveness she was all out of.

But he'd caught her, and the only thing left was to play by his rules—for now. Because her husband, the U.S. District Attorney of Maryland, would be revealed for the lying, abusive bastard he was in time. What she needed was a plan. She might not escape him tonight, but patience and placating Jack she'd mastered long ago.

"Because you pushed me to the limit tonight, to the point I thought I'd explode." He took a deep breath and continued. "When I said I didn't want to talk about it, I meant it."

"So to shut me up you took a swing at me. Twice."

"You left me no choice." He eyed her suspiciously. "Why were you rifling through my desk?"

Snooping. But she wouldn't admit to it. "I thought I left one of my case files in your office." His weight unbearable, she shifted. "You need to get up."

He slid down onto her thighs. "The drawer was locked."

"Okay, it was locked. I'm sorry." She needed to concentrate on her find, not what she'd done. Although it wasn't what she'd been looking for, she couldn't help her curiosity. "Have you always known?"

"If I did, how would that change anything?" he snapped and lowered his head, his eyes pinning her. "It doesn't concern you." He relaxed his hold on her wrists.

Not directly, but anything he'd go to such lengths to hide from her had to be something she could use against him. Too bad for her she'd only had time to glance at the document, and what she could gather in that split second wouldn't raise suspicion or tarnish a reputation . . . unless there was more to it.

"No . . . but I know how much the Reynolds name means to you. How long have you known you're—"

"I see." The corners of his mouth tipped into a smile, and he chuckled. "Kate, how much did you read before I walked in?" He tilted her chin up slightly.

"The header . . . your father's name." She took a huge breath through her nose. "You have to get up. You're squishing me. I'm going to freak out."

He hoisted her up to a sitting position and leaned her back against the wide trunk of a nearby tree. He squatted next to her, studying her briefly. "Where were you going, hmm?"

The truth would only earn her his anger. He'd done his best to reduce her world, starting with her family. Only, to his annoyance, they accepted what little time she managed to spend with them. They'd take her in, he knew, and he was baiting her.

"Away . . . away from you." Kate's hands sat restless in her lap, her fingers picking at her nails. She hated when she did that. He could read her every movement. She stopped, quelled her hands, and placed them on the ground on either side of her. "You get angry. You yell . . . throw things. I deal with it because I know the stress you're under."

The corners of his mouth lessened.

Pity was good—surprisingly easy to accomplish. But she'd take it and go for a few bonus points because she wanted him to know what he had done to her. How he had taken something so precious. Something she feared she'd never regain. "I'm a grown woman." She laughed, the sound mocking. "I sit next to and defend criminals every day. But I fear you more." She reached out tentatively and touched a lock of his dark hair that fell across his forehead, hoping to connect with him. "I want to love you—I do love you—I'm your wife." Her hand slid down against his face, his chest, and then the ground, resigned to rest against the cool, damp leaves.

How had she allowed a man to control her? To her credit, outwardly she appeared functional. Her colleagues would never guess the Kate Reynolds they knew and respected was a complete and utter mess who could not rid herself of one psychopathic husband. But why would they? No one else knew *this* Jack.

He looked deep into her eyes. "Yes, you are."

A knot formed in her throat, and she was unable to read him. He raised his hand to her face, and she remained stoic, refusing to flinch a second time. He touched her temple, his fingers gentle, and then slid his hand down her cheek, the palm of his hand resting against her beating pulse. Gliding fingers tightened slightly around the back of her neck, and his thumb pressed into the hollow of her throat. "No one leaves me, Kate." He paused. "Unless I say so."

He said nothing for the longest time, but his thumb remained. She swallowed hard, her throat bobbing against the pressure.

"Do you understand?" he asked.

She nodded. She understood completely. The only way to escape Jack was to bring him down. And abuse was a good start. Only if she went to the police, put a restraining order out on him, he'd find a way to make her regret adding a blemish to his fine reputation. Based on his reaction tonight after finding she'd jimmied the lock on his desk, he *was* hiding something, and she'd find it, along with the other information she'd originally gone in search of. Before long, he wouldn't be so hung up on divorce. He'd be too busy salvaging more than just his marriage.

And this was the biggie. She might just get a death penalty conviction overturned, after all.

He leaned in, his broad shoulders casting her in shadow against splinters of moonlight. He kissed her forehead, and Kate shivered.

Chapter Two

Taking time to consider her state of dress hadn't entered Kate's mind at the time. Catching Jack in the act of unfaithfulness did. Oh, she pretended to believe his unexpected meeting with Senator Bob Stevens at the Chartwell, a country club the Reynoldses had been members of since it was founded in '61, was on the up-and-up. But as Jack had pointed out so earnestly, wherever Bob went, so did his flighty silicone-and-lipstick daughter, Joelle.

Kate slipped from her BMW, the biting November rain driving sideways under the halogen lights of the parking lot. It had been weeks since she'd been out in public. Black eyes and split lips didn't mix with politics, making a leave of absence necessary, and easy to arrange since Jack and her boss George Seiler were tight.

Tonight would be her first public appearance. She swallowed hard—*don't get caught.*

Sloshing through the puddles in a pair of red lace-up canvas mules, she huddled against her thin North Face waterproof Windbreaker zipped high and tight against her neck, the hood pulled over her head with only the brim of her Baltimore Ravens baseball cap showing. With her head down, she slipped inside the doors of the club, hoping to avoid detection.

She didn't resemble the U.S. Attorney's wife or the professional trial lawyer she portrayed in court. It didn't matter, she kept telling herself. All she needed was a couple minutes—tops. She'd scan the dining room, and if anyone approached her, she'd flash her membership card that she'd shoved into her coat pocket and tell them she left her raincoat in the coat check the last time she was there.

The aroma of prime rib, the club's dinner special, permeated the entryway as she walked inside. The sharp pain and the embarrassing gurgle low in her stomach reminded her that she hadn't eaten since lunch. She'd blame Jack for that. Maybe he wasn't aware of the trouble she'd gone through to prepare his required evening meal. After his phone call, she'd tossed the chicken marsala in the trash, too ticked off to eat. She paced the two floors of their Tilghman Cape Cod until she couldn't stand the suspense. She grabbed her digital camera. Adultery, if proven, could aid her in escaping Jack.

Laughter from the bar brought her out of her reverie. She needed to get her head in the game. The only way to beat Jack was to outsmart him, keep one step in front, and stay focused on what she desired above all else—ridding herself of Jack.

The crowd, typical during the heavy dinner hours, continued into the evening, an advantage she hadn't counted on as she sent up a silent prayer. It took a moment for her eyes to adjust as she moved deeper into the entry-way of dark walnut paneling and soft lights aglow from several brass wall sconces. The maître d' busy with a lively crowd, the men in jackets and ties, the women dressed the opposite of Kate all fit well within the half-century-old club that catered to the affluent of nearby Annapolis.

This place, this world of Jack's so different from the farm she grew up on in western Maryland, needled her, making her feel somehow deficient. In the five years since she'd been married to Jack, she could count on one hand the times she had accompanied him to the Chartwell.

Kate slunk toward the brick archways bordering the main dining room, giving her a partial view of the guests. Jack usually enjoyed a view of the golf course, not that he could see it now at close to nine, but he was predictable. It would be easy enough to spot him. Kate scanned the dining room, her gaze locking on a familiar set of broad shoulders in a navy-blue suit jacket. He blocked any chance of Kate getting a view of his companion—until he motioned the waiter over. Kate caught a glimpse of a petite blonde tucked in a burgundy stunner of a dress that barely kept her plastic surgeon's masterpieces veiled. Joelle's bronzed, bare arm rested across the table, her fingers interlocked possessively inside Jack's hand.

Paralyzed and cold, Kate stared at the two. She wanted desperately to charge them and make a scene. Snap a few photos and be done. But then the gregarious, silver-headed senator approached the table, along with another older gentleman who sat next to Jack. Senator Stevens took a seat next to his daughter. Kate blinked and reconsidered what was actually taking place in front of her *and* the entire dining room of respected professionals and thanked the senator for his intrusion. Was she reading too much into the scene prior to the senator's arrival? If Jack were having an affair, he surely wouldn't flaunt his transgressions publicly. It would be political suicide.

God, she must look ridiculous dressed down in jeans, eyeballing the four-some. She remembered her Ravens baseball cap, and her hand flew up. Her hair still remained tucked inside. She definitely didn't fit in there, and she was silently cursing her reasons for rushing out tonight. She turned sharply, kept her head down low, and headed in the direction of the doors to escape. Steps away, she reached for the brass handle resembling a lion's head and tamped down the anxiety thrumming through her chest. She'd be out of here in a matter of seconds.

"Kate."

She cringed when his ample hand compressed her shoulder, urging her to face him.

Kate turned slowly and smiled ruefully. "Hey. What brings you two here?"

Tall and blond, he towered above her, dressed in a gray suit and tie and frowning down at her.

Dumb question, Kate thought.

Bryan Wexler and his wife Ally were Chartwell members, had been since they relocated to the area over two years ago. Under normal circumstances, Kate would welcome their company, but not tonight. And judging by the gleam in Bryan's eyes, he'd already gathered she was up to something.

Kate glanced toward Ally, her only hope of surviving the night. Looking more childlike with her auburn hair cut in a pixie, standing next to her husband, Ally came to just below Bryan's wide shoulders. Her trendy black maternity pantsuit revealed a baby bump Kate envied.

Ally smiled sympathetically.

Besides Kate's sister who was three hours away, Ally had become Kate's only support when it came to confiding her suspicions about Jack's infidelity. Which said a lot about their friendship, considering that Bryan and Jack were best friends and had been since college.

Bryan gave Ally a sideways glance. "I've been accused of not spending quality time since coming to work for your husband."

Being Jack's press secretary couldn't be an easy job, Kate knew. "Let me apologize for my husband," she said. "But I can't say I regret your decision to move back to Maryland." Out of all Jack's acquaintances and those he considered close friends, she most enjoyed the Wexlers and their disjointed comedy relief that included their four children, aged eighteen months to six years.

Visiting their colonial home in Cape St. Claire was a mishap of adventures, ones that reminded Kate of life growing up on her family farm in Clear Spring. It didn't surprise her that Jack didn't share the same sentiments. *He* had been content being the only child growing up, which was why it still remained just the two of them in their expansive but empty Cape Cod—to her relief, considering the way things were with Jack now.

Bryan peered over her head, and his brows knitted together before he leveled his gaze on her. "Meeting Jack?"

"Not unless I plan on catching his disapproving eye for breaking the dress code." Kate moved toward the door. "I should go." She nodded to Ally. "Give me a call."

Bryan looked from one to the other. "What's up?"

"Nothing." Ally's voice came out shrill.

Kate winced.

"Come on, Kate, have dinner with us," Bryan said. "We're sitting in steerage. The powers that be around here haven't recognized the high class running through our hillbilly blood."

Kate smiled at that. Bryan was born and bred in Annapolis. Just like Jack, his family was wealthy and had been members of Chartwell since he was a small boy. He swam at their Olympic-sized pool and learned to play tennis on their professional clay courts. But he'd been removed from the selective mindset of the Chesapeake elite since relocating to North Carolina and the Blue Ridge Mountains after college, where he met and married Ally, whose family was working class, not high class.

"I can't. I only came by to pick up my raincoat in the coat check." Kate turned to push through the intricately carved mahogany door when Bryan called out to the maître d'. "Justin, Mrs. Reynolds will be dining with us tonight. Could you add another place setting to our table?"

Great. Her odds of Jack finding her shot up exponentially. And if he didn't catch her, someone would. This group was notorious for their gossip, her name whispered in condescension as the farmer's daughter who snagged Annapolis's most eligible bachelor.

Her jeans, still damp from the rain, made her legs itch. She looked as if she'd come from a rained-out baseball game, and God only knew what her hair looked like under the baseball cap. Not pretty. The rules were stringent—she'd have no choice but to lose the cap once she entered the dining room. But refusing Bryan's invitation, at this point, could bring more unwanted attention.

"Bryan, you're making Kate uncomfortable."

"Kate?" He waited for her answer.

God, she wanted to tear her hair out, but she was starving, wet . . .

"Come on. We're next to the fireplace," Bryan coaxed.

Done. And it was her damp derrière that would be facing the fireplace if she was going to be coerced into having dinner. "You've talked me into it. Lead the way."

DEFIANT   11

Ally was left staring at Kate for a frowning moment.

Kate reached out and pressed Ally's hand and whispered, "I'm good."

Before she took another step, she shed her baseball cap. Her hidden blonde mass of hair tumbled out, and she gave it a quick shake, hoping it rested smooth about her shoulders. They entered, which was a relief, through the last arch of the expansive dining room, a fair distance from her husband. Kate glanced once toward the general vicinity of Jack and his dinner companions, her group rounding to the left of the arched wall, relieved his back was toward them. As they neared their table, one of the maître d's pulled out the chair nearest the fireplace, and Kate slid down onto the welcome red paisley brocade chair, relishing the heat of the flames against her back. She slipped out of her Windbreaker and folded it twice before placing it underneath the table.

Bryan assisted Ally into her chair and took the remaining one strategically positioned across from Kate's. He surveyed the distance between him and his wife and pulled Ally's chair up next to his, kissed her cheek lovingly, and placed a possessive hand on her thigh. He then concentrated on Kate and smiled contentedly, which, if she were guessing, meant victory to Bryan because he'd badgered her to the point of surrender.

The wine steward in his burgundy jacket appeared, and Kate lifted her empty glass, needing the wine to calm her tangled nerves. Taking a sip she relaxed, and her body sank deeper into the soft cushion of her chair. To her relief, the waiter appeared to take their order, delaying Bryan's inquiry as to the "Perils of Kate."

If it had been anyone else's life, then maybe she'd find humor in it. But it wasn't, and she certainly couldn't discuss Jack with his press secretary—no matter that her inner voice told her this man, who showed his sincere feelings for his wife out in the open, could be trusted with whatever confidence she shared.

That was what gnawed at Kate the most. She wanted something so simple, a love so deep—the love of a good man, like Ally had. And she ached to possess it.

The more time passed during dinner and the wine steward filled her glass, the more Kate's nerves unfurled, and she found herself enjoying the conversation that centered around the antics of Bryan and Ally's life and their four inquisitive children. It wasn't until Bryan leveled his gaze on Kate between the entree and dessert that she realized he wanted to resume where they had left off over an hour ago in the entryway of the club.

Kate motioned the wine steward to their table for another round. Was it her sixth glass of merlot? Her wine-fogged brain couldn't keep track.

"Drunk or not, Kate, I . . ." He motioned toward Ally. "We want to know what's got you so jumpy tonight."

"I'm not jumpy." Which was true—after the wine.

"Then I won't mention the obvious."

Ally gave Bryan a sideways glance. "What are you talking about?"

Bryan nodded toward Kate. "She knows."

"Kate?" Ally looked to Kate.

Kate shrugged. "Jack's here."

"Without you?" Ally waved an exasperated hand. "I mean with you here, without you." She frowned. "You know what I mean."

"The club was on the way—"

"From work?" Bryan eyed her suspiciously.

"Yeah, work."

"You always wear jeans and a baseball cap?"

Ally tugged at Bryan's arm. "Stop it, Bryan. Jack's the one—"

Oh sweet Jesus. Kate gave Ally a look.

"I saw that." Bryan glanced at his wife and then back to Kate. "For the last time, what's going on?"

"We think Jack's having an affair with Joelle Stevens," Ally blurted out.

She'd make a prize witness for any attorney, Kate thought.

Ally's head sank, and she gave Kate a fleeting smile. "Sorry." Ally then raised a questioning brow toward Bryan. "Don't act innocent. You run interference for him all the time."

"I do not," he said. The tanned face of Bryan ripened into a red flush.

"Whatever." Ally turned to Kate and added, "He's a man who also thinks with his—"

"Okay." He gave Ally a look of reproof. "I won't confess to knowing about some torrid love affair with Joelle Stevens, but on occasion, your husband—" He gave Kate a penetrating stare. "—needs a guiding hand to keep him on the straight and narrow."

Kate leaned in. "And you believe that's all it is, a glance here and there?"

Bryan shrugged. "Sure."

"Look don't touch?" Ally said. "Bryan Wexler, what planet are you from? I've heard the gossip, even if Kate . . ." Ally's face contorted, the color draining from her cheeks. She held her breath.

Bryan pushed back from the table. "What's wrong?"

"The baby."

"Jesus." He knelt down beside her and pulled her chair from the table toward him, placing his hand on her belly.

Ally placed her hand on Bryan's head and looked at him. "I'm okay, baby. He just kicked me really hard."

"You're sure?"

"Yes." Her hand slid to his shoulder, and she squeezed it reassuringly. "I'm fine. Stop worrying."

Bryan kissed her lips hard. "You scared the hell out of me." He connected with Kate, his expression grim. "I should have never let her talk me into another child. Every one of these pregnancies gives me more gray hair." He turned to Ally. "Worrying about you."

Ally's lips quirked, and she nodded toward her husband. "He can be overly dramatic."

"He loves you," Kate whispered to Ally.

Bryan straightened Ally's chair and took his seat. "She's right. I do." He gave Ally a quick kiss and opened the menu. "Who's having dessert?"

"He's crafty, too. We weren't finished with our conversation." Ally gave Bryan a deliberate look, but he ignored her.

"I am." He nodded toward Kate. "Kate's heard enough. It's her husband we're gossiping about and the man who pays my salary." He buried his face back inside his menu.

Ally opened her mouth, but Kate shook her head in response, a definite no. Even though Bryan had asked for it, she understood why he was back-pedaling now—he owed Jack. Or was it more an issue of Jack owning Bryan to the point he felt compelled to make excuses for him?

Guilty for pitting husband against wife, Kate sank dismally lower. She tired of the conversation, her belly heavy from the five-course meal, and the chill from the rain hadn't left her. The urge to crawl into a nice warm bed was overwhelming. But alone, because Jack was the last warm body she wanted spooned beside her.

"I shouldn't have agreed to dinner. I knew this would happen."

"Trust me." He reached for Ally's hand. "We've had more-heated discussions than this." He smiled adoringly at his wife of eight years and then reengaged Kate. "I'll talk to Jack."

"No." The desperation in her own voice shocked Kate. "I can handle Jack."

"Handle me how?"

"You were holding her hand," Kate protested when Jack leaned in from the open passenger door of her silver BMW and snapped her seatbelt in place. Her mind preoccupied with her defense, she stared blankly as he shut the door and came around to the driver's side and slid into the bucket seat beside her. She gave him a bewildered stare.

"Maybe I'm a sucker for a grief-stricken woman who just confided in me that her mother's dying of breast cancer."

"The senator's wife?"

"Of course his wife," Jack snapped.

"Oh." Kate pushed back into the heated seat of her BMW, deflated.

"Yes, oh." The planes of Jack's jaw sharpened. "I told you. There's nothing between Joelle and me." Jack placed his arm along the back of her headrest.

"Then why was she there with . . ."

"Jesus, Kate." He scrubbed his face hard. "I have no control over what Bob and Joelle do. Next time I'll deny her a seat at the table, if that makes you feel better."

He reached up, taking her by surprise, trapping a wayward wisp of her blonde hair between his fingers. "You're beautiful." He kissed her, taking the fight out of her with the heat of his firm lips. She elicited a traitorous moan when he brushed the inside of her mouth with his tongue, then pulled away.

She didn't want to feel anything but contempt for him. He was the enemy. But when he was being complimentary or loving, she found herself struggling to continue with her plan to destroy him, because along with all the bad, there had been good memories of the man she'd fallen in love with.

"Kate, I can't have you rolling around like a pouch of loose marbles every time you get a wild hair up your ass about my fidelity." His strong hand cupped her chin and brought her inches from his face. "I love you. But you're starting to piss me off. There are a lot of people who would love to put credence into the rumors circulating about my relationship with Joelle."

She wanted to laugh at his proclamation of love. That was what baffled her the most. He actually believed he knew what love was—selective memory and Jack were synonymous. And then *she* remembered Joelle and made a move to protest.

"They're not true, sweetheart." He kissed her again, fast and hard, and turned away to put his key into the ignition. "I'm asking you to stop obsessing over this and trust me."

Charming. But still an edge to his request, and it didn't go unnoticed.

Kate pushed further into the supple leather of her seat and looked away from him. Wrapping her arms around her waist, she hugged herself tight. He always had an answer for everything. Either he was telling the truth or he was well versed in deception. She'd heed the encrypted warning for now. There were consequences for pissing him off, and escape, once hard fought, was no longer an option. Yet.

CHAPTER THREE

IT GALLED KATE THAT SHE'D BEEN SUMMONED BY JACK FROM Annapolis to Baltimore on a moment's notice, leaving behind a stack of case files on her desk and subjected to the crush of rush-hour traffic. Kate forever rearranged her schedule so that Jack could showcase a marriage that, to the outside world, appeared to mirror Camelot. She took an irritated breath and entered the building, hitting the elevator button.

They were not Jack and Jackie Kennedy.

She stepped into the elevator, the doors closing in the high rise that was home to the U.S. Attorney's Office, and the profundity made her laugh.

Yes they were.

No longer amused, Kate gripped the handle of her shoulder bag, her reflection in the shiny brass doors of the elevator a scowl of contention. Not even the Christmas season could lift her sagging spirit.

Scrooge was alive and well.

The soft ping of the elevator alerted her to her floor. The slight dip as the car stopped made her stomach flip more with anxiety over having dinner at Morton's Steakhouse with the mayor and police chief of Baltimore and their wives. Her attendance, for appearance's sake, made her stomach sour.

After stepping out of the elevator, Kate made her way down the hallway and to the double wooden doors of the U.S. Attorney's Office. She smoothed down the jet-black skirt of her suit, tugged on her jacket sleeves, then, plastering a smile on her face, she opened the door.

"Kate. It's so good to see you." Janice Decker, Jack's paralegal, greeted her with a smile before an immediate frown set in. "He won't be down for at least forty-five minutes. He's up with the SAC discussing a case the FBI and the attorney's office are working on."

A reprieve—she'd take it. "I can wait."

"I'll wait with you." Janice grabbed her Baltimore Orioles canvas bag sitting on her desk and placed it on the floor, her feet prepared for her walk to the MARC Train in a pair of Nike tennis shoes she slid back under her desk.

That would not do. Kate liked Janice—in her late fifties, a thin blonde, impeccably dressed, and shouldering a responsibility far greater than baby-sitting Kate. "Janice, I'm fine." Kate glanced up at the clock. "You still have time to catch the five-fifteen train."

"I don't mind."

"I do. You're off the clock. Jack wouldn't expect you to stay. Besides, I have a few messages to check on my phone."

Janice hesitated.

Kate came around and lifted Janice's bag from the floor. "It's an order. And say hi to Emily for me."

Janice's eyes softened, a smile tugging at her lips.

Emily, Janice's granddaughter, was the theme of Janice Decker's desk. Having lost her daughter and son-in-law two years ago to a drunk driver, Janice had become Emily's guardian and cheerleader.

Kate picked up a small gilded frame of a ballerina, pretty in pink. "She's beautiful."

Janice's brown eyes, lit with pride, teared up. "That was taken last month. She's six and growing so big."

"All the more reason for you to go home." Kate put out her hand and pulled Janice to her feet and slipped the bag to her shoulder. "Let her know I was thinking about her."

Janice squeezed her hand. "I will." She grabbed her coat off the back of her chair and slid her arms into it. Hesitating, she peered over her shoulder. "I could buzz the office upstairs and let him know you're here."

Kate's chest constricted. "No." The word came out too harsh, and the heat of embarrassment, immediate, rode up her cheeks. "I mean, he's busy." She waved Janice off. "I'm fine."

Interruptions, she'd learned, only earned her Jack's wrath. If she had to endure two hours with Jack and his colleagues—and the mayor and police chief were heavy hitters—playing the dutiful wife, she didn't need to infuriate him with a suspension of thought to consider her well-being.

He'd find a way to make her regret her error in judgment for the distraction.

Her agitated fingers dug into her handbag until she came up with her iPhone and offered it up in excuse. "I have enough to keep me busy with returning e-mails."

Janice patted her arm. "It's good to see you, Kate." Janice's well-manicured nails disappeared behind the heavy wooden door as it swooshed before clicking shut.

Kate stood alone.

Alone . . .

She gripped her cell phone.

What are you wearing? Concrete shoes? Move!

Kate slipped down the hall. Jack's office greeted her, wide open and vacant. His massive desk sat to the left, a huge picture window behind it, the Baltimore skyline a jagged row of rooftops cutting into purple hues of night. To the right, a row of file cabinets drew her interest.

Skeletons didn't live in closets. She could dig for bones, and she knew just where to excavate first.

Kate dropped her handbag in one of the chairs in front of Jack's desk. She skirted a table and began ripping through the first file cabinet. Standard files, nothing to suggest a hidden impropriety. Same with the second. Her fingers damp with nervous sweat, she pulled on the third, the metal clinking resistance in her hand—locked.

Kate spun and went for his desk, skimming the papers on top for a set of keys. She checked the drawers—all easy access, full of pens, highlighters, but nothing to pique her curiosity. And no keys. With her hands on her hips, she struggled for a solution. If there was something smoldering, waiting to fan into flames, it would be in Jack's personal file cabinet.

Damn it. The key, just like every key in Jack's possession that held some dark secret she wasn't privy to, would be on his key ring. He'd have it with him. Kate's shoulders slumped. The opportunity, handed to her like an unexpected gift, dwindled.

Think, Kate.

Her gaze bounced off the matching leather black chairs and small table in front of his desk and settled on the doorway she'd come in. Her breath caught and held at the sight of the edge of his dark-blue suit jacket. Hidden behind the door, it sat on a hanger, hung over a hook of his hall tree.

Go, go, go!

Kate dodged the furniture. Trembling, she reached inside his coat pocket— nothing. She poked around in the next one and smiled with success when her fingers touched metal.

Bingo.

She pulled out his key ring. The silver Scales of Justice medallion glittered. Flipping through the ring, she picked out three small matching brass keys—three keys, three cabinets.

Kate jammed the first key in. It didn't budge. Pulling it out, she fumbled them, her stomach tightening when they slipped with a clang to the carpet. She snatched them off the floor, checked her watch, and calculated the time since entering the U.S. Attorney's Office—five for Janice, almost ten searching Jack's office.

What if Janice guessed at the meeting's duration? If Jack walked in on her now, Kate couldn't explain herself. The consequences of finding her sifting through his files a second time wouldn't stop at a black eye.

Worth the risk. She shoved the second key in and jiggled it in the lock with no luck. With a silent prayer, Kate took the last key and slid it in. Holding her breath, she turned it slowly, the metallic click and give of cylinders sending a tingle of accomplishment racing over her skin.

There were four drawers, no labels to determine what drawer would be the first logical choice. What *was* she looking for, anyway? The file from the house? Maybe he'd moved it here for safekeeping. Or was it the original file she'd been looking for when she'd gotten caught? It was a definite place to start.

She yanked on the top drawer and flipped through the manila folders, searching for a familiar white tab: John M. Reynolds, Sr. There was something about that file Jack feared. Having gleaned he'd been adopted was newsworthy only because she didn't know; Jack had never told her. But it didn't change the fact he was still John and Victoria Reynolds's son. And if he was concerned about his inheritance, he had nothing to worry about. He'd already received the Reynolds shipping fortune, after the tragic plane crash that claimed his parents years before she'd ever met him. His millions were safe and secure, procreating baby millions. But what was it about the file? Why had he become so enraged when he found her reading it?

Concentrating on the alphabetized files, she found not one out of sequence, the R's void of Reynolds. Maybe he'd renamed it? Or would it be in code? Something clever only he would recognize. She pressed a clammy palm against her forehead and moaned.

Enough, secret agent girl—stop with the drama and think.

The next drawer contained a hodgepodge of stationery, boxes of pens, business cards—a catchall. She shut the drawer and moved to number three. More files. Crammed tight together, they were difficult to look through. She examined them quickly, then a second time.

Last drawer, she opened it holding her breath. Only telephone books; she shut it with more force than she'd intended. Her spine straightened, and she poked her head up, eyes and ears alert. Only the clock's rhythmic tick reminded her to pick up the pace.

In a frenzy, she went back to the third drawer with the tightly packed files and pulled it open again. Maybe she missed it? Or maybe it was hidden? This time, she wedged her long fingers under the files, the metal bottom cool against her fingertips. She pulled her hand out and shoved it down more toward the center. She reached as far as she could go, sliding her hand side to side along the bottom, until she touched a slim file folder lying flat. She struggled to get hold of it. With the file firmly between her thumb and pointer, she tugged.

Tiny hairs along her neck spiked with recognition. The familiar block-style strokes written by Jack's hand in black marker on the tab: Trooper Jenna McGuinn.

Murdered on the interstate, one bullet lodged in her shoulder, another at point-blank range to the head.

Kate shuddered.

Five years ago, she had been Kate Fallon, fresh out of law school and the greenest of trial attorneys at the prestigious law firm of Seiler and Banks in Annapolis. Finished with one uneventful year defending clients, Kate had a bright future ahead of her, until she was awarded the case from hell and forced to navigate a judicial system against a seasoned vet—the Anne Arundel County State's Attorney.

Looking like Mr. GQ and doing his best to unnerve her with his good looks and cutting stare, he enjoyed gobbling her up for breakfast each morning.

Jack *was* that state's attorney.

And this file, or something similar, was the one she'd hoped to find.

The rough imprint of Jack's bold strokes ran along her palm on the front flap of the folder, and she stopped ruminating over what was and tried to concentrate on what she had found.

He'd jotted down notes inside the folder, names she recognized from the trial, dates—nothing unusual there.

Prosecutors were known for keeping files on cases they personally prosecuted. She'd banked on it. So the file, rather its existence, wasn't odd. Except why was this one strategically hidden? She flipped it open.

Kate's mind raced, and her fingers eagerly began flipping through papers. There were online articles about the trial he'd printed out, one on Trooper McGuinn's murder. But, oddly enough, one article was a simple embezzlement case Kate had assisted on prior to their marriage and before the McGuinn trial. There were several more printouts. One dated several months ago from a local Brazilian news agency website *Zero Hora*.

The water cooler in the hall gurgled, and Kate bobbled the file, a photo wafting to the ground. She picked it up and stood, flipping it over in her hand. It was of her. Kate blinked and glanced back toward the door with wobbly legs—no one. But it was her warning she'd been lost too long in the past. She slammed the file shut. She couldn't take it with her. He might go looking for it. Plus, when would she have an opportunity to return it?

Copies.

She glanced at the copier next to the file cabinets. God, how long had it been? Thirty minutes, possibly. She couldn't leave without it.

With agonizing slowness, the light of the copier flashed under the cover. One page at a time, she pressed them to the glass, grimacing and bobbing on the balls of her feet, willing it to move faster. With the last page, she retrieved her copies, shoved the papers back in the folder, and stuffed the file back exactly where she found it, locking the file cabinet.

Kate folded her copies in half and grabbed her handbag, jamming them deep inside. She snapped it shut. Clearing the chairs once again, she reached the hall tree. Careful to dump the keys in the correct pocket, she turned to trace her steps back to Janice's desk, and ran full force into a wall of muscle sheathed in an expensive, Blacke Label, gray-striped dress shirt.

"Whoa, Kate!" Jack's strong hands had her by the shoulders. "What are you doing?"

She couldn't catch her breath. "Your jacket," she said. "I'm sorry . . . I—it scared me . . . the way it hung. I—I thought it was a person through the frosted glass." She looked up at him. She had to look scared. She was scared. But he didn't need to know the reason. Did her story seem believable?

Jack pulled her away from him, his expression grave.

Shit!

"You're shaking." He motioned her to one of the chairs in front of his desk and took the one next to it, placing his hands on her knees. Their eyes locked, and he frowned. "From now on, if you're visiting after dark, have Janice call me when she leaves. I'll come right down or have a security guard come up."

Seriously?

Her bottom lip dropped in wonderment. She'd expected him to berate her for her foolishness. He was a true opponent. One who could change his stripes, and she could almost believe it.

Almost.

Chapter Four

THE LIBRARY BECKONED, WEIRDLY WONDERFUL, THE MOMENT
Kate pushed the glass door of the local Annapolis West Street Branch.
Books on every shelf—didn't matter if they were law books or the latest
racy novel, the diversion to immerse herself into something, anything, other
than her life, was always tempting.

But the usual affect was lost on her tonight. Books were not to be her focus.

When they had returned from dinner in Baltimore last night, she'd stayed
up until two in the morning, pretending to catch up on work in the small
office down the hall from hers and Jack's bedroom, reading the copies from
his file. The more she read, the more bribery, no longer theory, became fact.

Except the most compelling piece of evidence, the article published almost
six months ago in an obscure Brazilian news agency's website of *Zero Hora*,
had never reached U.S. law enforcement. If it had, Jack wouldn't be terrorizing her. He'd be in prison serving three to five for bribery and obstruction
of justice.

Kate clenched her briefcase and skirted several occupied library computers
until she found one empty. The cheery fluorescent lights above bounced off
the dark computer screen when she sat down. One thing she'd learned as a
defense attorney: If you want anonymity, you *do not* use your own computer.
An IP address was a fingerprint for the FBI and their computer crimes unit.

She touched a computer key, and the screen saver disappeared. With jit-
tery fingers poised above the keyboard, she glanced around, pulled the file
from her briefcase, and accessed the FBI website, specifically the Forms
page, and the FBI Tips and Public Leads form.

She pondered the first fill-in blank—first name. That would not do. She
wanted to bring Jack down. She wanted him to know it was her. But self-
satisfaction would have to wait until Jack could not retaliate.

Kate tapped away. Any box that didn't require filling in, she skipped. In the end, she'd only given her e-mail—IrishEyes@yahoo.com—new and void of any information linking her to Kathryn Fallon Reynolds.

The difficulty came in filling out the tip. Ample space, with a 3,000-word limit, she could write and still have room. But sitting in the hot seat with the bright royal-blue FBI website and the black, bold letters shouting the words "FBI Tips and Public Leads" made her sweat.

What were the three B's her law professor had taught her? Be brief, be blunt, and be gone. She began to type.

I HAVE PROOF U. S. ATTORNEY JACK REYNOLDS IS GUILTY OF BRIBING A WITNESS DURING THE TROOPER JENNA MCGUINN MURDER TRIAL HE PROSECUTED AS THE ANNE ARUNDEL COUNTY STATE'S ATTORNEY FIVE YEARS AGO.

Kate's finger hovered over the Enter key while she reread her words. So intent on her message, she almost missed the reflection of a man standing behind her in the glossy screen of the computer. Her spine stiffened and she froze in midstroke; then, with deliberate speed, she jammed her finger down and spun around, forced a smile, and tweaked six-year-old Brady Wexler's nose. "Hey, sweetheart, what brings you to *my* library?"

Brady leaned against her leg, his small hand resting comfortably on her bare knee below her skirt. "Daddy brought me for story time."

Kate glanced up into the brooding brown eyes of Bryan Wexler. He gave her a tight smile and turned back to his son. He pushed Brady toward a group of kids filing into the reading room. "Brady, I need to talk to Aunt Kate. I'll be here when you're done."

Aunt Kate, her honorary name, smarted with the tartness in Bryan's voice.

Brady smiled up with his gap-filled mouth. "See ya." He hugged his dad's leg and took off.

Bryan, dressed in jeans and a striped shirt, pulled out the chair next to Kate, his large, athletic frame dwarfing the chair when he sat down. He shot his hand out before she knew his intention and hit the Back button of her computer. The form reloaded. With her text no longer visible, Kate's shoulders relaxed slightly. But how long had he been standing behind her?

His lips thinned. "Nice try. But I'd caught the gist of it before you sent it."

Great! I have my answer.

"What the hell, Kate?" He pinned her with unsmiling eyes. "Who the hell are you? What the hell are you doing?"

His booming voice brought heads around. With embarrassment warm against her cheeks, she sent him a blazing look of rebuke. "Shh." She grabbed the file and held her chin level against his accusing gaze. "It's true," she whispered.

"He's your husband."

Among other things. She saw no need to list them. Bryan Wexler didn't see the abusive bastard she saw.

He shook his head and glared. "I never took you for the vindictive type." The bite, no longer in his voice but in his words, was maddening.

I haven't done anything, damn it.

Now she was pissed. "You can go to hell." She kept her voice low, which was difficult. Every ion in her body wanted to scream it at him. She shoved the file in his face. "It's all right here."

He reached for it, and she pulled it away. "Forget it." She stuffed the file into her briefcase on the floor and pushed back the chair to stand.

Bryan reached out and gripped her arm. "I'm processing. Give me a minute." He rubbed the back of his neck.

"You're his press secretary. Process this. Jack Reynolds is a cheat and a conniver. He's conned you and he's conned—"

He jerked her down so their heads were even. She shot him a look of surprise for manhandling her and opened her mouth.

"Shut up, Kate." He looked around, his blond eyebrows bunched in anger. "Sorry, I can't wrap my press secretary brain around this one. But you are talking about my friend, your husband, and my boss. What in God's name is wrong with you?"

His blank expression warned her that he found her accusingly out of touch with reality. Freaking crazy, even. She shivered.

He's going to tell Jack.

Kate rolled her lips in. "I'm not making this up, Bryan. I don't accuse people of bribery, especially my husband, unless I know the facts." She eyed the folder shoved haphazardly into her briefcase and plucked it out. "I hear story time is an hour." She handed it to him.

He made no move to take it, only kept his hand gripped on her arm, as if holding her there would somehow change one push of a keystroke. It wouldn't. Somewhere in cyberspace, her tip, with expedient service, was being directed to the FBI. She couldn't take it back. Nor would she, given the option.

What were the odds she'd run into Bryan? Like in an old Bogart movie, she wanted to say, "Of all the libraries in the world, he walks into mine."

"Why are you here?" she said. "You live in Cape St. Claire."

Bryan let her go and snapped up the file. "Private school in Annapolis." He flipped the file open and buried his head in it.

Kate slumped into her chair and clicked out of the FBI's site, relieved when it disappeared.

Where did this leave her? If Bryan didn't come to the same conclusion . . .

Twenty minutes later, He raised his head. "It's compelling." He tossed the file onto the table. "But bribery?"

She didn't miss the inflection in his voice. He was humoring her. He patted her on the knee. "If it will make you feel better, I'll talk to him."

"No." Kate pulled her knee away and swallowed. "You don't know this Jack Reynolds, Bryan. You tell him about this and I'm . . . I'm . . ." What was the worst Jack could do to her? That thought black and forbidding, so she focused, instead, on the face of a friend, who try as he might to deny the truth, would have to come to the same conclusion.

Kate flipped through the file, glanced around, and scooted her chair forward. "I defended the Stolzes. Jack prosecuted the case when he was Anne Arundel County State's Attorney. I knew of Jack, but did not know him prior to the trial. He was fixated on Renato Barbosa, his star witness. My clients claimed they were innocent. Claimed Barbosa was the trigger man. The only mistake they made was picking up a stranded motorist packing a gun with a penchant for violence. I believed them. Jack believed Barbosa. His testimony sealed both my clients' death penalty sentence. Barbosa said Kristie handed Jason the gun and ordered him to shoot Trooper McGuinn."

She waited for her words to sink in. The spy game was off the table. She wouldn't admit how she came by the file. Bryan didn't need to know. She'd stick to facts.

"You read the *Zero Hora* article." Kate pointed to a photo of a slick, dark-haired South American. "Six months ago Barbosa was arrested in Porto Alegre. While in custody, he admitted to receiving a payoff for his testimony in the U.S. several years ago." She cocked her head. "How many cases do you think he testified in, here in the States?"

Kate dropped back in her chair and folded her arms, waiting.

Bryan chewed on his bottom lip. He didn't like it. She could tell. Didn't want to consider that Jack was capable of such venality.

Bryan closed the file and slid it toward her. "Let me look into this."

"You promise not to tell Jack?" She twisted the hem of her skirt.

He leaned forward and placed his elbows on his knees. "What are you afraid of?"

"Nothing." She shrugged. "Everything, maybe. My clients are still sitting on death row, and I just exhausted all my appeals on the husband. His execution is set for June second. Is it fair to him—them—to ignore this when they may very well be innocent?" She hoped that last nugget of truth would make him reconsider telling Jack.

Bryan scrubbed his face hard. "Let me verify the information." He tugged at the file under her elbow.

When she refused to lift it, he leaned in. "I won't tell Jack."

The doors opened to the reading room, and small feet dashed and scurried against the carpet several feet away. Brady ran toward them, a flimsy coloring book and small pack of crayons in his hand.

"Daddy, they gave us an Arthur and D. W. coloring book!"

Bryan ruffled his son's blond hair. "That's awesome, buddy." He nodded at Kate. "Give Aunt Kate a hug and a kiss good-bye."

Brady wrapped his arms around her, and Kate now regretted the awkward position she'd put Bryan in. If Jack found out, could it cost Bryan his job? He had a family to support.

"Tell her to stay out of trouble." Bryan gave her a wink and stood, stretching his back.

He would be gone, and she'd be left with his word. But she trusted him. She just hadn't planned for it to be with her life.

He gave her a hug and let her go, nodding toward the computer. "I want to know when they contact you." There was no leeway in his voice.

She offered him the file.

"Keep it. I've got all I need right here." He pointed to his head.

Bryan was in now.

God help them both.

CHAPTER FIVE

THE SPY GAME THREATENED KATE'S SANITY. SHE COULD NOT access her e-mails from her own laptop, or her office desktop she'd glared at for most of the day. Even her intended lunch break that would have given her time to swing by the library had been gobbled up by her boss, George Seiler, and a DUI case of a prominent legislator.

Never mind, it had been two full days since she'd had access to any public computer thanks to Jack's maddening see-and-be-seen-with-wife-in-tow events.

So now, the library that usually gave her unexplained pleasure aggravated her. With all the computers in use, she staked out a grandmotherly sort who fumbled through a tutorial and had one of the librarians stapled to her side. Gambling that the woman would give up in frustration, Kate strategically paced behind several twirling racks of paperbacks, with covers of scantily clothed Englishwomen, breasts heaving, and hot, muscled to-die-for rogues, and her irritation soared.

Jack could pass for the rogue in deed and design—heavy with tight muscle, engaging steel-blue eyes when they weren't shooting daggers her way, and a silver tongue. She'd been susceptible to his charm, once. She'd married the bastard. Believed his proclamation of love after they battled each other in court over a case she now knew she should have won.

Her hand tightened on the handle of her briefcase. But the anger lost its punch when a silver-blue head moved past—her signal the computer was free. Kate rushed over as if she were in a game of musical chairs, afraid she'd find her ass on the floor. Her bottom hit the plastic chair with a thump. The computer was still up and running, so she accessed her e-mail account. She had a message. Her heartbeat bumped up a notch, and she quickly clicked in and onto the message from the FBI.

Her heart plummeted at the auto response message.

What the hell? Over forty-eight hours since she'd sent the tip—could it be possible they, too, believed IrishEyes was a crackpot? Prepared to initiate another tip, she blinked. A new message popped up, the e-mail address from a JParker.

She hit the Enter key and held her breath. One freaking line of text.

JParker: CAN WE MEET?

Her contact's credentials splayed across almost seven lines of text—impressive—but she narrowed in on what was truly important. JParker was an agent—Special Agent Jess Parker, specifically. Jess, a possible nickname for Jessica, left the he or she a mystery. Okay, but what was important was she was communicating with an agent. So they took every tip seriously. Good to know.

Answer back.

Right. She might just get a response.

IrishEyes: NOT POSSIBLE.

She hit the key and sat back waiting, chewing at her cuticles. Two minutes later, the response came.

JParker: THESE CHARGES ARE SERIOUS. IF YOU ARE A WITNESS TO A CRIME, I NEED YOUR COOPERATION.

IrishEyes: WHAT DO YOU WANT TO KNOW?

JParker: WHERE CAN WE MEET?

Persistent. Very well, meet your match.

IrishEyes: ARE YOU FAMILIAR WITH THIS CASE?

JParker: I'M FAMILIAR WITH TROOPER MCGUINN'S CASE. THERE WAS NO EVIDENCE TO SUGGEST MR. REYNOLDS BRIBED RENATO BARBOSA.

So the agent knew the star witness's name. Excellent. The FBI had done their homework. Kate pulled on her bottom lip—good point. She leaned forward and opened another tab to *Zero Hora*'s site and copy/pasted the URL of the article in Jack's file.

IrishEyes: BARBOSA ADMITTED IT. CLICK ON THE LINK: HTTP:// ZEROHORA/BARBOSA/RT

JParker: I'LL GET BACK TO YOU.

Kate made a face at the screen. *Typical fed. Dictate their timeline.*

IrishEyes: I'LL WAIT.

Kate sat, her arms crossed over her chest, her Gucci pump tapping the floor. She had read the same file in two minutes. It had been at least five since her last message, to which the arrogant Special Agent Jess Parker refused a reply.

"Hey."

Kate jumped, her head spinning around. "You scared the crap out of me."

Dressed in a gray suit, Bryan grabbed a chair from the next table, slid it over, and sat down.

Kate wrinkled her nose. "You stink. You smoke?"

"Cigars. There's a difference." He gave her a satisfied smile.

She covered her mouth and coughed. "Ally lets you smoke at home?"

He laughed. "No. But we have an understanding. Every Thursday night I get my cigar and cognac night with the boys on Main."

"Ah, that cigar bar."

"That's right. It's a few blocks down from your office."

"Why are you here, then?"

"I cut it short since Jack's working late tonight, thinking you might be here."

Her iPhone rang, and she jumped. Grabbing it from her briefcase, she checked the screen and grimaced. "Speak of the devil. I have to take it."

Bryan sat back in his chair, pulling his cell phone out, and began checking messages. The baby-blue case of his iPhone and the characters from *Scooby-Doo* printed on the back of it made her smile. She doubted he'd picked it out for himself.

"Hi." As usual Jack's call wasn't about seeing how her day had been or that he missed her. "I have one more deposition I have to go through," she said.

He wanted timetables: Where are you? How long before you'll be home? What are you making me for dinner? And it better be waiting for me when I get home! She'd never made it a habit of lying. Never had to until she'd married Jack and realized he couldn't handle the truth. So the lie she told in front of Bryan rankled.

Kate grabbed a sheet of paper and jotted down his required menu for tonight and tightened on the pen, realizing she didn't have the cut of meat he wanted grilled for dinner. "Yes, I have it." Another lie and an additional stop to the market. She checked her watch: five forty-two. "I'll see you at eight thirty." She disconnected and tossed the pen.

Bryan leaned in. "You serious? He actually dictates dinner. Right down to . . ." He slid the sheet of paper over. "What the hell is a freaking Bosc pear?"

"Their thick, brown, shiny skin and crisp flesh makes them an elegant dessert," she said with the utmost of seriousness before cracking a smile.

Bryan laughed. "He's an ass."

"Welcome to my world."

His laughter subsided, his lips forming a fine line. "What happens if you don't make his deadline?"

Kate shrugged.

"None of my business, right?" Bryan shoved the paper aside. "You hear from the feds?"

Kate relaxed and motioned to the screen. "I finally received an e-mail tonight, sent by an Agent Jess Parker. I sent the link to *Zero Hora*'s article on Barbosa. I'm waiting."

Bryan snorted. "You don't actually think he's going to respond tonight?"

The sarcasm she didn't appreciate. "You come by to give me a hard time? Tell me I'm delusional?" She eyed him.

His smirk disappeared. "No. I did some checking." He leaned in, his eyes searching hers. "You're scaring me, Kate."

"You found something."

He shook his head. "Not on Jack. No." He took a breath. "Don't know how you came by the file you found." He grinned. "Well, maybe I do. But I got to thinking. If I can disprove your theory, will you let this thing go?"

She couldn't agree to his terms. Truth? She wanted Jack to be guilty. Her clients would be exonerated. Jack would be in prison. She would be free. "How are you going to do that?" A good defense was a good offense.

He shrugged. "Let me worry about that." Determined brown eyes beaded in on her. "Will you agree?"

She could say yes. But the reality was, it wasn't just about her anymore. "What about the FBI?"

He slumped back casually in his chair. "From their initial response time, I'd say they're humoring you."

His comment prickled, and she had every intention of a rebuttal, but considering her empty Inbox, she had none to give. Instead, she'd concentrate on his question. Other than what she'd found. She didn't know where else to look. There was Jack's father's file. Based on Jack's reaction, he didn't want her reading it. But she had a pretty good idea of its contents, and it wasn't what she was looking for. She could agree not to dig. She'd let Special Agent Jess Parker dig for her. Maybe the FBI was humoring her, but they had to take every tip seriously. Right? Whoever Agent Parker was, he/she promised to get back to her. She'd keep the faith.

"I promise to let it go." She smiled sweetly.

"Why do I not feel comforted?"

"It's the best I can do."

He straightened in his chair and snapped his phone onto the clip on his belt. "I gotta go." He stood. "You be here same time tomorrow?"

Tomorrow was Friday. She had court all day and a few errands on Main Street in Annapolis, and then she would be at the library. She glanced at the computer. Seemed her contact had decided she wasn't the priority. "You afraid I might self-destruct?"

He reached in his pocket. "I almost forgot. You dropped your earring."

Kate grabbed both her ears, feeling for the sapphire studs. "I have . . ."

Bryan opened his hand. She recognized the black pearl earring, oddly out of place on the palm of his wide masculine hand. Jack had given them to her last year for Christmas, just in time for his annual New Year's Eve party. Her spirit sagged at the thought.

Only a few weeks away.

She would have liked to think he bought the set because he loved her without end. But Jack was a pragmatist. The pearls were expensive—Tahitian black pearls, to be exact. Farmed and nurtured to maturity, they could cost two hundred for an average set, unless it was of exceptional quality. Hers were exceptional. He'd shared the expense shamelessly last New Year's party. The oohs and aahs of his guests—because they were not hers, well, except for Bryan and Ally—had made him an even bigger ass in her eyes.

He'd done it. Spent ten grand to boost his already inflated ego.

Jack would recognize them anywhere.

She'd been looking for it the night . . .

Her hand shot back up to her ear. "Jack's office."

"Inside Jack's file cabinet to be precise."

Shit.

Bryan gave her a curious look. "I've known about his locked file cabinet. Most of our file cabinets hold sensitive U.S. Attorney case files, Jack's included. Never had a reason to consider he would stash a file in it from when he was the Anne Arundel County State's Attorney—until I ran into you last night." He dropped the pearl into her hand. "Okay, Nancy Drew, you need to hang up your spyglass. You're going to get caught." The laughter left his eyes, and he gave her a consoling pat on the shoulder. "Will you be here tomorrow, same time?"

"You were in his file cabinet." The words fell soft from her lips in quiet restraint. But inside she heeded his warning. Running into him the other night had saved her ass.

"Jack's not as slick as he appears." He pulled out a set of keys, his fingers gripping a small, brass, two-sided key she recognized on sight. "It's only one of his many hiding places."

Kate's mouth popped open.

A smile curled his lips, confident and amused. "Gotcha covered, Kate." He checked his watch. "Gotta go. But just so you know, I didn't find the file you got your copies from."

"It was . . ."

"Okay, I think I'll surprise Ally with a gallon of her favorite mint chocolate chip ice cream. See you tomorrow." He stood up and headed for the exit.

His wide shoulders, strong and dependable, disappeared through the double glass doors, along with the sense of security his presence brought.

She'd been so secretive for her own good. If she'd have told him on the front end where to look, then at least he'd have found the file and maybe believed it existed. All she had were copies of Internet articles and a copy of a file cover. Anyone with a vendetta could have put a file together like that and tried to make more of it than there was. And that was Bryan's mindset toward her—actually, "vindictive" was the word he'd used.

Kate swung around, prepared to exit her e-mail screen, and finally had a reason to smile. Looked like Agent Parker had read her link after all. She clicked it open.

JParker: Why didn't you tell me Barbosa's awaiting trial for assassinating a high-ranking official in Porto Alegre, Brazil?

Because you know it all, Kate wanted to type.

If she gave them the meal, they'd push away from the table, wipe their face and hands, and have done with her. She wanted to be involved.

Bread crumbs kept you hungry.

IrishEyes: An assassin. Imagine that. Makes you wonder who really killed Trooper Jenna McGuinn.

JParker: You're not amusing. Ever heard of obstruction?

Her mouth fell open with disbelief and outrage. How dare . . . !

Her fingers typed furiously.

IrishEyes: Amused? Hardly. Jason and Kristie Stolze are sitting on death row for a murder, I feel certain, they did not commit.

JParker: Very confident. Are you trained in matters of investigation?

No. Not specifically. How to answer? Before she could formulate her response, another Agent Parker e-mail popped up.

JParker: Trooper McGuinn's fingerprints were found on Jason Stolze's van.

IrishEyes: I'm not denying the Stolzes weren't pulled over by Trooper McGuinn.

JParker: Stolze's fingerprints were on the gun. Gunshot residue on his fingers and hands. Not Renato Barbosa.

IrishEyes: Barbosa could have wiped his hands down. Gunshot residue doesn't stay on your hands very long.

JParker: What about Stolze?

A stabbing pain shot through the base of her neck. Obviously he had not read the case file in its entirety. Or maybe he only searched online.

Redundancy she abhorred, along with time schedules and making Jack dinner. It was already a little after six. He'd be home by eight. No time to feed Agent Parker intelligence.

IrishEyes: YOU CAN GET ACCESS FROM THE CASE FILE. ANNE ARUNDEL CIRCUIT COURT DOCKET.

Kate typed in the number.

IrishEyes: READ IT AND GET BACK TO ME. I'LL BE ONLINE AROUND 5:30 TOMORROW EVENING. BTW, IF BARBOSA HAD A BOTTLE OF HAND SANITIZER, THE GSR, MOST LIKELY, WOULD HAVE BEEN GONE. JASON ADMITTED TO HANDLING THE GUN. IT WAS AN ORDER, AGENT PARKER. OTHERWISE BARBOSA WOULD HAVE KILLED HIS INFANT SON.

She hit Send. Maybe she had been a bit rash. She knew the acronym law enforcement used when referring to gunshot residue. Showing a knowledge of law and police procedure could eventually give up her identity.

But it was a foregone conclusion. If the FBI took her theory seriously and opened an official case on Jack, his wife, and specifically the Stolzes' defense attorney, would be interviewed.

Only she'd not admit to her third identity. IrishEyes@yahoo.com.

Chapter Six

Bleary-eyed and staring into an empty Inbox at the public library was no way to spend a Friday evening. Kate didn't need to worry about Jack. He'd made plans with his golfing buddies.

A dark flash pulled out the chair next to her and slapped a newspaper on the computer table. "We've got bigger problems than you snooping through Jack's file cabinet." Bryan scooted his chair close. His expression grim, he nodded to the day's *Washington Post*. "Jason Stolze's execution date has been moved up to March 1."

Kate's fingers, clumsy and shaking, grabbed the paper. Why hadn't she been notified? Or caught it on the news? She had been in a vacuum since she'd found Jack's file. She'd do her job by day and her spying at night, which left little time to read the paper or watch TV. She skimmed the front page, recognized the family photo of the Stolzes, and shivered with the unexpected urgency her life had taken.

"He's innocent, Bryan." She lifted her head, aware her eyes were swimming in tears. "Whether you choose to believe me or not, I need your help. It's not just crazy, vindictive Kate anymore."

He squeezed her hand, and she connected with him. "Kate, I don't know what to believe," he said, pain evident in his eyes. "Jack and I go back a long way. We've always had each other's back. Call it a guy thing. I don't know." He released her hand and rubbed the back of his head. "There's something else."

"What?"

"I overheard a phone conversation of Jack's today." He gave a wan smile. "Since I ran into you, I've shadowed your husband, trying to prove you wrong. Only I think I've managed to prove you right. I was in the file room next to Jack's office. The vent system from his office runs straight into there."

She didn't need to know the HVAC plan of the building. "You're killing me. What did you hear?"

He bent over, and she did the same. "Barbosa's in prison. Right?"

"As far as I know."

"You think they allow them phone calls from a Brazilian jail cell?"

"Why? You think it was Barbosa he was talking to?"

"The phone conversation was definitely heated. He flat out told whoever that he'd paid them, and it was the end of it."

"Anything else?"

Bryan nodded. "Jack warned him not to threaten him. He wasn't seeing another dime."

"Why would he threaten Jack now? It's been five years."

"Maybe he's looking for a defense fund. He's facing murder charges. Counsel doesn't come cheap."

"Or maybe he got wind of Jason's execution and decided to squeeze Jack for more."

It made complete sense. He'd been agitated that week she'd broken into his file drawer. Maybe this wasn't the first time he'd contacted Jack with new demands. Explained why his usual verbal tirade turned physical, even though, in the end, he'd realized she had the wrong file.

Kate frowned at Bryan, who looked like a man solidly punched in the gut. "I'm sorry."

"No. I'm sorry." His eyes hardened, and he squeezed her knee. "Don't escalate this, Kate. Let the FBI handle it."

"Then you need to stop, too."

"I will once . . ."

"Once? What does that mean?"

"If Jack paid Barbosa, it was either cash or direct funds."

"You think he had an offshore bank account?"

"I sure as hell don't think he wrote him a personal check."

Her expression must have revealed her thoughts because Bryan's face tensed.

"Don't even think about it," he said. "If there's an offshore account, I'll find it. Don't make me worry about you."

She would trust Bryan. He knew Jack—knew about his hiding places. He'd find what they needed. "Okay."

"My gut's telling me we need to march down to the FBI and lay everything out to them." He waited, his expression hopeful.

Kate shook her head. "I can't."

"There is protective custody."

"You ready to do that to your family?"

"I wasn't planning to."

Of course he wasn't. Men. Because they were bigger and stronger than women, they thought they were invincible.

"Neither am I."

He shook his head. "I'm taking the family to North Carolina over Christmas break to see Ally's parents. We leave Monday after Julia's basketball game. I'll be back before the New Year's Eve party." He smiled. "I know how you look forward to Jack's big black-tie affair."

Right.

"Seriously." His lips compressed to a fine line of concern. "Just be Kate Reynolds until I get back. No digging. We know what we're looking for. I'll handle it when I get back."

Truthfully, she was a little afraid to dig after what she and Bryan suspected. The possible existence of an offshore bank account and Jack's mysterious phone call made everything frighteningly real. She lived with the man. How would she keep up the pretense without him noticing something was amiss? And if things got out of hand before Bryan got back, she was essentially alone, except for Agent Parker. She needed to focus on behaving like a supportive wife.

"I promise."

Bryan stood to leave, and Kate grabbed his arm. "I'll contact you. He figured out my security code to my phone. I think he's been checking it periodically."

"Damn. He's that paranoid?" He shook his head. "I'll think of another way we can communicate."

"What'd you have in mind?"

"I'll figure something out when I get back."

Kate nodded toward the exit. "You better go. You've got a lot to do before your trip."

"Right." He squeezed her arm. "Remember, just be Kate. I'll be back for the party."

After Bryan had cleared the doors, she remained at the computer. Through the glass of the large windowed walls of the library, Bryan's dark SUV rounded the corner and disappeared. Kate turned to the computer screen. It was a little after seven and still no response from Agent Parker. Maybe the inattentive Agent Parker needed a reason to reengage.

IrishEyes: Jason Stolze is scheduled to be put to death March 1. Time's a-ticking . . .

So the last part was an unnecessary jab. But Agent Parker was taking her for granted.

Funny, Kate was starting to recognize the woman she had been prior to her life with Jack, and it felt wonderful to slip into that woman's skin again. Hoping for a response soon, she read the article Bryan had left. A total rehashing of the trooper's murder, the trial, and verdict had her tense when she'd reached the end. She dropped the paper in the trash can next to her and stood, her empty Inbox a reminder there was a strong possibility Agent Parker did not live and breathe the FBI. Since it was now close to seven thirty, she gathered her belongings.

She'd passed the little café in front when she came in. She was starving, and the aroma of fresh-baked muffins drew her to the counter, where there was an assortment of blueberry, cranberry, and banana nut. Kate made herself a cup of tea at the self-service area, greedily grabbed a fat banana nut muffin, paid, and sat down in the designated dining area.

She finished the muffin and covertly walked back to the computers, carrying the plastic foam cup of tea under her jacket.

She took her seat, clicked into her e-mails, and sloshed hot tea on her hands when Agent Parker's e-mail popped up in bold, announcing it was recently sent. She dried her hands on a napkin, shoved her jacket behind her, and pushed the cup to the side, hitting the Enter key.

JParker: UNLESS YOU HAVE SOMETHING SUBSTANTIAL TO ADD, MY HANDS ARE TIED.

Substantial. What about everything as a whole? There was enough preponderance of evidence to open a case as far as she was concerned. What more could she give the FBI? Bryan's serious face flashed before her, and she remembered her promise.

Sorry, Bryan.

IrishEyes: BARBOSA CONTACTED JACK REYNOLDS TODAY ASKING FOR MORE MONEY. I'M SURE BRAZILIAN JAILS WOULD HAVE A RECORD OF HIS CALL AND THE NUMBER HE DIALED.

She typed in the U.S. Attorney's number and Jack's personal cell.

IrishEyes: MAYBE YOU'LL FIND A MATCH.

She didn't need to get Bryan involved in this. The FBI could verify what she'd said by simply contacting the Brazilian prison and checking their phone records. Unless Barbosa used a personal cell phone—contraband was synonymous with prisons. Drugs and cell phones were big business. Kate sagged in her chair. If Barbosa had a cell phone, it wasn't likely sitting out in plain view.

She'd worry about that later. First the FBI had to get off their duffs and follow up the lead.

JParker: HOW DO YOU KNOW JACK REYNOLDS PRIVATE CELL PHONE?

Shit.

Simple. She wouldn't comment.

IrishEyes: WILL YOU AGREE TO SEE WHAT YOU CAN DO ABOUT AN EMER-
             GENCY STAY OF EXECUTION FOR STOLZE IF YOU CAN PROVE
             BARBOSA CONTACTED REYNOLDS?

JParker: WILL YOU AGREE TO MEET WITH ME?

The loss of her anonymity and the security to herself seemed a small price
to pay to save Jason Stolze's life. Protective custody . . . She could manage.

IrishEyes: YES.

JParker: I'LL BE IN TOUCH. AND, IRISHEYES, I WILL NEED YOUR FULL
             COOPERATION IF THESE ALLEGATIONS PROVE FACTUAL.

Agent Parker is a man.

Call it her Irish intuition, but there was something irritatingly male and
demanding about his response. And the use of her screen name, as if he
were trying to connect with her on a more personal level.

He was good. But she was on to him.

CHAPTER SEVEN

KATE SLIPPED THROUGH THE GLASS DOORS OF THE KENT MANOR Inn's banquet room and onto a veranda overlooking the hotel grounds and the Miles River, leaving the festive music behind. The cold, salty wind raced across her skin, and she shivered. It had been over a week since Agent Parker had promised to look into Jack's mysterious phone call. Maybe he had gone away for the holidays or maybe he believed her Barbosa theory was way off base. Either way, the suspense of no answer made her uneasy. She needed answers. Because next year she would not be subjecting herself to this New Year's Eve farce.

The bastard better be in jail.

She moved away from the doors. The gazebo lights in the distance twinkled, reminding her of past childhood Christmases on the farm, and she frowned. She wished she could be home with her family.

"Kate." The voice was harsh and impatient and familiar—Bryan's.

Her heart warmed, and she couldn't stop smiling. Lumped together for three nights in the library before Christmas and digging for clues into the McGuinn murder trial, she'd grown closer to Bryan and felt secure knowing she wasn't in this thing alone. She'd actually missed him.

"What?" She spun around.

"Where's Jack?" The spotlight tucked in the eve of the roof backlit him, his blond hair reminding her of an avenging angel, except more dapper in his tux.

She balled her hands into fists at her side.

"He's schmoozing Senator Bob Stevens and his daughter Joelle." Kate made a face and wrapped her arms around her bare skin, silently cursing the strapless black evening gown Jack had picked out without consulting her—never mind it fit perfectly.

Bryan took his jacket off and placed it over her shoulders. "We need to talk."

Obviously this was not about his vacation. Kate grabbed hold of his jacket and slipped her arms into the sleeves and motioned him to the corner of the veranda that rounded the expansive glass windows overlooking the mouth of the river and the bay beyond.

"You heard from your FBI agent?"

"No." She frowned. "He wouldn't help me with Stolze unless I gave him more to work with. I told him about the phone call."

Bryan's face tightened.

She grabbed his arm. "I didn't have a choice."

"I take it you didn't tell him our identities?"

"No." She gave him a curious look. "What's happened?"

"Jack was informed today by the FBI he is officially under a federal investigation for bribery and witness tampering."

Kate stared wide-eyed. There had been no clue in Jack's demeanor that he'd suffered such a blow. No anger or curtness toward her in the least. He seemed as he always seemed prior to his gala event—arrogant. Of course, arrogance could be another reaction if he still believed he was untouchable—investigation or not.

Bryan shook her arm. "Hey. Pay attention. There's more, so keep with me."

She nodded.

"I can prove he bribed Barbosa."

"You found the offshore bank account?" She straightened. "What bank?"

He gave her a stern look and shook his head. "No way, Kate. I'm leaving you out of it."

"I want to know, Bryan. I want to know what you found."

"I'm Jack's press secretary. I'll confront him. Get him to turn himself in."

That worried her. Bryan had only gotten a glimpse into her world. "It's not that simple. We should do it together."

Bryan scrubbed his hands roughly over his face. "Jesus, Kate." He grabbed her by the shoulders, his usual warm brown eyes now frantic with worry. "He doesn't have to know—"

"Know what?" Jack's voice caused them both to stiffen, and Kate had no choice but to look away from Bryan's troubled expression.

Her body swayed. If it weren't for Bryan's tight grip holding her in place, she would have slipped right through the sleeves of his jacket.

"I've been looking for you two." His steps closed in. "Aren't you cold, sweetheart?" Jack rubbed Kate's arm. "You need more than Bryan's jacket. Where's your coat?" He kept a steady bead on the two of them.

"I'm fine, Jack." She pulled away from him.

Kate removed Bryan's jacket and returned it. Stepping between them, she excused herself, then turned her back and walked away.

"Kate, where are you going?" Jack called after her.

She answered him by slamming the glass door behind her. Hidden against the wall, she slumped and took the breath she'd been holding.

Good cover-up.

She only hoped Bryan waited until another time to confront Jack about the evidence. Because he'd be pissed, and she was too tired to be Jack's punching bag tonight.

Kate had taken the scenic route to the suite. Reaching for the crystal doorknob, she pushed the door open. Leaning forward, his elbows on his knees, Jack raised his head from where he sat on the sofa, and she stopped.

"I can explain." Jack stood and took a step closer. "Kate, I'm asking you to listen to what I have to say."

Kate moved backward, her expression dubious as she negotiated in her mind whether or not to stay. "Do I want to know?"

"I think you need to know." His eyes didn't leave hers. Jack moved closer, and her hand clenched the doorknob. "Can I talk to you without you slamming the door in my face?"

Remorse from Jack made her wary. She assumed after snubbing him in front of Bryan, she had a fifty-fifty chance he'd make her pay. She'd remain repentant, hoping not to escalate the situation. What he needed now was to believe he had her support. "You shouldn't have left your party."

"This is more important." He motioned toward the sofa. "Will you come in so we can talk?"

She nodded, biting down on her bottom lip. He took his time, every step calculated, until he stood inches from her. Reaching over, he placed his hand on hers. Wrapping his arms around her, he pulled her snug and closed the door.

"I'm sorry, sweetheart, if Bryan upset you tonight." His lips moved against her ear. Pulling away he motioned to the sofa. "Let's sit down."

She walked past him and took a seat down at the end, pulling a throw pillow to her chest.

"Would you like a drink?"

"No. I want you to explain what Bryan told me."

He sat down next to her, took the pillow from her grasp, and held her hands in his. "I'm just as shocked as you are. The last thing I expected was to get a call from the FBI advising me I'm under investigation."

Kate sat, afraid to blink for fear he'd catch something in her expression that hinted she'd been the one responsible for the FBI's probe. "For what?"

"The FBI's probe centers round the Stolze trial."

Play it, Kate.

"Trooper McGuinn's murder?"

He shook his head. "I hoped we'd never have to revisit that saga in our lives. I'm sorry."

"Bryan said they're investigating you for bribery." She swallowed hard in an effort to appear concerned for him.

"It's crazy, Kate. They suspect I bribed Barbosa."

"Barbosa? Why? Wha . . . what would you have to gain?"

"Your guess is as good as mine. I know you and I had our differences at trial. You believed the Stolzes were innocent. I had an eyewitness, the murder weapon, and Stolze's fingerprints on the gun. I did my job. Why would I even need to bribe Barbosa when the evidence spoke for itself?"

She gave him one of her looks.

"Okay, I know how you felt about Jason and Kristie. You believed them." He shrugged. "You're soft, Kate."

She pushed his hands away. "I'm not soft, Jack. You didn't spend time with them. I did. They were innocent."

"Are we going to rehash this tonight?" He gave her a meaningful gaze. "We did this five years ago. I don't want to argue over what *is*."

Kate hesitated, afraid she'd overdone it. But his eyes remained trained on her and thankfully didn't turn to flint.

She gave him a conciliatory expression and put her hand on his shoulder. His muscles relaxed, and so did she. "What are you going to do?"

"Let it run its course, I guess. The FBI investigates thousands of cases every year. Most people don't even know they're being investigated. They follow it through and then close the file, if there's nothing there to substantiate the investigation." He shook his head. "It's nothing."

"Right . . . you're right . . . I know that."

His brows furrowed together, and he reached over to tilt her chin up. "Do you think I'm guilty?"

"No, of course not. Bryan just caught me . . ."

"I only wished he'd have let *me* tell you." He pulled her face close and placed his lips on her mouth, giving her a chaste kiss.

"Are you mad at him?" she asked.

"Bryan?" He smiled. "Angry as hell. I didn't want this news to ruin your evening."

Always the charmer. She resisted the urge to tell him he was a liar.

"Don't be angry with Bryan. He assumed I knew."

"I should have told you."

"It upset me at first, but you're forgiven. Right now I'm more concerned for you." She caressed his cheek. "If this goes public, it could ruin your political future."

"That's why I need your help. The FBI may want to question you."

She pulled back from him.

"It's okay, sweetheart. You were the Stolzes' attorney. They'd only want to ask you a few questions. If it should come to that, just tell them what you know, that's all."

"But I don't know anything. I admit, I believed the Stolzes were innocent, and still do. I disliked you during the trial. I never made that a secret. But that goes with the territory. Technically, we were enemies." She remained quiet.

"What's bothering you?"

"Why would they think you bribed Barbosa? If you thought Barbosa was the trigger man, you would have gone after *him*."

"Yes. I would have. But there was never any information to support he was the killer. Barbosa didn't know the Stolzes until he got into their van after he broke down. Besides, Jason Stolze was the one with the record."

The record he spoke of didn't amount to much. Jason had been arrested years ago for breaking and entering as a teenager.

She couldn't stand his hands on her. Kate pretended to yawn and let her eyelids flutter with what she hoped to Jack was sheer exhaustion.

Jack reached up and touched her cheek. "You're tired, Kate. I've told you everything I know." He glanced at his watch. "It's after ten. Why don't you get ready for bed? I need to go back to the ballroom. Since I threw this party, I should be the last one to leave."

Kate yawned again, but this time it wasn't forced. She was so drained, sleep sounded good. But knowing sleep would not come, she needed to continue the ruse. Wanting to go with him would reaffirm she was still behind him. "I'll go . . ." She tried to cover up a yawn.

"To bed." Jack pulled her up. "I won't be long."

CHAPTER EIGHT

K ATE'S EYES POPPED OPEN, HER HEART PUMPING FURIOUSLY AS SHE gasped for breath, her arm swiping the cold sheets on Jack's side of the bed. Empty. Glancing at the digital clock on the nightstand, she strained to see the numbers: two oh seven.

Intuition, she'd been born with it—sometimes a blessing, but most times a curse. Her instincts told her it weighed heavily, this time, on curse.

Get up.

Moaning, she turned on her side and ignored the little voice.

Now.

"All right. Fine. I'm up." Kate kicked off the covers, slid out of bed, and walked toward the terrace doors to view the Miles River, a glinting snake under the moonlight that tantalized. Over her shoulder, the deserted crumple of cotton sheets and cream-colored eyelet duvet reminded her of her wayward husband's absence. Not surprising, booze a remedy for whatever ailed Jack. He'd no doubt be saddled up on the nearest bar stool in the Purser's Pub, located on the main level of the historic inn.

Kate searched the floral wingback chair for her jeans. She slid into them, the denim cold against her legs. Once dressed, she snagged her corduroy jacket and headed toward the French doors. She slipped out onto the stone terrace.

Right away, the chill brushed her face. As she breathed in, the cold air filled her lungs. The moon, a plump egg yolk against a blackened sky, lighted her way; her shadow in front seemed to guide her toward the water.

Complicated didn't begin to describe her position in all this. Being the defense attorney for the convicted and now the wife of the prosecutor alleged to have bribed the star witness, she was only now thinking about how the FBI would construe her relationship with Jack and the case. Or what Jack might ask of her in the near future.

Dealing with Jack as the obnoxious prosecutor doing his best to undermine her defense was one thing. But standing by her husband, when she herself would applaud his arrest and conviction, could prove difficult.

Was it time to meet Agent Parker face to face and admit she was IrishEyes?

Kate continued to stare at the river. She bent down and picked up a few rocks, tossing one into the river only to have it sink. She frowned.

Shivering, she dropped the ones remaining in her hand and pulled her corduroy jacket tight. It had to be close to three, which meant the bar was closed. He'd be there waiting for her when she returned. She couldn't stay out here forever wandering and obsessing over her relationship to the accused and a decision to become a federal witness.

And that was exactly what she'd be if she came forward and admitted her role in all this.

Heading back up the path, the inn, looking quite antebellum with its porticos and columns, beamed in the distance. Pathway lights sparkled like a diamond necklace, encircling the grounds. Kate headed up the small slope away from the river. Pulling her jacket tighter, she hugged her chest. She rounded the corner of the path and came upon the gazebo she had seen earlier in the evening from the veranda. The tiny Christmas tree lights threaded around each post sparkled.

Kate continued up the grassy slope but stopped. Hushed voices mingled, and a woman's voice gasped with pleasure. Kate's face warmed with embarrassment, and she took the long route down the path, avoiding them altogether. But the man's voice, the deep laugh hanging in the night air, caused her chest to tighten. Crouching down, she made her ascent up the hill toward the gazebo. Staying low with the shrubbery, she followed the path around the structure until it met up with the steps.

The voices stopped, and she peered around the steps. The couple, their bodies seared together, lips entangled. The woman moaned seductively when he pushed into her middle, his meaning obvious. They didn't notice her footfalls climbing the wooden steps. They only continued to grope one another. Heart pounding, she moved stealthily across the gazebo floor. Her eyes strained against the haze of lights in her attempt to bring them into focus. Her voice, a jagged bolt against the soft sounds of their lovemaking, broke the calm of night, the word desperate as it left her lips.

"Jack?"

Jack swung around, his expression one of shock as he zipped up his pants. A curse escaped his lips before he pushed the woman away. He stepped forward. Joelle Stevens let out a gasp, dropping back against the railing, her dress falling into place.

Kate edged away, eyeing him. "You . . . bastard." She turned sharply, took off down the steps heading toward the inn, her boots clipping against the stone path.

His footsteps, heavy against the walkway, came up behind her. She refused to look back until his hand clamped down onto her arm, the sheer force spinning her around.

"Stop running from me." He pulled her closer. Their breaths labored from the burst of exercise, now visible against the cold, melded into one. "It's not what you think . . . I love you."

His maddening proclamation of innocence provoked her. Did he really think she believed her eyes had deceived her? It appeared he was fool enough to think he had a chance of redeeming himself, and that pissed her off even more.

Kate slapped him across the face. "You son of a bitch." She welcomed the sensation of pins and needles spreading through her palm and fingers. Retribution, although new with Jack, never felt so good. Glancing down, his hand remained, anchoring her to him. "Let go of me."

Their gazes locked and held.

"Not until you hear what I have to say." His fingers tightened around her arm.

She laughed. "There's nothing to say." Tears stung her eyes and escaped down her cheek, and she was confused she would feel anything, especially hurt. "You're a liar and a pathetic one at that." Peering around his broad shoulders, she spotted Joelle Stevens coming up on them, an expensive fur drawn tight around her shoulders.

Kate turned to Jack. "I'm leaving you."

"You're upset . . . Let me explain . . . It's not what—"

"Let go of my arm before I scream." Her voice carried an undercurrent of warning, and she wasn't above bringing down the house on this one. Jack stood to lose more if they woke up the inn, with him in the middle of a lover's triangle.

"You're not leaving me." Although he spoke the words, his expression hinted at his true feelings. His usual steel-blue eyes, confident and knowing, appeared uncertain. He stood in front of her, his shirt rumpled, his hair in need of combing, and the bowtie of his tux lying haphazardly against his open shirt on either side. For once in his life, he looked ill-prepared to deal with anything.

She yanked hard against his grasp. "Try and stop me this time."

His hand fell away; the unexpected release caused her to stumble backward. Catching her balance, she brought him into focus one last time. A burst of irrepressible laughter escaped her lips at the sight of his mistress, now clinging to Jack's arm, whining his name.

"You really need to train her better," Kate said, before giving them her back.

She slipped through the sliding door of the guestroom, grabbed her overnight bag, purse, and keys, and bolted toward the lobby. This was her chance. Public place. She had driven. Jack otherwise occupied. And this was a new one—she'd gotten her wish.

Jack's life had just imploded.

CHAPTER NINE

K ATE PACED HER NEPHEW FINN'S BEDROOM SHE'D BEEN OCCUPYING since arriving on the family farm early New Year's Day. She'd told Bren and Rafe the whole truth; her dad, only of Jack's infidelity. "Come on, Bryan. Answer your damn phone." The last word came out on a growl, and she kicked at a soccer ball next to the wooden desk.

It had been two days since her hasty departure from the inn. She'd called Bryan on New Year's Day on his cell to let him know she'd left Jack and why. They didn't talk long. It was his day to be with Ally and the kids. He promised he'd fill her in when he got to work today after confronting Jack.

They agreed she should call him after seven—plenty of time for him to gauge Jack's reaction. Now close to eight, he still hadn't returned any of her calls.

"Kate, Dad's leaving." Bren's voice traveled up to the second level and into Finn's bedroom.

She shoved her cell phone into the pocket of Bren's borrowed sweatshirt after getting Bryan's voicemail. "I'll be right down."

Kate took the steps and found her family in the foyer. Bren stood next to Rafe, his hand secure and resting on her shoulder. Her heart sank a little. *I so suck at picking men.*

She was happy for Bren. She'd managed through all the heartache of losing her husband, Tom, to pick another winning husband. Kate grimaced. She'd all but abandoned her sister the last year—including her wedding. *Not anymore, asshole.*

Kate clenched the banister and took the last step before letting go of the oak rail, her foot hitting the landing.

"Hey." She gave a quick smile to Bren and Rafe and took a step toward her father.

"I love you, Daddy." Kate leaned into her father and kissed him on his ruddy cheek, glad to be home in Clear Spring and the farm she had come to know as Grace.

Daniel Fallon's twinkling blue eyes held no hint of their usual mischief. He'd never been fond of Jack. His Irish intuition, which he'd shared with Kate on many occasions, told him that Jack, the highfalutin prosecutor with his family fortune worth millions, was full of horse hockey.

And he'd been right.

"I love you, too, Katie girl." Her father kept her close and whispered against her ear, "I pegged Jack ol' boy from the start. I just didn't figure he'd be a lecher to boot. I'm sorely tempted to pay that son-in-law of mine a visit and kick his miserable arse."

"Daddy." Her voice shook with reproach. That was the last thing she needed, her father defending her honor.

"Or a shotgun between the eyes," Rafe offered.

Bren nudged Rafe hard in the stomach.

"Ouch, darlin'." He winced but managed to wink at Kate. "A brother has a right to protect his younger sister."

"Well, you're not going to point a gun at his head." Bren eyed her father. "And neither are you, old man."

Her father released Kate from his arm. But his scowl remained. "Don't worry. I'll not be confronting him. In the grand scheme of things, that would only cause more trouble. You've suffered enough." He tweaked Kate's nose and then placed his tweed cap on his thinning downy white hair. "You'll stay with your sister, then, until we get this sorted out. And if that husband of yours has any ideas of reconciling, you tell him to go straight to hell." He pulled on his bottom lip. "On second thought, it'd be better you tell him Daniel Fallon said he can go straight to the Devil."

He slipped on the suede jacket her sister Bren handed him from the entryway closet and kissed Bren on the cheek. "Dinner was delicious, sweetheart." He craned his neck. "Rafe, tell the boys we'll try our luck at ice fishing tomorrow, then. The pond looks to be frozen well enough."

"I might join you myself."

Her father gave a quick nod. "It's a date. I'll come by bright and early. Let's say seven thirty or so."

"Then I better get our tackle in order." Rafe kissed Bren on the head. "I'm going out to the barn, and I'll pick up some more firewood for you girls. We'll see you tomorrow, Daniel." He patted his father-in-law's back and moved toward the kitchen, the side door shutting behind him.

Her father gave Kate a pout as he opened the door. "Don't be holding back on us, Katie girl." He clucked his tongue and shook his head. "Secrets. And we knew nothing about it, until now."

Kate wrapped her arms around her father. "I'm sorry I upset you," she whispered against the side of his head.

Her father slipped out the door and down the front porch step.

The night breeze caught Bren's hair, a deep red flowing past her shoulders, before she shut the door behind him and frowned at Kate. "You know it's because he loves you that he worries." She cocked her head. "I still don't understand why you didn't tell him about the investigation."

Kate took a deep breath. "I should have. But I didn't want him to worry even more. That's all. I'll tell him. Actually, I'll have to. I don't want him to read it in the paper in the coming weeks." She checked her watch. "How late is the library open?"

Bren shrugged. "I think until eight. Why?"

"I need a computer."

"I have one."

"One the feds can't trace."

Bren opened the hall closet and grabbed her coat and threw Kate another one of hers. "Let's go. I'll drive." She shook her head. "I always told you Jack was an asshole."

Too bad I didn't listen to you when I brought the asshole home.

Kate shoved her arms into Bren's leather coat and grabbed her purse off the bench. Good thing they were close to the same size. She'd been living out of her sister's closet for the last two days.

Relieved she could share her secret life with Bren, she was glad she'd chosen the family farm to hide out. It was also strategic. Jack would never come here.

The two traveled down the steps and to Bren's pickup. The truck gained traction in the snow-packed driveway leading from the farm to Route 68. The weather in western Maryland differed vastly from the weather of the eastern shore.

Bren settled into the driver's seat after making the turn. "What's your plan?" She glanced over at Kate and then transferred her attention to the road. "You can't hide out forever."

"I'm not hiding out, I'm planning, remember?" Kate pulled out a business card from her borrowed sweatshirt.

Bren reached for it, her finger touching the edge of the card. "What's that?"

"My new life, for now. I've had Sydel Baker's business card hidden in my wallet for months. She works for RE/MAX realty. I meet with her tomorrow to sign a lease on a townhouse in Annapolis, fully furnished and mine, just as soon as I want to move in."

"What's the address?"

Kate hesitated. She wouldn't be confiding her new address to Bren or her family. Jack was unpredictable at best. She didn't want to think about his worst—memories of lying on her back in a ravine with Jack defying her to leave him. She didn't want her family caught in the crosshairs when Jack flexed his muscle—and he would flex his muscle. It was just a question of opportunity. As long as the bastard didn't know where she lived—and the Millersville RE/MAX office had sworn confidentiality—she should be safe. At least for a while.

"My secret . . . for now."

"You can't be serious." Bren's hands visibly tightened on the steering wheel. "What's going on in that trial lawyer brain of yours?"

Why Bryan isn't answering his cell phone, for one.

"With the headlines, Jack's working damage control. Maybe that's why Bryan hasn't contacted me. He's probably been flooded with calls with the FBI probe." Why hadn't she thought of that before? "Anyway, I'm the low priority on Jack's radar screen. Eventually, he'll want to collect what he thinks is his. Keeping my address to myself will ensure he never finds it."

"Like I'm going to tell him."

"No. But he knows we're close. He could follow you to get to me. I've got enough to worry about keeping him off my tail, let alone wondering if he's on yours."

"I seriously don't—"

"Maybe not. But the less you know, the better."

Bren pulled into a parking spot, and the two hopped out. Once they cleared the doors, Bren waved her on. "I'll find you at the computer section. You want hot tea?"

"That'd be great."

Kate kept an even pace, though every nerve in her body shouted for her to run toward the computer area of the library. With the holidays, she'd been unable to use a public computer. This morning she had dressed early with every intention of hitting the Clear Spring Library when it opened. But opening the door and finding her father on Bren's doorstep, with fresh-cut flowers for her mother's grave, made it impossible.

She'd spent the day having breakfast as a unit, visiting her mom's grave, followed by lunch, then dinner—all the while checking her cell phone in case she'd missed a call or text from Bryan. Now with an hour left until the library closed, her heart thumped in her chest. She had so much to share with Agent Parker.

Kate sat down and accessed her e-mails. She wanted to know why Agent Parker hadn't told her about the opening of an FBI probe, then she wanted to tell him about the evidence Bryan had found and the possibility of there being an offshore bank account. Bryan had never confirmed it, but something about his expression told her she'd guessed right. Plus, she wanted to know how the hunt for Barbosa's cell phone had gone. It had been well over a week since she'd notified him of Jack's phone call. And that was where she would start—with her displeasure.

IrishEyes: YOU'RE IGNORING ME, AND I DON'T LIKE IT.

Call it immature, but she felt like throwing a tantrum. Being ignored and left in the dark made her cranky.

"He answer you back?" Bren took the seat beside her and set Kate's tea next to the keyboard.

Kate shrugged her shoulders. "It's a long shot—if he's even in his office."

"So we wait."

She wouldn't have expected anything less. Bren had always been there for her. Kate hugged her, careful not to tip Bren's tea in her hand. "Thanks."

Bren pulled away. "What if all your hard work doesn't get Jack indicted? What then?"

"I hadn't thought that far." Kate shrugged. "Get a divorce, for one."

"You think he'll let you go that easy?"

She'd gotten away for now. Had she been naive to think physically excusing herself from his life would be the end of it?

Bren raised a well-shaped, russet brow, and Kate remembered all the trouble that small gesture of Bren's caused when growing up.

"Oh, no." Kate put up a hand. "I don't even want to know what's cooking in that brain of yours."

Bren grabbed Kate's hand and tugged it down. "It doesn't hurt to listen. I got to thinking, and your timely townhouse is perfect for what I have in mind."

For an hour Kate and Bren discussed a backup plan if the FBI fell short of the mission Kate had started or if there was a game changer that required a Plan B. As far as plans went, Bren's was diabolically ingenious. Kate just didn't know if she had the guts to go through with it if her situation turned dire.

"I think your FBI agent dissed you, sis." Bren nodded at the computer screen.

"Give me a sec." Kate started a new e-mail. She was done with breadcrumbs. She'd be taking up residence in the townhouse tomorrow, and she couldn't guarantee when she'd have access to another public computer. This time her agent needed a whole loaf.

IrishEyes: CHECK OUT REYNOLDS'S BANKING ACCOUNTS. FOCUS ON OFF-
             SHORE BANKING INSTITUTIONS, ESPECIALLY ONES THAT DON'T
             MAKE IT A HABIT OF ASSISTING U.S. LAW ENFORCEMENT.

That was what she feared. Things had been changing in international banking. But there were a few holdouts fighting the new transparency laws governing a client's privileged information with law enforcement, specifically, the FBI.

She hit the Send button.

"Come on." Kate grabbed her trash from earlier and her jacket. "I'm tired. You've got to be beat, too."

Snowflakes batted Kate's cheek the moment she stepped from the library with Bren. They crossed the parking lot, and she shivered, the cold stealing her breath. She gripped the frozen door handle and waited for Bren to open the truck. The automatic locks clicked at the same time Kate's cell phone pealed in the bottom of her purse. Struggling to get the door open, dig for her iPhone, and climb onto the running board and into the seat was multitasking to the extreme.

Her butt hit the seat with a thud, and she tucked her phone in between her chin and shoulder while she shut the door without a thought to the identity of the caller. "This is Kate."

"Kate?"

Immediately Kate's senses went on high alert. "Ally? What is it?"

"I need you." Ally sniffed into the phone. "Bryan was mugged tonight."

"Oh my God. Where?"

"In the garage in Baltimore. They shot him, Kate. I'm here with Jack at shock trauma. Please come." Her voice broke. "Bryan's asking for you, honey. He's not making sense. They just wheeled him into surgery."

"I'll be there."

Ally disconnected, and Kate went numb, her fingers a vise on her phone.

"Kate?" Bren shook her by the arm. "What is it? What's happened?"

The back of her eyes stung, tears dangerously close to spilling. "It's Bryan. He's been shot. Ally and Jack are at shock trauma." Her hand flew up to her mouth. Tears running down her face made Bren a dizzy blur, and the urge to vomit was so real she had to swallow to keep it down. "I have to get to him."

Chapter Ten

Kate pushed the key into the lock and turned the knob until it clicked. Stepping inside the dimly lit office of Seiler and Banks, she closed the door behind her and continued toward her office and hit the light switch. She promised herself no more than an hour to go through her mail and clean out her Inbox. Slipping into her chair, she pressed her back into the ergonomic curve of her chair and closed her eyes.

Bryan was gone. He never made it through surgery. It had been three days since his death, and Kate remained numb. Her last memory of him had been on the veranda when Jack had interrupted them, his brown eyes pinning hers, and she'd had to look away.

Bryan's eyes would forever haunt her.

She wanted to believe his death was a senseless killing—the alternative too frightening and painful to consider. Jack had been at the hospital early Friday morning. Cried like a baby when the surgeon came out of surgery and told them Bryan had succumbed to the gunshot wound. It didn't seem possible he could have had anything to do with Bryan's death. His murder was a random act of violence. Right? Or had her need to escape Jack—punish Jack—gotten Bryan killed?

If that were true, how long would it take Jack to figure out they were working together—if he hadn't already?

Kate shook her head. She could speculate. But without Bryan, she had no idea what had transpired between them or if he had even approached the subject of the evidence at all.

She wiped the tears off her cheek and tried to clear her mind. But memory of Ally's shaken eyes resurfaced. Ally had been through hell—difficult didn't begin to describe the last three days Kate had spent with her friend. Again she questioned that little voice inside, and she shut it down. There was no way. Jack was a lot of things, but a cold-blooded killer? It didn't fit.

So she spent the weekend in Cape St. Claire caring for Bryan's children while Ally made their father's funeral arrangements and never said a word.

Kate hated herself.

Taking a deep breath, she opened her eyes and began sorting through the stack of memos and files Marlene had left in her inbox. After forty-five minutes of nonstop paper shuffling, she managed to redistribute the pile into file cabinets, folders, and George Seiler's desk for review.

The last item—the mail. There wasn't much since the office had been closed for the holiday, mostly junk mail and her monthly subscription to *The American Lawyer.* A letter-sized manila envelope with her name and the law firm's address written by hand sat on top, stamped from a post office she didn't recognize, with no return address.

She picked it up, and something hard slid to one corner of the envelope. Curious, she grabbed her letter opener and sliced through the top. Popping the envelope open, she let the contents fall out. A brass key, which she caught between her fingers, radiated cold, the jagged teeth rough when she closed her hand around it. She examined it, and her face tightened. Engraved on the top of the key's head was ANNAPOLIS CIGAR COMPANY and the number 17.

Bryan . . . oh my God!

With shaky fingers, she set the key down and accessed the cigar bar's website and sighed. They closed at eleven. Even if she left the office now and traveled the block it took to get to the shop, it was ten fifty-two by her watch. She'd never make it before they locked their doors, leaving her in suspense until they opened on Monday. She shook her head in bafflement. Why would he send her a key from his cigar bar? She didn't smoke. But the locker that members received upon joining, as noted on the website, intrigued her. She doubted Bryan's locker held cigars and cognac.

That thought made her shiver—the evidence. He'd left her the evidence. Kate pushed back from her chair and stood, shoving the key in her jeans pocket. She grabbed her purse and coat, flew out of her office, and locked the door.

Pocketing her key, she quickly made her way down to the street and ran the few blocks, hoping to catch the bar before it closed. When she reached the darkened storefront, the outside lights remained on, so she banged on the glass. "Can you open the door? Please!"

Come on! I know you're in there.

She banged harder. "I'll bust the glass," she whispered to herself. "Hello. I need you to open the door."

With that, the outside lights went out, and Kate was left in the dark. She let her head fall against the cool glass window and the imprint of the office hours stenciled on the door. She lifted her head. *Damn it.* They wouldn't be open until noon tomorrow. Same day as Bryan's funeral. Fine. As soon as the funeral was over, she'd be at this door tomorrow with her key, and if her intuition proved correct, she'd have the evidence the FBI needed to put Jack in jail.

Over her shoulder, the red lights of the word HILTON pulsed. She gathered herself and walked the two blocks down to the hotel. Cold and in need of a computer, she stole inside the double glass doors of the hotel and pretended to be a guest and sat down at one of the computers.

IrishEyes: COME ON, PARKER. I NEED YOUR HELP.

Kate waited. Any minute someone would figure out she didn't belong here. Every muscle tensed, and she chewed her cuticle, silently willing a response. Almost five minutes later he e-mailed back.

JParker: THEN LET'S SET UP THAT MEETING YOU PROMISED.

Kate hesitated. Was she ready to give up her anonymity?

JParker: YOU NEED TO TRUST ME, IRISHEYES. IF IT'S REYNOLDS YOU'RE AFRAID OF, I'LL PROTECT YOU.

She was mentally and physically homeless. The Tilghman home she shared with Jack would never be her home again. She was not a child where she could hide from the big bad wolf on the family farm. There was the townhouse, of course, but it wasn't a home—more a refuge until she could create a life *she* wanted.

Kate squared her shoulders. First, she wanted her own questions answered.

IrishEyes: NO ONE CAN. LET'S MOVE ON, AGENT PARKER. ANY WORD FROM BARBOSA'S PHONE RECORDS?

JParker: BARBOSA'S DEAD.

A sick dread, cold and paralyzing, rushed over her.

IrishEyes: How?

JParker: IT'S CLASSIFIED, IRISHEYES.

IrishEyes: I NEED TO KNOW, PARKER.

JParker: HE HUNG HIMSELF TWO DAYS AGO. THERE WERE NO PHONE RECORDS TO CONFIRM HE CALLED REYNOLDS. THEY DIDN'T FIND A CELL PHONE.

Kate fell against the chair back. Just because they didn't find a phone didn't mean Barbosa hadn't called Jack. Bryan had heard the call. That was good enough for her. But a lot of good it did when the only one connected to the truth was dangling at the end of a rope.

God, I can't breathe.

Her eyes welled up, and the screen blurred. She clicked out and grabbed her briefcase and ran out of the hotel.

He was going to get away with it. And then he would come for her.

CHAPTER ELEVEN

T HE GROUP OF MOURNERS BLANKETED THE SMALL ST. ANNE'S
Cedar Bluff Cemetery off West Street in downtown Annapolis.
Dressed in black and gray hues, interspersed throughout the headstones,
they jockeyed for position behind the row of burgundy velvet chairs
positioned in front of the casket. Kate clung to Hannah Wexler, her soft,
pudgy toddler arms wrapped tight around Kate's neck. Hannah was the
youngest. The other three, ranging in ages from six on down, stood next to
their father's casket, sitting above the open grave. Their small hands rested
against the smooth oak. Ally wept next to them, her parents who had made
the trek up from North Carolina on either side of her and Bryan's mother
and father holding one another, his mother wiping away her tears. The
burgundy chairs meant for the family remained empty.

The wind whipped, and Kate snuggled her face next to Hannah's. A hand
touched her waist, lips grazing her ear. "I need you." Jack's voice broke.

Kate trembled with grief and a little anxiety. She had freed herself of
him. Maybe he was suffering with loss. Or he was trying to lure her back.
Either way, she didn't trust him. Kate allowed his hand to remain. She didn't
comment. As soon as the service ended, she'd pass Hannah to her mother,
give Ally a solid hug, and sidestep Jack. Her goal—the ornate wrought-iron
gates of the cemetery and the cigar shop a few blocks' walk on Main.

She'd purposely chosen not to tell Agent Parker about the locker. If she
had, he'd have staked it out, knowing she'd be there when it opened at
twelve, ready to pounce on her the moment she walked through the door.

This was between her and Bryan, for now.

Father Dooly concluded the burial mass, and Ally grabbed one of her
children's hands, nodding to the rest of her brood. She rounded the chairs,
one big blur through Kate's tears. Hannah let out a cry and reached out for
her mother, slipping from Kate's arms.

With Hannah on Ally's hip, she reached for Kate. They hugged, their bodies one soft jerk of emotion.

"I'm so sorry, Ally. I loved him." Her tears fell on the black velvet collar of Ally's coat.

"He loved you so much, Kate."

She pulled away, her lips quivering. She smoothed down Ally's hair. "I have to go. But I'll be back in time for the luncheon."

She turned, careful to keep her heels from sinking into the spongy earth. Keeping her eyes on the open gate, she tightened the sash of her black raincoat and moved in that direction.

She'd lost track of Jack, hoped her lack of response had given him her answer. Clearing the gates, she let her breath out and skirted the two limos when the door to the last swung open, causing her to stumble.

A hand shot out to steady her, followed by a tall, well-dressed man with the unmistakable air of conceit.

Kate went cold. "God, you scared me."

"I'm sorry. How about I give you a lift?"

"No, thanks." Kate shook her arm away. Jack's grip remained tight.

"He's dead, Kate." His usual demanding voice gentled, and she connected with his eyes. They were a mix of what she believed to be pain—and loss. Kate questioned if he had anything to do with Bryan's death at all.

"I-I'm sorry, Jack. I know you loved him."

"Come with me," he urged, tugging her arm forward toward the dark hole of the limo.

"N-no, I can't." She pulled back.

"Don't—"

The edge, or what she imagined to be anger, disappeared with the approach of footsteps on the cobblestone street.

"Jack, I thought that was you. Kate."

Jack's grip lessened, his hand sliding down and away from her to shake the hand of her boss, George Seiler. "George, thanks for coming."

"Well, of course, I know how tragic this is for you and . . ."

Kate kissed George's cheek. "I'll be in tomorrow. I'm so glad you came." She started to walk away.

"But where are you—"

"To the office. I need to . . . catch Marlene before she goes to lunch."

"Oh, okay." George shook his head and gave a confused lift of his lips.

Kate didn't acknowledge Jack again. One thing George Seiler excelled at was bending one's ear. He'd bend Jack's for a good fifteen minutes. Enough time for her to clear the crest of Main Street, which happened to be the way to her office as well as the cigar shop.

Kate cut across to Church Circle and hopped the curb onto Main. Ignoring the pinch of her black stilettos, she kept up a brisk pace, her heels clipping along the brick sidewalk. She glanced back more than once, sensing someone. Each time she found only the usual stream of pedestrian traffic. No Jack.

Kate recognized the green lights of the cigar shop protruding from the brick building on the other side. She passed the Chesapeake Art Gallery and crossed the narrow thread of gnarled inlaid brick making up Main Street, the cobblestone continuing its lazy sprawl before the Chesapeake Bay seemed to swallow it whole. Kate peered inside the expansive shop window encased in weathered brick, her reflection the only thing visible. She double checked the sign, the lights lit and shining down on a wooden scroll painted in deep red and canary yellow—ANNAPOLIS CIGAR COMPANY.

She took a breath and opened the door, a small bell ringing.

Stale cigar smoke lingered in the air. Unexpected pink walls surrounded her, with green leather couches to the right.

"Need help?" The voice made her jerk.

"Locker." It came out on a croak. Kate swallowed and started again, her words much smoother. "I have a locker." She dug into the pocket of her raincoat and held up her key. "Seventeen."

A portly gentleman filled a reception window. He leaned through, pointing past the sitting area. "Around the corner."

Kate frowned.

He shook his head. "You have been here before, right?"

"Ah . . . sure." She nodded and cleared the couches, moving toward the wall. "You're an idiot," she whispered to herself. Kate rounded the wall and relaxed. Right in front of her on the far wall stood a row of green lockers, seven across and six down, all the same size, square and about the size of a ruler either way.

She began to sweat. Her fingers gripped the key hard, and she scanned the numbers of each locker until she came to 17.

She put the key in the lock and turned. It clicked, and Kate opened the door. Her hand shot out touching bare metal.

It was empty.

The tears she'd held back since her nightmare came streaming down. *Why this damn locker, anyway?* Kate replayed the events of the last week in her head, from the moment she found Jack on the veranda with Joelle, to the farm, trying to reach Bryan.

She stopped.

She'd been calling him the night of his death, had even gone so far as to leave a few desperate messages. It was Bryan's phone, not hers. But what if his death wasn't random?

Oh God.

They'd never found Bryan's cell phone.

Her throat tightened. The bell rang, and a hard-soled shoe hit the tile floor. Kate peered around the corner. A new man had entered, wearing a black designer trench coat. His back was turned, and he was speaking with the man behind the window.

Kate shut the locker and locked it, holding the key tight in her hand. Clearing the wall, she managed to take several steps before colliding into him. Her purse slipped down her arm, and the key slipped from her fingers, falling to the ground with a clink. He reached out to steady her, and her stomach tightened.

"I'm sorry. You all right?" Warm blue eyes held hers.

She nodded. "It's my fault. Really," she offered, bending down to pick up the key when their heads collided.

"Relax." His eyes connected with hers and then her bare knee pressed against his thigh in their crouched positions. He squeezed it softly. "It's okay, I've got it." With the key firmly between his fingers, he reached for her arm and pulled her up simultaneously with him and handed it back to her. His fingertips brushed against hers.

They exchanged a glance again. His hand reached out tentatively. Then he slid her purse back onto her shoulder. "I think you're good."

She gave a fleeting smile. "Yes. Thank you. I'm sorry for—"

"It was my fault."

She touched his arm. "Thank you."

She headed for the door and slipped out, running up Main Street and into the parking garage. Her hands shook while she struggled to open the door. The key turned, and she was in, clipping her seatbelt, and starting the car before she backed out and drove toward the exit.

Kate hit the brake to avoid the man crossing right in front of her in the parking garage. Her heart still pounded in her chest. He remained a dark figure when she passed him to the right. She couldn't be sure, but he resembled the one in the shop. She fed the machine her parking pass, and the gates opened.

If it was the same guy, he'd been following her. Had Jack put a tail on her? She swallowed and gripped the steering wheel with one hand and searched for her cell phone in the pocket of her coat, her fingers trembling.

In less than ninety minutes, Kate made it to Bethesda. She stepped from her car and hit the lock on her BMW key. The car chirped, its lights flickering once. She hit speed dial on her phone and placed it to her ear. "I'm here. Where are you?"

"Behind you." A hand landed on her shoulder, and Kate let out a sharp cry.

"You're a mess." Bren spun Kate around on her heels.

Kate's legs trembled.

"No shit." She pulled out the key from the pocket of her raincoat. "Like I said on the phone earlier, one key and no evidence. I can't do this without it."

"Oh, yes you can." Bren grabbed hold of her quilted handbag and placed her other hand in Kate's. "We have no choice." She pulled Kate. "Come on. I called, and they're waiting for us."

The two stood in front of the smoke-tinted glass—the double automatic doors embossed with the words NIH's DEPARTMENT OF TRANSFUSION MEDICINE.

Kate turned toward Bren. "Last time it hurt like hell. Are you getting yours done, too?"

Bren shook her head. "I did mine last week."

"Great." Kate's head dropped, and the two took a step forward, the doors opening. They checked in and made their way back to the donor area.

Kate sat in the reclining chair, madly pumping the red ball in her hand. She hated needles.

"Hey, lighten up." Her nurse, Marissa, brought her plastic-gloved hand down on Kate's fingers, the ball smashed between them.

Kate grimaced. "Sorry."

Bren leaned against Kate's chair and smiled. "She was always the sissy."

Marissa removed the warm compress from Kate's arm. She had promised it would ease the pain of the needle, this time around, and she laughed. "I have a sissy sister, too. She's actually older." She removed the compress and swiped Kate's arm with iodine. "So we'll cut this one some slack." She winked at Kate. "It's in."

"Really?" Kate checked her arm. Sure enough, blood pumped through the tubing, filling the bag close to the floor.

She relaxed.

Marissa reviewed her chart. "Your numbers were slightly high last time. I think we need to up your protocol to every month until we can bring it down."

Kate slumped in her chair. *Wonderful.*

The clock on the wall, directly in front of her, clicked by the minutes. She kept a tight grip on the ball, pumping it. Marissa sat at her desk, typing in Kate's information while Bren paced the floor.

Another nurse checked the bag. "Marissa, I think she's done."

Marissa came to Kate's side. "She's right." After she removed the needle, she bandaged Kate's arm. "You're all set." She nodded toward the cantina where they kept snacks and juices for the patients. "No excuses. Sit down and eat a Danish and have some orange juice."

Kate got to her feet. "I feel fine."

Bren stood next to Marissa's computer and gave Kate a slight shake of her head.

Really? This was the part of the plan Kate didn't agree with. She hesitated, and Bren bore into her with a stern expression.

Kate took a step, then dropped. Her head hit the leg of the table on the way down, and she wanted to pull Bren's hair.

She kept her eyes closed, and the shadow of bodies hovered above her. They chattered, called out orders. A finger lifted her right eye, the beam of a penlight spearing it, and her eye watered. She remained unmoved. Her head ached. A lot.

The only words running a race in her head—*hurry the hell up!*

Kate struggled for breath. Ammonia, strong and stinging, burnt her nasal passages before her eyes popped open.

"She's awake. Kate, you okay?" Hands had her by her arms, bringing her to her feet, placing her bottom on the chair. Marissa stood next to her, frowning down.

Kate's face warmed, and her nose ran. "I'm fine," she sputtered and caught Bren hiding a grin as she moved forward.

Marissa checked her blood pressure and shined the light into her eyes again. "Your pressure is good. I think you stood up too fast."

Kate shook her head. "I'm not dizzy anymore." She made a move to stand.

Marissa grabbed her arm. "Easy."

Bren stepped over. "Let's get you something to eat." She steered Kate through the cantina's door and sat her down. "You okay?"

"No." Kate made a mean face. "My head hurts like hell."

"The chair leg wasn't part of the plan." Bren opened the refrigerator and gave her an orange juice with a straw. "Drink it."

Kate grabbed it, sucking on the straw. "Did you delete it?"

Bren leaned in. "Yeah. No one saw me. They were too busy taking care of you."

"And you—"

"Yep." Bren gently patted the quilted handbag.

Kate nodded. "Hand me that sticky bun."

"You okay enough to take it with you?"

Kate shoved the plastic-wrapped Danish in her pocket. "Let's go."

They cleared the sliding, smoke-tinted doors, and Kate turned cold. "Did you notice anyone following me when I drove in?"

"Hard to tell. A few cars came in the garage right after you." Bren's head swiveled around the general area of the parking garage. "Do you think you were followed?"

She couldn't be sure, only a feeling. "It's nothing." She took Bren's hand. "Let's get out of here."

"Wait." Bren placed the quilted handbag resting on her shoulder onto Kate's and winked. "Your clothes from New Year's. Remember? And something special at the bottom I've been meaning to give you."

"Right. I almost forgot." Kate cocked her head. "What'd you get me?"

"You'll see." Bren motioned her toward the garage with her hand. "You go. I'll watch from here."

Kate's eyebrows lifted.

"Just in case you were followed. I'll call you later tonight."

Kate hugged Bren, emotion welling up in her chest. "Tell me we're doing the right thing."

Bren's head nodded against Kate's. "It's the only thing."

CHAPTER TWELVE

KATE SHUT THE BLINDS TO HER OFFICE AND WENT STRAIGHT TO her desk. She cleaned out her drawers, dropping her personal effects into a brown box on her credenza, grabbing picture frames of her and her family, leaving the ones with Jack. After her revelation in regard to Bryan's cell phone and the messages she'd left, it had become clear: If she was right, Jack would be using every means available to get to her.

The man in the cigar shop, the fact he'd been right behind her and in the garage, concerned her.

Giving Jack or his hireling open access to her at work could get her killed. She'd be keeping a low profile once she walked out the doors of Seiler and Banks. She'd call George later. He'd grant the leave of absence considering the recent circumstances.

Tears hit the back of Kate's eyes. She would never get over Bryan's death. Her hands stilled on the file cabinet drawer. She'd caused it. Her throat tightened. She should have never involved him.

Kate quickly continued her search, climbing on the credenza behind her desk. She was reaching for her law degree hanging on the wall when the front door to the office opened. Her grip tightened on the frame, and she let it go. Her heart caught in her chest, and she remained suspended.

Jumping back off the credenza, she dodged her office chair and went for the blinds, tilting them up a fraction, to catch a glimpse of Jack coming through the office door. Dressed impeccably, Jack flaunted a perfect smile, though his teeth took on a fang-like quality. His eyes were no longer glacial pools of blue but fireballs pulsing red-hot when their eyes locked. Did he know she was on to him?

Cold panic seized her, and she jumped back, stumbling, her body trembling when the box on her credenza drew her attention. Shit!

She snagged the box, shoving it under her desk right as his footsteps neared her office door. She couldn't stop shaking but managed to reach the wand to the blinds, twirling them open. Witnesses were good.

Marlene smiled through the glass, and George was in his office. Kate relaxed. Jack couldn't harm her. Still, it didn't make him any less frightening. But his visit did confirm what she hoped—the townhouse remained elusive where Jack was concerned. So she took a deep breath.

A quick knock and Jack popped his head in the door, his smile still in place. "Is this a good time?"

Her eyes narrowed in on him. *Damn it.* If, in fact, Jack knew nothing in regard to her activities with Bryan, they would betray her. She reined in her expression and worked hard to keep her heart skittering in her chest, from controlling her speech.

"Sure." She waved him in.

From his expression, he seemed to be over his snit from yesterday at the cemetery when he tried to physically force her into his limo.

"You look a little more rested."

"I wish I felt it." She motioned to the chairs. "Have a seat."

"Have you heard from Ally?"

"Not since the funeral. I'm sure she's busy packing for the trip home. I offered to help, but I think it was time for me to give them their space. I left on Sunday night."

He sat down in the chair and crossed his leg. "What are you up to, Kate?"

Her throat tightened, and she swallowed. *He knew.* "Can you be more specific?" She caught her hands fidgeting on her desk and moved them to her lap. If he noticed her nervous reactions, she was done.

He leaned in. "I've given you time to cool off. I've apologized for my indiscretion. I think it's time you gave up this ridiculous notion that we're separating."

The tension washed from her shoulders, and she relaxed. She could disguise her fear and turn it into pique. "Is that what this is, a little indiscretion? Forgive me for being offended, but sticking your dick where it doesn't belong is egregious to me. So excuse me if I don't share your sentiments about your affair with Joelle Stevens." For good measure she stood up, stepped away from her desk, and gave him her back. Feigning her distress, she bobbed her shoulders, pretending to cry.

His chair skimmed against the commercial-grade carpet, his hands coming down on her shoulders. She trembled when he whispered in her ear, "Kate, don't cry, honey. I'm sorry. I've ended it with Joelle. Just come home, and let's try to put this behind us."

She wanted to heave with him near, his hot breath moist against her ear. She snuffled. "I'm not ready, Jack. I need time to sort out . . . this."

"Okay." He kissed the back of her head, and she bit down on her lip. "I'll be patient. But cut me some slack, Kate. At least give me your address."

Not on your life.

"Jack . . . I really need to get back to work. George is expecting me in the conference room to discuss our caseload." She squeezed her eyes, confident they watered enough. She turned and gave him a halfhearted smile, which she hoped indicated she wanted to try and work on their marriage. "Let's agree to get through the work week. I have court tomorrow—all day. Friday I meet with this Agent Parker in the morning."

She'd almost wrecked her car coming home from the blood bank yesterday when she answered the phone. Parker's voice was the last one she expected on the other end, and it took a moment to register he was calling Mrs. Jack Reynolds—not IrishEyes. She had no choice but to agree to a meeting.

"Yes, I'm aware." He smiled and then caressed her cheek. "I was apprised. Thanks to *your* hectic schedule, this Agent Parker and Agent Powers have decided to fit me in on Thursday. We'll be meeting in my office in Baltimore. I think they're looking to get their hands on my computer." Jack stiffened.

"You're innocent of the charges." For more emphasis, she pulled on his lapels and then smoothed them down against his suit coat. "Don't let it bother you." She gave him a conciliatory smile and then shifted gears. "I want to get beyond my feelings of betrayal . . . I do. Let's allow each other to get through this horrendous week and agree to meet for dinner. We can discuss our future. Saturday?" She beamed up at him. "I was thinking maybe Sherwood's Landing at the Inn at Perry Cabin . . . where you surprised me for our anniversary."

She clenched her teeth. *Don't gush.*

In a more subdued voice, she continued, "I love you, Jack. I always will . . . I just need to be able to trust you again."

"Let me make this up to you, sweetheart." He kissed her forehead, and she cringed. "I'll book the room we had last April." He had a curious look to him just then as though he were trying to call something to mind. "Room 362 with the great view and the double Jacuzzi tub." He smiled.

Of course he'd remember the tub, and the room number, compliments of his photographic memory. Well, he could picture this—*not happening, you murdering bastard.* Kate let her anger go and concentrated on the best way to reply.

She pressed against him, placing her cheek against his chest, and wrapped her arms around him. "I'd like that very much."

She sighed, and slid her eyes around his broad chest and caught sight of Marlene. Her secretary enjoyed eavesdropping on her conversations. The glass walls of her office had become a gaping peephole into Kate's private life. Today Kate's interaction with Jack could rival the most popular soap opera on television. Marlene with her grand smile and wink made no excuses for her prying eyes.

Damn fishbowl.

CHAPTER THIRTEEN

KATE SHOOK FROM THE INSIDE OUT. NOT FROM THE BITING WIND or that she sat waterlogged inside her car in front of the Cape Cod she'd shared with Jack. She shivered into the collar of her raincoat. The zippered pouch and a small wooden horse figurine with the name of her black horse "Jet" inscribed on the brass base, which she'd tucked inside to keep from getting wet, poked her.

Her ploy had worked. Jack believed she was tied up in court today. He'd not suspect she'd sneak into their Tilghman home while he was at work in Baltimore. It took her longer to find what she'd come for. Afraid Jack would leave early from work, she'd almost left without it. Thank God she had decided to climb the mahogany ladder attached to Jack's towering bookcase; otherwise she'd have never seen the brown pouch with her passport and bonds taped to the fan blade above his desk. What a bastard. He had actually hidden them from her.

When they'd built the bookcase, she'd warned the shelves were too high and thought the ladder was overkill, but a nice touch. But now that ladder was a stroke of fortune for her, or a bad omen, she wasn't sure which. Either way, when he found the documents missing, she was dead. Really dead.

Now as she sat in her car, shivering from adrenaline, she pulled the pouch and small horse from her coat and picked up her purse, opening it. She moved her wallet and the legal manila envelope that held her past, present, and future, trying to make space. She shoved her horse into the cramped space and tossed the purse onto the passenger seat. She'd need her bonds tomorrow when she cashed them in. Searching her car without the interior light, she reached for the glove compartment and laid the pouch inside, locking it.

She never believed she'd take her client Davey Bollinger up on his offer that day he was released on a technicality. He had been so elated, he promised

Kate, "Anything you need, you call me, doll. I'll hook you up." Well guess what? She needed him, and he came through. She wouldn't concern herself about the legality of their business transaction on the dock this morning before sunup. Choosing life over death seemed to override any law she had violated. Kate put the car in Drive and headed toward Annapolis.

Kate parked and slipped into a grocery store, miles from Annapolis, and purchased a dozen doughnuts, coffee, cream, and a few odds and ends to get her through. She chewed her cuticle. She should forget the meeting. Every moment she remained only added to her hysteria. Jack would put the pieces together—maybe not today, or even a few weeks or months from now, but eventually.

Kate paid, grabbed the two brown bags, and headed up Route 50. After pulling into a parking space to the side of her townhouse, she stepped out of her BMW. Her raincoat flapped vigorously in the wind, rain pelting her skin. She didn't have time to deal with Mother Nature and her wrath. Not today. It wasn't just the wind and rain swirling. Close to five, darkness had settled in, and she struggled with the key to her townhouse. She wanted to scream. The wet brown paper bags filled with groceries made it impossible to see the lock. Her shoulder bag slid to the crook of her arm, and the briefcase handle slowly slipped between her wet fingers until she let go. Finally, the key eased into the jagged slot, and she hesitated, the usual friction of the key against the inner mechanisms nonexistent.

It wasn't locked.

Kate wanted to believe it was her oversight. She shoved her head over the brown paper sacks and gasped. The wooden doorframe was splintered around the strike plate. Her stomach tightened. The door pulled wide, and she fell forward, the grocery bags pulled from her arms.

"I've got it." His voice was gruff with irritation.

Cold radiated to every part of her body, her mind a disjointed mess that couldn't decide if she should run or take the next step forward, and then the words fell from her mouth. "You're resourceful." It came out clipped, and a pang of regret surfaced in her chest.

Don't piss him off.

She should have known he'd find a way to get to her before their agreed Saturday night rendezvous.

"You need to be more choosey when it comes to real estate agencies, if you wanted your address to remain a secret." His voice was slurred.

He stood there staring at her, content to bar her entrance to *her* townhouse and allow her to stand in the rain. "Jack, do you think you could step aside? I'm freezing."

"Sure, sweetheart." He turned to the side to allow her entrance. The two grocery bags rested comfortably in his left arm, and his right hand clenched a bottle.

She eyed him and then his hand. Her body began to tremble. "You're drunk."

"Completely." He smiled, looking quite satisfied with his accomplishment.

She grabbed her briefcase and placed her purse back on her shoulder, moved inside, and shut the door. Stepping out of her shoes, she sat her briefcase down in the foyer and dropped her purse next to it. Rainwater dripped from her raincoat, and she shed it, tossing it to the floor. Without a word, she took the bags from his arm, walked down the foyer to the kitchen, and started putting the food away.

She felt completely violated, his resources unlimited. The rubber soles of his dress shoes tread stealthily against the oak floor leading into the kitchen.

She kept her back to him, her hands shaking around the soup can—her only weapon.

Even drunk, he wouldn't miss the opportunity to give her his smug look—gotcha, Kate. More reason to keep her back to him. Her fingers tightened around the soup can she so wanted to send crashing into his skull. The kitchen chair glided across the tile, and his muscular frame dropped into it, the chair creaking under his weight.

She swallowed. "Are you hungry?"

"What do you have?"

Her own stomach gurgled, and she ignored it. She needed to equalize the effects of the liquor. One wrong comment from her could send him into a blind rage.

"There's a sub in the bag on the table," she offered and kept her back toward him.

He grunted and stood up, rooting through the contents of the paper bag.

Her nerve endings tingled. He wanted something. The fact he stood in her kitchen was a silent reminder he was still in control.

His grip came down on her shoulder, and she jumped. "Shit!"

He laughed into her ear.

"That's not funny, Jack. You scared me." Her heart pumped furiously, and there was nothing she could do to slow it.

"Sorry, sweetheart."

He nuzzled her hair that had begun curling into long, loose ringlets about her shoulders. His large hand reached above her head, and he grabbed a glass in the cabinet she had left open. She no longer felt him pressed up against her, and she relaxed.

"I'm thirsty," he said. "What do you have to drink?"

Her stomach lurched. The refrigerator . . . *shit*. Kate scampered across the floor in her bare feet and slammed the refrigerator door shut as Jack opened it.

"What the hell. What's wrong with you?" His steel eyes tunneled into hers.

She laughed. "You know how I am about smells."

"No, I don't." Jack gave her a hard look and refused to let go of the door handle.

She smiled and grated under her breath, "Because you never listen when I'm talking to you, unless it *involves you*." She kept her hand pressed up against the door. "The last tenants were from India. The refrigerator smells like old curry. I'm trying to get rid of the smell with baking soda. If you open that door, I'm going to puke." She let go and waved her hand. "Go ahead, but I'm warning you—you're going to clean it up, because I can't. You know how I am about—"

"Okay, *enough*."

The last word—his tone—froze Kate in place.

He gave her an irritated glance and let go of the handle. "Water. You do have water?" His outstretched hand held out the glass.

She took a deep breath and filled his glass at the tap, handing it back to him, the glass shaking slightly. Jack took his seat and wolfed the entire sandwich down and, thankfully, drank the water she had given him.

Cautiously, Kate sat down in the chair across from him next to the whiskey bottle. "There's no liquor in this house." She nodded toward the bottle of Black Bush Irish Whiskey.

Jack smiled. "Mick." His eyes darkened, and his hand shot out before Kate could jump back. With his fingers now wrapped around her pendant, a pendant he would not approve of, he tugged. She could pull back and let the thin silver chain break, but she loved the necklace. It meant more than any other piece of jewelry she had, including her wedding rings.

"What's this?" He scrutinized the dainty silver butterfly.

"Bren gave it to me." The surprise at the bottom of the bag. It was meant as a birthday gift. But Bren had decided to give it to her earlier to cheer her up.

"Bren? With all the gold jewelry I've given you, why would you wear this? It's ugly."

As usual, everything was about Jack. What Jack liked. What Jack wanted. Needing space, she pulled back and relaxed when his fingers slid off the pendant, and the silver, warmed by his fingers, fell against her chest.

She prodded, "Mick who?"

"Mick McGarvey . . . McGarvey's Saloon on Market." He grumbled, "I had to park on Main. I passed Mick's place and thought, why not? My little

Irish lass has tortured me long enough." He snuffled. "This is your fault, Kate. My state, or lack thereof, can only be traced to you and your behavior."

She rolled her eyes, pushed her chair back, and immediately regretted her actions when his steely grip clamped down on her wrist.

"Pack your bags, Kate. You're coming home."

Jack pressed down on her wrist. One more ounce of pressure, and her bones would snap. She reached over for the bottle of Black Bush but only managed to knock it over. The whiskey came pouring out, splashed onto the table, and rolled quickly over the lip and onto Jack's lap. He howled, the cool liquid flooding his dress pants.

He released her hand. "What the fuck?"

CHAPTER FOURTEEN

SECONDS, KATE HAD SECONDS. SHE TOOK OFF DOWN THE HALL, her options limited, and then her eyes locked onto her purse. Davey's manila envelope had emerged from the bottom of her handbag, its corner now visible and catching her eye when she rounded the banister of the steps.

She needed to get to it.

"Kate, get your ass back here," he bellowed down the hall, his chair clattering to the floor.

Her detour took five seconds—precious time if she wanted to escape him. The teeth on the zipper of her handbag bit into her palm. The throw rug at the bottom of the steps slid, and she fell to her knees. On all fours, she climbed the steps and froze when his hand snagged her foot. She kicked hard, and his hand fell away. She pushed up off the tread and continued the climb to the second level. If he caught her, he'd go straight for her purse. The fact she snagged it right in front of him made it a bull's-eye. The envelope had sunk back into her purse, but once he dumped it, the envelope and its contents would be his focal point. And then she would be his next target.

She slammed the thick pine door of the master bedroom, hit the switch to the overhead light, and then reached up with quivering fingers to turn the antique-style key sitting in the lock. Her heart fluttered like wings taking flight, except there was nowhere to fly, nowhere to hide. The room seemed to twirl, and all she could do was stare.

The pounding of his fists brought her out of her stupor. "Open the goddamn door, or I'll level it. Do you hear me, Kate?"

She had to stall. "Not until you calm down. You're scaring me. I didn't mean to spill the bottle."

He laughed derisively. "Like hell, you were aiming for my head."

Kate winced. *Damn.*

She scanned the dresser. No good. The mattress . . . he'd look there. Closet—forget it. She eyed the frame. It sat neglected against the back wall under the window sill, the watercolor of Thomas Point lighthouse. She had picked it up in the art gallery on Main the other day and had every intention of hanging it. But she hadn't gotten around to it. She laid it down on the bed and sighed with relief. The back hadn't been enclosed in brown paper.

She tried to clear her mind. Ignoring his verbal tirade and the blows against the door, she reached inside her purse, searching for her nail file. Her fingers became agitated—there was so much crap in her purse. Heart pounding, she grabbed the envelope and tossed the bag across the room. She dug her fingernail under the first tong and gritted her teeth when the metal slipped under her nail. A drop of dark blood appeared in the underside curve of her French manicure. She sucked her finger and ignored the bitter taste. If she left a fresh trail of blood on the frame, he'd become suspicious. She continued to struggle with every stubborn piece of metal until she could clear the cardboard back. She positioned the envelope in one corner, replaced the cardboard, and pressed flat the tongs.

How long had he been in the house? An hour, possibly? Enough time to thoroughly search it. She turned the frame around, moved past her bed, and placed the picture back in its exact location beneath the window. A loud crack brought her attention around. The entire doorframe tore from the wall. The door itself hung like a piece of split skin, still attached, but barely.

She swallowed hard as he charged her. Still on her hands and knees, she pretended to pick up the contents of her purse. His fingers laced her bicep, and he yanked her to her feet.

"What's in the purse, Kate?"

"N-nothing," she replied, caught like a rag doll in Jack's angry grip.

He released her, and she stumbled sideways, trying to remain upright. "You're lying," he said. He kicked at her lipstick, stepped on her compact mirror, the crunch an indication he had cursed her with seven years of bad luck.

She laughed.

"You think this is funny?" He eyed her speculatively.

She sobered. "No."

He raised his hand, and she flinched. "Are you afraid I'm going to hit you?"

She bit down on her lip and shook her head. "No, you promised you wouldn't do that again." She pleaded with her eyes. "I'm trusting you won't."

He pointed toward the bed. "Sit down."

Kate clasped her hands in her lap and sat down, her bare feet only skimming the floor with her toes. Jack scooped up her purse and dumped it next to her on the bed.

"What are you hiding, hmm?"

She shrugged her shoulders. "I told you, nothing."

Jack ran his fingers through the contents lying on the plaid comforter. Nothing out of the ordinary—her cell phone, reading glasses, a pack of cinnamon Dentyne, hair ties, hairbrush. But then her eyes landed on the delicately-carved, black wooden horse, and she swallowed hard, wondering what he'd make of it in her purse.

He angled his face. "Why were you running?"

"You looked so pissed-off when I spilled the whiskey. I was afraid."

His cool demeanor concerned her. She knew silent rage when she saw it. His face was flushed. He clenched and reclenched his fists. "Afraid?" He narrowed in on her, his voice surprisingly normal, pleasant, in fact. "I'm not going to damage your pretty little *face*." His tone sharpened, and he tilted her chin up. Releasing her, he grabbed hold of her horse resting against her thigh. "I can think of other ways to upset you without raising a finger to your face." He flung it across the room, shattering the oak-framed mirror above the dresser, shards falling to the floor.

She winced and turned away from him, her gaze transfixed on the little black horse lying on its side, broken. Tears stung the backs of her eyes.

"Oh, I'm sorry," he said. "Wasn't the horse a gift from your mother? Was it important to you?"

"No," she croaked.

"Same old Kate, always have to get the last word." He stepped around her and clamped on to the Victorian lamp on her nightstand. Not an antique, but she liked it. It would be a shame if he destroyed it, but better the lamp than her face.

He flipped it on. "Pretty the way the light shines through the different colored glass, isn't it?"

He was baiting her. Rather than play his mind game, she remained quiet, allowing her head to dip forward, her blonde waves of hair shielding the sides of her face.

With one swift yank, that side of the room darkened, and the ornate glass globe disintegrated into tiny mosaic pieces scattered across the oak floor. He moved on, pulling out dresser drawers, tossing them into a heap, the wood smashing together and splintering. Her lingerie littered the floor. And then he stopped. She peered through her veil of hair. He stood in front of the Thomas Point lighthouse print, bent down, and picked up the frame.

"Thomas Point. I've always envied the son of a bitch who lived there. Privacy. No intrusions . . . and no wife to fuck with your mind." He turned and gave her a menacing grin. "What do you say, Kate? Would you have married me if I was a light keeper?" He shook his head. "Probably not." He turned and sat the picture down where he found it.

Too close. Kate let out the breath she was holding.

He faced her now, his hands on his hips. "I couldn't keep you in your designer suits and French shoes. Little farm girl marries a millionaire," he scoffed. He moved closer. She huddled on the edge of the bed and didn't dare look at him. His angry fingers reached out and pushed her hair behind her ear. "It was the money, wasn't it?"

The money? She had no idea what he was talking about. Between the two of them, Jack was the one riveted on money, hence, the pre-nup. He'd had it all his life—money. Jack always played it safe in the stock market and real estate. Unless he developed a compulsion to gamble, it would be hard to lose seventy-five million dollars.

She lifted her head and refused to look away from him. He actually looked in pain. Jack never talked about his childhood. She had never met his parents. Something or someone was responsible for the man he had become.

"Is that what you believe? I married you for your money?" She tucked her feet underneath her. "I never cared about your money. I make a six-figure salary, Jack. High six figures. I can buy my fancy suits and designer shoes. And as far as the farm girl crack, maybe I grew up on a farm, but I'm not some country bumpkin. I'm a successful trial lawyer. I paid my dues—college, law school, taking on every case deigned beneath the highfalutin lawyers at Seiler and Banks."

He towered over her, his hands strong and angry. He could crush her skull. If she was going to die tonight, she wanted to know the truth before she left this world. "Did you bribe Barbosa, Jack?"

He didn't answer, only looked away.

"Was I right? Are Jason and Kristie innocent?"

He turned toward her. "Is that what you think?"

She searched his face. "I want to know the truth."

"Yeah, they're innocent. I bribed Barbosa. I'm loaded, right? I could afford to pay some slick bastard for his testimony because I'm so inept at my job."

He reached over and grabbed her by the arm and yanked her across the bed. Her feet skimmed the comforter, and her toes hit the hardwood floor where he dropped her. He kicked at the mangled dresser drawers and pointed toward her undergarments. "Pick it up." He crossed the floor and threw open the closet and scooped several hangers filled with blouses, suits, and jeans and flung them on the floor next to her. "If you want them, then I suggest you get them in order." He headed back to the closet and grabbed another handful.

She pinched her eyes but couldn't stop the tears. She blinked, and they escaped down her cheeks. Her nose ran, and she wiped it with her sleeve.

She struggled to her feet and rushed him. Her hands tugged at his shoulder, and she tried to push him away from her closet. "Don't!" she cried. "You're ruining them!"

He turned on her, his eyes sharp and unyielding. "I'm not fucking with you anymore. You're coming home. And if you believe I'm capable of bribing witnesses to get what I want, then you'll have no trouble believing I'll use whatever means to keep you where you belong." He cocked his head. "We both know who you care about most."

He didn't have to say their names. Her family meant everything to her. Deep down, he resented them, especially her close relationship with her sister. She couldn't risk him hurting Bren—or worse.

"I'll go. I will." She grabbed his arm, pulling on his dress shirt, and begged him to acknowledge her. "But, please, let me do this myself."

He smirked. That mannerism, his way of letting her know he had won. He let go of the clothes resting in the crook of his arm. Still on the hangers, they swished back into place.

He checked his watch. "You do that," he said in a condescending tone. He speared her with his icy blue stare. "I'm late for a meeting."

She didn't know the time. Maybe it was close to seven or seven thirty. He was like a mechanical doll. He was done terrorizing her, and now he was going to casually resume his regularly scheduled life.

She hated him.

"If it's all right with you, I'll return tomorrow. I want to call Sydel and see if I can break my lease." She looked at the door hanging precariously by one of its hinges. "I'll need to get the door repaired." She looked around the room. "And the mess," she said. "I need to clean up."

The meeting scheduled for tomorrow with the FBI must have eluded him. He made no mention of it, and if he did, she would lie about the location. She had no intention of cleaning up or fixing the door. Maybe the FBI would be more inclined to believe her when they walked in on the destruction.

It was time to say good-bye to IrishEyes.

Toes softly on the steps, after the front door slammed shut, she crept downstairs. He was gone. She tried the lock, but found it weak after Jack's handiwork, and chained the door. Padding to the kitchen, she stared at the whiskey bottle tipped over. The smell of Ireland's finest teased her nasal passages. After what she had been through over the past two hours, drunk would be a nice state of consciousness. She moaned and walked away. There wasn't enough to fill a shot glass, much less catch a buzz.

The cream she had bought for coffee tomorrow was probably room temperature by now. After her theatrics, there was no way she could have put it in the refrigerator right in front of Jack. So she had shoved it in the cabinet.

She twisted open the cap and took a whiff. It smelled fine. She peered inside the fridge, the chilly air a relief to her flushed arms and face.

The sealed translucent bag with its precious contents was still there lying flat against the wire shelf exactly where she'd left it. She placed the cream next to it and sagged against the refrigerator door. If he had insisted on looking inside, there was no way to explain it—none. She might as well offer herself up as a sacrificial lamb and save herself the trouble of trying to escape him.

Head throbbing, she downed two Advil and headed down the hall to the living room, grabbed her phone from her purse, then continued to the overstuffed chair. She sighed, placed her water on the oak table next to it, and sank into the softness, its arms embracing her, keeping her secure. She lifted her legs, sore from trembling, up onto the matching ottoman and pressed the glass filled with tap water against her temple. She remembered her passport and bonds still locked in her glove compartment of her BMW.

Thank God for FBI agents and doughnuts.

With her hands full of groceries, she had decided to leave her passport and bonds in the glove compartment. Otherwise, she would have had them in her hands, and it would have been the first thing Jack would have grabbed the moment he opened the door, her spirit halfway between heaven and hell. She glanced at the time on her phone she'd dropped in her lap. If Jack had killed her after opening the refrigerator, her spirit would be halfway there. To heaven, that is, because she had already spent her time in hell.

Kate awoke. The pounding in her head had her sitting straight up. She glanced at the time on her cell phone, the numbers still blurry from sleep— eleven forty-two. *Shit!* She had dozed. Her eyes felt crusty and heavy. Her lips, as she licked them, sharp and cracked. She reached up with the back of her hand and swiped against the dried layer of slobber on her cheeks and groaned. It must have been a deep sleep.

The pounding . . . why wouldn't it stop? It was as if it was outside her head. She jumped to her feet and tripped over the ottoman.

It wasn't her head—it was the door.

Creede

Here's a land where all are equal—
Of high or lowly birth—
A land where men make millions,
Dug from the dreary earth.
Here the meek and mild-eyed burro
On mineral mountains feed—
It's day all day, in the day-time,
And there is no night in Creede.

The cliffs are solid silver
With wondrous wealth untold,
And the beds of running rivers
Are lined with purest gold.
While the world is filled with sorrow,
And hearts must break and bleed,
It's all day in the day-time
And there is no night in Creede.

— Cy Warman

CHAPTER FIFTEEN

Colorado, three years later . . .

THE BRIGHT RED PICKUP CAREENED LIKE A BULLET DOWN THE thin Colorado mountain road, with little room for driver error. A cloud of dust followed in its wake when the pickup caught the turn sharp onto 149. The Silver Thread Byway cut a swarthy path through cliff palisades painted in layers of tangerine and cream hues. The one-lane highway in either direction was deserted at seven in the morning on Charlie Robertson's way to downtown Creede and the office of Sterling Log Homes.

Wide open spaces greeted her. The Rio Grande, which ran parallel to the highway, a surging flow of snowmelt left from spring, gurgled and pulsed in the distance. The serenity was lost on her. Not even the warm summer breeze and the scent of pine, wafting through the back slider of her pickup, reduced her anger.

Route 149 rolled her right into town and onto Main Street with its narrow two-lane road and side streets tightly gripped between towering mountain rock. She slowed her speed and maneuvered the parallel parking space with ease. Reaching across to the stack of contracts strewn on the passenger seat, she grabbed the paper neatly folded on top and got out, shutting the door.

After hopping the curb, Charlie swung open the door of Sterling Log Homes and cleared the doorway to her partner Ben Sterling's office and tossed the letter on his desk. "I think that should take care of it." She turned abruptly to leave.

"Whoa, where are you going?"

She spun around, her gaze locking in on him. "To clean out my truck."

"Your truck?" He gave her a quizzical look. "Do you want to tell me what this is all about?" He snapped the paper open, glanced at it, and flung it on his desk, laughing.

Charlie's cheeks warmed. "You're a jerk."

"And you're emotional." He sat back in his chair. "Do you actually think I would accept your resignation?"

"From where I'm standing, it looks like you have no choice. I'm done. If you weren't so hung up on my sex, we wouldn't be having this conversation. I thought we'd worked through the issue of your partner being a woman, but I guess it's still an embarrassment for you."

"What are you talking about?" Ben's brows furrowed.

"The Fielding deal. Scott Fielding called me this morning. Seems he is under the impression that Charlie Robertson is your *male* partner."

Ben laughed again.

Charlie fisted her fingers. "It's not funny."

"I'm sorry. He's old school. I'd have lost the deal."

"Hiding me isn't the answer."

He scratched his head. "I wasn't hiding you. Granted, I didn't make it clear. He must have assumed the name on the business card was a man's."

She eyed him. This wasn't the first time he'd strategically chosen to be vague about her identity. She got it. With the economy, not many tourists were plunking down six hundred K and upward for a vacation home made of logs. She and Ben needed every sale.

"What?" His lips twitched, forming a faint grimace. "It wasn't intentional."

"So it slipped your mind."

"What?"

"The fact I'm a woman."

"Trust me, I'm well aware."

"What's that supposed to mean?" She took a step closer, hoping he had a good enough answer before she beaned him in the nose.

Ben stood and came around his desk. "I'd have to be either blind or stupid not to notice," he said, his eyes intent on her face. "Look, if it will ease your pain, I'll call Scott back and explain—"

"Don't bother. I'm resigning, effective immediately." She turned to leave.

Strong fingers wrapped around her upper arm and pulled her back, rolling her up against him.

Lines bracketed his mouth; eyes locked into hers. "Listen, I'm not going to let your bruised ego dictate to me. I'm sorry, it was an oversight. This paper means nothing. Remember, you signed a contract, and I'm not about to let you slide."

"You can stick that worthless piece of paper up your—"

His hand caressed her cheek, his mouth crushing down on hers. She pushed against his chest, totally confused, frightened even. But the scream fighting toward her lips turned to a soft moan. Her hands moved over his shoulders, her fingers sifting through the chestnut hair at the nape of his neck.

Ben's tongue caressed the inside of her lips, and she cautiously unclenched her jaw, allowing her timid tongue to explore his mouth. He pulled her closer. His callused fingers, intertwined in her hair, trembled.

Charlie smiled to herself. Under his tough-guy act, he was as soft as a marshmallow. They had a good thing going; each knew what the other was thinking before their thoughts could be formulated into words. They argued constantly, but harsh words were a reality, especially with deadlines and inspections looming on every project.

His own reaction made her aware of how much she cared for him. Charlie pulled back, breaking the kiss. She was breathing hard.

Ben's usual hard-line eyes gazed at her questioningly, and he angled his head to taste her again.

She pulled her head back, whispering, "No." Sliding her hands down his chest, she held him away. "I'm not ready for this."

She closed her eyes. He had to touch her, make her aware of him in that way. They smelled good together. Wasn't that silly, but they did. He smelled earthy, a blend of Irish Spring soap and sawdust. Or did she smell like sawdust? It didn't matter; she liked the smell. Her eyes opened, and she considered him thoughtfully. Ruggedly handsome, well respected, that was Ben.

So what is the problem?

A stupid vow she'd made to herself long ago over a man who didn't come close to measuring up to Ben. This couldn't happen. With a relationship came honesty. She could never be honest with anyone—ever.

"Charlie." His words came out rough. He moved to kiss her again.

She smacked her hand across his lips. His wide eyes made her bite down on a laugh, and she tried to remain serious and let go of him. "Don't get any fool ideas about you and me. I'm not mixing business with pleasure."

"Does that mean you enjoyed it?" He grinned.

"No . . . I mean . . . yes, it was . . . Ben, stop. This isn't good for business, and you know it."

"Funny, as of about five minutes ago you were no longer employed at Sterling Log Homes. So, as far as I'm concerned, there's not an issue." He went to kiss her once more.

She pulled her head back. "We need to focus on work." Then sidestepping him, she added, "After careful consideration, I've decided to accept your apology." Charlie reached for the sheet of paper with her hasty ultimatum on his desk and crunched it up in a ball, tossing it in the trash can. "Plus, I need this job. My first mortgage payment's due."

"Sobering, I know."

He couldn't even begin to comprehend the gamble she'd made by putting down permanent roots. It could be her biggest error in judgment since arriving in Creede.

"Exactly. So let's concentrate on getting our second draw on the Lockhart site. I'm going to see Quince."

"That recluse." He was frowning at her, his forehead creased in irritation. "Why?"

Ben sat on the edge of the desk and crossed his arms over his chest like an Indian chief questioning his squaw. A little too command and control.

Charlie found it amusing and placed her hands on her hips. "Then I'm assuming you have expertise in dynamite."

"You hit rock?"

"Yep. If our clients want that ten-foot-deep basement below grade, I need someone qualified to set dynamite." Quince was top-notch when it came to explosives. He'd told her stories about working the Last Chance Mine until it closed.

"We can't . . ."

"No. It's volcanic—too dense for a bulldozer."

Ben's mouth moved in preparation to lodge a complaint.

"Hey, you helped pick the site. I'm only doing damage control."

"Fine. I'll go with you. It'll be dark before—"

"He doesn't like you." If there was one person Quince wished dead, it was Ben. Years before Charlie came to Creede, Ben had kicked Quince off land that Quince claimed fell under squatter's rights. Not that Quince owned the land, but it was kind of like ownership being nine-tenths of the law—in his mind, it was his. She squared her shoulders, her expression serious. "Besides, I've been there at night."

"I see." He was laughing, again, looking as gorgeous as ever. "How about I stop by later tonight to make sure you get home okay."

His eyes shone dark and restless with wanting her—or was that just her sexually deprived imagination?

Get a grip.

Charlie pointed her finger at him. "I think it would be best if you keep your distance from me tonight." Charlie moved to the door and then swung around. "One more thing. In the future, your partner and co-owner is a woman."

"I'll work on your last request, but I'm afraid keeping my distance from you is going to be a challenge."

Charlie threw her head back and groaned, then leveled a serious expression his way. "This didn't happen, understand? We're partners."

Before he could offer a rebuttal, she stepped out of his office and closed the door.

CHAPTER SIXTEEN

CHARLIE MANEUVERED THE GRAVEL ROAD AND PULLED OFF TO the side, parking below the rock ledge leading into the forest. Back when she came to Creede, she had met Quince by accident while hiking one of the "Fourteeners"—San Luis Peak that reached fourteen thousand feet in the San Juan Mountains surrounding Creede. Lost in the Rio Grande National Forest for nearly three hours, out of water and granola bars, and nearing dusk, she came across his camp.

His home leaned to the left considerably, the weathered boards running vertical, emitting light through cracks wider than a man's thumb. She'd been standing with one foot poised on the first unsteady step leading to his small front porch when he flung open the barely hinged door. He reminded her of a troll; though not short, his expression ripe with agitation made him appear trollish.

He snarled at her through rotten teeth. "State your business and move on."

She had no business, and his German shepherd made it clear: One scant move in either direction and she was chow.

They had come to a mutual understanding that day. He demanded solitude, and Charlie was desperate for civilization. During the two hours she spent with him maneuvering around the Fourteener, getting her to a reference point where she could navigate back into town, he wasn't particularly polite, sweet-smelling, or agreeable. But he intrigued her. Against his fiery complaints, she searched him out regularly, forging an unlikely friendship. Protective of the man she had come to know as Quince Maynard, she didn't appreciate Ben's earlier comment.

She took a breath and cleared her mind. This was where it got tricky. Once she crested the jagged mountain ledge, she'd have to go on foot the rest of the way. She wasn't concerned about the loss of daylight. She'd made this trek often enough, but she grabbed her flashlight for her return. By then the last remaining twilight lingering against the cool, still strength of the San Juan Mountains would turn into darkness.

Quince's shack rested about a mile deep inside the Rio Grande National Forest. Charlie shoved the flashlight into the back pocket of her jeans and searched the rock wall for a foothold. The rubber soles of her work boots made the ascent manageable. The thin saplings shooting through the crevices assisted her to the top as she grabbed hold of them, hoisting her body over the ledge. Pushing up from her knees, she dusted off her legs.

The man really needs to rethink his Josey Wales lifestyle.

Charlie entered the dense forest and pushed through the brush, its once spindly branches now thick and leafy in summer. Immediately the temperature dropped. Above, the declining light filtered through the crowded pines, shafts of shimmering pixie dust, lucent, floated about her. She breathed deep, a combination of pine and decay filling her lungs.

She kept moving deeper, a choir of crickets and bullfrogs serenading her. She knew she was getting close from the thin, worn path of Quince's wheelbarrow. She came up short when she encountered a new addition to his fortress—barbed wire. "What the hell?" She strained her neck. Darkness had dropped like a veil, the light spilling from the cracks of his shack. "Quince! It's Charlie."

The bark of his dog split the calm of the forest solitude, and Charlie screamed. She lit the area. Gimlet eyes glowed yellow against the light of her flashlight. The dog bared white teeth and growled a warning from several feet away.

Shit.

Charlie put out a steady hand. "Hey there, pooch. Nice doggy." She craned her neck, searching for Quince, whispering under her breath, "Where the hell are you, old man?"

"Her name's FeFe."

Charlie spun around. Quince stood stock-still, his long gray hair tied back. His bushy gray eyebrows knotted together, eyes dark with aggravation, lips twisted and barely visible through the shroud of whiskers.

"You really need to rethink her name."

"She came from the pound." He dug his heels into the soft earth and gave her a once-over. "Why you here?"

"To visit a friend."

He gave a snort. "Like hell. You want something."

"Okay. Doesn't mean I didn't miss you."

"Hungry?"

"A little."

Quince moved past her, took two steps to the right, and unlocked a makeshift door of barbed wire. "*Nein,*" he commanded to the shepherd. She gave one regretful whine because she wasn't going to get to eat Charlie for dinner and bounded toward the shack.

"Ever think of moving back to civilization?"

Quince looked over his shoulder. "You're one to talk."

"What's that?"

"I told you, I don't like people."

Charlie followed close behind, climbing the single slanted step to the covered porch. She caught a whiff of something warm and meaty and wondered what creature Quince might have killed to fill the pot. After unlatching his crooked door, he stomped in first with his heavy boots, the floorboards creaking against his weight.

She came up behind him, the shepherd rubbing against Charlie's legs, her tail slapping the shelving along the wall filled with amber-colored liquid. Quince tossed down a metal pie plate, his fine china, and a single metal fork.

"Whiskey?"

"Sure." She never turned down the offer of Quince's corncob whiskey, made from his very own private still. She didn't want to risk hurting his feelings, especially when she needed his help. Of course, she'd pay him and well, but if she offended him, he was notorious for rebuking an offer no matter what the money.

He poured a generous portion into a metal cup, and Charlie winced behind his back. She'd be drunk off her ass if she finished it. Who knew the proof of his homemade concoction? If she had to label it, she'd use the word "lethal."

"How'd you come by so many bottles?" She nodded toward the shelf.

"Lightfoot." He smacked his lips. "He runs a mean bar and 'eats' in town. I swing by once a month. He saves the empties."

Tommyknocker Tavern—she knew the place well.

"You selling it now?"

Quince gave her a sly smile. "Man's gotta make a living."

Now the fence made sense.

He handed her the cup, his hands rough and cracked with dirt permanently imbedded in his skin. "Sit." He motioned toward the table and two mildew-stained barrels he used for chairs. "Stew's almost ready."

Charlie balanced herself on the barrel and took a tentative sip of her drink, the heat resting on her tongue before she found the courage to swallow. When she did, the burn washed down her throat, and she blew out a heated breath.

Quince eyed her expectantly.

"One of your best batches," she lied.

He grinned, exposing a set of gnarled teeth stained from tobacco. Wiping his hands on his dirty overalls, he reached for the pot on the stove and slammed it down on the table. He ladled out each of them a generous portion, and her mouth watered. The mystery meat notwithstanding, it smelled eatable.

She blew on her fork covered in brown gravy and chunks of meat, the steam curling above her nose. Her tongue darted out tentatively to test the temperature. Not scalding, so she sampled it.

"Good?"

Actually, yes. "Delicious." She smiled.

The rest of the meal was eaten in silence, except for Quince who grunted as he ate. By the time she helped him tidy up after dinner, she was surprised at the warmth of her face. She glanced down into the cup of rotgut and realized she'd drunk two-thirds. Not good if she expected to find her way out of the forest and to her truck tonight.

"Let's sit out on the porch." Quince motioned toward the door and waved her out first. Judging by his manners, he was on his way to becoming inebriated as well. He sat down next to her, their backs against the wall of the shack, their legs drawn up with the gallon bottle of Quince's finest between them. FeFe, more accepting of Charlie, stretched and settled down next to her and took a labored breath, her chin resting on her paws, her eyes heavy.

Charlie relaxed and extended her cup when Quince held out the whiskey, reminding herself she still needed to broach the subject of hiring him to blast the rock.

"I want to hire you."

"I'm retired."

"I know. Ever think of coming out of retirement?"

"No." He said it with conviction.

"Why not?"

"I told you. I don't like people."

"You like me." She turned and smiled sweetly.

"I didn't have a choice."

"Direct. I've always liked that about you."

He nodded and took another sip from his cup.

"When can you start?"

"Tell you what. Tell me what you have in mind, and I'll name the price."

"You'll be reasonable?"

"You've got my word."

Charlie went into detail in regard to the job site, the volcanic rock, and the depth of the basement. Quince listened intently, sipping his whiskey.

He nodded throughout, giving her hope he'd be agreeable to her proposal and wouldn't try to gouge her on his price.

"I'll do it."

"How much?"

He gave her a devilish smile. "No money. Tell me who you're running from."

Charlie stared round-eyed, and the chill she thought could never again ride up her spine returned. "I think you've had too much to drink, my friend." Charlie wiped her mouth of whiskey and didn't like the sound of her own slurred voice trailing off her lips.

"I served two tours in 'Nam. I know when someone's running scared."

"You're drunk, old man."

"Girl. You can't run from the past. The past eventually catches you."

Slightly intoxicated—no, extremely intoxicated—she still wasn't sharing her past with Quince.

"Is that why you're a hermit? You're—"

"Damn it, girl. I told you—"

Charlie raised an arresting hand. "I got it." She pushed up with one hand, balancing her cup in the other, and tittered.

Quince pulled her back, her butt coming down hard to rest on the wooden planks of his porch, the whiskey sloshing over the rim of her cup. "You're not going anywhere tonight."

The sky began to pitch.

"What's it going to be?" Quince set his beady black eyes on her.

She eyed him back with disdain. "My story for the job?"

"That's what I said."

It was almost a relief someone had figured her out. She trusted Quince. He'd saved her life. He allowed their friendship when he could have easily sent her away. If there was someone she could trust with her secret, it would be a man who doesn't like people.

"If I tell you, it goes no further than you and me."

Quince spit into his palm. "Shake on it."

Charlie laughed. Even the sight of bubbling spit in his weathered, filthy hand didn't turn her stomach. Feeling like a kid sealing a deal, she shook on it. "Not a word."

"Done."

While Charlie divulged her secret past, her true identity, Quince listened intently, never interrupting once.

She took a deep breath. "That's it."

Quince pulled on his scraggly beard in contemplation and then turned toward her. "He'll find you."

"I covered my trail." With her fingers, she ticked off the items in the envelope she'd gotten from her pal Davey. "New identity complete with birth certificate, Social Security card." Her stomached dipped. She'd almost forgotten the envelope tucked inside the frame that night.

"You always have brown hair?" He nodded to her head.

"Nope." She yanked on it. "Compliments of Excellence-to-Go by L'Oreal, Medium Reddish Brown number 5RB—after I arrived in Denver."

He pulled his lips in, considering, then shook his head. "Trust me. He'll find you."

Charlie thought back, and her body went cold. She had left a trail—*her blood*. It had never occurred to her that Jack could track her through the blood donations. Those were a must, if she wanted to keep her iron levels at a safe level.

Quince's words reawakened that frightened woman back in Maryland. The possibility of Jack finding her weighed in the back of her subconscious.

Even if her family had heard Jack was looking for her, they couldn't warn her. Their plan never had a contingency for that. They didn't know where she had ended up.

Charlie shrugged. "I'll run."

"Until he catches you." Quince moaned and pushed up from the porch and disappeared inside the cabin. When he reappeared, he gripped a double-barreled shotgun. He held it out. "Take it."

"Hell no. Last time I handled a gun, it almost landed me in jail."

Quince laughed out loud. "You should have aimed higher and shot him in that miserable ass of his."

Charlie smiled. She could see the humor in it now. But at the time, having a gun seemed prudent. She just hadn't counted on her heavy trigger finger.

"It was dark; he scared the hell out of me."

Quince let the butt fall to the porch with a thud. "You still have it, then?"

"Top shelf of my closet."

"Then learn some self-restraint and get some target practice in. Bastards like your husband don't just disappear for good."

CHAPTER SEVENTEEN

NICK FOSTER ASSUMED THE POSITION—LEGS STRADDLED, ARMS apart—while Deputy Shepherd, a lanky looked-to-be-twenty-something full of piss and protocol, did a quick pat down.

If this isn't a bunch of bullshit.

He wanted to say "screw it." Especially since he knew damn well that Charlie Robertson, the construction worker from Creede, Colorado, was *not* the Kate Reynolds he sought.

"He's good, Mike. Clean as a whistle." Still in a squat, the deputy peered up. Nick met pale-blue eyes fringed in blond lashes, fair complexion, freckles, and a cheeky grin with dimples.

Jesus. What are you—sixteen?

Nick angled his head. Sheriff Coulter, don't-piss-me-off-by-the-book lawman, had everything under control. About sixty, yet fit for his age, he leaned against the front of a silver four-door pickup, the words MINERAL COUNTY SHERIFF stenciled around a five-point gold star. "Then let's move on to the next phase." He tapped Nick's driver's license and military ID against his thumb and handed them to Shepherd. "Run him, Shep."

Walking for hours, lugging his duffel bag, since the piece of shit rental car had sputtered and died miles back, Nick should have been thankful he had a ride into town. Drawing attention to himself from local law enforcement wouldn't have been his first choice.

"Will do." Shepherd sauntered away and sat in the passenger seat, tucking his long legs inside the patrol vehicle.

Coulter's wary hazel eyes locked on Nick. "What brings you to Colorado?"

Nick laughed. "Relaxation." He surveyed his predicament—eyeballed and interrogated by Mineral County's finest after being forced to walk fifteen miles in boots he didn't have the chance to break in. "Not quite what I had in mind, huh?" Nick grimaced.

Coulter's tight expression lessened. "I know what you mean. Course, being in the military, I'm sure you've faced greater hardships. See much action?"

"Afghanistan . . . mostly."

Shepherd strode toward them, and Nick was thankful for the interruption. "Comes back to Nicholas D. Foster. He's good. License is up to date, no warrants or speeding tickets." Shepherd handed Coulter Nick's identification.

Coulter pushed off his patrol car and focused on Nick. "Looks like you check out." He rubbed his chin thoughtfully. "You say you have a gun, eh?"

"Yes sir."

Coulter motioned for his deputy. "Shep, give his duffel a once-over." His thick brows puckered, and creases formed around his full mouth. "There should be one firearm, correct?"

Nick stiffened. "Correct." *And a multitude of questionable devices hidden in a side compartment. Shit!*

Shepherd bent down and rifled through Nick's bag in an orderly fashion. Glancing down, Nick noticed that the deputy's shoulders barely cleared the wide brim of his Stetson. Appearances notwithstanding, he had learned never to discount a man's strength on first impressions. Although slender, Deputy Shepherd's arms flexed with lean muscle. Within seconds the deputy held only his gun, and Nick relaxed. "Got it. Glock 22, magazine and gun separated."

Coulter rapped Nick on the back. "Good man. Glad to see you still practice gun safety, even in retirement." He chuckled. "You wouldn't believe the yahoos we get from out of state. Just because Colorado allows people their God-given right to openly carry and bear arms. You'd be surprise how many leave one bullet in the chamber and think it's not loaded." He laughed, and the fine lines imbedded in his leathery face softened. "Greenhorns, the whole lot of 'em. All it takes is one trigger pull and *bam*." He slammed his meaty hand against the roof of his pickup.

Nick jumped.

A sly grin snaked across Coulter's lips, making it clear he enjoyed Nick's response.

Nick's adrenaline spiked. *Asshole.*

The amusement in Coulter's countenance shifted, his gaze now quiet. He gave Nick a nod. "Okay, son, how 'bout we get you into town."

Shep grabbed Nick's duffel and shoved it in the back seat with him. With no recourse but to assume the front, Nick took his eye off the bag reluctantly and climbed into the passenger seat of the truck, and Coulter started the engine. The rush of pine trees and the double centerline of Route 149 looked better going fifty-five miles an hour. His feet ached like a son of a bitch.

"How long you say you'd be staying in Creede?"

It wasn't the words, but quite possibly his tone, although to anyone else it would seem friendly enough. Nick made his living reading people—and in Coulter's words he definitely sensed an underlying meaning. His question wasn't based on simple curiosity. Although he smiled when he asked, it bordered on something more disquieting, like, *I got my eye on you, boy.*

"A few weeks. Just looking to relax. Do a little fishing."

"Hmm, let me see if I can hook you up." The sheriff settled back in his seat and remained quiet. For a small-town sheriff, Coulter seemed squared away. Nick would keep that in mind during his stay in Creede.

"I'd appreciate that." Outside, a tortuous path of asphalt cut through emerald valleys, mountain ledges interspersed with layers of rock and ponderosa pines. The ceiling of clouds looked more like cotton he could reach out and pick.

Nick relaxed against the back of the seat. He listened to the sheriff's and deputy's conversation, the two sounding more like an Andy Griffith rerun, except more Western. Seemed nothing much happened in Creede.

And as long as Charlie Robertson cooperated, it would stay that way.

CHAPTER EIGHTEEN

I N THE UPSTAIRS ROOM OF TOMMYKNOCKER TAVERN, CREEDE'S ONLY true tavern where the locals hung out, Toby Keith belted out one of his songs while the pinball machines along the back wall pinged. A few of Charlie's guys from Sterling yipped when their score grew higher.

Charlie nestled her head against the plump vinyl back seat of the booth and closed her eyes. Her head throbbed, big time. If she kept her eyes closed and tried to tune out the pool balls slamming into their designated pockets and the cheers that followed, the pain would subside. Charlie smiled. Now would be a good time to begin target practice. The gun she'd bought when coming to Creede now, after her conversation last night at Quince's, rested comfortably in a small holster on her hip, hidden underneath her Sterling Log Homes sweatshirt—easy access.

"What are you smiling about? Doesn't it hurt?" Charlie's eyes popped open just in time to catch Ben reaching over the table and touching the bandage over her left eye.

Charlie took a huge breath through her nose, her back pressing deeper into the booth. "Yeah, it hurts. Next time Joe decides to have a heart attack while driving a seven-thousand-pound bulldozer, give me some advance warning."

Ben leaned across the table. "Next time don't pull Superwoman and jump aboard the damn thing."

"I guess I should have let it crush you and Jim. Only I'd be out a partner and a stone mason, not to mention a pissed-off client with his cabin on deadline." She smiled at him and leaned over the table. "It was a self-serving act. I need my paycheck."

He laughed and opened up the dessert menu. "Want to split an ice cream sundae?"

He liked to tempt her with his obsessions—and one that could easily become hers. Although, she did treat herself occasionally to la crème de la crème of homemade ice cream at The Old Firehouse Restaurant on Main, a refurbished building from Creede's wild mining days. Ben would be lucky to get a bite in, then. "Hot chocolate sauce and I get the cherry."

"Deal," Ben said and waved Shelley over to their table.

They were back to just Ben and Charlie, and she couldn't have been more relieved.

Shelley moved in their direction, and Charlie's stomach clenched. Maybe no one else noticed the hunted look in the young mother of a four-year-old son. Or the way Shelley had changed her hairstyle tonight to accommodate the bruising behind the soft blonde curls that framed her face, more apparent now that she stood at the end of the booth next to Ben, her hand resting comfortably on his shoulder.

"Hi, guys. Thinking about dessert?"

"We'll have the usual." Ben's fingers reached up and patted Shelley's hand.

Charlie sat back. *Huh.* She bet they didn't even realize they were doing it. Shelley and Ben . . . how'd she not see that before?

Shelley squeezed his shoulder and let go. "Vanilla ice cream, hot fudge, and two cherries," she recited, smiling when she wrote it down on her pad. Then she winked at Charlie, adding, "Make sure you share the cherries with Ben."

"You could be a little more generous considering I'm injured." Charlie pushed out her bottom lip.

Shelley frowned. "How about some Advil? I think we have some in the back."

Charlie dug into the pocket of her Sterling Log Homes sweatshirt, a catchall these days, and set down a bottle of Advil. "I've been popping them all day."

Shelley clicked her pen off and shoved it into her apron. "Let's get you that dessert, then, and see if it makes you feel better." She moved away and disappeared down the stairs.

Charlie clenched her fists. "Did you see the bruise on her cheek?"

Ben craned his neck to look behind him.

Charlie kicked him lightly with her work boot. "You can't see. She's too far away."

"Which cheek?"

"Her left one."

"It's time I paid that son of a bitch a visit."

Charlie leaned in. "You can't do that. He'll only take it out on her."

"Then what the hell you propose I do? Let him beat her senseless?"

"If she's not willing to leave him, intervening is only going to earn her another beating."

DEFIANT
105

"This is bull—" Ben's cell phone rang. "Hold that thought."

Charlie cupped her ear, trying to hear. They'd been waiting for word from the hospital about Joe.

"Yeah." He smiled. "That's great news." He continued the conversation, nodding, his expression giving her every indication he was getting an update. He ended the call. "Joe's going to pull through. He'll be out for a few months. We might have to put him on light duty when he returns."

"That's great."

Ben looked around then settled his eyes on Charlie. "About Shelley . . ."

Yeah, about Shelley . . .

Charlie nodded to his shoulder. "What's up with the hand squeezing?"

"What?" His face folded in confusion.

"Don't play stupid. I never noticed it before, but you two do that—" She motioned toward his shoulder again. "—thing a lot."

He looked as though she'd caught him stealing copper from a job site.

He leaned over, the light catching the amber in his chestnut hair. "She's in a relationship."

"With an *asshole. Jeez.*" Charlie slapped both her hands on the table. "She's not even married to him."

He shrugged.

"Hey." She kicked him with her boot again, harder. "Instead of trying to screw with the good thing we've got going, you need to invest some time and energy and let Shelley . . ."

Shelley sat the sundae between them with two long spoons. "Shelley what?" Her blue eyes darted from Charlie to Ben.

Charlie swallowed. "Your hair looks different. I don't remember you wearing it that way before."

Pink crept into Shelley's pale face, her hand shaking when she touched her cheek.

Ben glanced up at her face for the first time. He tightened his grip on the ice cream spoon, his knuckles turning white. He opened his mouth slightly.

"Shelley," Charlie said, louder than she'd planned. Concentrating on more composure, she continued, "Can you refill my water?" She picked up the bottle of Advil at her elbow, shaking the pills inside.

She nodded. "Sure. I'll be right back." Shelley let the tray drop to her side and headed back down the stairs toward the kitchen.

"Damn it. You were going to embarrass her."

He narrowed in on Charlie. "What's the right answer, then? You seem to know a lot about the subject. You want to enlighten me?"

Charlie sat back in her seat. That's the last thing she needed: Ben suspecting she spoke from experience. "I don't know any more than you do. Maybe we need to approach this situation together."

"Double-team her?"

Sports analogy. That would work. "When she comes back," Charlie said, snagging one of the cherries sliding down into a soup of melting vanilla ice cream, "talk to her about anything except her face or Bobby Ray."

Ben took a large spoonful and ate it. "Then what?"

Charlie yawned and took one last bite of the sundae. "I'm going home. I'll talk to her on my way out and offer to take her in. If she's willing to leave, she and Gunner can stay with me as long as she wants." Charlie glanced at her watch.

"Hey." Ben reached over and tapped his spoon on the table in front of her. "What do you want me to do?"

"Hang around until she gets off in about fifteen minutes. Offer to walk her to her car." Charlie shook her head in bafflement. "You act as though you've never engaged a woman in conversation."

Charlie kept her eye on the opening by the steps leading down to the main dining room. "She's coming. Just make sure you let her know we both want to help her. But for God's sake, don't you threaten to confront . . ."

"Here you go." Shelley smiled and placed a tall glass of water on their table.

"Thanks." Charlie downed the pills and got up, clearing the booth. "I'm going to head on out." She winked at Ben. "Check?"

"Got it covered."

Charlie rapped him on his shoulder. "Good man. See you tomorrow."

Ben raised his spoon, his mouth full of ice cream. "Be careful driving home, and try some ice." He pointed to his own head.

Before Charlie could reply to Ben or formulate what she wanted to say to Shelley, Shelley grabbed Charlie's arm and pulled her onto the landing leading down the steps and whispered "You two were talking about me."

Charlie reached out with tentative fingers and carefully pushed the curl strategically hanging across Shelley's ivory skin. The purple hue and slight swelling caught the recessed light from above, and Charlie gritted her teeth. "You tell me how awesome Bobby Ray is, and I'm walking down those steps and out that door." If she wanted to stay with him, or if she was too afraid to leave, she understood. Her words were not meant as a threat, and she didn't plan on confronting Bobby Ray. But Charlie wouldn't allow Shelley to excuse Bobby Ray's actions and expect her to believe it.

Shelley slumped against the wall, her sweet blue eyes tearing up. "You don't understand."

Charlie wrapped her arms around her and struggled to find the words.

"Trust me—I do. Let me help you," she whispered against Shelley's hair.

Shelley pulled away and wiped her tears with the back of her hand when a busboy passed by on the steps on his way to clear a table. "He pays the bills. I . . ."

Charlie placed her hands on Shelley's trembling shoulders and kept her voice low. "I get that, Shell. But when a man hit's you, that's bullshit all the way around."

Shelley's head dropped, and she stared into her hands. "I can handle Bobby Ray."

"Until he what? Kills you or Gunner? Leave his ass. You two can move in with me." Charlie cradled the side of Shelley's head, avoiding the bruise, and tried to pull her face even with hers.

Shelley shook her head, keeping her eyes directed to the ground. "I can't."

"Or won't." The headache that had begun to subside returned, and Charlie let go of Shelley and pressed the heel of her palm into her temple. "I'm going home." She needed a hot shower and sleep. Now it was Ben's turn. Sadly, she doubted he'd make any headway, either. Charlie pushed off the wall and grabbed the banister leading down.

Shelley caught her arm. "Don't be mad."

"I'm not."

Shelley's hand slid down Charlie's arm then fell away.

Charlie turned and took a step down toward the main dining area.

"Charlie," Shelley called after her. "Mike was asking about you. I told him about today. He wants to see you before you leave. He's out front having dinner with a retired Navy SEAL who's new in town."

Great. She didn't need his overzealous, fatherly interference in front of some old man she didn't even know.

"Thanks, I'll catch him on the way out."

CHAPTER NINETEEN

CHARLIE QUIETLY TOOK THE STAIRS DOWN TO THE MAIN LEVEL and hung back by the bar, which gave her time to assess Mike's demeanor before she approached his table.

She missed her own father—Mike had filled the void. But lately he was suffocating her. She caught the three men sitting in the far table by the picture window that faced the corner of Wall Street and Main. Mike and Shep were easy to spot with their uniforms. She couldn't make out the third until he turned a short-cropped brown head, and she caught the jut of his rough, unshaven chin and face.

Her body went warm, the frisson of tiny sparks of awareness tumbled inside her, and she blushed at her instant attraction. She expected a sixty-something gentlemen, not some hot, good-looking guy close to her own age.

No way was she going near that table.

She moved down the bar, heading toward the kitchen and the back door, running full force into a busboy, knocking his tray with empty beer bottles to the floor.

Chairs scraped the floor, heads turned, and heat crept into Charlie's face.

"I'm sorry." She bent down to pick up the broken glass.

A strong hand encircled her upper arm. "You're cut."

She angled her body, her eyes coming to rest on a pair of serious baby blues darting over her face and body. "Let him pick it up," the stranger said.

A youth came from behind her with a dustpan and broom. Charlie dropped the green shard of a Rolling Rock beer bottle and allowed the man to bring her to her feet.

"I . . ."

Mike stood next to her now. "What the blue blazes, Charlie?" He frowned at her, then reached up to examine her head.

She pulled away, yanking her arm from the SEAL's grip. "I was just on my way out."

Mike gingerly touched her bandage. "What Mack Truck—"

She stepped back. "It was a bulldozer, and I'm fine."

"The hell you are." Mike gave her a curious look. "You planning on driving yourself home?"

Charlie gripped the truck keys in her hand. "Same as I always do."

Mike opened his mouth a second time and then snapped it shut when his police radio went off. He grabbed the radio off his belt, holding up his hand. "I need to take this." He motioned toward Shep. "Don't let her leave."

"But I'm fine," she called after him. Charlie's shoulders slumped, and she caught the sympathy for her in Shep's eyes. "Just tell him I gave you the slip. I'm fine to drive. It's a bump on the head—not brain surgery."

Shep shook his head. "No can do, Charlie."

Her arms dropped to her side, her head falling dejectedly. "This is stupid." She raised her head and took a decisive step toward the door when the SEAL blocked her exit.

"I think you need to . . ." The SEAL's commanding voice faded, and the room began to spin. Strong arms held her, placing her bottom on a chair. He reached up and pulled her eyelid, opening it wider with his thumb, his rough face inches from hers. "How long ago did you hit your head?"

She pulled away, giving him a disagreeable look. "Around three."

He remained on his haunches, his muscular legs filling out his jeans in an appreciable way, and the tingle of unexplored newness to the opposite sex returned.

He stretched the strong column of his neck toward Shep. "She has a concussion."

"I don't," she snapped. "They checked me out in the hospital."

The SEAL leveled a serious gaze in her direction. "If it were me, I wouldn't let you drive."

"But you're not, and it's my call." She made a move to stand, and a familiar wide palm pressed down on her shoulder.

"I'm not a doctor, Charlie," Mike said. "I'll trust Nick's judgment on this. He's been through three tours in Afghanistan. I think he knows a concussion when he sees it."

Nick. Who the hell was Nick? Who cared what Nick thought?

She smiled convincingly at Nick, who seemed to be making the decisions in a town he had just recently ridden in to and had become an authority for her friend the sheriff. "Really, Nick. I'm fine. I drove in on my own. I can drive home the same way."

He clucked his tongue and stood.

His mannerism was annoying. Charlie clenched her fingers.

"You do what you want, sweetheart," Nick said. "I'm just passing through. But I know a thing or two about head injuries."

"He's right," Mike said. "Someone's going to drive you home."

"Fine, grab my partner. He can take me home."

"Last I saw he walked out with Shelley," Shep added.

She could blame herself for that.

Mike pulled on his chin. "I've got a single-car collision on Bachelor Loop Road. No injuries, fortunately, but an ambulance on the way for good measure." He nodded to Shep. "Betty Phillips called as well. Seems the Henderson boys are out destroying mailboxes again. One of us needs to swing by and take a report." He looked at Nick and grimaced. "No major unsolved mysteries around here, just petty misdemeanors and accidents that keep you hopping."

Charlie stood up, placing her hand on the railing of the steps leading upstairs. "Well there you go. Too busy to worry about me." She made a move to leave.

"Not so fast, slick." Mike held her in place. "I think I have a workable solution." He nodded toward Nick. "Nick here's staying at my cabin. He's had a hell of a start to his vacation with breaking down."

Mike eyed Charlie. "We picked him up just outside of Creede."

This had to do with her because . . .

"Nick, you can drive Charlie's truck to my cabin. That'll take care of you." He scratched his head, his eyes landing on Charlie. "Shep can swing by, once he gets the other pickup, and take you home, and I can head on out to the highway."

"Hell, no," she said. "I need my truck. Plus, all my tools are in it. I don't even know him." She pointed an accusing finger at the SEAL. Not that she had a problem with him, per se. In June, tourists flooded Creede. But this was different. "Nick . . . Nick . . ." The throbbing pain returned, and she cradled her head with her hand. "I don't even know his last name."

Nick frowned at her. "It's Foster."

"Thank you," Charlie bit back. Insanity. It was like she had no say in the direction she wanted her night to take or end. Had anyone considered how the hell she'd get her truck back? And she certainly wasn't allowing a perfect stranger, whether or not he passed Mike's rigid test of trust, drive her new pickup.

Mike took a deep breath and blew it out his nose. "Regulation prohibits him driving a patrol vehicle."

"That's not my problem."

"Fine, you ride in your truck, and he drives."

Charlie's gaze landed on Nick Foster. Standing tall, wearing a form-fitting, long-sleeved shirt outlining the contours of his muscular frame, he had the air of quiet composure. Nice for him. He wasn't the one being forced to ride with a stranger.

Actually, she was just as much a stranger to him. Only he seemed perfectly fine with the arrangements.

His eyes connected with hers and held. Something registered. Perhaps he actually felt some responsibility for her anger and anxiety. Because of his misfortune—lack of transportation—she'd been made to suffer.

Not happening, no way, no how.

CHAPTER TWENTY

C HARLIE WAVED MIKE ON AFTER THEIR POWWOW ON THE CORNER of Wall and Main outside of Tommyknocker's. "Got it—over top of the door jam." She found Nick standing alone outside the tavern. He stared at her intently, which made her uneasy. But Mike assured her he was safe—even ran his history through NCIC, the National Crime Information Center. She continued toward him. Shadows deepened the hollow below his eyes. Tight lines edged his pouty, tough-guy mouth. Her stomach fluttered.

Okay. He's good-looking—not interested.

"Change of plans. I'm driving."

He pushed off the picture window of the tavern. "How's your head?"

She gave him a tight smile. "Better." Not that he had helped her situation with his Dr. Foster M.D. act.

He nodded. "I didn't mean to cause you trouble with your friend Mike."

"We're good." She nodded to the ground and his duffel. "You must be tired. Let's get on the road. Mike's cabin is on Love Lake, about thirty minutes away."

He slung his bag over his shoulder.

"I'm the red Chevy truck." She pointed out the Silverado across the street by the Creede Post Office.

He glanced over and laughed. "A half-ton pickup?"

She clenched her fingers. "Is that a question or a statement?"

"No." He raised his hand in defense. "In your line of work, I guess it's required."

She ignored him and started past him, crossed over Wall Street, turned around, and noticed him several yards back. Strange, every time she stopped and peered over her shoulder, he stopped. Almost like a game of Red Light, Green Light.

Was he checking her out? She bit down on her lip and kept a steady pace, hopped the curb, and continued toward her pickup, three or four spaces ahead. Thinking better of it, she stopped and faced him abruptly.

"What are you doing?"

"Walking." He gave her a questioning look.

She retraced her steps toward him. "You're not a very good liar."

"I'm fine." He waved her on.

She tapped her finger to her lips. "You're in your early thirties, give or take." She invaded his personal space, grabbing his upper arm, the touch of him solid beneath his navy Windbreaker and her fingertips. "Strong, yet you can't seem to keep up with me." Her eyes swept over him again, lingering longer than was prudent, and the heat crept into her cheeks.

Stop staring and help the man.

She grabbed his duffel bag off his shoulder. "Let's lighten your load." He started to open his mouth but closed it—the bag already on her shoulder. "Let's go, Foster, ten yards."

Charlie kept her eyes trained on her truck, glancing down at his feet. "Your boots are new."

"Yeah." She caught the pain in his voice.

"Blisters hurt like a bitch. I know. Same thing happened to me when I first started in construction."

"You any good at it?"

She liked his voice. It had a slight rasp to it. "I'd like to think so."

"I'll have to come see for myself and visit you."

Charlie stiffened. "I don't date." The words were out before she could take it back, and she regretted it immediately.

His body shook, and a deep-throated laugh lingered in the cool June mountain air. "The polite thing would be to wait until you're asked."

She glared up at him. "You're a jerk."

He laughed again.

Charlie's face warmed, and she dumped his duffel bag on his feet.

He grunted.

She smiled, gave him her back, and walked to her truck.

"Hey, you're mad." He continued to laugh at her.

Charlie climbed into the truck and started the engine. She hit the high beams and snickered when his arms came up to shield his face. Not so tough anymore, Mr. ex-Navy SEAL.

She pulled out and had every intention of leaving him. He grabbed his duffel bag and limped toward her, and she couldn't do it. She lowered the passenger window when she got even with him. "Get in."

He threw his duffel in the bed of the truck, bent down for a second or two, she assumed to tie his boots, something, maybe the zipper to his jacket clinking her truck, and then he hopped into the cab. "I'm sor—"

"The deal is you don't talk to me."

"No problem." He pulled up the collar to his jacket and let his head fall back against the headrest.

Charlie's eyes lingered. Tight-cropped, golden-brown hair and the hardened planes of his face, rough with a light beard, gave him a dangerous look. But, then, weren't Navy SEALs trained to kill?

She shivered and kept driving, heading toward Middle Creek Road. Nick remained quiet, and Charlie turned to find his eyes closed, his breathing heavy.

Relieved that he'd fallen asleep, Charlie put more pressure on the gas pedal. As soon as she got him to Mike's, she'd set him on his way, hoping she could avoid him until he moved on. The turn came up quick, and she made a left. She gasped when Nick slumped against her.

How the hell?

She eyed him. *Great.* He hadn't put his seatbelt on. Charlie pushed back. He didn't budge. Her grip tightened on the steering wheel.

Just drive the truck, Charlie.

He flustered her—not good. She kept to the road, now dirt. The back road to Mike's cabin would be coming up soon.

Nick moaned in his sleep, his chin snuggling into the hollow of her neck. Charlie bit down on her lip, looking for the turn. An arm snaked around her waist, pulling snug, and his action had her swerving quickly to make the left to Mike's cabin.

Damn it!

He smiled in his sleep, and she swore he'd done it on purpose. But his breathing remained deep, totally unaware of the liberties he took with her body. She assumed he mistook her for someone else, perhaps his girlfriend? Wife? Someone he obviously enjoyed snuggling with based on the grin smeared across his face.

The narrow, unmarked forest road ran right up next to the cabin, and she parked in front, turning off the ignition. The stillness of the truck unnerved her. He remained against her, his breath even waves, tickling her neck. Those firm yet pouty lips of his grazed her skin.

Warm tingles spread through her. This didn't come close to what she'd experienced with Ben the other day, and that made her tremble.

Charlie nudged him. "Foster, wake up."

He didn't move.

She moaned. "Come on, Foster, help me out here." She pushed harder on his shoulder—nothing, his rugged face serene in sleep.

He made an inaudible sound, smiled in his sleep, and snuggled deeper into the soft curve of her neck.

"Foster, get off me!" Her voice, reverberating thunder, clapped inside the cab of the truck.

His eyes shot open.

His face tightened, and he blurted out, "Oh shit!" He released her and pushed back against the passenger door. Scrubbing his hands across his face, he stared at her. "Charlie, I'm sorry."

"It's late, I'm tired—you don't owe me an explanation."

He opened his mouth and then, looking as though he thought better of it, clamped his lips shut.

Speechless. Well, good.

She'd gotten him to his destination. Next she'd find the key and then she was outa here, wishing him a pleasant stay in Creede and a nice life.

"Come on, Foster, wipe that surprised look off your face."

He smiled. "What look?"

"You know, the 'I was asleep so I can't be held responsible for my actions' look." She slid out the door, leaving it ajar.

Nick kept his eye on her as she climbed the steps to a small log cabin, several yards, he assumed, from this Love Lake glistening to his left. He mentally took notes of her finances sitting in the passenger seat of her brand-new, red Chevy pickup—looked like building premier log homes had been and remained lucrative for Sterling Log Homes *and* Charlie.

He flipped through the files left in a loose pile on the passenger seat. The one's he'd crunched between them when he'd fallen asleep. He glanced back through the glass slider. She remained on the porch, her hand above the jamb searching, he'd guess, for the key. Flipping through the folders revealed supply lists, surveys, and handwritten notes, presumably to keep her on deadline. But judging by the hodgepodge in her truck, she was no longer the organized trial lawyer she'd once been.

The creak of a door made him tense. She had stepped inside the cabin and turned on a light. He chuckled at the events of the day that had him at the ire of a woman who, until a few days ago, he didn't believe existed. She'd been giving the sheriff an earful since walking out the door of the tavern. Her head injury had been an unexpected perk.

Nick went back to work and cautiously examined a small, silver, tape recorder in one of the two cup holders pulled out from the front console until the passenger door swung open. Nick gave a jolt, his body falling back when a small, sturdy hand pressed up against his back.

"Foster," she said. "Whenever you feel the need to pitch in and give a little assistance, let me know,"

"Yes ma'am." He pulled himself up and slid out of the truck, bumping into her, his shoulder knocking into the side of her face, a soft moan falling from her mouth.

"Shit." He reached out to steady her, smoothing back a wave of her auburn hair, a stark contrast to the blonde she'd once been. He slid his hands down to her small shoulders. "I didn't see you. You okay?"

"Just fine." Irritated brown eyes held his and softened, her body moving closer. He'd made her life difficult today. He could understand her frustration. But he'd never counted on the attraction they would both have for each other.

She was attracted to him—no question.

Nick removed his hands from her shoulders, angling his head to check her out—slender build, nice-sized breasts that filled out her green Sterling Log Homes T-shirt, and a small waist. He had an immediate appreciation for the woman, and that included the job site story he'd heard from the waitress.

She handed him the keys. "Door's open." She turned and rounded the truck, the right side of her sweatshirt slightly raised, a holster and snub-nosed revolver visible.

He called after her. "Hey, no 'good night, Nick'?"

She laughed and stood on the running board, peering over the roof of the truck. "Good night, Nick," she said on a laugh and then shut the door, started the engine, and pulled away.

He nodded to himself. She may have begun to settle into this hole-in-the-wall called Creede, but she hadn't let down her guard.

Nick would keep that in mind, and Annie Oakley with the fine ass and sexy, long legs wouldn't distract him.

Chapter Twenty-One

C HARLIE SHUT AND LOCKED THE DOOR OF HER LOG CABIN. Holding the keys to her chest, she closed her eyes to those rough fingers of Nick Foster's along her cheek. She rolled her lips in, holding her eyes closed. When he'd bumped into her, she should have given him the keys, wishing him a nice stay in Creede and a nice life somewhere far away from her. Instead she'd taken a step closer. To what?

Her eyes popped open, the lights brighter than usual in the foyer of her new log cabin, and the dull ache returned. She checked her watch—five after ten. Charlie groaned. With two hours of work ahead of her, she'd be lucky to get to bed by midnight thanks to Nick Foster and his brooding good looks. Her stomach gave a giant flip-flop.

Get real. Any relationship with a man, but especially one like Nick Foster, was not a consideration. She let those serious blue eyes of his fade and went back out, retrieved the plans for the Fielding site, and locked her truck, heading back to the cabin. Towering pines bordered her property, their branches bumping against one another in the wind. Charlie quickened her pace. She stopped on the top step, the door creaking with the wind. *Crap.* She forgot to close it. She continued toward the front door, hesitating in front of the threshold, her grip tightening on the plans.

She'd never have given it a thought until recently—leaving a door open unattended. Jack would have to be a phantom to have slipped in without her knowing it. She took a step toward the open doorway.

Always leave an exit.

Thinking better of it, she left the door open and took her first step. Laying the plans on the closest table in the entryway, she unholstered her gun.

The home she swore would be lived in, messy if she chose, appeared neat and orderly under the recessed lights.

She still lived by Jack's rules.

She moved tentatively out of the foyer area, toward the great room. In front of the stone fireplace, with thick drapes drawn on either side, sat two brown leather couches, evenly spaced to form an L with matching coffee and end tables. The tables contained knickknacks and books, strategically placed.

She checked the great room. Nothing was out of place. The kitchen revealed the same. Charlie retraced her steps, moving toward the stairs and the basement door. It remained shut, her eyes veering in the direction of the steps leading upstairs, and she froze. The rectangle rug at the bottom of the steps leading up to the second level ran wide to the left.

She made it a point every morning to kick it back against the riser of the step, leaving no gaps. A chill slipped up her spine, and she tensed. Charlie's grip tightened on the gun. Fingers trembling, she put her boot on the first step and eyed the top landing, then the rug, and then the top landing again.

She fell back against the wall. All the adrenaline pumping through her veins redirected toward the black cat sitting perfect and pretty, his green eyes blinking down at her from the top landing.

"Scooter!"

She bounded up the steps after him. "Damn it, cat. You scared the living hell out of me." She searched the rooms one at a time until she came to her room. The warm light from the colorful globe, similar to the one Jack had broken, lit the master bedroom with its king-sized, wrought-iron bed. Charlie bent down with the gun and peered underneath. "I know you're here, Moochie." He knew he was in trouble. She hardly used his given name Scooter unless he'd done something egregious. "Do you want your two-finger spank now or later?

Charlie stood and placed the gun on the nightstand and yawned. Throwing off her sweatshirt, she let it land on the pine floor. Her heart regained its natural rhythm, and she sat down on the bed and removed her boots. Pulling up the pillows, she lay back.

The bed gave a little. Moochie padded toward her and nudged her shoulder blades with his face. He let out a cheerful meow, his insides rumbling like a NASCAR engine. "Is that the best you have for an apology, hmm, pretty boy?" She rubbed his ears, and he curled up beside her.

Charlie settled into the pillows and turned on her side, drawing up her knees. She continued to stroke Moochie's soft coat. The last few years had been full of defiant acts, her cat one of them. He had become her only kin. Charlie frowned. Although she enjoyed her new life and the freedoms it brought, she missed them—her family. Charlie's hand stilled on Moochie's side, her lids fluttered shut, and she slept.

Charlie shot up from her bed. Something had woken her . . . She checked the clock: twelve thirty-two. *Shit!* She had left the front door open.

She scurried to her feet, her socks sliding on the wood, and listened—silence. Then footsteps, heavy and moving up the steps, had her heart pounding in her chest. She fumbled for her gun on the nightstand, keeping an intense grip on it, her knuckles white with pressure. Her body trembled, the gun shaking in her hands. She took measured steps and swallowed hard, creeping toward the door. She swung into the doorway and turned toward the hall.

Her scream, followed by a slew of obscenities, echoed up to the cathedral ceiling. His fingers wrapped tightly around her wrists while he shoved the gun above her head, pointing it at the ceiling.

"*Jesus*, you almost shot me clean through!" Ben bellowed. "What the hell are you doing, Charlie?"

"What am *I* doing?" Both their arms remained entangled in the air. "What are you doing? This is *my* house. You're damn lucky you're not lying in a pool of blood. Why are you here?"

"I came to check on you. If you recall, you hit your head pretty hard today."

"It's a bump on the head."

"Oh, that's right. I forgot how hard your head really is." He followed the length of their arms, caught sight of the gun still pointed at the ceiling, and nodded upward. "How about you slowly take your finger off that trigger and hand me the gun before you really do some damage?"

Exhausted, she slid her finger off the trigger, leaving it in the trigger guard, the gun dangling on her fingertip before Ben snatched it out of her hand. Popping out the cylinder, he emptied the six bullets into his palm and shoved them into his pocket. "I thought after what happened you'd stored this thing away."

She shrugged. "That was an accident."

He gave her an incredulous look. "You kidding me?"

Charlie ignored him and headed down the steps. "You didn't see Moochie outside, did you?"

"You even listening to me?" His cowboy boots clomped the pine steps behind her.

Charlie peeked out the door and, finding the porch empty, shut the door to her cabin and locked it. "You carry a gun sometimes," she accused.

"Charlie, I'm warning you. If you don't answer me, I'll place you over my knee and tan your hide."

She rolled her eyes. "I swear, Ben, it's like you walked out of some Western movie."

He caught up with her as she headed toward the great room. "How long you been carrying this thing around?" He held out her snub-nosed revolver, and when she reached for it, pulled it behind his back, shoving it in the back waistband of his jeans. "Why would you leave your cabin door open?" His face creased with worry, and his eyes searched hers. "Charlie, what's going on? Did you black out?"

"No." She'd simply forgotten, and that was more problematic.

"You sleep with the gun?"

"*No*," she added with emphasis. He'd seen her bed. The gun had been on the nightstand, and she wasn't under the covers. "I mean I fell asleep, by accident."

"With the gun?" He placed his hands on his sides, his fingers flexing, eyes tunneling into hers.

Give him enough to make him happy.

"It's nothing. An active imagination on my part. I usually straighten the rug at the bottom of the steps." Her eyes veered over to it—straight, now. "It was crooked when I came home."

"You saying someone was in your cabin?"

Moochie stole down from the top of the stairs, and Charlie pointed in his direction. "I think he's my culprit. I found him at the top of the steps, *after* he totally freaked me out."

Ben eyed her speculatively, running his hand through his thick chestnut hair before letting it drop to his side with a big sigh. "What about the door?"

"It was an oversight. I got distracted tracking the cat down to give him a what-for."

The haze of a blue and red light danced on the pine floor through the two side windows of her front door. "What the hell . . . ? You didn't—"

"'Fraid so. I got concerned." He shrugged his shoulder.

A car door slammed, followed by a jiggle of the lock and a knock. "Charlie. Ben. You in there?"

Charlie motioned to the door. "You can explain."

"This is not my fault," he said, taking long strides across her entryway, turning the lock and opening the door. "False alarm. Just a rug out of place and a knot on the head, *and* she forgot to shut the front door."

Mike stepped in and whipped off his Stetson. "You're joking right?" He gave them both an incredulous look. "I just pulled into my own driveway when you called."

Charlie came up behind Ben. "And it was all for nothing." She motioned them out the door. "In case you two have forgotten, it's late and I'm tired."

Mike gave her a quizzical look. "Ben, you go on. I'll make sure everything's secure."

Charlie didn't like the sound of that. More like he was going to give her the fatherly chat he gave his own children.

Ben patted Charlie's back and moved past Mike. "Why don't you sleep in?

There's not much going on tomorrow except the electrical punch-out on the Jameson cabin. If you can take care of that after the electrician does his final, he's working late to finish, say . . . around eight thirty, we'll be good to go."

Charlie nodded. "No problem."

Ben placed his hand on Mike's shoulder. "You, Tess, and the kids coming to the open house party for our new neighbors?"

"You bet. This Saturday—Rio Grande Club at seven sharp. Tess is looking forward to it. So are the kids."

"Great. We booked a trio of fiddlers." He glanced back at Charlie. "Take care of that head." He crossed over the threshold, her gun poking out of his jeans.

Hell no. Charlie took one step forward, grabbed the gun, and shoved it in the back of her own waistband.

Ben flung around, his hand reaching for the same spot. He shook his head and eyed Mike. "You deal with her." Ben shut the door.

"What the hell just happened?" demanded Mike.

"Nothing." Charlie walked back toward the couch and shoved the gun behind the overstuffed cushion.

He followed her. "I don't even want to know what you shoved behind that cushion."

She smiled sweetly. "Want something to drink before you head home?"

"How about some conversation?" He bent down and grabbed the coffee table edition of *Colorado's Fourteeners* then set it down, the corner of it hanging off the edge of the table. He touched the coasters, moving them from their assigned spots. "Anything else out of place?"

Now there is.

He went for the wooden horse statue her mother had given her when she was ten, sitting strategically on the end table with part of his ear missing and minus his tail.

Charlie grabbed it out of his hand. "Stop rearranging my stuff! You're screwing everything up."

His head came around. "What the hell's up with you? Why does it matter?"

"It doesn't, okay? You're just making something out of nothing." Her head throbbed. "You need to go home."

He frowned. "You know I have my own demons, Charlie. It always struck me odd the way you—" He reached behind the cushion and pulled out her gun. "—marched yourself down to Ramble House and purchased a gun first thing after arriving in Creede."

Charlie cursed under her breath, vowing that if she ever bought another gun, it wouldn't be through the local sporting goods store.

Mike popped the gun open. "Ben have the bullets?" A pair of determined hazel eyes connected with hers. "I can't have you shooting up the town because you're running scared."

Her insides shook. Did he know?

"I've got the permit. I'm allowed to carry it concealed."

He opened his mouth.

"But I won't until I learn how to shoot it." She held her hands out, motioning with her fingers.

"I don't think that's such a good idea."

"Mike, give me my gun. I promise not to load it, and I'll keep it upstairs in the closet for now."

He stood there like the stubborn man she knew him to be. He had no choice. She had purchased the gun legally. His shoulders dropped. "Fine. But I'm asking you, as a friend and someone who cares about you, to keep it locked up in your closet with the ammo separate." He handed her the gun.

She slipped it in her waistband. "I promise."

"Well, good." He took a breath. "Walk me out."

She followed him to the door. "See you Saturday."

He grabbed his Stetson from the small table near the door and placed it on his head. "Think about what I said earlier. I'm here if you want to talk."

She nodded and shut the door, careful to lock the deadbolt, and slumped against the rustic wood she'd stained only a few weeks ago. Right now, her head spun with a multitude of oddities that seemed to spring up overnight. Rugs out of place, handsome strangers, a feeling of foreboding she couldn't shake thanks to Quince's unwavering belief that her past would eventually catch up to her.

And the gun, very deadly, and easily turned against her if she allowed the enemy to get too close.

CHAPTER TWENTY-TWO

"**M**ORNIN,' NICK."

Nick met the welcoming face of Sheriff Coulter dressed in his crisp uniform and Stetson.

"Hey, how's it going?" Nick wasn't surprised the good sheriff stood on his front step. "Before I forget, thanks for the use of the cabin. I plan on taking you up on your offer to use the boat. Looks like you have a great fishing hole here."

"You got that right. Well, good." He jutted his chin toward the cabin's interior. "If you need a pole or tackle, it's in the supply cabinet back in the kitchen."

"That's generous. Thanks."

"Nick, we're a small town—a close-knit family, so to speak. Long as you're in Creede, we'll consider you family."

"I appreciate that, Mike."

Mike shook his head. "About Charlie . . . you didn't see the best of her last night. She's a great gal."

"Yeah, I've been meaning to ask you about her." Nick moved back. "Come on in."

"Sure." Mike removed his Stetson and stepped inside. "She settle down once the two of you got on the road?"

"She seemed fine." Of course, he'd slept most of the way. Nick cocked his head. "She wary of men in general?"

"I wouldn't say wary." He scratched his head. "She started working for Sterling not long after she came to Creede. Now they're partners. They seem to have a good working relationship."

"Huh? Maybe it was the concussion."

"From the way Shelley told it, she hit that damn dashboard hard."

"About that . . . You don't often run across a woman that pretty who gets her kicks playing in the dirt."

"So you think she's pretty?" He took a step closer "A word of advice: If you have any notion of getting to know her better, be forewarned, she doesn't take kindly to male advances."

Not where Nick had stood last night outside her truck. He smiled at that. It wouldn't take much to change her mind.

"Look, Mike." Nick put up his hand. "I'll likely see her in Creede while I'm here. I thought since we got off on the wrong foot last night, we could meet on neutral ground."

"I see what you're getting at."

"Thought I'd ask her to lunch."

"Well, there's no harm in that, I suppose." Mike pulled on his chin in reflection.

From where Nick stood, Mike Coulter had appointed himself Charlie Robertson's guardian. He decided to steer the good sheriff in a different direction. "Know where I can rent a car in town?"

"You read my mind. There's a place called Sam's." Mike glanced at his watch. "Thought I'd swing by while things were slow and give you a lift into town. I know he's got something you can rent."

"Great, just give me a minute." Nick headed back toward the bedroom to grab his wallet and keys.

Mike's voice rose. "I was thinking with you being new in town and all, maybe you'd like to enjoy a real Western dinner. Sterling's having a get-together in South Fork at the Rio Grande Club tomorrow in the Timbers Restaurant, seven sharp. It's informal—jeans, a nice shirt, and cowboy boots if you have 'em."

Nick thought about that for a moment. If Sterling was having a get-together, his partner would be there. He needed to get close to her. Personally, he liked things neat. If he could get her alone, he'd take her. Simple as that. But if she had anything on Reynolds and he rushed things, it could come back to bite him in the ass.

From what he'd witnessed back at the tavern, she liked things on *her* terms. She'd have to decide on her own to trust him, and he'd have to make it damn easy. He'd start today easing his way into her life. Saturday would be the natural course of things. Mike had invited him. He felt obliged to go. She just happened to be there. That would work. "Thanks for the offer." He cleared the bedroom and smiled. "Looking forward to it."

Surrounded by soaring pines and several stands of aspens near the banks of the Rio Grande and the muffled rat-a-tat-tat of pneumatic nail guns, Charlie crested the steep incline of the gabled roof of the Brickman cabin, nearly forty feet high, carrying a load of green shingles. The brisk air tugged at her ponytail. Shafts of auburn hair, a color that had taken some getting used to, caught the wind before she pulled them behind her ear.

Once she had arrived in Colorado and changed her hair color, she wasn't going anywhere without a Colorado driver's license and a car. First step—the license. At first glance, the driver's license of Charlie Robertson didn't resemble Kathryn Reynolds until she'd gotten lost in her eyes—hunted—just like Shelley's. Charlie dropped the shingles with a thud.

Hunted or not, those first few days on the run she'd had to keep moving. With cash she'd bought a reliable used Honda Civic and let fate guide her. Several days later, after following the willful flow of the Rio Grande carving its way through valleys dotted with ponderosa pine, she'd driven into Creede. A town that could easily fade into the days of the Wild West, with historical buildings lining the main street, wedged between mountain rock, her gut told her: *This is it*.

Charlie took a deep breath of sawdust and pine and smiled contentedly. She'd gotten in her much needed five-mile run on one of the snowmobile trails near her cabin this morning. The extra sleep and exercise had been the best remedy for her head. Charlie put a tentative finger against her temple. The knot had gone down considerably since yesterday. She'd removed the bandage this morning before showering and decided she could live with the bruising and the small gash.

Charlie grabbed a shingle from the top. Laying it even with the next row, she joined in with the rest of her men and fired several galvanized nails into the shingle.

Between shingles, she kept an eye on the gravel road below leading into the job site. Quince had agreed to meet with Ben before lunch to talk about the Lockhart site. His beat-up 1987 El Camino, which he kept parked off of Bachelor Loop Road behind a junkyard, made it easy to spot. She had no expectations of the two playing nice with each other.

The noon sun warmed Charlie from the inside out. Sitting her hard hat down in front, she ripped off her sweatshirt and laid it next to her. Charlie took another shingle, lining it up, and angled the nose of her nail gun toward the roof when she peered down and caught a ray of sun reflecting off a black Harley pulling into the job site. The rider lifted the helmet and her finger yanked back on the trigger. Shit! She glanced down, the tip of the gun resting in the soft green material of her company sweatshirt.

"Son of a . . ." She dropped the gun and pulled on the green sleeve and grimaced when the material ripped, the sweatshirt flying up with her hand, her butt falling back against the roof. Her stomach dipped, and she relaxed when she caught her balance, the edge of the roof still several feet away.

She examined her sweatshirt, two gaping holes the size of quarters on either side of her right sleeve. "You kidding me?"

Down below, Nick Foster had hopped off the bike. "Why are you here?" she moaned. He hadn't mentioned being in the market for a log home. From what Mike had told her, his visit to Creede centered round vacation. His determined strides moved closer, his head tipped up, searching. "Crap," Charlie said to herself, crunching down close to the roofline.

Shorty, one of her crew, walked up to him, said something, she assumed, based on the way he moved his face toward the side of Nick's head and then pointed directly at her. Charlie shoved the nail gun into the holder on her hip and threw her sweatshirt back on, resigned to making the trip down the . . .

"Charlie."

She jumped at the crackle of Shorty's voice and grabbed for her radio, her boot catching the edge of her hard hat left sitting on the roof. It rolled and went over the lip before she could grab it. The crack that followed made her cringe. *Damn it.*

Charlie grabbed her radio from her hip and keyed it. "What's up?" she asked, her voice sharp.

"I got your hard hat."

She shook her head.

"It's broke."

No shit.

"I got that. Anything else?"

"There's a Nick Foster here to see you."

Her body slumped. "Coming down." After securing her radio, she cleared the roof and climbed down the ladder, willing the flush of anger—or was it embarrassment?—to fade. What could he possibly want with her? She hadn't been the most gracious of Creede residents to him last night.

Charlie's boots touched down on the dirt, and she began walking in Nick's direction. She skirted the forklift with its monotonous drone, as it plodded over rich, russet earth, carrying fieldstones to the corner of the cabin's foundation wall.

The door to the office trailer popped open, and Ben stepped out. He headed toward Shorty and Nick with his bike and reached the two before Charlie did. A conversation took place, followed by a handshake. Charlie kept walking, and Ben turned around. "Hey, you hear from Maynard?" He checked his watch. "He's twenty minutes late."

Still several steps away, she wanted to do an about-face. She didn't need to get into an argument with Ben in front of Nick Foster. She smiled pleasantly when she reached them. "No. Maybe his car wouldn't start." He hardly used it, and he didn't care for the walk down the mountain. It wouldn't have surprised her if he hadn't gauged the time and distance correctly from his shack to the junkyard, and the car didn't start. "He'll be here."

Charlie's gaze met Nick's. His eyes were warm and blue and smiling at her. "Hey, how's your head?"

She hadn't noticed his dog tags last night. They weren't like dog tags she had ever seen. These had a thin rubber casing around each metal tag. They rested against his collarbone and the edge of a gray T-shirt, its short sleeves hugging his muscular biceps.

"He's asking about your head." Ben shoved her yellow hard hat at her, a crack running the length of it from front to back. "Take it."

"What?" She took her eyes off of Nick's smooth, tanned skin and grabbed the hat from Ben, the heat returning to her face. "Got it. Thanks."

Ben gave her a disagreeable look. "How'd you crack the—"

"She kicked it off the roof," Shorty said.

Jeez. She beaded in on Shorty, handing him her hard hat. "There's another one in the office. You mind getting it?"

"Nope." He took it and moved away without a word.

Charlie touched her temple, the scab rough, and connected with Nick. "It's not pretty to look at. But it doesn't hurt today."

"Nick tells me you drove him to Mike's cabin last night." Ben crossed his arms. "You never mentioned it." His words came out agitated.

"A favor for Mike. He had a call and . . ." She leveled an irritated gaze at Ben. Why was she explaining herself to him?

Nick took a step closer, standing directly behind her. "She didn't have much of a choice."

"Thank you," she said, glancing back at Nick, and caught him eyeing Ben with what looked to be annoyance.

Ben zeroed in on Nick. "How long you in town, then?"

"A few weeks."

"Nick's looking for a little relaxation. He just retired from the Navy," Charlie added.

"Huh, what branch?"

"SEALs," Nick said.

"I know a guy. Good guy. I did a cabin for him a while back." He looked at Charlie. "Before your time. His name's Rockingham. Brad Rockingham."

"The Navy's a big place." Nick shook his head. "Don't recognize it."

"Ah, well, figured you might have heard of him."

Ben's two-way went off, and he grabbed it off his hip. "Excuse me." He nodded to Nick. "Nice to meet you. Enjoy Colorado." He walked away, and Charlie relaxed. Then Ben turned back. "Charlie, don't forget the electric punch-out on the Jameson cabin." Then his brows snapped together. "Strike one for your pal Maynard."

"Got it," she called back and clenched her hands. Quince wasn't helping her or his case with Ben.

"He upset?"

"Probably." Charlie moved away from Nick. "Nice bike." She ran her hand along the slick, black paint job.

"Sam hooked me up."

"He's a good guy." She frowned up at him. "I thought we had pretty much parted ways last night."

"About that." He stood next to her, the sun picking up the flecks of gold running through his brown hair, cut neat around his ears, a little longer on top. She liked the look and his high forehead, the way his ears laid flat against his head, straight nose, firm lips, rough cheeks . . .

"You're staring." The hint of a smile tugged at the corners of his mouth.

Charlie straightened, heat creeping back in her own cheeks. "Sorry." More like she'd been taking inventory.

"Have you had lunch?" Nick asked.

Lunch?

"Why?" It came out louder than she intended.

He laughed. "I've never had to work this hard before."

"For?" She gave him a quizzical look.

"I'm asking you out."

This time she laughed. "On a date?" She glanced around.

"I'm making you uncomfortable."

"*No*," she snapped, her hands fidgeting at her side, and grabbed hold of the handlebar of his bike. "You caught me off guard. That's all." She shrugged. "Plus, my truck's kind of a mess."

"Thought we could take the bike."

"I don't have a helmet."

Nick nodded toward something behind her. At the same moment, something pressed into her side, and she turned around to find Shorty shoving a yellow hard hat into her stomach.

"Not even a scratch on this one," Shorty said with his protruding pug eyes and smug look.

She took it from him. She couldn't remember the last time she had damaged equipment, unlike Shorty, who'd been written up for leaving a chop saw with its diamond-tipped blade in the bed of his truck overnight, then gave her shit when she wrote him up and collected $382 to replace it. She beaded in on him. "Find something to do."

"Ah, right. I'll go check on the rough-ins." He turned, whistling a tune, and Charlie made a mental note—Tommyknocker's, upstairs, eight ball. She smiled. *Paybacks are hell.*

"Problem solved." Nick tugged her hard hat from her hands and flipped it over, adjusting the band and placing it on her head, his arms brushing her shoulders before stepping back.

No, the problem wasn't solved. *He* was the problem. She hadn't expected to see him again. She didn't date. She couldn't date. But she wanted to go to lunch with him. *Damn it.* He knew, too. She could tell because . . . *Damn it.* She could just tell.

"I'm really busy here."

"You like barbecue?" He swung his leg over the bike and sat down. "I bought two of those Creede Caldera sandwiches in town at that tavern last night—supposed to be delicious. They're in the saddlebag." He tipped his head toward the seat. Behind it, on both sides, sat a black leather saddlebag with decorative silver studs running along the corners.

Reaching back, Nick patted the seat.

Hell no. Even if her butt could fit, she'd be right up against him.

"Come on, Charlie." He grabbed hold of her hand and shook it playfully, his eyes connecting with hers. "You want to come with me."

His hand remained wrapped around hers. She liked his hand, too. Perfectly male and tanned, she wondered what he could . . .

She pulled her hand away. "One hour."

He smiled. "Then hop on, Cinderella."

Charlie hesitated. She didn't believe in fairy tales or happy endings. Her life came with strict instructions, and damned if she knew why she was threading her leg over Nick Foster's Harley, her hands awkwardly hovering around his broad shoulders like she'd get a case of cooties if she touched him.

He reached back and grabbed her hands, bringing them around, placing them on his flat stomach. Her insides fluttered when her fingers settled on a set of washboard abs.

"Hang on," he called back and put on his helmet, bringing the kickstand up. He turned on the ignition. The motor rumbled beneath her thighs, and they pulled out with a roar.

She cursed herself silently the moment they hit the open road, leaving Ben, the job site, and her sensibility behind. He hadn't said where they were going. She didn't even think to ask. She opened her mouth but snapped it shut. He seemed fine, friendly, and flirtatious.

Don't act like a jerk, Charlie.

She let the wind take her hair, whipping it about her face, and grimaced at the cool air flowing through the nail holes of her sweatshirt sleeve. She needed to think back before Jack and her anxiety about men. Nick made her uneasy—but in a good way. She tightened her hold on him and leaned in. They zipped along the highway, Nick taking the curves easily. He seemed to be comfortable driving it. She'd never been on a motorcycle. They made her nervous.

He turned off Bachelor Loop Road and followed a narrow path, weaving through the wood line until it opened up to a familiar grassy incline.

Nick rolled the bike to a stop and hit the kill switch. Charlie hopped off. She'd been here before. She dropped the hard hat next to the bike and ran up the hill. Once she reached the crest, her breath caught. The view lunged downward. Pines and mountain ledges jutted and sprawled. The horizon rose and fell in purple hues of rock, the mountain ranges nameless sentinels in the distance.

Nick stood behind her, his hand coming to rest in the small of her back, and she tingled.

"You hungry?" He took her hand and stepped onto the boulder that cantilevered over the cliff, and she followed.

"How'd you find it?"

"What?"

"This place."

"When Mike brought me into town. I figured it had to be off that side road we just came in on." He tilted his head toward her. "You been here before?"

She shook her head, pulling him down to sit with her. "Once. I could never figure out which way I came. I got lost."

His brow rose.

"I was on foot."

"How'd you . . ."

"My friend Maynard."

Understanding lit his eyes. "The guy Ben mentioned."

"Yep. He's a character." She laughed, "It's a long story. You ready to eat?"

"Sure." He pulled out a foil-wrapped barbecue sandwich and handed it to her with some napkins and a bottled water, nodding toward the panorama below. "Do they fish much in that stream?" He pointed down toward the slinking silver chain cutting through the basin.

She laughed. "That stream you're referring to is the Rio Grande, the longest river in North America."

"Oh, yeah." He grinned. "I never excelled at geography."

She unwrapped her sandwich, and he did the same. "Honestly, when I saw it for the first time, it looked like nothing more than a stream to me, too.

The word 'grande' refers more to its length than its width. In some places you can hop across the river rocks to get to the other side."

He took a bite of his sandwich, barbecue sauce running along the side of his cheek.

Charlie laughed. "You're a mess." She reached over with a napkin and wiped his face. The moment her fingers touched the roughened planes of his chin, she regretted it.

His hand came up, brushing her knuckles before he took the napkin from her. "Thanks."

Her stomach dipped—not from the height, but from Nick's pale-blue eyes so blatantly holding hers. "Now *you're* staring."

"I am." His gaze softened, and he laughed. "I'm sorry. I keep trying to figure out how you ended up in construction."

"By an accidental discharge."

"A what?" He gave her an incredulous look and laughed.

"I'm serious. Laugh, but it wasn't funny then." She took another bite and a sip of water.

"You're kidding. You can't just throw that out there and casually eat your lunch and not elaborate!"

"Look, I got in a lot of trouble. So if I tell you, I don't want to hear the story recirculating."

"Who am I going to tell?"

"Good point." She set down her sandwich and leaned in. "I shot Ben in the leg." She sat back and let Nick's jaw drop.

"With a gun?"

"No, a water pistol." She shook her head. "Of course with a gun. Everyone has one in Colorado. I figured it was necessary." She waved her hand. "Short and sweet. I didn't know him. It was dark. He snuck up behind me in the alley in back of the Creede Hotel where I was staying, and I shot him."

His eyes grew serious. "Did he try and hurt you?"

"Nope. The hotel lets him throw small scraps from the job site into their dumpster. It was a misunderstanding, and a big one, that brought me to the attention of Mike Coulter."

"Ben press charges?"

"I was lucky. In the end, they coded it as an accidental discharge, and Ben, great guy that he is, offered me a job when he found out I was new in town and looking for one."

"Huh?" Nick's expression changed to one of reflection, and he continued to eat his sandwich.

"You and Mike. You two related?"

She shook her head. "He seems to think so. But, no, he's more like a teenager's worst nightmare. Only he's forgotten I'm thirty-five, not fifteen."

"I'm thirty-five, too."

"They retire SEALs that early?"

"Some. I chose to leave. Seen my share of collateral damage on both hard and soft targets."

She sat up. "Soft? Meaning people?" She hadn't meant for her words to come out on a quiver.

He gazed over the ledge. She couldn't say how high it was; maybe a thousand feet. High enough it fluttered her stomach when she stood on the edge.

His eyes came back to her, steady, unwavering. "You ever been in a fight for your life?"

She gripped the rock, hesitated. "N-no." What the hell kind of question was that? He'd seen strife, a land burgeoning with radical views and hatred of the Western world.

He'd seen terror in a man's eye. She was sure of it. Even death.

Could he see it in hers?

Charlie took small bites and a couple of swigs of water and grew more uncomfortable with his silence.

His hand reached out and touched her temple before she knew his intentions, and her gut clenched. "I was concerned about you today."

"Why's that?"

His fingers caressed her cheek, and then he pulled them away. "I thought for sure you were going to tumble off the roof along with your hard hat."

Yeah, because of *you!*

She wasn't careless, and she knew how to do her job. Only if she admitted her behavior had to do with the way she felt about him and how he made her feel, she'd die from embarrassment. Her anger rising, Charlie beaded in on him. "I wasn't even close."

"It doesn't bother you being forty feet up in the air?"

"Nope." She grabbed her trash, shoving the napkin inside the foil, and rolled it up in a small ball, tightening her grip on it the more he stared at her without so much as a word. "You know, if you keep looking at me that way, with your eyes bugged out, they'll grow crossed."

"Sorry for staring, you're curious." He shrugged, giving her a most sincere expression.

"Curious in what way?"

"You're mad."

"No. Just trying to figure out where this conversation is going."

He laughed. "I'm still trying to figure out how a gorgeous woman like yourself landed a job with Sterling in the first—"

The heat rose in Charlie's face. Did he actually think the line about a gorgeous woman would ease the sting of questioning her ability to run a job site? She had news for him. She could run one just fine until he showed up. And the bulldozer incident didn't count because she hadn't met him yet.

Charlie stood up, maneuvered across the boulder where they sat, and headed toward his bike.

"Wait, Charlie, I didn't mean anything by that. I only meant—" He scrambled across the rock where they had been sitting. "Charlie. Come on. You're being ridiculous," he called after her.

She grabbed her hard hat off the ground and hopped on the back of his bike. If she'd had the key, she'd have driven away, leaving him to thumb it.

When he reached the bottom of the hill, his usual neat hair stuck up in places, probably from pulling on it, and his eyes were a mix of confusion and a little anger. Not the so-put-together Navy SEAL he'd been a few minutes ago. Charlie turned her face away and smirked, putting her hard hat on.

"I'm sorry if I offended you." He squeezed her shoulder.

This time she couldn't stand the weight of his hand, and she jerked her arm away.

"So you're not going to talk to me? Okay. Have it your way." He grabbed his helmet from the handlebar and swung onto the seat. After revving the engine and popping up the kickstand, he pulled out.

Charlie wobbled and grabbed the seat. No way was she putting her arms around him.

He turned. "Grab hold of me," he yelled over the engine noise.

No.

Something between a grin and a smile tugged at his lips before he turned around, shut the visor on his helmet, and gunned the engine, letting go of the gas. Her body lurched and then slammed forward against his back, and she grabbed hold, her arms sliding around his middle, trembling.

Jerk.

Chapter Twenty-Three

C HARLIE PULLED INTO THE GRAVEL DRIVEWAY OF THE JAMESONS'
soon to be vacation home in Bristol Head Acres on the outskirts
of Creede. She shut off the truck and got out. Shoving her keys into her
pocket and grabbing the one for the house, she shut the truck door. With
the house key firmly between her fingers, she straightened the holster
hooked to her jeans and smiled. She'd agreed with Ben and Mike's request
in theory, but in practice it belonged on her hip.

In the distance, a full moon sat high over the jutting mountain rock and
dense trees in the Rio Grande National Forest, making nine thirty at night
all awash with eerie shapes. From the cottonwood she'd planted at the corner
of the cabin, its wispy limbs dusting the gravel drive with its silhouette, to
her own shadow becoming one with the dark outline of the gabled roof,
Charlie shuddered.

She kept a steady pace, the driveway stones crunching beneath her boots,
and climbed the steps to the front porch framed up with thick ponderosa
pine. With her hands on the intricately carved mahogany door and rustic
doorknob and lock, she wanted to pinch herself. It still amazed her, the
natural gift she had for architecture.

The only thing a law degree had given her was Jack.

Standing in the dark in front of a vacant house with five thousand square
feet of hiding space with him on her mind made her . . . *an idiot*. She jammed
the key into the lock. She'd been in plenty of empty houses, alone, in the
dark, since moving to Creede.

Charlie hit the light switch, her body giving one big jerk when she
remained in darkness. She flipped the switch several times and shook her
head. Typical. She'd run out of fingers if she counted the times the electrician
had forgotten to throw the main breaker after he'd finished a job. Charlie
shoved the key in her back jeans pocket and reached inside the front pocket

of her sweatshirt and pulled out her flashlight. Clicking it on, she shined it back and forth until the walnut-stained door leading to the basement caught the light.

Clearing the expansive hall, where fresh varnish filled the air, she opened the door, its hinges creaking, and took the steps quickly. The flashlight danced on the newly painted faux walls until she found another stained door to the mechanical room. Once inside, she located the two gray electrical boxes and the main switch, as usual, in the off position. She flipped it on, keeping her flashlight on for the return trip. Had she thought about it, she would have left the light switch upstairs on.

She'd had enough of the dark.

Charlie climbed the steps and shut the door behind her, walking swiftly to the first wall switch, and stopped midstride when a shadow crossed in front of her on the knotty-pine floor. Her back went rigid, and she held her breath. To the right, in the great room, a stream of moonlight spilled onto the floor, and she let the air dwindle from her lungs. Charlie gathered herself.

Check the lights and get the hell out of here.

Ten steps ahead sat the switch. She tightened her grip on her flashlight and kept the beam on the wall, moving closer toward it when angry fingers reached out—only to dance along her face and beyond while she stood in its shadowy path,

The cottonwood.

"You're being ridiculous. It's the wind." It must have picked up since she entered the house, but with the walls made of twelve-inch solid-pine logs, she couldn't tell for sure. She turned off the flashlight, the erratic beam a beacon. The light pouring in would guide her to the switch. She started in that direction. Her heart ticked away the seconds, growing louder in her ears, her own footsteps giving her the chills.

Another shadow passed by a window in front of her. Definitely human. Charlie dropped to the ground in the great room, her body trembling. She couldn't move. Now on all fours in the dark, she remained rooted to the floor. No one knew she was here except Ben. He'd have walked right in calling her name. It wasn't Ben. But Ben had mentioned it today in front of Nick. Why would he be here? He'd come to the job site looking for her. She shook her head.

She knew why.

Still on her knees, Charlie grabbed for her gun on her hip and moved to the wall of windows only eighteen inches off the floor where he'd passed by moments ago. She peered out. Only her truck, exactly where she parked it. She needed another vantage point. Heart pounding, she kept low, heading toward the front of the cabin.

Boots climbed the steps and clomped along the front porch, and Charlie ran, heart pounding, toward a small hexagon-shaped window near the door. A head crossed by the window. *Shit.* His steps continued down the porch, and Charlie peered out.

A face smashed itself against the glass, and Charlie screamed. Adrenaline ripping through her body, she held tight to the gun and fell back. The face remained a hideous distortion still pressed against the glass, its beady eyes searching.

She shot out the door, the gun shaking in her hands, her own boots biting into the porch. "I'm going to kill you, old man!"

He laughed. He stood there and laughed, his body jerking, lips sputtering, gray hair wild and sticking up, lit by the moon behind him. "Ah, God, you should have seen your face, girl." He shook his head. "I almost pissed and shit myself."

"You're an asshole." She shoved the gun into his gut, his rough fingers juggling it when she turned to walk away.

"Where you going?" He followed her.

"Home." She swung on him. "I've been walking around this town packing for almost a week because of your bullshit."

She put her face in his, her hands on her hips. "He's not coming for me. Got it?"

He smacked his lips, his whiskers twitching. "You don't have to get so indignant."

"Indignant." She let the word fall from her lips and shook her head. When she got back to the job site today, after being made to feel like an incompetent idiot who couldn't manage to keep from falling off a freaking roof, Ben had been waiting for her. "How about pissed? Yeah, pissed. Why the hell weren't you at the job site at twelve?"

His head fell slightly. "Something more important came up."

"Than a job?"

"That don't pay *shit.*" His raspy voice rose. He handed her the gun. "Your story for the job, remember. I had other business."

"Like I wasn't going to pay you." Charlie took the gun and tossed it into the open window of her truck where it landed with a quiet thud.

He shrugged.

"Then how about your word . . . *to me?*"

Quince huffed a breath through his nose and scratched the back of his scraggly head. "I didn't think of it like that."

"So what was so important?"

"I have customers."

"Customers?"

"My concoction. I was bottling it . . . got caught up in filling the bottles. Plus, I had some deliveries tonight." His shoulders slumped. "My car took a crap in town, and Macon Davis, I sell to him, gave me a ride."

"And you saw my truck back off the road, thought you'd make amends and hitch a ride the rest of the way. End of story."

He threw his hands up. "That's it."

Charlie opened the door to her truck. "Get in. You think you can climb the ledge where I normally park and come in on foot?"

He smiled his rotten-tooth-filled smile. "Aw, nothing to it." He came around and got in and shut his door the same time Charlie did, the deafening slam only adding to her annoyance.

Charlie started the truck, powering up her window. It didn't take long before Quince's dirty hair, filthy clothes, and the unmistakable stink of alcohol leaching from his pores made her gag. She inched her fingers toward the window button and glanced over. He looked straight ahead, his head heavy against the seat back, his old hands lying one on top of the other in his lap, and her heart broke. She slid her fingers away from the remote.

"You think you can make it on Monday?"

"Yep." He smacked his lips together and tapped his head without acknowledging her, almost as if in a trance. "I got it right here."

She pulled out of the development onto Middle Creek Road and hopped on 149, heading in the direction of the narrow road and the area where she usually came in near the ledge. Her shoulders slumped a little at the thought of the old man next to her. Whether either of them wanted to admit it, they needed each other. Now that her heart wasn't in near heart attack mode, she chuckled to herself. She'd been so angry when she'd realized it was him in the window, flying out the door, hunting him down on the porch, his laughter floating on the wind. Since she'd known him, she'd never seen him laugh. Maybe a chuckle when he was being a smart-ass but never belly-hurting laughter like tonight.

Charlie wouldn't have believed, three years ago, she'd come to know a man like Quince. The thought of Jack's reaction to her choice of occupation, the vehicle she drove, and the company she kept made her smile. Charlie took the turn for Bachelor Loop Road and followed the road, her headlights catching bugs zipping in every direction, trying to escape her windshield. She'd been that bug once, flitting about, dodging Jack's wrath. Even the simple act of helping someone, other than him, would set him off.

She pulled into the familiar spot plenty large enough to park and keep her truck a safe distance from the shoulder at Allen's Crossing. Putting the truck in Park, she turned toward Quince. "I have to go to Denver in the morning on Monday. You be available in the evening? Let's say around six thirty, if I pick you up?"

He waved a gnarled hand. "That's out of your way."

"Maybe. But I want to make damn sure you make it." From what he'd said about his car, that was a no-go.

"How about we make it a dinner meeting and Sterling's buying."

"Ah." His head perked up. "If that cheap ass is buying, I'm eatin'."

Charlie laughed. She figured that would get him going. She could have easily slipped the meeting in when she returned in the afternoon. If she admitted she cared enough to make his life easier and feed him, he'd fight her.

He opened the door. "I'll be waiting, girl." He reached over and patted her shoulder. "Thanks for the ride. And I've got some money put by for car repairs. Promised Grady from the Last Chance Mine I'd help him out while he's on vacation."

"You're going to run it?" She gave him a look of disbelief. He'd have to make change, collect credit card information, and be courteous.

"Hell, no. Can't stand tourists. He's closing it down for the week. Just wants me to do a sweep. Make sure no one's messing with it." He pulled on his beard and smacked his lips, leaving his hand suspended in the air. "Plus, he's paying me."

"Aren't you the entrepreneur."

"Sounds like," he said, the unmistakable hint of humor in his voice. "I'll be more dependable after Monday."

He got out the rest of the way, climbing onto the back of the truck bed, and she hit the button and brought down the passenger window so she could listen to be sure he made it up the ledge with no problems. "Thanks for the ride," he called out, and then hoisted himself up. Once the rustling stopped, she powered the window up, made a tight U-turn, her gun sliding off the seat with a clunk next to her feet. She stopped and reached down, shoving it under her seat. It could stay there for now.

Every stupid thing that had happened to her lately had been because of her obsession with the past.

Jack could go to hell.

CHAPTER TWENTY-FOUR

A COUNTRY BALLAD HUNG ON THE GENTLE BREEZE. THE SCENT OF pine and honeysuckle wafted past Nick's nose. If he closed his eyes, he could almost imagine the life of a cowboy working his ranch just before the turn of the twentieth century when a horse, a bedroll, and a campfire were all you needed to set the world right.

But for Nick, he'd have to settle for the forgiveness of a bewitching bronze maiden and a refresher course in Dating 101. He'd get what he came for. His jaw tightened—by force if necessary.

He followed Mike's suggestion. While digging in the closet, he found a pair of cowboy boots size eleven, surprisingly comfortable, in worn brown leather. Decked out in his Levi's and a crisp, copper button-down shirt, the only thing missing was a Stetson.

The roar of the Harley gave one last sputter before Nick turned the ignition key and lifted his helmet off. The Rio Grande Club stood solitary, a combination of climbing fieldstone accompanied by glossy, crisscrossed logs stained the color of whipped caramel. The scene was anchored by the jagged peaks of the San Juan Mountains—stair steps to the heavens like no place Nick had ever seen.

Nick bit back his pride and headed in the direction of a lone fiddle and the dramatic entranceway framed up with sturdy ponderosa pine logs and pine trusses. The music, a timeless waltz, emanated through the open doors of the Timbers Restaurant. Entering, he found a sizable crowd of men, women, and children from babies on up to teenagers, sitting at round tables or milling about in Western wear. The men dressed comfortably in jeans and crisp long-sleeve shirts, some accented with Western bolo ties and sterling-silver cabochons, others preferring the casual open collar. Nick slipped into the swell of bodies crowding the rustic, pine planks and scanned the room in search of Charlie.

A hand clamped onto his shoulder, and he turned to find Mike holding a frothy glass of beer and smiling down at him. He wondered what they ate out West. Except for Shep and his lanky form, the men he had met so far towered over him by several inches. At six foot one, Nick was no slouch, but he certainly felt small in comparison.

"So, you found the place."

"No problems." He reached to shake Mike's hand.

"Good." Mike's expression widened. "How'd that lunch date go for you yesterday?"

First of all, he'd never mentioned, specifically, when he planned on asking Charlie to lunch. And, secondly, judging by Mike's expression, he already knew the answer. Charlie didn't seem the type to go running off at the mouth. That left Ben Sterling. Nick had obviously stepped into a breach Sterling had only thought of occupying. Irritatingly enough, Nick had failed himself.

Nick could only grin. "I should have taken your advice."

"Ah, she shut you down. Don't say I didn't warn you. Charlie's not one for entertaining a man's eye."

"I didn't give her the eye," Nick argued. "I merely asked about her choice of occupation. She seemed to take it the wrong way."

"Jeez, Nick, you questioned her abilities?" Mike winced, sucking air through his teeth. "I don't know what's worse—an unwanted advance or some knothead deciding she's ill-equipped in a man's world."

"That bad, huh?"

"If I was you, I'd cut my losses and move on. If I know Charlie, you don't have a snowball's chance in hell of redeeming yourself."

A chair slammed to the floor, and Nick went on alert, searching the room. He looked to Mike.

He shook his head. "I knew he'd be trouble." Mike straightened. "Fifth table from the right, toward the middle. Bobby Ray Hanson."

A lumbering, belligerent asshole with greasy black hair, face pumping red, had the petite blonde from Tommyknocker's by the arm, pulling her up from the table with a small boy sitting on her lap.

Nick nodded. "What's his deal?"

"Shelley's live-in boyfriend. A real piece of work."

The day in the tavern came back to Nick. "Those bruises on her face the other day? He put them there?"

Mike's brows rose. "You noticed that?"

Nick's jaw tightened. "She press charges?"

"Nope. And there's not a damn thing I can do about it." He took a step in their direction. "But tonight's different. I'm a witness." Mike took another step then froze. "*Shit.*"

An attractive blonde in her late fifties came up on the couple with the child. Her voice rose, and she pointed her finger in the boyfriend's face. He eyed the woman, who stood her ground in a brown pantsuit.

"Who's that?"

"My wife."

Nick held back a chuckle.

Mike advanced, and Nick held his arm. "I think she has it under control."

The boyfriend dropped Shelley's arm, straightened his jacket, and stormed out.

Mike smiled. "God love her." He turned toward Nick. "Seeing as you screwed up with one female, I'll let you try your luck with another." He waved her over. "Tess, honey." She smiled, catching his gesture, gave him a tilt of her head, said something to Shelley, and started toward them, skirting the myriad guests offering a quick greeting as she passed. Mike reached out and scooped her toward him, giving her a big kiss, whispering in her ear.

She grimaced. "I told Shelley we'd take her home."

Mike's face stiffened. "Not sure that's such a good idea. She can stay with us the night."

Tess nodded and smiled at Nick. "You must be Nick Foster, the SEAL who's staying at the cabin." She reached out her hand. "Tess Coulter. I hope you're enjoying your stay in Colorado."

Nick shook her hand. "Nice to meet you, too. I can see Mike has an eye for beauty."

"You're making me blush." Tess turned playfully toward her husband and slapped him lightly on the arm. "We need to keep Nick around. I like the way he thinks."

"He may be quick on the uptake with you, sweetheart, but trust me, his silver tongue almost got bit off yesterday by a hard-ass general contractor we know and love."

Tess stopped laughing. "Charlie? What did you say to set her off?"

Nick shrugged his shoulders. "Not much. Before I knew it, she took off."

"What he's leaving out, Tess, is he questioned her ability to work construction."

"Oh, that's a sore spot for sure." She leaned in toward Nick. "When Ben hired Charlie, the crew figured he had a thing for her." She laughed, shaking her head and looked toward Mike. "I guess I can tell him about the . . ."

Mike motioned with his hand. "Go ahead. It's no secret."

"Charlie shot Ben in the leg."

"She told me."

"Ah, then you know that part." She waved a hand. "Anyway, if Ben had romance in mind, Charlie set him straight on that. She took to construction, surprisingly. Proved to the crew she could handle the work and had an aptitude for architecture. In the end, she became his partner, taking every dime she'd made to buy in."

"I guess an apology is in order."

"A good place to start." Tess made a wry face. "She's a beautiful woman. I thought for sure some single, good-looking man from Creede would break through her turtle-shell exterior. But I can only count on one hand the men she's allowed to get close to her." She held up three slender fingers.

"Whoa, you two have me confused," Mike protested, turning a bead in Nick's direction. "I thought you were just passing through?"

"Still am." Nick nodded toward Tess. "Thanks for the history lesson. I'll try to steer clear of the subject."

"Just passing through, huh?" Mike flashed his don't-cross-me smile at Nick. "If you're thinking of toying with her heart and then making tracks for parts unknown, you better think again."

Tess turned her attention to her husband. "Michael Coulter, have you given any thought as to *why* Charlie hasn't had any male suitors?" She tapped her foot and folded her arms over her chest. "Could it possibly be because there's not one man in Creede who's willing to cross over you first in order to get to her? You really need to back off." Her eyes narrowed, and she pointed an accusing finger at him. She turned to Nick. "Ignore this bully over here. I like you, and contrary to Mike's actions or reaction, I know he respects you. My advice, approach her again." She smiled at Nick and gave Mike a look of reproof. "I'll take care of this one."

Mike gave Nick a sheepish grin. "Guess I've been told." Mike's eyes moved up over Nick's head. "She's hot."

Tess followed his line of vision. "You better go talk to her before she goes out after him."

Nick turned. Charlie let go of Shelley's hand and made her way to the back of the room.

Damn. Ghosts had no business looking like that.

If there was one yard of material making up her dress, he'd be surprised. He couldn't quite say what the color was, blue . . . green . . . but he liked it. He chuckled to himself; she certainly had traded her cosmopolitan ways for a Western lifestyle. She wore a pair of soft cowhide boots that came very close to matching her skin tone.

Nick glanced back toward his guests. "If you'll excuse me, I think I'll try and make amends. And don't worry—I have only good intentions where Charlie is concerned."

What a crock.

He smiled just the same and glanced back for a moment at Charlie.

"I'm counting on it." Mike angled his gaze toward Nick before Tess pulled him on to the dance floor.

Nick kept his eye on Charlie. With determined steps, she headed toward the rear exit, sidestepping several lines of dancers stomping to "Cotton-Eyed Joe" when she was abruptly spun around by the tall bronzed giant—Ben. Her expression softened, and she let him pull her onto the dance floor. The trio of fiddlers changed up to a waltz, and Ben gathered her into his arms. When he snuggled her even closer, Nick ignored the overwhelming urge to politely interrupt. Then Ben kissed her.

What the hell was that? Partner my ass!

Nick chided himself through gritted teeth, "This is none of your business." He knew why he was here, and it was only for one purpose. Once he handed her over, she wasn't his problem. With that thought, he turned on his heels to get some air.

Charlie stiffened and stared straight into Ben's eyes. "What was that for?"

"What?" The innocent look just wasn't Ben. The glint in his eye gave him up.

"You know what I'm talking about, the kissing." Her shoulders rose, and she tried to shrink from view. "You're going to give everyone the wrong idea."

"I don't think it would surprise anyone. We've known each other for the better of three years now. What are you afraid of?"

"Nothing."

Everything. Charlie hadn't seen this coming. They had their moments, but at the end of the day it was respect and, yes, love that held them together. She trusted him with her life. But her heart?

"What is it?" His eyes bore into hers, the laughter fleeting. "This Nick Foster, he upset you the other day."

No. It wasn't Nick Foster.

He lifted her chin up to face him. "Did he upset you? I want the truth, Charlie."

"No. I was being a jerk." She refocused on Ben and added, "*To him.*"

Ben was pensive for a moment. "There's something about the guy that rubs me wrong."

Competition. Well, Ben needed to get over his idea that they would eventually hook up. She pointed a slender finger in his direction. "I'll worry about Nick Foster."

The tempo changed, and he reeled her out and then brought her back into his arms. "You will, will you?" His eyes roamed the dance floor and stopped on a pretty blonde, sitting at a table talking with Tess, while Mike did is best to corrupt little Gunner with a game of quarters, minus the beer.

He was dancing with the wrong girl.

She squared her shoulders. "And another thing. No more talk about me and you. We're going back to the way things were."

"Business?"

"*All* business."

Ben grinned, throwing his hands up in defeat as she made straight for the door, and then called out over the music, "Monday, my office. I want to discuss that old fart Maynard with you."

Charlie glanced back. "No discussion. He apologizes profusely. Oh, and I'll be in Denver in the morning—"

"Your blood?" His brow rose.

She nodded. "So mark down dinner for three at Tommyknocker's, six thirty, Monday, after I get back. Be nice." She smiled sweetly and slipped out the door.

CHAPTER TWENTY-FIVE

SHE WAS DOING IT TO HIM AGAIN. KATE . . . CHARLIE, THE NAME didn't matter. It made him irritable, and damned if he could pinpoint the exact cause. And then Sterling kissed her, and he wanted to grind his fist into the man's face.

Put it in perspective, my friend.

Breaking it down, she was married to a dirty federal prosecutor back East who Nick knew very well, faked her own death, and assumed a new identity, giving him three years of grief trying to locate her. She had something he wanted—evidence his boss needed that spelled prison time. That was it.

So put your testosterone back in your pants and focus.

Walking the grounds, he followed the narrow path of asphalt, bringing him to the banks of the Rio Grande. Charlie had been right. The river in this particular location was no wider than a stream.

Finding a towering tulip poplar to lean against, he studied the rise and fall of the water as it lapped and gurgled over rocks on its southern flow toward New Mexico. Bending down, he tugged a piece of wild grass to chew on and contemplated his next move.

He'd been in Creede a total of three days. By Thursday, he'd have no choice but to let the boss know he had located her. The boss had his timeline, and he wouldn't deviate. Nick had a week to do things Nick's way.

Twigs snapped, and he went rigid.

Charlie stood on a flat rock at the river's edge and removed her boots. Casting them up the bank, she placed her foot in the running water and whistled through her teeth. Undaunted, she plodded forward, maneuvering river rocks slightly below the water's surface. She bent down in search of some unknown treasure resting on the bottom. Pulling up several rocks, she threw them in the water, only to have them hit with a thud before sinking to the bottom.

Her dress reflected the moonlight; she sparkled. Her hair was pinned up loose, wisps of auburn silk escaping to frame her face. Who was he kidding? He couldn't take his eyes off her.

The still air carried only the gurgle of the river's current. He couldn't have asked for a more isolated area, his prey within striking distance. It would be so easy to end this thing now if he was the one calling the shots.

Charlie's piss-poor attempts to skip a stone made him grin. He wanted so badly to correct her form, and the thought of how he would proceed with his method had him rock hard.

The chilly water lapped the bank. *God, don't tempt me.*

Charlie lobbed another, but like the throws before, it only made a loud *kerplunk*. She dipped her hands in the water again and grabbed several more rocks.

He stood mesmerized. The wisps of material from her dress, shimmering and dancing with the breeze, exposed tight thighs and the sexy curve of her legs. He groaned to himself. A spectacular view he'd soon forfeit. "Flat rocks work better."

She froze. As if remaining that way would make her invisible to him. The rock slipped from her fingers. Charlie kept her back toward him. "I suppose you're going to tell me I'm incapable of skipping rocks, too."

Nick pushed off the tree and slowly made his way toward the river bank. "I never implied you were incapable of anything. To the contrary, I believe if you're good at what you do you should pursue your dreams. And from what I've seen and heard, you're top-notch in your trade. If you hadn't bolted yesterday, I would have told you so."

She turned toward him. "Can you teach me how to skip a rock?"

"Sure." He bent down to find a good, flat rock and stood. "It's all in the wrist." He manipulated his wrist to show her the motion.

"No, I mean show me. Here, where I'm standing." She pointed to her bare feet, her toes wiggling in the water.

Nick surveyed her location. She was nimble enough to hop the rocks, but he was twice her size. "Mike would have my head if I ruined his boots." He stared down at them for her benefit.

"Then take them off." She lifted her toes from the water for emphasis. "See, I don't have mine. Just take your time. You won't fall."

Shit. She was baiting him, and he knew it, but a challenge had been made, and he'd be damned if he was going to let it go unchecked.

Nick reached down and yanked off his boot, stuffing his sock way down deep, deciding if he'd made a hasty decision.

"Come on, Nick." Charlie's laughter floated in the night air. "One more boot to go." She swayed her hips, and Nick cast his other boot and sock onto the bank.

He stepped out onto the first rock. The rush of water washed over the top of his foot. "Shit." He sucked air through his teeth. The stab of cold spikes coursed straight up his legs. "This water's freezing."

"I thought Navy SEALs were used to cold water?" He could tell by the curve of her kissable mouth that she found herself—his situation—amusing.

"Wet suits and flippers, beautiful," he said and quickly traversed the rocks, holding his breath and collided into her.

They swayed, and Charlie squealed, "*Jeez*, Nick, you're going to knock us in."

He steadied them, grabbing hold of her slim waist, his hands sliding to her hips. "We're good." Nick reluctantly let go of her.

She smiled up at him. "See what a little coaxing can accomplish?"

"So, does this mean you're not angry with me anymore?"

"You said your piece, and I accept your explanation. I guess I overreacted." She rubbed her hands together. "Okay, show me what you got. I've been trying to master this rock-skipping skill for as long as I can remember."

He laughed. "Patience, grasshopper." He eyed the riverbed. "First, you need a nice, flat rock." He snagged a few from the bottom of the river. Gazing over the water, his eyes came back to the curve of Charlie's bare shoulders and the tantalizing slope of her firm breasts. *Damn* but she was asking a lot of him. "Do you mind if I put my arm around you?"

She hesitated, biting down on a perfectly shaped bottom lip, and Nick clenched his jaw, trying to curb the arousal, snaking through his body.

She nodded.

Nick turned her away from him, his arm coming around, and pulled her snug to his chest. The wide spread of his hand resting against the shimmer of her dress and her flat stomach had him swallowing a moan. He took the rock and slipped it inside her palm, her fingers closing in response. "Do you feel the difference?"

"Yes, it's smooth to the touch."

She fidgeted, her shoulders tense. She was uncomfortable—with him. But she made no move to leave his arms, and he couldn't help but wonder if she felt the same rush as he. Even though he'd tried to ignore it—ignore her and her sweet, round ass pressed intimately against his crotch.

He brushed the whiskers of his face alongside her smooth cheek, her hair teasing his nose. "No pressure, beautiful." He kept her hand in his, his fingers wrapped around hers. "Just follow my motion, but don't release the stone until I tell you."

"Got it."

He guided her arm forward a few times until she was able to make a fluid motion. "Good, you've got the hang of it."

Charlie held the stone firmly between her pointer finger and thumb and practiced flipping her wrist. "Like that?" She looked over her shoulder.

"Perfect. Now give it a try." He let go and moved his hands down to her hips.

She took a deep breath and blew it out slowly and then flung the rock. It flew from her hand, and she tilted her head to see it tip the water before dipping below the surface.

Her shoulders sagged, and she angled her head back to him, her expression one of disappointment. "What did I do wrong?"

"That was good, for your first try." He couldn't help himself. The curve of her neck taunted him, and he touched her there, his rough fingers gliding down her silky skin, her muscles tense. "You need to relax, Charlie." He massaged her neck with slow, easy strokes, enjoying the feel of her beneath his fingertips, when he ran across a thin silver chain he'd not noticed before. He tugged on it. "What's this?"

She wrapped her fingers around the pendant. "A necklace."

"Can I see it?" He turned her toward him, sliding his finger down to the intricate piece of silver. "What is it?" He strained to make it out under the moonlight.

Her head rose, her warm brown eyes connecting with his. "A butterfly."

He studied the craftsmanship. "It's unique."

"The designer only made one like it," she said, her voice soft, almost reflective.

"Why a butterfly?"

"They're pretty." She smiled up at him, her supple, long black lashes fluttering against her tanned skin. "It's not just that." She wet her lips and gave him a curious look. "You really interested in this?"

"I wouldn't have asked."

"Do you believe in mythology?"

He shook his head. "Nope. Never got into all that."

She nodded her understanding. "In ancient mythology, they believed the butterfly was linked to the human soul." She swallowed, her eyes taking on a faraway look, and continued, "When a loved one dies, they become a butterfly, their soul transcending into a new life and a new world."

Now it clicked. Charlie's butterfly pendant symbolized her journey. Her new life had taken her to an obscure Western town in the hopes of remaining hidden, with the ability to start anew. She had managed to re-create herself—changing her appearance, taking on a career dominated by men in an attempt at transformation.

His fingers tightened on the pendant. No one had ever come close to making him human. He lived for the job. He didn't let anything cloud his objective. She'd managed to make him consider her feelings—that was a problem. He let the pendant fall softly between the swell of her breasts.

"You ready?" he asked, his voice slightly gruff.

She frowned at him and awkwardly turned around on the rock they shared.

Nick dug into the front pocket of his jeans and handed her another stone, kicking his conscience to the curb. He continued to aid her in the exact form needed to send each stone on a precise trajectory. Finally, on their seventh attempt, he unwillingly let her go, allowing her a full range of motion.

Nick slanted his head and caught Charlie's determined bronzed profile, her jaw set. She held the stone tightly in her fingers, angled back her arm, and flung the river rock. Keeping an eye on its course, she tipped back on her heels as it hit the water, counting its rhythmic dips skidding across the water before sinking in silence.

Nick's mouth fell open. "Holy shit!" He was laughing—*unbelievable*. And not at Charlie Robertson's skill. As amazing as it was, he liked her grit—he liked her.

"Oh my gosh . . . did you see that fly?" She swung on him, laughing, too, her hand raised for a celebratory high five.

Nick met her hand with a slap of congratulations, threading his fingers through hers, still wet, the water warming between their palms. The pressure of her fingertips, like tiny electrodes, sent sparks through him. Their bodies collided with a whirlwind of excitement. He grabbed onto her, struggling for balance, her soft curves pressing into him. He held her tight, steadying them, the icy current rushing below. "Whew, that was close."

She was breathing hard, as was he, his lips grazing her ear, her hair teasing him with the scent of coconuts. His hands moved down the small of her back and lingered. He wanted to keep them there, frozen in time, untouched by the future.

She pressed closer, her warm breath tickling his neck. "Nick, that was awesome," she whispered against his ear.

Nick stiffened, his hands sliding to her slender waist, and he gave one solid push, separating her from him.

"What's the matter?" Those well-shaped brows of hers snapped together, and Nick realized his mistake. "Oh, I get it," she said. "I'm sure your idea of a Saturday night isn't standing in the frigid waters of the Rio Grande teaching a grown woman how to skip a rock."

Shit! This was going straight to hell, and fast, if he didn't turn it around. "You're kidding me, right? I'm standing here in my bare feet, freezing my ass off, to help a challenged rock-skipper. I don't subject myself to that kind of pain unless I'm enjoying myself."

"Okay, you don't have to get so indignant," she shot back. "If you say you're enjoying yourself, then you're enjoying yourself. Who am I to question it?" She cocked her head, her eyes taking him in. "I've been trying to put my finger on you, and now it's clear. You're just plain weird."

"Weird!" Without a thought, Nick scooped her up. Her long, bare legs dangled from the crook of his arm, the shimmering dress rode up her tight, muscular thighs, and she giggled like a teenager as he crossed the rocks toward the bank, their laughter mingling with a melodious tune choired by tree frogs and crickets.

"Put me down, you nut," she snickered.

Carrying her to the grassy bank, he said, "Not till you take it back." Falling to his knees, he laid her down gently. Her hair spilled out of its silky knot and fell past her shoulders.

"Or what?" Winded, she breathed deep, tempting him with every breath, her breasts expanding over the neckline of her dress.

Nick rolled over to his side, propping his head up with his hand so he could study her. Reaching up, he pushed a strand of hair from her face with his finger and traced her cheek down to the soft hollow of her throat. "You're beautiful," he said, his voice rough.

Her laughter subsided, and her body went rigid.

"What?" Nick leaned in.

Her sultry eyes took on a glacial stare, and she threw his hand off of her. "Get off me." She rolled away from him, grabbed her boots a few feet away, and ran barefoot up the dark slope into the stand of shadowing ponderosa pines and tulip poplars.

"Charlie!" he called into the night. "Where are you going?"

The silver-dollar moon filtered through the wide crown of leaves, kept her visible, making her look more supernatural than human before she disappeared up the path.

Charlie's heart beat so fast it thumped against her chest. *God—the guy must think I'm a total head case.* Everything had been fine. They were laughing.

She hadn't counted on him touching her there—that spot—soft and vulnerable where Jack had touched her long ago, and the memory seized her in an unavoidable wave of panic.

Is it always going to be this way with men?

In the past seventy-two hours, Charlie had more male attention thrown at her than in years. First Ben, now this wanderer making her pulse race. He was slick. One minute he was the patient instructor, the next he was making her feel inadequate with his faraway stares. Then carrying her in his strong and capable arms across the water, causing her to laugh like a silly teenager enamored by his chivalry.

But he ruined it when he gave her that serious look, touched her, the way Jack had touched her. Oh, she heard his voice—very male, very seductive. "You're beautiful." She wasn't falling for it. She wasn't falling for him.

She reached her truck, popped the lock, tossed her boots on to the passenger seat, and sat behind the steering wheel. She slammed the door and punched down the locks, her way of shutting out the memory.

The best thing she could do was stay away from him.

Charlie threw her head back against the headrest, took a cleansing breath, and counted off all the reasons she shouldn't be attracted to him. He was a drifter only here to take in the sights. He'd move on, taking her heart with him, and, this was the biggie—she knew positively nothing about him. Tall, rugged, errant hotties were not an everyday occurrence in Creede, especially one that seemed curious about her.

Maybe too curious.

Chapter Twenty-Six

CHARLIE SAT BACK ADMIRING ALL THE PRETTY BOTTLES BEHIND the bar and finished her beer, ignoring the two men sitting next to her bickering. She gave a nod to Tommyknocker's owner and bartender, Pete Lightfoot, whose family had ties to Creede long before the first silver vein had ever been discovered. One hundred percent Apache, he wore a single braid of raven-black hair down his back. His deep, inset eyes glinted with an all-knowing wisdom, or maybe it was a bartender thing. Charlie raised her glass. "How about a refill, Pete."

"Coming up, Charlie." He nodded toward the bandages wrapped around her elbows. "Been to see the doc in Denver."

Charlie grimaced. "Just got back this afternoon." She'd thought about skipping her blood bank appointment, realizing, now, she'd left herself vulnerable. But the thought of dying a horrible death, if she didn't keep up on it, changed her mind.

"You're an ass, Sterling." The craggy voice of Quince Maynard made Charlie's heart dip with disbelief and a little anger. As much as she'd stressed good behavior, she'd hoped the man could muster some self-control.

Charlie gave him a sideways glance, prepared to give him her full ire, and frowned. He couldn't see her displeasure with his wild gray head dipped down toward the top of the bar, his finger, with a ring of dirt beneath his nail, pointed squarely at the plans for the Lockhart site. "You set the charge here. No way around it." He threw himself back in his stool.

Ben shook his head earnestly. "Too much risk of collateral damage. Not losing the pines to the right."

"Charlie," Quince called over. "Tell your partner, we do this my way, or I'm out."

Charlie swiveled her bar stool toward them, prepared to knock both their heads together, when the door to the tavern opened. Her fingers tightened on the edge of the bar. "*Jesus.*" She hopped off and grabbed Ben's arm. "Call 9-1-1. *Now!*"

"Why?"

Charlie concentrated on the woman coming toward her. She recognized her only by the soft blonde curls framing what was left of her pretty face. She staggered, grabbing hold of an empty chair at a table several feet in front of Charlie. The tears hit the back of Charlie's eyes, and she ran to her, clearing people and tables. "Shelley! *God, Shelley!*" Her name fell on a whisper.

The small frame of Shelley Evers leaned into Charlie. Charlie held her and slid a chair out and sat her down. "H-help me." The words left Shelley's swollen lips, the bottom one split, oozing with blood.

Charlie's hands hovered around her face. Shelley's eyelids were a purple, protruding mess, pupils barely visible through slits. Blood trickled from a gash gaping open above her eyebrow.

Charlie's stomach roiled.

This is my fault.

She'd always feared the backlash if others took it upon themselves to interfere between her and Jack. Charlie figured Shelley had the right to deal with the abuse in her own way, too.

She'd been so wrong.

Charlie crouched down beside Shelley. "Bobby Ray do this to you?"

She nodded, and her hand, scratched and bloody, reaching up unsteadily, clutched Charlie's arm.

Charlie's stomach pitched. "Shelley, honey, where's Gunner?"

Shelley swallowed. "I-I d-didn't get a ch-chance. H-he's with my m-mom."

Technically Gunner didn't belong to Bobby Ray. He had no right to him. That didn't mean he saw it that way.

Charlie moved closer to her, speaking softly, smoothly, though her body trembled with rage. "Where is Bobby Ray now, Shelley?"

"Gr-Gruenewald Sawm—"

"Shh. Relax." She shouldn't have pushed. But she needed to know. Of course, the asshole would simply head off to work, and Charlie's jaw clenched.

Ben rushed over with a cell phone to his ear. He dropped to his knees next to Shelley, his other hand coming to rest on her thigh. Quince and Pete stood behind him looking on, their expressions grave.

Pete handed her a cold rag with ice and nodded toward Shelley. "Put it on her lip."

"The front room by the bar and hurry the hell up," Ben said, his voice sharp before he clicked off and shoved the phone in his back pocket. His face stiffened, his eyes veering from Charlie to Shelley. He whispered, his voice low and controlled, "Ambulance is on its way."

"They taking her to the clinic?" Charlie asked.

"Rio Grande Hospital in Del Norte."

Charlie's shoulders slumped. That was what sucked about living on the frontier. Shelley had a good forty-five-minute ride. But the gash above her eye looked bad. They'd have to stitch it, and judging by the bruising, Charlie wondered if her eyes had suffered trauma. The hospital would be the best place.

Ben caressed Shelley's hair, then said to Charlie, with a ruthless look in his eye, "Call me when you get to the hospital." He rose to his feet, and Charlie grabbed for him.

"Where you going?"

"He wants to pick on a woman half his size." He raked his fingers roughly through his hair. "Let's see how he fares with me."

Shelley moaned, "No," and reached up to snag Ben's hand. "Stay with m-me." Tears emerged from the slits of Shelley's lids, rolling down her cheeks.

Charlie's heart cried with her, and she clenched her fingers.

Stuck between a hunch and a standing position, Ben looked to Charlie. "I'm going to kill the son of a bitch," he growled.

Shelley started to shake, and she pulled Ben's hand downward.

Quince's gnarled hand landed on Ben's shoulder. "Sterling, don't upset her," he snapped.

The heat rose in Charlie's face. There was nothing left to break or bruise or split, and that had Charlie so fired up. She could kill the son of a bitch herself.

Just like Jack, Bobby Ray had become emboldened. Untouchable. And Charlie wondered if this last act of violence would get him a jail cell tonight. They were witnesses to the aftermath. But if Shelley wouldn't press charges, it would be the same bullshit.

Charlie motioned to Ben, pulling out another chair next to Shelley. "Come around here. She wants you close to her."

He hesitated.

Now she mouthed, her gaze locking into his

He stood and took the chair, moving close to Shelley, and took her hand in his, her fingers curling in response.

Charlie patted Shelley on the shoulder. "Ambulance is on the way, Shell."

Shelley angled her head toward Charlie. "I-I just want to . . ." Shelley began to tremble, and Ben took off his Sterling Windbreaker and draped it around her.

Ben smoothed down her hair. "Shelley, sweetie, relax. It's best they take you. I'll follow behind, honey." His brown eyes, etched in concern, remained fixed on Shelley's face, his jaw tightening.

Charlie came around to Quince and pulled him aside. "When Mike gets here, tell him Bobby Ray's at home." She waved to Pete. "Put the beers on my tab, would you?"

"On the house, Charlie."

"Thanks." Then she turned back to Quince. "Have him notify Shelley's mom, and it wouldn't be a bad idea for Shep to sit on her house. She's got Shelley's son."

He nodded. "You think he'll grab the kid?"

Charlie shrugged. "Not taking that chance."

Quince gave her a wry look. "What you up to, girl?"

"Just do it."

He rolled his lips in like he always did, his eyes beading in on her. "Don't do something stupid."

Her hand came down on his shoulder, a vicious smile upon her lips. "Y. O. L. O."

He gave her an ornery look. "What the shit?"

She winked. "You only live once, old man." Charlie took one last look at Shelley and caught the curious and troubled eyes of Ben. "Checking on the ambulance." She pointed to him. "Stay with her."

Charlie pressed through the glass door of Tommyknocker's, letting it slam behind her.

CHAPTER TWENTY-SEVEN

NICK GOT PAID TO DELIVER. GET THE JOB DONE AND KEEP HIS boss apprised. That was what he wrestled with as he pulled in front of the Creede Repertory Theatre, parked, and headed north up Main Street toward the Tommyknocker Tavern. He'd checked in earlier, sidestepped the issue of why, after five days, he remained in Creede.

Hell if he knew.

But it seemed prudent after the debacle on the bank of the Rio Grande to give her space. He could kick Reynolds's ass for making this more difficult.

He shook it off and kept walking, maneuvering around tourists coming in and out of shops. The town had seemed to swell overnight with the anticipated annual Fourth of July Mining Day Celebration on Wednesday. American flags hung on almost every business he passed, flapping in the wind vigorously—festive. Only his mood could be described as anything but. Nick kept moving down the sidewalk and waited for a group of soccer moms and young girls with matching uniforms to pile into a van after leaving San Juan Sports.

When the group cleared, he ran full force into Charlie. "Whoa." He steadied her, his hands gripping her by the upper arms, the edge of his palm rubbing against gauze bandages at both her elbows. "What the hell happened to—"

"Not now, Nick," she snapped and tried to jerk away, but he held her tight.

"I didn't see your truck." Her body trembled slightly in his grip.

"It's parked on a side street." Their eyes connected. Hers were determined and growing slightly moist.

Screw it. He didn't need this, and Nick let her go. She headed away from him, crossing the street.

Nick concentrated on the corner and making a left on Wall. Soon he'd be sitting at the bar ordering a nice, cold brew. A siren wailed in the distance, growing louder, until the swoosh of an ambulance, its lights flashing, passed by.

Nick picked up the pace and rounded the corner of Main and Wall, the ambulance now parked in front of Tommyknockers. He cleared the doors of the tavern and practically ran into Sterling, who was assisting two EMTs lifting a woman onto the gurney. Nick grabbed Sterling's arm. "What's—"

"Shelley Evers."

He barely recognized the waitress, her face a distortion of swollen purple flesh. "Her boyfriend do that?" Nick's fingers clenched.

Sterling nodded while the EMTs next to him ran Shelley's vital signs and began wheeling her out. Ben headed out with them and turned back. "You seen Charlie?"

"I ran into her up the block—"

One of the EMTs grabbed Sterling's arm. "You following?"

"I'm right behind you." He glanced back to Nick. "You see Charlie, tell her I'll give her a call once I know something." Then he yelled back to the old codger. "Maynard, tell Coulter she's pressing charges, and I want his ass thrown in jail. No excuses."

Ben hustled out with the emergency personnel, and Nick was left to fill in the gaps. Charlie had mentioned some old guy at lunch that day. Nick moved in on him. "You know Charlie Robertson?"

Wary black eyes rested on Nick. "Who wants to know?" His head moved up, then down until his mulish face landed on Nick's.

Nick rubbed the stubble of whiskers against his cheek and took a drawn-out breath. The woman, he thought for sure, had come from Tommyknocker's. He didn't know how the bandages fit in. From what he'd gathered, Bobby Ray Hanson had caused the trauma to Shelley's face. She and Charlie were friends, and she looked upset and angry when he'd run into her. *Damn it.* She wasn't that stupid?

He grabbed the old guy's arm. "She go after Hanson?"

His leathery skin crinkled around his eyes, and he narrowed in on Nick. "Gruenewald Sawmill. Hanson works the night shift. He done it to Shelley. And Charlie's gone after him."

"Where?" The word unexpectedly a mix of anger and concern.

"Gruenewald Sawmill," he repeated like Nick was stupid and then stood. "Follow me."

The two hotfooted it through the front doors of the tavern, the old man surprisingly keeping up with him as they sprinted down the sidewalk of

Main Street, dodging townsfolk on their way to Nick's bike. They hopped on, the old man pointing. "Take 149 west out of Creede. You can't miss it."

Nick revved the bike to life, weaving through the main thoroughfare with Maynard against his back, heading out of town. The moon cast their shadow on the asphalt as Nick whizzed past, the watchful columns of evergreens on either side of him a blur, and he pushed the bike to top speed. Who did she think she was? Avenger of all women who had ever been lorded over by men with a penchant for violence? If she was so damned capable of fighting everyone's battles, why the hell didn't she stay in Maryland and fight the bastard she was married to?

Now he was headed out on a desolate stretch of highway, hoping to save the hothead from being crushed by a man he wasn't so sure he could take on and win.

CHAPTER TWENTY-EIGHT

C HARLIE'S CHEST CONSTRICTED, AND SHE CONTEMPLATED WHAT
the hell she was doing. Avenging a friend? She could hide under that
pretense. But reality, cold and stark, prickled her senses, and those icy,
steel-blue eyes from her past surfaced. Pushing them from her mind, she
concentrated on Shelley's swollen face and split lip and the scene before
her in the gravel lot of Gruenewald's Sawmill.

There it sat, freshly waxed and gleaming under the moon's silver threads
of light. Bobby Ray's baby, according to Shelley, a 1969 Mustang fastback,
painted in flaming red to match his flaming ass. Well, it was about time ol'
Bobby Ray was brought to his knees, and she knew just where to strike first.

Reaching into the Mustang's window, Charlie laid on the horn. Easing
up, she waited.

Sure enough, the heavy work boots of Bobby Ray clomped against the
concrete floor of the mill. "What the shit?" His deep, slow voice echoed
through the open doorway.

Ignoring the dip in her stomach, Charlie walked over to the bed of her
truck and, under the hodgepodge of construction debris, pulled out a piece
of gas pipe.

She headed back to the sports car and stopped short at the lumbering
figure filling the doorway of the sawmill. He stood almost seven feet tall.
She swallowed hard, ignored the tremble in her hands, and tightened her
grip on the metal pipe.

"You screwing with my car?" he asked before spitting a stream of chewing
tobacco onto the gravel.

Charlie's stance widened, and she dug her boots into the gravel, her eyes
focused on him. Her auburn hair wild and hanging past her shoulders caught

her attention, and she wished she'd had the sense to secure it back out of her way. She quickly tucked it inside the collar of her Sterling Log Homes T-shirt. Charlie slapped one end of the pipe into her open palm. "This is for Shelley." The pipe slashed downward, ripping off the driver's side mirror.

"What the hell?" Bobby Ray snapped straight up, mouth agape. "I'm going to fuck you up, Charlie." He came at her fast, jumping off the step, all two hundred and eighty-five pounds of height and muscle. His shadow, cast by the moon's glow, expanded and loomed over her.

Shit! Now she was in trouble. The motor of her truck rumbled to her right—reassurance she had a quick escape, if she could reach it in time. Charlie held up the pipe one more time. "I suggest you stop, Bobby Ray. You come any closer, and I'll let you know real pain."

He froze on the gravel lot no more than twenty feet in front of her and gave her a curious look. "Shelley's *my* girlfriend, and I can do what the hell I want to her. It's none of your damn business."

His words, although different, echoed another's hauntingly familiar sentiment, and she went rigid with defiance. "Well, jackass, I just made it my business. It seems you're either hard of hearing or you're just plain stupid." She lifted the metal pipe and sent it careening down into the windshield, forming a spider web. "That's for Shelley's black eyes. Now, you want to go for broke? Then keep spouting off. I hear you can get a pretty penny for scrap metal these days."

Bobby Ray came at her, the gravel crunching under his weight.

Pistons snapped and popped. Charlie stopped, her head swiveling to the left.

Bobby Ray did the same, his head turning cautiously.

Charlie took several steps away from his car, cupping her ear. She quickly scanned the area. Sandwiched between the two wooden buildings of the mill sat the log conveyer. She smiled. The belt on the conveyer moved forward, the screech of metal spitting logs out.

Bobby Ray unleashed a flow of obscenities. He grabbed his head between his meaty hands and growled. "Get the fuck away from my car. Tell Shelley she can go to hell. I don't need that bitch." He turned and thundered away toward the conveyer belt.

Charlie lifted the pipe above her head. A strong arm encircled her waist and jerked her backward. A masculine hand yanked the pipe from her grasp.

"Do you have a death wish?" the familiar voice growled quietly into her ear.

"Let go of me." Her face contorted, and she thrashed against his hold. What the hell? Did he have a tracking device on her or what?

"Look, baby, that little diversion I created is only going to keep Jethro occupied for a couple more minutes. After that, he'll regroup and kick both our asses. So settle down, and let's get the hell out of here."

Nick settled behind the wheel of Charlie's truck and, after recognizing the crossroads coming out from the sawmill, took a right toward Charlie's cabin. Tomorrow he'd hook up with Maynard and get his bike.

He'd traveled a good mile with only the red glow of the truck's rear lights and a dark tunnel of roadway in his rearview. He reduced his speed. If Hanson was behind them, he would have caught up to them by now.

Nick glanced over. Charlie sat stone-faced in the passenger seat next to him, and he shook his head. As remarkable as it was, this woman who resembled the soft defense attorney was nothing compared to the well-toned, indignant tight-ass, her arms crossed over her chest.

"What were you thinking?"

"You wouldn't understand." She gave him her back and stared out the passenger window.

Nick's grip tightened on the steering wheel. "Try me. I think you owe me that much, since I saved your ass."

With her arms remaining crossed, her fingers digging into the bandages at her elbow, she turned to face him. "First of all, you didn't save my ass, and, second, I don't recall asking for help. Frankly, Mr. Foster, it's none of your damn business."

What had she done with the woman from Tilghman? Kate Reynolds was a butter knife compared to the serrated edge of Charlie Robertson. This woman beside him had a temper, and, when needed, an arsenal of obscenities to make a Navy SEAL blush. He refused to smile at that. "Look, don't get your panties in a wad."

"Don't tell me what I should do with my underwear. Who the hell are you, Nick Foster? Do you make it your business to shadow one particular resident of a town and dog her every move? Seems you have a particular interest in me, and don't think people around here haven't noticed." She threw her head against the back seat of her truck.

The two sat in silence. She had summed up the evening in two sentences, and Nick was left with nothing more to say.

A familiar song began to play, and Nick looked to Charlie who grabbed her phone off her hip, the music interrupted when she took the call. "How is she?" She nodded. "Bring her to my cabin once they release her." She shook her head. "Doesn't matter. I'll be up." She turned her back on Nick, her voice dropping to a whisper, "He's with me. I can't talk right now. I'll see you later." She disconnected the call.

"How she doing?"

"They're stitching her now." She waved him off and leaned her head on the window, drawing her legs up onto the seat. She sighed. "Will you take me home?"

Nick reached over and stroked her hair. "Charlie?"

She sniffed, her shoulders trembling.

Shit! He'd done his best to avoid women and tears. His gut knotted up. "Honey, I need you to give me directions."

She nodded, her voice quivering, "You're good. It's down a few miles, Moonshine Mesa's straight ahead."

He kept to the winding gravel road, the homes scattered acres apart, the valley sloping up to meet pine trees sprawling up the mountain side. To the right, another mountain range rested, its peaks topped with snow.

"Driveway coming up on your right with pines on either side."

"Got it." He took it, cresting a small hill before taking the dip of the short driveway. At the bottom sat a log cabin with a nice-sized front porch, warm light spilling from almost every window. He'd have found it without her help, but showing a knowledge of where she lived would have raised suspicion. He pulled in front and parked, turning off the engine.

Charlie sat quietly next to him.

"Do you want to tell me why you're bandaged up like a busted piñata?"

No response.

He touched her arm closest to him, his fingers tracing a path along the edge of the white bandage. "Did you have another accident at work?"

She looked over her shoulder. "That's right, I'm a woman who doesn't belong—"

"I didn't say that." He caressed the side of her cheek. "Turn around so we can talk."

Her head slumped, and she faced him. "I have a disease. Okay?"

"How bad?" The tendon in his jaw flexed. He'd been told about it—the disease. Didn't care to listen about how it affected its victims until now.

"Are you actually feeling sorry for me?" She made a face. "You don't even know me."

He knew quite a bit about her and her former life. Her current one—a learning curve. "I'm not as horrible as you seem to think I am."

Charlie fell back against the seat. "I have hemocromatosis—too much iron in my blood."

"Is it . . ."

"Fatal?"

"Yeah."

"It can be. But mine is under control."

"What does this have to do with it?" He slipped his finger under the edge of the strange gauze wrapping, that reminded him of an ace bandage, along the crook of her arm and tugged.

"Hemocromatosis causes high iron overload. They take a pint of blood to reduce the iron and also test it, and if my levels are within normal range, I don't get a phone call." She laughed. "Today, I got a taste of what a voodoo doll feels like."

"They couldn't find your vein?"

"You got it. Stuck me a few times, actually." She held out her arms to him and nodded to the right. "Three times in this one and two in the left before they could fill the bag."

Son of a bitch. Nick fell back against his seat. He'd gotten his hands on the police report for Kate Reynolds's townhouse. It had been everywhere—the blood. He'd guarantee a good pint's worth. It had taken the feds a couple months to determine the blood spatter patterns were staged. Damn good for an amateur.

The woman was diabolical and scoring points with him in a major way. He moved his hand to the base of her neck and pulled her close and kissed her hard on her mouth. When he pulled away, her lips were moist and slightly open.

"What?" He couldn't help but chuckle. Speechless.

"I didn't say you could . . . you know . . ."

"Kiss you?"

"Yeah, that."

"You didn't have to. It was written all over your face." He chuckled, again, and she became pensive.

"How are you going to get home?"

On the way back to her cabin, he'd been pondering that same question. "That's a dilemma. I gave my bike to your friend Maynard after he got me to the sawmill and sent him on his way."

"Quince?"

He nodded. "Grumpy bastard. But he cares for you. Eventually, I'll get it back." He connected with those brown eyes of hers that were slowly growing larger. "I'm thinking, after last week, you're not keen on me borrowing your truck."

She remained quiet.

"And I'm assuming Bobby Ray knows where you live."

She nodded.

"The sheriff will catch up with him in due time. But until then, I'm not comfortable with you staying here alone."

He gave her a minute to digest the situation and then ran his finger down the soft inside of her arm just below her elbow and the bandage. He laced his fingers through hers and then connected with her eyes again. "I got the gist of the conversation with Ben. But I'm thinking his arrival is sketch, at best, considering the speed of hospitals. I'd feel more comfortable if I spent the night."

She made a move to protest.

"On the couch, of course."

She cleared her throat. "I think that's prudent, and I'll feel better knowing I'm not alone." Her fingers tightened on his. "You don't have to sleep on the couch."

Damn. He hadn't been going there. Not that he wouldn't like to *with her.* He just hadn't counted on her being so agreeable.

"I have two spare bedrooms. You can pick whichever one you like best." She gave him a sweet smile, grabbed her keys out of his hand, and turned to exit the truck, laughing when she shut the door.

Nick got out, slamming the door, and chased her up the steps. When he grabbed her around the waist, she shrieked then giggled when he pulled her to him. "You did that on purpose."

"Ah, Nick, you're so easy." Her eyes danced with laughter under the recessed light of the porch; her hands gliding up his T-shirt teased him. "I do want you to stay," she whispered, the humor fading from her face. "Thanks . . . for earlier. That was really stupid of me."

Nick held her gaze. He needed her alive. His arms tightened around her slight waist, his hands resting on the curve of her shapely ass. But when he cut through the bullshit, the truth he'd rather ignore troubled him—she *should* fear him. He would bring her face to face with the evil she had so desperately sought to expunge from her life: Jack.

Chapter Twenty-Nine

CHARLIE EASED HERSELF FROM NICK'S ARMS AND OPENED THE door. She was a mess of tingly nerve endings. Things were moving too fast. Actually, things shouldn't be moving at all. But that didn't stop her from wanting them to . . . with him.

She walked in and sat her keys down. The door shut, and she couldn't bring herself to turn around. Moochie came around the corner, rubbing the side of his face on the edge of the wall, and she reached for him. He sidestepped her, and she frowned, turning around.

"Hey, buddy." Nick picked him up and held him in his arms, scratching the back of his ear, the rumble growing louder.

"Mooch, you traitor." She smiled at Nick with bemusement. "How'd you . . ."

He grinned. "They like me."

She narrowed in on him. "But do you like them?"

He cradled Mooch in his left arm, rubbing him under his chin. "You like that, buddy." He smiled at her. "They're easy, independent . . ."

Her brows rose.

"Yes, I like them." He sat him down. "And . . . I like you." He kissed her forehead and moved past her, eyeing the open space, cathedral ceiling, his hand coming to rest on the varnished curve of the log wall. He turned. "You build it?"

She nodded. "A few months ago."

He gave her a lift of his brow. "Moonshine Mesa, huh?" He glanced into the great room to the left, giving her a sideways glance. "You have your very own still, Ms. Robertson?" he asked, a grin tugging the rugged curves of his lips.

"You're not funny, Foster. It's named for the stills built during the silver boom in the forest behind me." She tried to remain serious, but her lips wouldn't cooperate.

"I like your smile, Robertson."

She fidgeted. "You hungry?"

"Whatcha got?" He moved into the kitchen and grabbed the refrigerator door and looked back. "You mind?"

"Knock yourself out."

He pulled out eggs, mushrooms, an onion, milk, and cheddar cheese and placed it on the counter. "You like omelets?"

"Sure." She motioned up the stairs. "I'm going to get a quick shower, and I'll get your room ready. It has its own bathroom. Towels are under the sink. I'll show you after we eat." She picked at the wrappings on her arms. They itched.

"Come here," he said in a demanding voice that didn't match the concerned look in his eye—she assumed for her.

She walked cautiously toward him. "What?"

He took her hand, pulled her toward him, and cleared a space on the counter before grabbing her by the waist and sitting her on top.

Charlie gripped the edge of the counter. "What are you—"

He pushed her hair behind her ears, his warm, soulful eyes intent on her face. "Relax." He reached down to her arm and touched the bandage around her left elbow and started to unwrap it. The movement of his wrist, and the masculine, black, waterproof diver's watch he'd worn since she'd met him tantalized her. She struggled against the warmth growing inside her, the more his tough-guy fingers worked the bandages free.

"Nick . . ." She touched his hand. "You don't have to . . ."

His hand stilled under hers. He brought his head up, brows furrowing over a pair of gorgeous blue eyes. "I want to." The slight rasp of his voice made her go all shivery.

She rolled her lips in and allowed him to continue. He moved closer, his flat stomach pressed to the granite countertop, with him between her thighs, heat racing through her. He let the last bandage fall to the floor and ran his fingers up her arms, examining the puncture wounds. "How often do they have to take your blood?"

"Once a month."

His head rose, his eyes intent and holding hers.

Charlie caressed the strong angle of his jaw. "You're staring," she whispered.

"If things were different . . ." He angled his head, the warmth of his mouth suspended over hers like a spell, and then broke it when he rested the side of his rough face against hers, his lips grazing her hair and ear beneath. "You better go upstairs before I do something stupid." The heat of his lips and the way the words ripped from his throat—low and harsh—made every nerve ending tingle. She wanted to tempt him—tempt herself. She pulled her face away, her eyes lingering on the hard angles of his face.

His jaw tightened.

"Nick . . ." She gave him a questioning look.

He took her by her waist, the pressure of his hands making her more aware of his strength. Serious blue eyes searched her face. "It won't stop with a kiss," he said, the words rough and, maybe, a little angry.

He sat her down and lifted his chin toward the steps. "Not kidding."

He meant it, and that had her turning away from him and heading for the steps, a nervous mix of confused and frazzled, definitely rusty, untapped hormones.

What the hell was she thinking?

She wanted him, and it all came back. The kiss in the truck, his lips, strong and controlled, gliding over hers. Her nether region tumbled softly, and she grabbed the banister and climbed the steps to her bedroom and shut the door. Once in the bathroom, she turned on the shower, tossed her clothes off, and stepped in. Soaping up the washcloth, the rough terry cloth running across her nipples tingled.

Damn it.

He wasn't even in the room, and she couldn't stop him from touching her. She quickly finished her shower, brushed her teeth and hair, threw on her underwear, pajama pants, and t-shirt. She headed down the hall with bare feet to the top landing and took a minute before taking the stairs.

The aromas of eggs and onions filled the air, and her stomach growled. She rounded the archway into the kitchen and stopped. The small oak table in the kitchen was set, omelets and toast on each plate and two glasses of orange juice beside them. The cookware was washed and drying in the rack next to the sink

She fell back a step.

He could cook, he could clean, and . . . he wasn't in the kitchen.

"Nick." She traveled a few steps into the great room—empty. She took the steps two at a time to the upstairs, walking swiftly to check out the bedrooms, calling his name. He didn't answer, the rooms vacant. Her heart sped up, and she flew down the log stairs, her feet squeaking on the floor as she rounded the corner.

He came from the basement, his back toward her.

"Hey." It came out with force and more frightened than she intended.

What was he doing in her basement?

His back straightened, and he shut the door. Slowly he turned, and Charlie trembled with an unknown fear until he grinned, holding Moochie in his arms. "Hey," he said, his expression changing to one of alarm. "You okay?"

"Why were you . . ." Charlie came up on Nick and snatched Moochie from him. "What were you doing down there?" She nodded to the door leading down to the basement.

"I heard him meow and went to investigate." He petted Moochie's back. "Found him on top of the hot water heater."

Usually she shut the door. Last time she had a reason to check was the night the rug had been moved. Funny, she thought it had been shut.

He touched her arm and headed into the kitchen, calling back, "Come on. I'm starving."

Charlie let the cat go, along with the uneasiness.

She'd left the door open, just like her front door the night Ben barged in—end of story.

Everything had a reasonable explanation, including the rug and Quince's surprise visit at the Jameson cabin. Charlie shook her head. Nick's arrival in Creede had nothing to do with it.

CHAPTER THIRTY

CHARLIE HAD WAITED FOR THIS GAME OF POOL AGAINST SHORTY, in the upstairs room of Tommyknocker's, since he had jammed that hard hat into her stomach. She bent over. "Two, left center." The cue ball smacked into the solid-blue ball. It rolled across the green felt, and she ignored Shorty's groan as it disappeared into the pocket.

Charlie smiled. She couldn't help it. She'd been smiling ever since Nick kissed her last night. She had a lot to be happy about, actually. Ben had brought Shelley to her cabin around one in the morning. She would be staying with her indefinitely, with Gunner to follow in a few days.

Ben had also set her mind at ease with the capture of Bobby Ray. He'd be in jail until trial. Good thing. Ben would have demanded he stay the night. She didn't want to have to explain Nick had already released him of that duty. Unless you counted the rush of water overhead from the shower pipes, he was clueless.

She broke down and told Shelley when they passed Nick's shut bedroom door. They talked in Shelley's room after she showered and slipped into a pair of Charlie's pajamas and got into bed. Mostly about Shelley's predicament and how she'd always had feelings for Ben.

No surprise there.

When they woke in the morning, Nick had already left, leaving his towels in a neat pile on the bathroom sink and his bed made with a note on the pillow that said, "See you later tonight, beautiful."

Her stomach dipped, and she realized she was smiling to herself.

"Take your shot," Shorty said with agitation, motioning with his head toward the cue ball and the tip of her stick.

Charlie let the memory fade along with the smile and reconnected with the game. She focused on her shot, enjoying Shorty's pain as he hung over his pool stick shaking his head. He'd asked for it, and she planned to give it to him. Her reward for a long day under the blistering sun, three stories up, finishing the roof of the Brickmans' cabin.

"Charlie!" She jerked. Mike filled the opening, standing on the top landing of the steps leading down to the main dining room.

"Your truck's illegally parked. You want to move it?"

She grabbed her keys from her pocket. "Will you move it?" She smiled sweetly and glanced back at Shorty. "Don't want to lose my concentration."

He nodded, hand up ready to catch the keys she tossed in his direction. "Appreciate it, Mike." She winked at him.

"You owe me," he called back and descended the steps.

"Six, right corner." She continued to call her shots. "Four, center pocket." The other men from Sterling gathered around the pool table.

With her back facing the steps, a view of the outside deck and the cliffs beyond, Charlie stood poised to sink the eight ball and win the game. She leaned over the table, her butt cocked out, her legs straddled one in front of the other. "Eight ball, right corner pocket."

A sly smile lit her face, the cue stick gliding between her fingers, the back of the stick gripped in her palm. She aimed and pulled back. The cue stick jerked hard, unexpected, striking the eight ball, the force sending the eight and then the cue ball slamming into the pocket. The crowd of men erupted into jeers and moans. Shorty's brows knit together, and he scratched his head.

"What the hell!" Charlie peeked under her arm to find a pissed-off sheriff—definitely not good.

"I need to see you." The words grated off his lips, and his smiling eyes from a few minutes ago bore into her, his finger pointing toward a booth.

"Why are you—"

"The booth, Charlie."

She straightened. "Fine, after I'm done." She met his hard stare with one of her own.

Mike stepped closer. "No, now." He took her pool stick and eyed Shorty. "Looks like this is your lucky day, Shorty. Since I'm the law, I'm deciding this game. Charlie's forfeiting."

Shorty hesitated. "You're sure, Mike?"

He nodded. "Take your money."

Shorty grabbed it like a vagrant on his last dollar. Shoving it in his wallet, he turned to Charlie, shrugging his shoulders. "Sorry, Charlie, no hard feelings."

"Take the money. My beef isn't with you." She turned, glowered at Mike, and whispered, "You can't just come in and take over."

"I just did, sweetheart. Now are you going to continue to make a scene? Or oblige me on this?"

She stood her ground. Sheriff or not, the mean old brow thing had her spitting mad, and she gave him an angry face. "Let's go."

Mike motioned toward the booth, and Charlie followed him, sitting on the other side. He folded his arms on the table and pressed his chest tight against the edge of it. "When you make me a promise, I expect you to hold up your end."

She had no clue what he was getting at. "What crawled up your butt?" She threw her back against the bench.

"I'll tell you what, smart-ass." Mike whipped off his Stetson, placed it on the table, and reached behind his back, pulling out a familiar silver snub-nosed revolver. "Found it under your seat."

She dropped back against the booth and threw up her hands. "That's Quince's fault. I—"

"What does he have to do with it?"

Nothing. After that night she had realized it truly *was* nothing except her own ridiculousness. Only she forgot she'd stuffed her gun under the seat. She'd leave Quince out of it. Mike already knew about the rug incident. She wasn't leveling with him and confessing her true identity—once he knew the whole of it, what she'd done, he'd have no choice but to turn her in.

"Charlie, did you not hear a word I said? Tell me what's going on!"

She slammed her hands on the table. "Why are you badgering me?" She closed her eyes tight.

"Charlie?"

Cracking open one eye, she peeked across the table. "Damn, you're still here." She opened both eyes and lay her head on her arms, resting on the table.

"I'm warning you, if you don't stop with your antics and level with me, I'll throw you in the pokey until you come clean."

Her head shot up to meet his threat. "You can't do that."

"Try me, Missy, and we'll see who comes out on top."

Charlie arched a brow, questioning his authority, but thinking better of it, conceded. She surveyed the room, catching a few curious eyes before they glanced away. "I'll tell you, but you need to keep your voice down," she whispered.

"Fine," he whispered back. "Let's have it."

"I forgot it, okay. Yes, I had been uptight that night with the rug before I knew it was Moochie. I had to check out the Jameson cabin after dark the next day and took it with me—where I left it under the seat. I should have put it away back on the shelf like I promised."

His shoulder's relaxed. "Charlie, we've been through this before. I have no problems with you owning a gun. But you need to take the time to learn to use it. Do you even know what a misfire is? Or a jam? Do you know how to clear a jam?"

All right, so she wasn't well-versed in firearms.

"For being so full of wind tonight, you seem awful quiet now. Give me the gun, Charlie."

"No."

Mike leaned in hard against the table. "You are the most hardheaded woman I know." His dark eyes bore into her. "Give me the gun before you hurt yourself or someone else."

"No." Her voice a whisper, she folded her arms over her chest.

Out of the corner of Charlie's eye, she caught the glimpse of a man standing tall and handsome at the end of the booth, his smile sympathetic.

With his eyes, Nick motioned for her to slide over. Charlie moved to the end, and he sat down, his thigh touching hers.

Mike glared up at Nick. "For a man just passing through, you certainly make it your business to keep up on all the scuttlebutt in this town."

Nick laughed. "You'd have to be a deaf mute not to know what's up between you two."

"I appreciate your thoughts, but this is between Charlie and myself." Mike drew in a breath and put all his concentration on Charlie. "Look, I don't have time to scratch my ass, let alone give you gun safety and shooting lessons, but let's see if we can work something in."

"If it's a hardship on you, Mike, I can teach her. I know a thing or two about guns. It would take a couple of days, a few hours each session. But if she's willing to make time, I'm available." He shot her a hopeful smile.

She wasn't giving up the gun. Not that she felt threatened at the moment, but it was security. There was no reason for Mike not to agree to Nick's offer, and she did agree—she *was* ill-equipped to protect herself, not that she would admit it to him.

Charlie reached over and squeezed Nick's arm. "Thank you." She was thankful and a little embarrassed when her eyes became moist. Refusing to blink and make herself an even bigger charity case, she looked away.

Mike searched both their faces. "Fine." He handed the gun to Nick. "I want Nick here to take it with him until you two set up some type of training schedule. Is that understood, Charlie?" He narrowed his eyes in her direction.

It would have to do, she decided. "Okay."

"Then it's settled. Once he feels you're adequately trained and won't blow a hole in someone by accident, he'll give it back to you. Agreed?"

Charlie nodded.

"Good. Now I can stop worrying?" he said, rubbing the back of his neck.

Nick slid out from the booth, stuck the gun in the back of his jeans, and grabbed Charlie's hand, pulling her to her feet. Looking back at Mike, he rapped him on the shoulder. "She'll be an ace when we're done."

Mike shook his head looking bewildered, and, if she was reading him right, wondering if he'd just been bamboozled.

Chapter Thirty-One

WITHIN FIFTEEN MINUTES, AFTER CHARLIE AND NICK WALKED out the doors of Tommyknocker's, they had loaded his bike into the back of her truck with the two-by-twelve she had in the bed. He could have followed her to Mike's cabin. But something told her he'd done it so he could spend time with her during the thirty-minute ride from Creede to Love Lake.

At close to five with the sun creeping behind the sharp juts of the mountain, they had a good two hours before dark to begin target practice. Charlie sat on top of the picnic table behind the cabin where a rocky knoll stood. Nick lined up several targets: an old tire, an empty Folgers coffee container, and two empty Corona bottles. He came toward her, his strides long, legs powerful cords of muscle flexing beneath his Levi's. His expression was one of pure confidence, and the world around her seemed to disappear.

"You ready?"

Charlie pushed off the picnic table and planted her feet on the ground. "I am."

"First, let's go over safety." He took her snub-nosed pistol. "Number one, never point a gun at someone unless you're prepared to use it." He paused to give her a knowing look. "Case in point, Ben's leg."

Charlie grimaced.

"Second, to avoid an accidental discharge, carry your gun pointed down with your finger on the trigger guard. That way, if you slip or something causes you to put pressure on the trigger, it will be the steel guard, not the trigger, you're pressing on."

"Got it." She lifted her chin and nodded. Their eyes connected and held, his stare intense. The heat shot up her neck.

Damn it, you're blushing.

Charlie concentrated, instead, on the backstop of mountain rock and wild-flowers behind Nick—different scenery, she hoped, equaled no pink cheeks.

"Are you paying attention?"

She jumped and once again was drowning in his blue eyes. "I'm sorry. I'm all yours."

He cocked his head and gave her a quizzical look. "Okay, let's move on." He angled the gun in his hand. "You purchased a double-action revolver. Good choice for a beginner." He turned it over to inspect it. "Easy to use, no risk of a jam."

He continued to go over the mechanics until she was comfortable with the gun's inner workings. He loaded the gun, slapped the cylinder into place, and held it up to eye the sights. "Okay." Motioning her toward him, he held the gun away. "Slide up in front of me, and I'll show you how to line up your sights."

Pulling her close, he stepped behind her, placing his arms around her shoulders, and then positioned her hands on the gun, making sure her fingers wrapped around the gun grip and the trigger guard. "Okay, close one eye. Look through these two sights and concentrate on lining them up." He pointed to the sight in the back and the front, both highlighted with a red strike.

Concentrate. Well, wasn't that easy for him to say? Here she was resting snug against his chest, his lips close to her ear whispering instructions. She squirmed, his breath warm, filtered through her hair.

"Are you listening?"

She swallowed hard. "Yes, like this?" She looked back for his approval.

"Yes, perfect. Do you see how the sights line up?"

Struggling for a moment, she eyed the sights. "Yes . . . yes I see it now."

"Good girl. Okay, let's move over here toward the targets. We are, give or take, fifty feet away." He steered her toward the intended targets. "Remember, when you're ready, line up your shot and then squeeze off a round. Oh, before I forget." He reached back and pulled a pair of yellow shooting glasses from his back pocket. "Found these in Mike's broom closet. It'll keep the glare down."

His hands came around, placing the glasses gently onto the bridge of her nose and over her ears. He took a step back. "Okay, just aim with your sights and shoot when you're ready."

Charlie took a cleansing breath, lined up the sights, closed her left eye, and eyeballed the target. "Red Folgers coffee can to the left of the rubber tire."

Nick chuckled.

Charlie lowered the gun. "Why are you laughing at me?" She glared at him.

"I'm sorry. You act like you're getting ready to sink a pool shot. So, you aiming for the small 'g' in between the 'l' and the 'e'?"

"Sure, why not?"

Nick shook his head and grinned.

Charlie went all shivery—definitely to-die-for gorgeous, and at the moment all hers.

"What?" Nick gave her a curious look.

"*Nothing.*"

"You're smiling."

"I do that sometimes." She held the gun up. "Let's not analyze it."

He winked. "Whatever you say, beautiful. Let's do this."

What were they doing? *Flirting.* Charlie smiled to herself and tucked that thought away for now.

With a sly grin, she concentrated on making the shot. "Red Folgers coffee can to the left of the rubber tire, going for the small 'g' in between the letters 'l' and' 'e.'"

With that, she placed her finger on the trigger, closed her left eye, lined up the sight, and squeezed off a round.

Nick fell back on his heels. "Damn, Charlie."

"What's wrong?" She frowned.

"Nothing—you're a natural. I've never seen anyone, including a man, not flinch the first time they shot a gun. But you just squeezed one off, no problem, and hit the target to boot."

She wouldn't remind him it had been the second time she'd shot a gun.

Jogging the fifty feet to the can and returning in an instant, he placed his finger through the hole in the coffee container. "Do you see the 'g'?" He searched her face.

"No?"

"Damn right, because there's none. You shot clear through it."

Charlie let out a holler. "How 'bout that? I guess I am a natural." She laughed and fixed him a wide smile.

"Okay, Annie Oakley, let's not get too cocky. There is such a thing as beginner's luck."

She took a wide stance and concentrated on the next shot. She made a challenge to herself. Let Jack come waltzing back into her life and try to mess with her. He'd find a gaping hole through his chest.

Nick followed Charlie, carrying steaks he had grilled after target practice, through the main room of the cabin. Teaching her the finer points of handling a firearm might not have been the wisest move.

Trouble was, he couldn't keep his hands off her—target practice had its advantages.

He smiled at that and stopped in the doorway leading to the covered porch. "What do we have here?"

Candlelight flickered on the table set for two, flowers lying loose in a bunch in the middle. The lake, a reflection of mountains and the setting sun, sizzled against a cobalt sky.

Charlie set the salad and a plate with their baked potatoes in the center. "Just sit down," she ordered, twisting the corner of the brown plaid vest she wore over a snug white T-shirt.

"You embarrassed?" He arched his brow.

She stiffened. "No." The word came out sharp.

Her behavior, although sometimes erratic and unpredictable, entertained him. But he wasn't smiling now. He considered himself hardened, his own life a road of hard knocks. Even though the table was set with mismatched plates and silverware, and two oddball glasses, she'd taken time to make it nice with wildflowers from the small garden out front. She'd done it for him, and that reached his core. No woman had tunneled that deep, and, frankly, it pissed him off. Even if he wanted to say the hell with Reynolds and take his wife and walk, he couldn't. This job owned him.

Nick set down the steaks. "I think it's ni—"

She leaned over and kissed him—hard and fast—the technique, one he had taught her. A smile tugged at the corners of his mouth. The tease of her supple lips that tasted like cherry ChapStick lingered on his. She gave him a curious look. "What? It was written all over your face." She laughed, and before he could pull her toward him, she took the farthest porch rocker and sat down.

Nick took the one across from her and chuckled. "Nice move. But this table isn't going to protect you from me."

Her brown eyes widened slightly, and he didn't have to elaborate. He may have meant it as a double entendre, but she only got the part about tempting him.

The single candle burning in the center of the table cast an orange brilliance around them. They both started on their steaks then moved on to their salad and potato at an easier pace. Sipping beer, they sat back, and Nick studied Charlie. For the first time she seemed relaxed. Maybe it was the beer? Even he felt a slight buzz, and if Charlie was 110 pounds, he'd be surprised.

"I have a question."

Charlie raised a well-shaped brow, and Nick held out his hand. "Without you taking offense, of course."

She laughed instead, and *he* relaxed.

"I'm sorry for biting your head off the other day," she said. "I don't know why I get so riled when I think someone is questioning my ability to live in a man's world."

Her eyes flickered with candlelight.

"You're not a man . . ." Charlie stiffened, and he realized he needed a quick recovery. "That's not to say you can't fare just as well, if you have the ability. Take the military—there's plenty of women that can 'walk the walk' of a soldier, and sometimes better than their male counterparts."

Charlie reached out to clink Nick's beer bottle. "My sentiments exactly. I'm glad we've come to a mutual understanding, Mr. Foster."

"So what brought you to Creede? Not that I'm knocking the slow pace out here. It's just I have a theory your blood didn't always run toward the Western Divide."

"Very perceptive, my friend," she said. "I'm not from around here. I'm from back East. A few years ago it became necessary for me to make a clean start, and Creede fit the bill. A quiet town, beautiful scenery, a population of less than five hundred who, for the most part, keep their noses out of other people's business." She gave a rueful smile. "Excluding Mike and Ben, of course." She laughed. "Not that I didn't give the others cause to wag a tongue in my direction, especially working construction."

"So Ben took a chance on you?"

"Yeah, gotta love Ben." She tipped her third beer in the air. "After I tried to maim him, I think he wished our paths had never crossed." A big smile lit up her face. "I have to say, I really didn't know how much I would come to love construction. But the creation of something from your mind to a sketch and then to something tangible is amazing."

Nick tensed his jaw. "You seem to care for Ben."

"Absolutely. If he hadn't given me that chance, I never would have realized my full potential. I love Ben."

She was in love with Ben Sterling—a hard slap in the face. Nick's fingers tightened on his beer.

She peered into his eyes, her pretty face folding into a pout. "Why so quiet?"

"Nothing. So you and Ben are a hot item?" His tone was sharp—angry.

Charlie sputtered with laughter, beer spritzing Nick. He jumped out of his chair, his own beer spilling in the process.

"Oh, Nick, I'm so sorry. Here, let me dry you off." She stood and reached over with a napkin and dabbed his face. Losing her balance, she listed.

Within seconds, Nick found his ass resting on the wooden planks of the front porch with Charlie in his lap, laughing hysterically.

He laughed with her. Holding her tight to his chest, he looked down into her eyes. "You're cut off." He glanced at their bodies, in particular his ass resting on the hard decking. "This is funny to you?" He tried to keep a straight face.

Charlie wiped the back of her hand across her mouth, still holding on to her bottle of Corona. "No. You, you're what's so funny. Ben and I are not *an item*. What I said *is* true. I do love him, but not in the way you're thinking. He's given me a beautiful home, allowed me to fulfill my dreams of becoming a builder. I needed a job." She sobered slightly.

"Then why was he kissing you the other night at the club?" he whispered, like it was a secret.

Charlie cocked her head and laughed again. "Oh, you saw that. Where were you? I don't remember seeing you inside the club."

"Well, I was there."

"Oh my, do your eyes always bore down on a woman when you're jealous?"

"I'm not jealous." He dumped her on the floor, stood up, and walked away.

Still laughing, Charlie rose and followed him. Grabbing him by the arm, she turned him toward her. "Yes you are," she said and searched his eyes. "I may be a little tipsy, but I know jealousy when I see it. For your information, that was Ben's doing, not mine. In the three years since I've known the man, he's been more like an older brother. We tell each other what to do or where to get off. But he's decided there's more. He's a great kisser, I won't deny it." She smiled and took a swig of her beer. "But that's as far as it goes, for me, anyway," she said with a sigh as she fell into him.

Nick wrapped his arms around her and pulled her snug against him. He peered down into her face, flushed from alcohol. She was right—she was tipsy, but completely aware of what she was doing. He slid his hand up her back and pulled at the band holding her hair neatly against her neck. Her hair cascaded past her shoulders. He ran his hands through the waves of auburn highlighted by the moonlight. Grabbing tightly to a mass of flowing hair, he pulled her head back, exposing the delicate curve of her neck. Moaning, he nestled his head into the crook where her neck and shoulder merged, fluttering wet, warm kisses as he made his way up her throat until he came to her lips, slightly parted. He touched his mouth to hers, tentative at first. Her lips were soft and driving him slowly insane. The taste, a combination of beer and her damn cherry ChapStick, had him deepen the kiss.

She urgently returned the favor, suckling and nipping his bottom lip, sending shudders through his body.

Reaching back, he fumbled for the doorknob. Grasping the handle he swung it wide. Finding himself stumbling backward, he steadied himself against the wall inside the cabin. He drew a deep breath when she raked her fingernails up his shirt.

"Charlie," he whispered in an attempt to free his lips. "Slow down, sweetheart. I'm not going anywhere."

"Nick," she whimpered against his parted lips. "Don't stop."

Kissing her forehead, he leaned into her. "I couldn't if I tried." Searching for her lips, he explored until his tongue found the warm recesses of her mouth. Her tongue darted between his lips playfully. He pulled away, nuzzling her ear. "Ah . . . baby."

He flicked open the button to her vest and pulled her T-shirt from her jeans. Slipping his hand under her shirt, his fingers traversed smooth skin. He searched upwards until he came to the swell of her breast hidden beneath a veil of thin lace. Finding her erect nipple, he stroked it, forcing a moan from Charlie as her lips slid to his ear.

"Damn, girl." He moaned. Pulling her up to meet his eyes, he kissed her, teasing her mouth open. Her tongue darted tentatively and then bolder, melding with his.

Her fingers making quick work of the last button on his shirt, she placed her hands on his bare chest, and he groaned with the contact. Her hands traveled past his pecs and stopped at the metal dog tags resting on his collarbone. She touched them, her fingers brushing his flesh, the simple act making him horny as hell. He caught her hands in his.

"Why do they have the rubber edges?" Her eyes wandered up until they found his.

"So they don't clink together behind enemy lines." He kissed her forehead.

"Oh." She remained quiet for a moment. "Did you ever . . ." She wet her lips. "Have you ever been . . ." She tunneled her hands through his short-cropped hair.

"No." He kissed her then, long and deep. For once he didn't want to talk, didn't want to probe. Well . . . not the way the boss expected him to with the infamous Kathryn Reynolds.

Her arms went around him, her fingers pressing into his back. "Nick," she said, kissing his chest, neck, the sweet curve of her lips grazing his chin. "Will you ever have to go back?"

He angled his head and gave her a questioning look. "If I did, would you care?"

Her brows puckered, and she rolled those luscious lips in, then out, considering. "Yes . . . I'd worry too much."

She said it like this thing between them could somehow turn into something lasting—permanent. It wouldn't. He kissed her cheek. "I'm here now, Charlie." He continued to travel down her neck, dropping soft kisses on her throat. He lingered there, the spot where she'd pulled away from on the banks of the Rio Grande. "Let's focus on the moment."

She pushed back his shirt from his shoulders, kissing him, taking nips with her teeth, moving lower until her tongue flicked his nipple, her mouth suckling him. His head fell back, a moan ripping from his throat. "Ah . . . Charlie." A ringer went off. *Shit!* He wanted to smash his damn cell phone as it pealed a second time on the mantel over the fireplace.

"Charlie, baby," he said, pulling her off him.

She stopped and jerked her head back, her lips swollen from his kisses. Her cheeks flushed, her eyes searching him. "What?"

"You're beautiful." He brushed his thumb over her swollen lips. "But I need to get that." He moved away and grabbed the phone, catching it as it pealed again. "Foster." He gave her his back. "*Shit*," he growled into the phone. "When? Damn it—that's not good." He glanced back at Charlie and gave her a quick smile. "Yeah, working on it." He rubbed the stubble of his chin and nodded to the words on the other end flowing through his ears—not registering as Charlie sidestepped the chair near the couch, closing the button on her vest.

Nick's eyes narrowed, and he whispered, "Charlie, where are you going?"

She tucked in her T-shirt, flipped her hair forward, and ran her fingers through it. She waved a hand at the front door of the cabin, and whispered, "I should go." She pointed to the phone. "You're busy."

Busy hell. He covered the phone. "I'll be one more minute." The news he'd just received would make his job that much more difficult.

Charlie walked over and kissed him square on the lips. "Will you meet me tomorrow?"

His brow shot up.

"Fourth of July—Miner's Celebration."

He nodded.

"I'll be helping Shelley with Gunner at the parade." She reached down to the coffee table and grabbed her own phone and snapped it in place. "We'll be at the ball fields in the afternoon." She kissed him once more.

"I'll meet you there."

"It's a date." She kissed him on the check, her hand sliding down his chest, and slipped out the front door.

Damn it.

He pressed the phone to his lips. "No, I didn't find it." He nodded, walking over to the front door Charlie had left open, her taillights growing smaller. "I'll wrap things up and call you tomorrow, late." He clicked off, irritated. Good thing the one on the other end didn't know what he'd been about to do with Kathryn Fallon Reynolds.

He looked down at his jeans, his dick pushing uncomfortably against his Levi's. He grimaced. He needed to cool down. What he really needed was a cold shower, and the lake, easy access, tempted him through the open door of the cabin. Gathering his thoughts and willing his erection to recede, he reminded himself. This wasn't real.

He slammed the door.

I'm screwed, and I didn't even get laid.

CHAPTER THIRTY-TWO

THIS WASN'T QUITE WHAT NICK HAD IN MIND FOR HIS DATE WITH Charlie. There was candlelight, if you counted the citronella candle on the picnic table behind him. But the private table for two he had envisioned had become a plaid blanket on the grounds of Memorial Park in downtown Creede at the Annual Fourth of July Miner's Day Celebration. Tess Coulter and her teenage daughter and son sat down in front, minus Mike who was on duty, and Shelley Evers and her energetic son, blond like his mother, had plunked their blanket next to his.

He'd been surprised last night when Charlie had mentioned Shelley would be here. He assumed a crowd would be the last thing she'd want. But she seemed in good spirits with Gunner, who was four—at least that was the number of fingers he held up when Nick had asked him his age. He'd also seen Sterling, briefly, before he excused himself to check on a few things at the office a block up, promising to make it in time for fireworks.

The gathering had become a friendly get-together of Charlie's closest friends. Only she wasn't here. She'd abandoned him earlier. Actually, they'd agreed, after the parade this morning, helping Shelley with Gunner with the games setup on the ball field in the afternoon, and a quick bite at Tommyknocker's, they'd both clean up and regroup at the park. His job—a blanket and the cooler.

"Nick, have you seen Charlie?" Shelley turned to him, letting go of Gunner's hand so he could play with the kids on the blanket behind hers. She smiled at him through a pair of stylish sunglasses with big black lenses that covered her eyes. Other than the split lip that had begun to heal, no one would know Bobby Ray had beaten the snot out of her three days ago.

He smiled. "I think she ditched me."

Shelley laughed and patted his hand across the blankets. "Trust me—that's not possible." She then turned around to help Gunner crack one of those glow sticks and put the string around his neck.

Truthfully, Nick was becoming restless. This job had taken longer than he had expected. Reality would soon dictate its swift conclusion.

The chatter of small-town living floated on the warm July air, mixed with laughter, lighthearted male posturing, and the occasional harmless female tit for tat. He took another sip of his beer and shook it off. Tonight he'd sit through a small town's Independence Day celebration and try not to despise himself, sitting in Memorial Park, drinking his beer, the pulse of patriotic music and Old Glory high above on the flagpole several feet away, snapping her displeasure at him.

Townspeople continued to fill the park, the fresh-cut grass becoming a sea of mismatched floral and plaid blankets in preparation for the light show set to go off against the darkening sky. He'd guess the town of three hundred, plus an influx of tourists, had shown up for the event. Families packed the sidewalks on both sides of Main Street, going both north and south, their lawn chairs set for a strategic view of the sky.

He envied this town—their easy way of life, which Charlie had found. He wouldn't mind sharing it with her if things were different. Nick's grip tightened on the beer bottle, and he took a swig. Soon all of it—this town, this woman—would be . . .

Nick let it all go for now and focused on the petite, auburn-haired beauty, her hair pulled up in a loose bun, wisps framing her face. She crossed Main Street in a sexy pair of cowboy boots, the contrast against her tanned skin turning him on in a major way. Her gaze connected with his, and she smiled.

Nick placed his beer on top of the cooler and stood, meeting her at the end of the blanket. His arms going around her waist, he pulled her to him, kissing the sensual curve of her mouth. He then nuzzled her ear with the side of his face. His eyes alert on the crowd, he whispered, "I thought maybe you were going to stand me up."

She pulled back, tipping her chin up. Her fingertips lightly brushed through his hair, making him breathe deeply, and he tried to ignore her touch—the attempt futile. Those expressive brown eyes of hers gazed into his, sweet and unyielding. "Not a chance. I have it on good authority this is a date I was destined to keep." Taking his hand and turning it over, she drew a line down his palm with her finger. "Do you believe in fate, Mr. Foster?"

Fate, destiny, whatever you wanted to call it—to him there was no romanticizing the events that had brought him to Creede. Their relationship had been coerced, created in the hopes of sealing a trust that, in the end, would allow Charlie to divulge her secret past and the evidence Reynolds believed she'd hid in an old mining town—evidence that could quite possibly indict him for bribery.

He kissed her again, his lips lingering longer then he'd planned. "You're beautiful, Charlie." He took her hand and led her to the spot he'd carved out for the two of them with the blanket and pulled her down with him. "How about a beer?"

"Sure." Charlie moved to the edge near Shelley and reached over, grabbing her hand. "How you feeling?"

Shelley smiled at Charlie. "I'm doing good. We took a nap, and Ben picked us up while you were in the shower." She nodded to Gunner. "He's having a ball." She shook Charlie's hand playfully. "Thank you . . . for everything."

Charlie gathered Shelley in her arms. "I love you, Shell." Gunner came at them full force, and Charlie caught him in her lap, messing with his hair and kissing the top of his head. "And I love this one, too."

Gunner squealed, "Charlieeee!" and then hopped off.

Nick's jaw tightened. With everything she'd been through with Reynolds, the woman had the capacity to love and love big. Nick's life suddenly became more complicated—given the right circumstances, or rather building upon these seven days, yes, he'd counted them, she could love him. He wouldn't get to find out. Nick brought his arm around Charlie. "Here you go, beautiful." And then he leaned over to Shelley. "How about a Corona, Shelley?"

"I'm good." Shelley grabbed for Gunner as he maneuvered around her. "So, Nick, given any thoughts to settling in Creede?"

He should have seen that coming. He'd heard the two—Shelley and Charlie—talking that night in the room next to his.

"It's tempting." Nick ran his fingers along the slender nape of Charlie's neck and then caught the black patent-leather shoes on the corner of the blanket. His fingers fell away from her, and he stood. "How's it going, Mike?" Nick reached out to shake his hand.

"A sizable crowd, no arrests, I'm doing well," he said, nodding down toward Charlie. "How's target practice coming?"

Charlie gave him a curl of her lips. "Hole in one."

Mike laughed. "That's golf."

Charlie mouthed the word "oops."

Nick put a hand on Mike's shoulder. "She's a natural."

"Does that mean she's cleared to carry a gun?"

"In my opinion, she's qualified. I think I should give it back to her."

"I trust your judgment." Mike tilted his head in Charlie's direction. "As much as I hate to admit it, Charlie, I can be a little overbearing."

"A little?"

Mike gave her a harassed look. "Okay, a lot."

"Doesn't mean I don't love you."

Mike finally gave into a smile. "Same here."

"Dad!" Mike's teenage daughter, Amy, Nick would guess fifteen, long blonde ponytail, shorts, and a red T-shirt with a star-spangled peace sign on the front, jumped to her feet. "Can I go sit with Jen?" She pointed to another teenage girl that could be her twin, same ponytail, waving over at them.

"What about your—"

"Mike, let her go," Tess said, lifting herself onto her knees, her gaze locking onto her husband. "I have plenty of company here."

"All right, then." He winked at Amy. "Go on." He pulled on his chin for a moment and called after her. "Where's your brother?"

"With Josh on the ball field," she called back.

"You seen Ben?" Charlie asked Mike.

"Last I saw he was heading for the office." He shook his head. "That man's never idle."

Gunner stepped over Shelley's leg, trying to get to Mike. Mike scooped him up. "Hey Gunner, whatcha got there, buddy?"

"Light stick." He pulled it up on its string looped around his neck. "It's purple."

"That's something, Gunner." He winked at Shelley. "How you doing, Shell? My girl Charlie taking good care of you?"

He'd have been pissed if he knew the extent Charlie had gone to protect her friend. Nick wasn't going to share, and he doubted the old man would give her up.

"Yes, she is." Shelley touched Charlie's hand and patted it resting on the blanket.

"All right, all." He sat Gunner down and gave a wave. "Show starts in forty-five minutes." He checked his watch. "O'dark thirty." He motioned to Tess, who stood and carefully sidestepped Shelley and Charlie to get to him. They embraced, and Mike gave her a hearty kiss. "I'll see you and the kids at home, sweetie."

He waved a final good-bye and disappeared up Main Street.

Nick sat down, his arm going around Charlie, and he pulled her snug to him. Tonight he'd concentrate on her. He couldn't look past her if he tried. Her smooth, tanned body molded to the white ruffled blouse, resting off her shoulders, the neckline revealing the swell of her breasts. Her shapely knees bumped his on the blanket. The fringe from her brown suede skirt fell away, exposing her toned, muscular legs.

Nick reached over and squeezed her bare upper thigh. Looking into her eyes, he bent down and kissed her cheek. Then positioning himself with his knees drawn up, he pulled her in between his thighs with her back against his chest and pulled her close. "You smell good."

Her body stiffened. "Oh shit." She made a move to stand.

Nick grabbed on to her. "What?"

She connected with him, a scowl creasing her pretty face while she tried to stand. "Ben, he looks like some loco bull that's been poked too many times." Charlie turned back, her eyes fixed on Main Street.

Ben crossed the two-lane road. His face set, his lips pressed tight. Once he reached the park, he sidestepped blankets and townsfolk, his gaze never wavering. He barreled toward them.

Nick looked down at Charlie. "What do you think's got him all fired up?"

Charlie grimaced. "I think it has to do with us."

"Us?"

She pointed at him and then to herself.

Ah . . . Except that's not what she led him to believe last night at Mike's. Nick directed stern eyes toward Charlie. "I thought you said you and Ben were only partners." He pulled her up with him, cocking his head, searching her face.

"I told him." Her brows snapped together.

"I don't think he got the message."

The crowd dispersed, grabbing children, blankets, shoes for the tall figure of a man dressed in a pair of Western-cut blue jeans. His shoulders broad under a navy button-up shirt, his Stetson set atop his head in a determined fashion, his boots kicking up loose grass clippings as he shortened the distance.

Behind Nick he caught Shelley grabbing Gunner and moving away. Tess fumbled for something on her blanket with Charlie refusing to move away from Nick.

"Out of my way, Charlie," Ben boomed.

"No," Charlie's eyes flashed, and she motioned behind the brown barn-style building of the Creede Historical Society. "If you have an issue, we can talk in private," she said through gritted teeth.

"This isn't about you." Ben peered over her head, zeroing in on Nick.

Nick placed his hand on her lower back. "Let me talk to Ben," he whispered, gently pushing her away.

Just what I need, a fistfight, and over a woman, no less.

Swearing under his breath, he squared off against the man, face flushed and clearly angry.

Ben sized him up. "Who the hell are you? Is your name really even Nick Foster?"

Whoa. Not what he expected.

Nick laughed it off. "Last time I checked." He waited a moment.

Ben stood stone-faced and quiet. Several more seconds passed, and Nick placed his hand on Charlie's forearm ready to vacate when Ben's steely grip came down on his upper arm. Nick released Charlie and turned to face Ben.

"Foster, remember my friend Brad Rockingham?" Ben asked smugly.

Rockingham?

"What's the matter, Foster, drawing a blank? Colonel Bradley Rockingham, my friend and the Commander of Naval Special Warfare, United States Navy. He would have been your commanding officer." Ben crossed his arms across his chest, looking rather proud of himself. "I found it odd you couldn't place him."

Right . . . the job site.

"Brad and I go back a long way. I sent him a quick message the other day. I got his reply a few minutes ago while checking my e-mails." He waited a moment, his eyes beading in on Nick's. "He didn't recall you, either."

Chapter Thirty-Three

"WHAT IN THE HELL? YOU TWO BETTER HAVE A GOOD REASON for interrupting tonight's festivities with this bullshit." Mike bore down on Ben. "What's crawled up your ass, Sterling?"

Ben grabbed his cell phone off his hip. "I just received an e-mail I've been waiting for." He shoved the phone toward Mike. "This is what's crawled up my ass. I have direct confirmation that this so-called retired Navy SEAL never existed." Ben sneered at Nick. "I don't know what kind of games you're playing, but it stops here."

Mike glanced at the phone and then turned his attention toward Nick. "Is this true, Nick?"

Nick swallowed hard. *Shit.* Who would have predicted the woman he was in search of would find a small community and become some sort of royal princess to the kingdom—their kingdom of Creede. What bullshit. She had men falling all over themselves to protect her. What were the odds that one of them would have connections so far up the chain of command in the Navy?

Nick gave Mike his most sincere expression. "Mike, I don't know what Ben thinks he has on me." Looking in Ben's direction, he continued, "Ben, I'm not going to argue with you. You seem dead set on believing your friend. And I can't fault you for that. But I don't believe you've ever served our country in the armed forces, so you wouldn't be aware of the lengths the military goes to keep our true identities secret, especially behind enemy lines. Maybe your friend needs to take a closer look."

He'd slam this Rockingham's reputation, knowing everything he had worked toward was about to go to shit. "I remember Rockingham. If I recall, he was more of a figurehead only promoted up the ranks because he kissed ass."

"You son of a bitch." Ben reached out and connected with Nick's jaw.

Catching Ben's tightly rolled fist against the side of his face, Nick stumbled backward. Everything tilted, and Nick shook his head, his face throbbing. *Touchy bastard.* "It wasn't meant as a personal attack."

"Like hell it wasn't." Ben pulled back again, pressing his fist forward, striking Nick in the stomach.

Nick doubled over, his breath whistling through his lungs.

Damn it. Now I'm pissed.

Nick dodged the next attack as Ben's fist came inches from his head. He shot an upper cut and caught Ben under the chin. Ben's head tipped back, and pain shot through Nick's hand like a son of a bitch.

Charlie's stomach soured. She looked to Mike frantically, anger building when she spied a grin plastered across his face. Striding forward, she grabbed Mike's upper arm and turned him toward her. "What the hell is wrong with you? This isn't funny. They're going to kill each other. Do something."

Mike sobered. "Charlie, relax, these two have had this coming. All I've done for the past week is watch them posture like two polecats. Let them get it out of their system."

Not that a fistfight could be considered an eloquent ballet. But there was a type of raw beauty—defensive jabs, countered by an offensive shuffle of the feet, thwarting off the connection of fist to flesh. They hugged, not like drinking buddies bidding a fond farewell, but like primal black bears fighting for the right to court the only female bear for a hundred miles.

Maybe Mike enjoyed the demonstration of male prowess, but she'd had enough.

Mike's body convulsed with pent-up laughter. Standing next to her, he nudged up against her hipbone, something hard and unforgiving between them. Service weapon? Yes, of course, the gun had become part of Mike. She hardly noticed it, until it caught her hip bone.

She reached over and clamped on to his pistol. Remembering the latest police dramas, she pushed it forward and straight up to release it from its holster. Mike turned and grabbed his empty holster. "What the hell?" He looked aghast, and if it weren't for the urgency, she'd have laughed at his confusion.

She aimed the gun straight in the air in the middle of the grassy area of Memorial Park and, thinking better of it, pointed it down and squeezed off one round into the dirt. The bullet pierced the night like the whistle of a train crossing the solitude of the Western Plains, and Ben and Nick's heads whipped around, and they fell apart, each rolling onto their butts. Those near and aware of the commotion paused—no movement, chatter nonexistent—no doubt wondering if what they had witnessed was a real gunshot or a firework. They'd been lighting them off sporadically all day.

She stared back at Mike. "How's that for your simple Western town?"

She grabbed Mike's hand and turned it over to place his gun in his palm. "Don't *even* give me the lecture. I've tolerated your meddling into my life because I love you. But it's about time you let me live *my* life. I'm a grown woman and not your teenage daughter."

She moved first to Ben and bent down. "As for you. Let me set the record straight. You're my partner in business and a dear friend. I owe you my life for taking a chance on me. I love you, Ben, but not the way a woman should love a man."

Searching the crowd, she locked onto Shelley, standing on her blanket in bare feet, holding Gunner's hand tight. She'd be mad that she had broken a confidence. Charlie couldn't tell if Shelley knew where she was going with this, her eyes hidden behind dark sunglasses.

"Wake up, Ben. The one you should be going after is Shelley. She loves you." Charlie turned and gave Shelley a rueful smile and shrugged her shoulders.

Ben followed Charlie's gaze, his own eyes softening. He knew, had known. He was just being a man—difficult.

Charlie turned her fury on Nick. He resembled a scrapping prizefighter, one on the losing end of a bout, judging by the streak of crimson beginning to flow from his bulging nose. Even in his disheveled state he was irritatingly handsome. "As for you, Mr. Foster, if that's even your name, I think it's time you considered another vacation destination. Creede's just been pulled from your itinerary."

Everything hurt—his nose, ribs, jaw . . . Before he could get up, she gave him her back and cleared Memorial Park and disappeared into the crowd on Main Street, preparing for the fireworks set at "O'dark thirty," according to the flyer he'd seen in town. Nick pushed forward with his hands to a standing position.

Mike handed him a napkin. "Here, son. Your nose is bleeding."

Nick took it, tilting his head back. "Thanks. Sorry for—"

"Like I said, Creede's a pretty hospitable place, just a few drunks and an occasional brawl." He offered a crooked smile. Mike shifted his gaze toward

Ben. "Isn't that right, Ben?"

Ben grumbled, "Whatever," while Shelley and Gunner grabbed him by both of his hands, lifting him to his feet.

Nick wasn't interested in making amends with Ben Sterling right now. He had more pressing business to attend to. He turned in the direction Charlie had headed but jerked back when Mike grabbed his arm. "Nick, we need to talk." His voice was stern this time.

Nick pulled his arm away, zeroed in on Mike, and snapped, "Sterling's a jealous bastard. There's nothing to what he's saying."

Mike's expression softened. "Can't say I don't agree with it."

"So we good?" Nick glanced over Mike's shoulder. The delay put him farther behind Charlie.

He nodded. "Go on. I guess you have some explaining to do." He chuckled. "Good luck with that." Mike waved him off.

Nick made a move, then swung back toward Mike. "Any idea where she went?"

He pulled on his chin. "Her truck's probably parked on one of the side streets. Not that she'll get to it until the fireworks end and the crowds clear out." He nodded north up Main. "If I had to guess, she's heading north to the cliffs toward West Willow Creek Canyon."

"Thanks." Nick pushed through the crowds, maneuvering around lawn chairs and bodies, and headed in that direction, the excited chatter and laughter growing fainter once he hit the dirt road inside the cliffs. Above him the explosion of fireworks, their dramatic display of color exploding in the western sky, and the oohs and aahs that followed filtering through the night air were far too cheery for his way of thinking.

He had been in town for almost a week but had no idea where to start searching for her. The road remained desolate, dark, and cool sandwiched between the cold mountain rock and the gurgle of Willow Creek running alongside the road. Charlie was bullheaded. Knowing her and her antics, she was sore as shit with him and would probably take to walking down this road until she calmed down.

After Ben's public decree, her head would be spinning with questions. She knew her partner well. She trusted him. Yes, Ben had acted like a jealous fool, but his intentions were admirable when it came to Charlie. She'd have to believe there was something to his story.

Nick picked up the pace. Her familiar silhouette wouldn't be hard to pick out. Everyone was at the celebration. They were probably the only two on this isolated stretch of road.

CHAPTER THIRTY-FOUR

CHARLIE KEPT WALKING WITH NO CLEAR DESTINATION IN MIND. She entered Willow Creek Canyon north of Creede, multicolored bursts of light fanning the Colorado sky, and she passed the Creede Fire Department and the Mining Museum built inside the mountain. The constant boom, reverberating off the solid rock walls inside the damp and incredibly dark canyon, had her trembling slightly.

She had thought having one insane husband who had little regard for her well-being was torture. Now she had too many men, although well-intentioned, who were completely out of control with their efforts to protect her. From what? The bogeyman? She knew he existed. But they didn't.

Thinking back at Mike's expression when she'd borrowed his gun, she laughed. The thought of shooting it off like she had rolled out of a Wild West saloon after a drinking binge and a winning hand at five-card stud had her snickering.

And Ben's face, after she delicately set him straight on a few things—priceless.

Charlie loved them both, and they knew it, but they had it coming. It had become incredibly stifling, especially after she struck up a friendship with Nick.

They wouldn't come looking for her. It was an unwritten rule with those two. She'd reach her boiling point with their incessant interference in her life, blow up like Mount Vesuvius, and then forgive them just as quickly as the dust settled.

But Nick Foster wouldn't be met with the same favor. He was a drifter, and his identity was now questionable. She had heard his lame excuse. *Top secret, my ass.* If your own commanding officer had never even heard of you, it didn't take an Einstein to figure something was terribly wrong.

Then again, Ben was a jealous fool. She'd been in the company of Nick Foster, here and there, for more than a week. If he was connected with Jack, if he'd come in place of Jack, she wouldn't be standing here questioning the man's intentions.

She'd be dead.

"Just a Kiss" from Lady Antebellum began to play, and Charlie jumped. *Shit.* iPhone.

She unsnapped it off her hip. The screen shone bright against her face when Mike's name popped up, and she let it go to voicemail. Well, guess he knew she was really angry. Too bad. She waited until it registered as an actual voicemail and went in to delete it.

Huh?

Two messages. She'd cleared them out earlier today. There hadn't been much, considering the holiday. She found Mike's first and hit Delete. Done. When the other message popped up, she slowed her steps. The blood bank in Denver. Her stomach dropped, and her breathing slowed. Something must have come back on her bloodwork on Monday. With nervous fingers, Charlie entered her code and put the phone to her ear.

She came up on the fork and kept going west onto West Willow Creek Canyon, heading toward the Commodore Mine. She kept walking with only the pulse and splash of the creek running parallel to the road.

The female voice of her doctor filled her ear:

"Charlie, it's Dr. Jeffrey," she said, her voice anxious. "First, your bloodwork is fine."

Charlie relaxed. She'd just assumed.

"I'm calling on a different matter." She paused. "Hate to call on the holiday. But this couldn't wait. Tried your cell yesterday, but your voicemail was full."

Charlie nodded in agreement. Some days it would fill up before noon—yesterday being one of them.

"I want to apologize upfront. This was just brought to my attention yesterday. We have a strict policy in regard to patient confidentiality." She cleared her throat. "Especially with the HIPAA laws."

Charlie's stomach dipped, her hand gripping the cell phone. She stood alone in the Rio Grande National Forest, a thin dirt road beneath her feet, with only abandoned, wooden mine buildings built into the steep mountainside—totally isolated.

"Last month, our intern, Ashley, you've met her."

Charlie nodded.

"She spoke to a gentleman. By the time the call ended—he was very persuasive—she'd given out your home address."

Shit!

"After seeing you on Monday, Ashley told me what had occurred. I'm so sorry, Charlie. This is unusual. Ashley realizes, now, the mistake she's made."

Come on, Doc, give me the bottom line.

"We've since gone back to check the specific date and time the call came in and located the number the gentleman had called from. Unfortunately, Ashley cannot recall his name. I'll leave it on this voicemail and hope that you recognize it, and that the person had obtained it in good faith."

Dr. Jeffrey read the number slowly and repeated it a second time. Charlie couldn't breathe. She couldn't move. She spun around and cried out, "Son of a bitch. He's here!" Her voice echoed up the canyon rock walls, blowing over the craggy cliffs above. The only sound that remained was her heartbeat, erratic and pumping deep within her chest. Charlie turned and ran toward town, her boots digging into the dirt road.

Quince's steadfast proclamation rang in her ears, "He'll find you." Charlie's stomach pitched. The finale filled the night sky, a distortion of shadows dancing inside the canyon, the sound more like rapid fire, and Charlie ran faster.

The threat of Jack remained, more frightening than it had been in years. Would he come for her himself? Nick flashed before her, a stranger with a questionable identity, and she shook.

Charlie touched the outside of her skirt pocket and the hard shape of her truck key. She quickened her pace, came up on the compression house where they used to make magazine powder, and caught sight of the ore bin, an abandoned five-story log structure built into the steep mountainside. The moon cast it in shadows looming on the dirt road. The last crackle of fireworks fizzled above. Quiet descended, eerie and bone-rattling. The town would be clearing out now. She needed to get to her truck parked behind the office.

Her hands became clammy. Her heart beat furiously against her chest. Charlie Robertson faded away with every passing step. She was Kate Reynolds, would always be Kate Reynolds. It didn't matter if she changed her name, moved two thousand miles away, and altered her appearance. She would forever be the wife of Jack Reynolds, always darting like a damned field mouse in search of a hole.

She crossed under the ore bin, her shadow now one with the massive structure. Skeleton walls of crisscrossed timbers rising from the dirt creaked with centuries past, and the air stilled. Charlie trembled, the chills racing across her bare skin, and she kept moving.

Her boots bit into the dirt trail, stirring dust. With no option, the mountain falling away to her left, she passed the crisscross openings of the ore bin, dark and forbidding, only an arm's length away. A force, sudden and fierce, jerked her around by her waist. A strong muscled arm pulled her back into the abyss of the chute. Darkness engulfed her, and she struggled to free herself. She opened her mouth to scream, but was silenced when a pair of warm lips crushed down on hers.

She pushed against the force, her fingers digging into muscled flesh beneath two shirt pockets. Arms came around her, almost lifting her boots from the pavement. She kicked wildly and flailed her fists at this head, shoulders, chest.

The pressure of lips fell away. "*Damn it.* Settle down." His voice was razor sharp, angry.

Charlie's eyes popped open. Her heartbeat slowed, then sped up. *Nick . . .* His hand clamped down on her arm, yanking her off her feet, dragging her out from the shadow of the structure and onto the narrow roadside. The moon's luminous halo of light caught the roughened hard plane of his jaw. It flexed.

She swung at him with her other hand.

Long, angry fingers caught her open hand. "Knock it the hell off." Angry blue eyes bore into her. "You done?"

"You want to let go?" Her brows snapped together.

He dropped her hand, and it fell to her side.

"Explain yourself," she shot back.

"Sterling's an asshole."

She threw her hands up. "That's it?" she said, blowing out an irritated breath, still shaking.

"Don't know what to tell you, Charlie." He reached into his pocket, and she jerked.

"Relax. It's my wallet." He gave her a guarded look. "What do you want to see—a driver's license, military ID?" He arched a brow. "Correction—retired military ID." He flipped through the wallet. "Even got a voter's registration card." His head dipped toward hers. "Republican, in case you're wondering." He kept digging and laughed. "Don't want to lose this." He held out a card. "Health insurance. Better keep that on top in case Ben—"

"All right."

"You're sure?" He raised both his brows.

The panic lodged in her throat receded. She motioned for him to put it away. She didn't have time for this—for him. "I'm tired. I'm going home." She turned to leave and then swung back on him. "You've got something of mine, and I want it back."

He gave her a confused look.

"My gun."

"Why the sudden interest in it now?"

"None of your business."

"You ever tried trusting someone?"

"Like you?" She laughed and then tears welled up in her eyes. She had no one. She swallowed more determined. "I want my gun, Foster. Is it on you?"

"Mike's cabin."

"Then I'll follow you over."

The ghostly glow of the moon above bounced off his rugged, and at the moment, frowning face. "Who are you afraid of?"

Standing there with a slightly swollen nose, his eyes edged in anger . . . concern. She couldn't tell. Was it for her? Her situation? His situation? He had to be in pain. The last time she looked, Ben had a pretty mean swing—with a hammer, at least. Could she trust him? Would he be angry to know *she* was the liar?

She bit down on her lip. "You don't want to know. Let's leave it—"

Two bright beams came up the thin road, lighting them up. Then a familiar spinning bulb cast the area with shades of red and blue as it flashed, reflecting off the canyon.

Charlie sighed. "Now what does he want?"

"Charlie, is that you?" A voice echoed from the PA system of the patrol car.

She peered down into the window. "Shep?"

"Yeah, it's me. I've been looking for you for a good half hour. Mike sent me to check up on you."

Right. Her babysitter.

"I'm fine." She reached into her skirt pocket and pulled out her truck key. "I was just—"

Nick snatched her key and placed his arm tight around Charlie's waist and pulled her snug to him. "We were just heading off to Mike's cabin to make up." Nick grinned.

What the hell? He has something I want. I'm not planning on bolting, yet.

She wanted to slap him. First, for stealing her key and, second, for making her look like some bimbo that was about to get lucky.

But as long as Shep thought she was fine with the situation, he'd leave. And then she'd deal with jackass.

CHAPTER THIRTY-FIVE

CHARLIE PULLED HER LEGS UP ONTO THE FRONT PASSENGER SEAT of her truck, parked behind the office of Sterling Log Homes. She had loved her job—this town. She hugged her knees tighter against her chest, her body slumping against the door.

She hadn't counted on Nick commandeering her truck. She checked her silver bangle watch—quarter to eleven. Now she was wasting time. Or he was wasting *her* time with his stupid bike. She would have fought him, but the Neanderthal would have no problems forcing his will.

Eventually she'd escape him. Creede had been a safe haven, but she had to leave—tonight. Get her gun, pack her bag, grab her cat and the cash she'd put by, and hit the road. She'd miss her friends and especially her job, but the uneasiness creeping through her bones told her Jack knew Charlie Robertson from Creede, Colorado, was his dearly departed wife.

She *should* take her truck and go, once she had the gun. But she wasn't leaving Moochie. She loved that damn cat.

The truck thumped from behind, the tailgate slamming into place, reminding her she wasn't alone. She needed a plan, one that would allow her access to her gun, which she knew was somewhere in Mike's cabin. Then she needed to lose the bodyguard who took the chivalry thing way too seriously.

The driver's door swung open. She jumped and then relaxed when he slid onto the seat.

His hand reached out to caress her cheek. "I'm sorry. I didn't mean to startle you." He bent his head to peer into her eyes. "I want to know."

I want to know? Right . . . She had told him he didn't want to know before Shep pulled up. She couldn't have kept her big mouth shut.

She stared out the windshield. "There's nothing to say."

"You're lying."

The deep rasp to his voice carried concern, and she closed her eyes—*not talking.* She'd be gone soon.

His long fingers kneaded her neck. She couldn't think.

Nick was definitely the enemy—but only to her heart.

Think.

Her head rested on the cool glass of the window. She was exhausted and those magical fingers, slowly moving up the base of her skull with their rhythmic strokes were screwing with her resolve. Her lids fluttered. Disappearing tonight would take energy. Energy she didn't have to even pack her bags.

Shelley flashed in her head. *Shit!* What if Jack was here, now? He'd go for her cabin. *Shelley.* Her heart plummeted into her stomach. She'd be there soon with Gunner and Ben. Reaching over, she grabbed Nick's arm. "He could be at the cabin."

"What cabin?"

"Mine. Oh God, Shelley and the baby. We need to—" She grabbed her cell phone and punched in Ben's number and got his voicemail. *Shit.* She disconnected and typed him a text.

Don't bring Shelley back to my house. Keep her with you. Don't ask. Just do it. I'll be in touch.

She grimaced. Just like Shep, she felt sure Ben would take it the wrong way. Her head popped up to find Nick staring at her.

"What the hell are you doing?" He turned in his seat.

Her phone buzzed, and she read the text and relaxed.

"Ben. I wanted to apologize." She shrugged.

"Right." He took her phone, viewed the messages, and handed it back. "I'm a patient man, Charlie. Maybe you should try the truth."

Charlie fell back onto the seat. "The truth about what?" She hadn't meant for her words to sound like a dare, but they had.

"Should I list them? The gun, for one. Your odd behavior earlier when I found you. Why you think someone would have any interest in your cabin, or you, for that matter?" The edge returned to his voice. "And I guess you're still going to leave me in suspense as to your cryptic answer. Who are you running from, Charlie?"

She waved him away. "No one. You were up my ass. So I threw you a bone hoping you'd back off."

Reaching, he pulled her over roughly. Holding her tight against him, his eyes searched hers. "You're lying. You're running from someone. Maybe it's time you trusted me."

She tried to wriggle free. "Let go."

"Not on your life. I've got news for you. You can keep quiet about what's really going on here, but if you don't want to end up my common-law wife, then I suggest you start talking because I'm not going anywhere." He pulled her even closer and placed his hand around the back of her neck to keep her from moving. He bent his face into hers and crushed his lips onto her mouth.

His kiss was desperate, angry, and frustrated all at the same time, and she knew why. He needed the truth from her, but she couldn't give it. And he was frustrated because there was obviously something happening between the two of them, and it was equally apparent neither one could admit it to the other or even themselves.

She gave into his kiss, his lips strong and passionate. Charlie ran her hands around his neck and reached up to splay her fingers through his hair. She melted to his touch, and didn't care. She was in . . .

He pulled away, leaving her a confused, tingling mess of raging hormones. Frowning down at her, he reached around and tugged at her arms encircling his neck and moved her across the seat. God, this was embarrassing. She was breathing hard, as was he. He was such a liar, even about this thing between them.

She wiped her mouth with the back of her arm. "You're a bastard." She stared out the window. "Let's go, Foster. I'm tired and I need a hot shower."

He reached out to touch her. "Charlie, I'm—"

She swatted his hand away. "Don't touch me." She narrowed her gaze and bore directly into him. "Don't *ever* touch me again."

CHAPTER THIRTY-SIX

THE WATER RAN IN THE SHOWER, AND NICK PULLED DOWN THE bed for her. He left a wrinkled powder-blue, long-sleeved dress shirt he'd forgotten at the bottom of his duffel bag out on the bed.

When they had arrived at Mike's cabin, she stormed off into the bedroom and slammed the bathroom door. When he went to check on her, he found a trail of clothes shed on the bedroom floor and a locked bathroom door that spoke volumes.

The woman was a freaking handful, and stubborn. Worse. He recognized the flight-or-fight reflex. If she flew, he'd never find the evidence. He'd searched her cabin on the main level, the night he stayed. The second level when Charlie remained downstairs waiting on Ben and Shelley, leaving the shower running as a decoy.

She'd be better off dealing with him than Reynolds. Scary part was, she thought she could handle her husband on her own. Only, the damn gun she believed would save her would end up in Reynolds's hands.

He'd thought about taking her phone. But after he read the text messages, it looked more like Charlie wanted her house to herself, perhaps to entertain him. He smiled to himself—not happening tonight. Bottom line: She had no one *to* call, unless she wanted to give up her true identity.

He'd gotten his own call when he'd reached the cliffs earlier, searching for Charlie. The boss had arrived, and he wasn't pleased. Not the plan. But he'd deal with Reynolds.

He was more worried how she'd react when she knew whom he was working for.

The door to the bathroom popped open, and steam wafted into the bedroom. She emerged wrapped up in a white terry cloth towel, her hair hidden beneath another.

"Do you mind giving me a little privacy?" There was no emotion in her voice. She brushed passed him.

A little pissed, hungry, tired, and taunted by a towel that barely covered her ass, he pulled her into his arms. "Talk to me."

"There's nothing left to say. If you want to keep me here against my will, I'll deal with it. But I'm calling Mike in the morning. And I'm pretty sure, once he finds out you're holding me hostage, he'll either arrest you or kick your ass out of town."

She looked so warm and clean, her skin a rosy pink from the heat of the shower. He smiled inwardly. Or was it indignation? "You're really pretty when you're angry."

She kept her eyes on him. "Please let me go." Her voice broke slightly.

She'd meant forever. Even though those eyes of hers said something entirely different. He'd have no choice in the end.

He released her. "I need a shower." He walked over to his duffel bag and straightened his dick, which was rock hard and growing increasingly uncomfortable, and grabbed his boxers. He gritted his teeth. Since finding Charlie Robertson, he couldn't remember the last time he'd had a hot shower.

"Shirt on the bed's for you." He hooked his chin toward the bed. "I'll sleep on the couch."

"I'll take the—"

"Damn it, Charlie. I'm tired of arguing. For Christ's sake, take the bed." He slammed the bathroom door.

Men. They were infuriating, bossy—and to think they called women moody. But he'd left her alone. The bathroom door whipped open, and she swung around. The steam of the shower created a halo effect, though he was definitely no angel. He stood shirtless, his well-defined bronze physique rippling, his slender hips still sporting his jeans, unbuttoned with the zipper partially down.

When she finally retraced the original path her eyes had taken, he was grinning at her.

"I thought I'd save you the trouble. I've got the truck keys with me if you're contemplating a jail break."

She gave him a rueful smile. "I'm not up for a jail break tonight," she said before giving him her back.

The door shut again, and she smiled. "You think you're so smart," Charlie whispered under her breath. She always had an extra key.

Relax, boss-man. I'm too tired to slip into oblivion tonight.

She'd get a good night's sleep, at least a couple hours. She knew he was exhausted, too. Eventually, Mr. Super ex-Navy SEAL would fall asleep. She'd make her move then.

Whipping off her towel, she grabbed for the shirt on the bed. The other towel, wrapped like a turban, she tugged off. Standing at the mirror, her damp hair framing her face, she touched the dark skin just below her blood-shot eyes. She tossed the wet mass on her head back and frowned. "You look like shit, Charlie, and your hair . . . it looks like a freaking bird's nest."

She dug in the top drawer looking for a comb. A remote control rolled to one side along with three shiny bolts. Ripping through the remaining drawers and coming up empty, except for a pair of Tess's jeans. She shut it and scanned the bedroom.

His duffel bag sat on a chair near the door, the handle of a brush poking out the top. She moved toward it, checked the bathroom door. The shower ran, and she began rifling through the bag. A zipper on the bottom caught the tip of her finger. She struggled against the clothes on top and tugged it open, digging inside it. Her fingers grazed hard . . . cold . . . steel. She grabbed hold and pulled until a black semiautomatic handgun was free.

Her stomach dipped.

Relax. He'd had his chance to use it on her. Being retired military, she didn't question it further. She'd trade him. If he wasn't going to give her gun back to her, then she would just have to borrow his.

She smiled contentedly. Things were certainly turning around. Before dawn, she'd be out the door with a set of wheels, armed, and making tracks to a new life.

Somewhat human again, Nick dropped his toothbrush in the cup on the sink and turned to open the door. Only the light on the nightstand remained on. Propped up against the pillows, she lay tucked under the blankets. She looked fresh but tired. Her hair combed and damp curled at the ends. But it was her eyes, big and dark and staring at him. And he was that close to saying "screw it." But fifty thousand was a lot of money. Not that he would see a dime of it. He owed it all to someone else.

"Do you want to brush your teeth?" he asked tentatively, wondering if she was still mad at him.

She shrugged and gave him a guilty smile. "I already used your toothbrush earlier." Her smile faded quickly, replaced by compressed lips. "I hope you don't mind."

"Nope, I'm good with that." He walked closer to the bed. "Can I get you anything? A drink . . . something to eat?"

She shook her head. "Not hungry—just tired. I borrowed your hairbrush, too. I found it sitting on top of your duffel bag."

He glanced back, the bag and hairbrush where he left it. Nick stepped closer and sat on the edge of the bed. Pushing a curl from her face, he tucked it behind her ear. "I know that look. You can trust me," he said softly.

She remained stoic in his powder-blue shirt. There was no emotion in those usual telltale eyes. "Good night."

Yep, she was still pissed. Tomorrow was another day, and, frankly, he was too tired to push the issue. Standing, he reached over and turned off the light. "Good night, Charlie."

CHAPTER THIRTY-SEVEN

Nick sat straight up on the couch. The scream had him struggling to orient himself. Throwing off the blanket, he dodged the coffee table only to make a direct hit with his knee into the end table. Cursing, he ignored the pain and headed for the bedroom.

Nick flipped one of the light switches. The lamp on the nightstand popped on, and he stopped.

"You're kidding. Right?"

"No. It's freaking huge!" she shrieked.

He shook his head and limped toward the bed where Charlie stood on the mattress with long bare legs, her back glued to the wall, her toes wedged between the pillows. "Kill it!"

At the end of the bed sat a spider that was no doubt more afraid of the woman. He didn't have the heart to smash it. Instead, he flipped the comforter up, and the spider flew up in the air before hitting the hardwood floor and scurrying off to hide behind the baseboard.

"What the—"

"I thought you were tough. It's harmless."

She stood there and didn't say a word. The trembling started and the tears began to flow.

Shit!

"Hey, don't cry. I'll find it and kill it."

She shook her head, and slithered down to the bed. "It's not the spider," her lips sputtered, and she started that hiccuping thing like she couldn't catch her breath.

Nick moved to the edge of the bed.

"Charlie," he whispered. "Don't cry, baby."

Charlie lifted her head, her auburn hair falling away from her face, her eyes swimming with tears. He loved her eyes, always having the ability to draw him in. At that moment, however, they tormented him.

Leaning over, he folded her into his arms. "Charlie, you're safe, sweetheart," he whispered against her ear, her hair tickling his nose.

"Stay with me." Her hold on him tightened.

Nick pulled back, searching her eyes. "Are you sure about that?" He gave her a stern look.

She nervously chewed on her bottom lip and nodded.

Standing at the edge of the bed, his brows knit together, he weighed his options. His jaw tightened. "Slide over."

She nudged her body several degrees to the right, and he slipped under the covers, pulling her body hard up against him, and lay down with her, kissing the crown of her head. "Charlie?"

"Hmm?" The sound rumbled against his bare chest where her cheek rested.

"I can help you. Will you tell me what's going on here?"

She lifted up on her elbow and stared at him. He moaned slightly when she caressed his face. "I just want you to hold me."

Still not talking.

"Okay, let's get some sleep." Keeping her in his arms, Nick adjusted himself and flipped off the light on the nightstand.

Of all the stupid things he'd done, this had to take first place. There was no way he was going to get any sleep with Charlie nestled next to him. He'd be lying if he tried to deny she wasn't making him horny as hell. And he wanted her more than he had ever wanted a woman in his life. The silky skin of her leg caressing his had him dialing back the urge to scoop her up in his arms and kiss her breathless.

She stirred and leveled herself up. Wiping her tears, she sniffed, and then pressed a kiss to his lips, the taste salty and turning him on big time. Her slender hands encircled his neck, and she sidled closer. Round, firm breasts jiggled and brushed his chest, pert nipples grazed and teased him through the dress shirt, and he moaned into the softness of her mouth. His arm wrapping around her shapely back, he pulled her tight to him.

Are you insane, man? Let her go. You can never have her.

That stab of reality had him pulling away.

Their lips fell apart, and she whispered, "Love me."

Her request—a given. He loved her. Probably since the first day he'd met her at Tommyknocker's, her indignant brown eyes marked with challenge, locking into his. She had to be perfect for him, and that had put him on edge from the start.

"Charlie, you need to—"

She kissed him again. He retreated slowly, his lips still dangerously close to hers. "It's not a race."

Her laughter, quiet and erotic, fluttered against his face.

He was losing it. Her slender legs intertwined with his had him reaching down. He caressed her thigh, his hand slipping beneath the soft cotton of his dress shirt she wore until it came to rest on her firm, round cheek. He groaned. "For the love of . . . you're not wearing underwear."

The moon's silvery light spilled through the slats of the blinds, and he recognized that tilt to her lips, her eyes wide with feigned innocence.

"I'm wearing exactly what you gave me." She placed her hand on his roughened cheek. "Touch me."

He moaned and swore inwardly. The oath, speech, reminder—whatever you called it—sounded all well and good, except his dick wasn't cooperating. He was weak with wanting her. Needing to push himself inside her and thrust until he exploded.

Now he panicked.

"Baby, you're killing me here."

God she felt so right and tasted so good.

Why did she have to be so damned real? If she had only remained his ghost, a figment of a woman safely locked away in his mind, he wouldn't be tormented by the woman lying next to him, so soft and sexy, wearing only his shirt.

Nick was half-tempted to take her—all of her—and tell the powers that be to pound sand.

Selfishly, he yanked the covers back. Straddling her, he reached for the buttons and popped each one slowly. Charlie's heartbeat pulsed into his hand. The moonlight cast shadows over them, and he was spellbound by the smooth swells of her breasts partially visible as the material parted. Unbuttoning the last button, he stopped.

Her brown eyes, curious, locked into his.

"What?" He kissed her hard and pulled back. "Change your mind?" he asked. Because this was the point of no return for him. If she didn't issue an objection, then, sweetheart, he was branding her his.

She shook her head. "Not a chance." She ran her hand along his bicep. "Just relax," she whispered. "I'm a grown wom—"

Nick bent his head down and kissed her. Her lips opened slightly, and she returned the favor by pressing back urgently, her tongue a frisson of sparks exploding as she licked into his mouth. He moaned and pulled away. "Baby, tell me something I don't know."

Charlie placed her palm down onto his hand resting on her abdomen. He liked her hand tanned by the sun, small and possessive on his. She glided his hand past her rib cage until his fingers found her breast warmed by sleep. He cupped it in his hand, its size that of a full and ripened fruit waiting to be sampled.

Charlie arched her back.

There was no doubt in his mind what she wanted. But usually he was the aggressor with only one thing in mind—good sex and no strings. He didn't appreciate the role reversal. What the hell was up with that? He chuckled to himself—his dick for one.

Charlie's eyes smoldered, definitely for sex, definitely to be touched. He wanted her to the point it ached. She'd weakened him.

She wiggled beneath him, silently begging him not to stop. Her lips sweet and wet beckoned, and yet he hesitated. "Last chance."

A momentary flash of annoyance shot through those all-encompassing eyes of hers, and he couldn't help but smile.

He kissed her hard, his mouth gliding along her pulsing throat. He dipped lower. The buttons no longer an impediment, he slowly pushed away the soft cotton shirt to expose perfectly shaped breasts and rose-tipped nipples. God, she was beautiful. He flicked a tender peak with his tongue and suckled her.

A sweet, feminine moan escaped her lips, and the desire to do her had him forgetting why this was a really bad idea.

He focused on Charlie, her pretty face, dark crescent lashes fluttering against her bronze cheeks.

He'd take his time with her. She was worth every agonizing minute. When he was through with her, he wanted her sated and withering beneath him—and as Neanderthal as it sounded, his.

All those covert glances, and Nick was now naked from the waist up. Charlie ran her hands along his back, took a nip at his chest. Nick's broad shoulders were muscled and sleek. The only wedge of soft, light brown hair extended from his belly button and disappeared into the waistband of his boxers. And it was that burgeoning erection hidden behind the rough cloth, the friction so erotic against her nakedness that had her wet with anticipation.

Her hands explored his wide, muscled shoulders. She followed the hard contours of his chest down past an impressive six-pack and delighted in his strong, tapered waist. Nervous fingers dipped inside the waistband of his boxers. His shaft was as soft as velvet, his head moist with expectation, and she reveled in her own ability to make him want her.

He grunted, kissed her hard and fast, stealing her breath. With quick dexterity, he shucked his boxers, pulling her tight to him as he rolled their bodies over so she rested on top. Her hair, a mass of spiraling curls, brushed her face and shoulders. Nick's long and capable fingers tucked a strand behind her ear. The pad of his thumb skimmed across her mouth.

She trembled, and for an instant questioned her decision to have him share her bed. Three years she'd kept to the plan—no men—her self-imposed sentence for getting it wrong the first time. But for reasons she couldn't quite grasp, she was going for it. His blue eyes, so hot and sexy, gleamed up at her, and she had her answer.

He trailed fire down her neck; his lips, firm and possessive, caused her toes to curl in automatic response. She was so out of practice she wouldn't be surprised if she just didn't succumb to the orgasm welling up inside her.

"I want you, Charlie." His words, thick and slightly breathless, shook her with desire for him, and she could deny him nothing as he tumbled her down next to him and lowered himself onto her thighs.

Her hands moved down to his lean hips, his flat stomach hovered above her. The tip of his rigid penis poked her thighs, and she cast her gaze downward.

"See something you like?" His voice rumbled with amusement for her avid interest in him.

"You were holding back on me." She grimaced. "This might be a problem. It's . . ."

"Trust me, it'll fit." His blue eyes twinkled with mischief for the deeds he had in mind that would prepare her for his entrance, and the thought shot through her like a syringe full of illicit mind-altering drugs.

She arched against his erection.

"Not yet," he whispered roughly as his lips brushed her breast, drawing her nipple into his warm mouth, turning it pebble-hard. Flicks of his tongue made her dizzy with the need to have him inside her.

He drew back and released her nipple, glistening wet and erect, the air cool against her damp skin. She raised her head, and the weight of their stares crashed like two waves on a collision course. The contact all awash with lustful fancies they were and would be performing on one another.

His strong, masculine hand, an imprint on her skin, burned blazing heat between her thighs. His palm pressed seductively against her mound, the contact hard and unyielding as his finger slipped inside her warmth. Deftly he stroked her cleft, teasing it until she thought she'd die of sheer ravishment. So close to cresting into pleasurable waves of ecstasy, she pressed into his hand and sighed when he withdrew his finger.

She frowned up at him. "You're teasing me."

"That's the point." He was breathing hard, and it shot a thrill through her to know this wasn't a one-way thing that was happening between them. Nick Foster was a true keeper of his feelings. But tonight he let go, and she could see the glimpse of the man who was just as vulnerable as she.

That thought caught and held, and her heart beat faster. Maybe this wasn't just red-hot, lusty sex for him, and that made her tremble with the knowledge she would never see him again after tonight.

And as hard as it was to grasp, this man had slipped past a wariness brought on by fear—fear she'd repeat hell on earth a second time with a man—and forged an abiding trust for him she could not deny.

Strong, attentive hands moved up her arm. "You're cold?" The sensuous curve of his mouth tightened, and those baby blues narrowed in on her.

Definitely not cold. More like, I'm falling for you, and it hurts.

"Just a little." This was her little secret, and she wasn't sharing.

He groaned and poured his hard masculine body down on top of her, wrapping her in his arms. He felt so damned perfect. She wanted to cry. His fingers lifted her chin and brought her face even with his. "Better."

"Yes," she said as she reveled in the strength of his embrace.

His lips slanted over hers, and she kissed him back with the desperation of a woman trying to burn a memory into her soul.

Slow and hot, he sampled her earlobe, shoulder, teasing her mouth with expert skill until she parted her lips to his hungry kiss. His knee and calf, rough with hair that felt so heavenly male, pressed in between her legs. The pressure of his hand traveled up her thigh until he came to the soft delta of springy curls and slid his finger inside her again. She was wet and warm and waiting for him.

"Charlie," he breathed into her ear. "You're so wet. I don't think I can . . ." He thrust inside her, and she whimpered with how good he felt.

Threading her arms around the strong column of his neck, she snuggled closer, and then he moaned into her mouth and froze.

At the touch of his lips in retreat, Charlie's eyes sprang open. Her passion-fogged brain scrambled to understand, and she gasped. "Nick?"

"I'm sorry, honey. You're so warm and tight." He frowned. "I wasn't playing, I promise. I don't want to hurt you."

Charlie caressed his cheek and looked deep into his brooding eyes. "It's okay. Don't stop. You feel so good inside me."

The hard planes of his face stiffened, and his eyes, dark with passion, searched hers.

Her laugh, gentle and reassuring, escaped through her swollen, thoroughly kissed lips. "I may be out of practice, but—"

Her words were swallowed by his firm mouth, and he murmured against her, "You're perfect, sweetheart."

Oh God. No, *he* was perfect, and he felt amazing. She wrapped her legs around his muscled thighs and pulled him closer until he filled her fully. Hot flames licked and spread through her, burning like wildfire. The weight of him pressed her deeper into the pillow-top mattress, and she welcomed the burden of his hard, lean body so sensual it made her woozy with delight. She had wanted him the first night they met. And she knew now this was where she was meant to be. If only time could halt, keep them here in this space—this moment. She couldn't stay. She wouldn't stay, and her stubbornness would pay her back in spades, because she'd go a lifetime without his touch.

His arms, so possessive, slipped behind her back and held her tight, and she closed her eyes to the future, if only for a while, so she could concentrate on him, all of him. Taking her hard and fast, he plunged into her. Her body convulsed, climbing higher. He rocked them with his thrusts, and she clenched around him, reveling in the sensation of having him inside her.

Her body began to crest, and she writhed beneath him as he dove into her. Mindless with pleasure, she dug her fingers into his sleek, muscled shoulders and closed her eyes. Her world exploded, and she was reduced to a million tiny nerve endings of delight. And she cried out in overwhelming delirium, and yes, pain, as her eyes snapped open.

She was in love with him.

Her heart hurt so bad that tears burned to escape, and she swallowed a sob. The last thing she needed was for him to know her true feelings.

He kissed the hollow of her neck, the stubble of his cheek rough against the smoothness of her skin, and she held tighter.

"God, you feel so good." He thrust into her again and again, the control she'd seen him cleave to dissolved, and he groaned in pleasure as he shuddered inside her. His full weight dropped, consuming her. She wrapped her arms around him and clung to him, pleasuring in the blessed contact of their dampened skin.

They lay there for a while until she began to stir. He rolled off and pulled her to him. Now in spooning fashion, he kissed the curve of her neck. "Charlie?"

She recognized that tone. He wanted more from her than what they had shared. She'd give her soul to tell him. "Hmm?"

He smoothed back a spiral of hair from her face. "I won't let him hurt you."

Her heart wept inside, tears hitting the back of her eyes. She'd made a huge mistake opening up to him. If it weren't for Shep's timely interruption in town, she would have told him. If she opened her mouth now, she'd be tempted to finish that conversation.

"You can trust me." He pressed a kiss to the back of her head.

He'd just put himself on her list of ones she cherished with all her heart. No amount of coaxing was going to get her to level with him.

Charlie's eyes fluttered, and she suppressed a yawn. "Tomorrow."

His body relaxed, and he snuggled closer, whispering against her ear, "I'll keep you safe."

CHAPTER THIRTY-EIGHT

CHARLIE WOKE UP TUCKED SECURELY IN NICK'S ARMS, HIS WARM thigh thrown over her legs. She turned to gaze at him. In his sleep, his arm tightened around her waist, and his hand found her warm breast as he cupped and squeezed it.

God, she needed him to stop touching her. Every inch of her craved him. Was it her imagination, or based on the smile forming on his lips, could he divine in his slumberous state that she was having a serious change of heart?

She concentrated once more on those well-formed lips and blushed, which was ridiculous, because shyness was a moot point—he knew every inch of her. Maybe shyness wasn't the issue, but perhaps her wanton behavior. Her cheeks warmed at the thought. She smiled inwardly. For being hands-off Foster, he had surprised her. She had sensed since they met that he was more tentative, or maybe wary would best explain his feelings toward her. But his lips and tongue could ignite a fire in her belly, and that was the surprise. He was an extremely confident and gentle lover.

She turned in his arms to check the time on the clock resting on the nightstand—quarter to five. Her heart hurt, and she blinked back tears. It would be light soon. She turned once more to gaze at him. She didn't want to think about how angry he would be when he woke up to find her gone. But it was necessary. She blocked out the ache in her heart. She couldn't tell him the truth. It would be unfair to bring him into her nightmare.

Sliding out from his arms, she hesitated as he readjusted himself and settled back to a soundless sleep. She reached under the bed and grabbed the bundle she had prepared when Nick was taking a shower last night. The clothes she arrived in were missing. Nick must have done something with them. Keeping her naked was definitely a resourceful tactic. Since escaping in the buff wasn't an option, she'd gone back to the dresser drawer with the pair of Tess's jeans. She'd salvaged her panties and bra from the bathroom after Nick had gone to bed and hid his loaded gun, which sat like a paperweight inside her bundle under the dust ruffle, before she finally settled into bed.

Snagging Nick's shirt off the floor, Charlie crept into the living room. She quickly slipped on her panties and her bra, and buttoned up the shirt. Slipping her legs into the jeans and finding them too long, she bent down to roll them up. Doing the same to the sleeves of Nick's shirt, she tied it securely around her waist.

She grabbed the gun and tucked it down into the back of her waistband, promising to figure out how to check the chamber when she had time. She still needed her boots. They were here somewhere. She had kicked them off during her fit of anger when she entered the cabin last night.

On her hands and knees, she searched the floor around the couch and spied them a few feet away. She sat on the couch to slip them on and caught sight of Nick's wallet on the coffee table. Looking around nervously, like a pickpocket open for business, she snagged it off the table. It didn't really matter who he was—not now.

Sure it does. She opened the wallet. She'd never gotten a clear view of his identification in the canyon.

With trembling fingers, she rifled through his billfold—an American Express card with the name Nicholas D. Foster embossed on the front, the medical card, his driver's license. Slipping his military ID out from the slot, she pulled it closer. The photo matched the California driver's license, the address going to an APO Box—military—Carlsbad, California.

What did she expect? She clenched her teeth. For all the shit with Ben and his accusations, he appeared to be Nicholas D. Foster after all. Feeling like a spy, she put the license back into his wallet and shut it. When she did, a small piece of notebook paper stuck out the top. She tried pushing it back down, but it only bent from the light pressure from her fingertips.

Irritated the paper wouldn't cooperate, she opened the wallet to shove it back down. Without a thought, she unfolded the neat square. The sketch, done in pencil, had become smudged, but she recognized it. Her fingers automatically clenched her butterfly pendant, the silver warm, a contradiction to the chill causing the hair on her neck to stand on end. Nick Foster and her necklace—she couldn't link the two. He had been curious about it. Had he been that wowed he'd memorized it and sketched it? Not likely.

Searching further, she came across a photo. Her heart sped up, pounding in her ears. She recognized it from Jack's file folder. A snapshot of Kate Reynolds looking very legal, blonde hair swept into a bun, serious expression, wearing a navy-blue suit. The photo had graced the front page of *The Washington Post* at one time, taken during the Stolze trial. For weeks after relocating she had searched the newspapers online, hoping the FBI, during their investigation of her husband, would find proof of an offshore bank account and a payoff linked to Barbosa so her clients would be cleared.

On Mar 1, on a Colorado morning, surrounded by ponderosa pines, the scent of freshly dug earth, and the monotonous grind of the skid-steer positioning logs around the perimeter of a log home, she had sat in her pickup reading the news on her laptop. RYAN STOLZE, HUSBAND OF KRISTIE STOLZE, FATHER TO LUKE STOLZE, AGE FIVE, EXECUTED BY LETHAL INJECTION FOR THE MURDER OF MARYLAND STATE TROOPER JENNA MCGUINN.

The reality of what she had done hit her. If she had stayed, picked up where Bryan had left off, explained everything to the FBI and asked for protection, there was a slim possibility she'd have survived Jack. But instead, she'd protected her own ass and allowed an innocent man to be put to death for a crime she was sure he didn't commit. Worse, his wife Kristie would someday meet the same fate. And yet, Charlie Robertson had been content to build million-dollar homes, live her new life, and never look back.

She, now, hated what she had become.

Quince's words, a one-two punch, slammed her with fear. "Trust me. He'll find you."

Jack's ability at recall had always astounded her. He had seen her necklace that night in the townhouse in Annapolis. It would be just like him to sketch it out by memory. He was extremely detailed like that. He knew Bren had designed it. It was the only one of its kind. If he sent someone to find her, the necklace and the photo would have been given to his hired henchman.

If he knew she was alive, he might believe she suspected him of Bryan's and Barbosa's death. Not that she could prove it conclusively. That being said, meticulous Jack would need to do a little housekeeping. Allowing her to exist was a complication that couldn't be ignored. Loose ends could unravel.

Still, it had been over three years. If she hadn't made a move to return and bring him down, why would she consider it now? She gave up trying to figure Jack out. It didn't matter. The man in the next room, the man she had fallen in love with, the man who had made love to her, wasn't who he claimed to be.

And his loaded gun, cold and biting into the flesh in her back made her shiver—the bullets meant for her.

The bed creaked, and Charlie gasped. Dropping the sketch and photo, she quietly snuck through the front door of Mike's cabin, leaving Jack's hired assassin behind.

CHAPTER THIRTY-NINE

CHARLIE HIT THE GRAVEL DRIVE LEADING TO HER CABIN. SHE parked, got out, and listened—only the intermittent chirp of a bird and the light rustling of trees. She bounded toward the front door.

Taking the steps, she cleared the porch and juggled her keys, looking for the one for the lock.

"Miss me?" His voice, a jolt, sliced like the glint of a razor—sharp. Deadly.

The nightmare had caught up with her.

Charlie's fingers tightened on the key. *Call someone, anyone.* She pocketed the key and grabbed her iPhone off her hip. The phone shook in her hand, and she accessed Mike's number. She'd get one chance. If he didn't answer, she wouldn't get time to leave a message.

With trembling thumbs, she hit Text, hesitated with a plan, and began typing.

HELP TAKEN TO LAST C M.

The stones of the driveway popped behind her, and Charlie hit Send and went for Nick's gun, cold and pressing into her back.

Footsteps hit the porch hard. "Not so fast, Kate." An angry hand smashed her head against the solid mahogany door. Her eyes shut, and she grunted through the pain. "You think I'm stupid?" He ripped the gun from her waistband and released the magazine, letting it drop to the ground, then racked back the slide and popped out a bullet.

Her eyes widened. *Shit! I could have shot myself.*

He spun her around to face him and sneered before tossing her gun into the stand of pines bordering her property.

He held a silver semiautomatic pointed at her. His eyes swept her, landing on her left hand. He went for her phone. Charlie threw it to the ground and stomped on it, glass, plastic, and tiny electronics, crunching underneath her boots.

Jack's hand shot out, grabbing her ponytail. Pulling her face up even with his, and she shivered with the desperation in his steel-blue eyes. "Who were you calling?"

"N-no one."

He twisted her hair, yanking it higher. Kate whimpered but refused to scream. "I saw you punch in numbers," he growled.

She'd let him think that. "I didn't get to finish." He couldn't check it, wouldn't know it was a text. He hadn't heard her speak. Her answer made sense.

He let go and pushed her. She stumbled back, hitting the door, the pain radiating through her back.

An arm's length away, he aimed the gun toward her head.

She couldn't keep her teeth from chattering.

He studied her for a moment. "Dyed your hair." He tugged on the elastic band holding her hair in place, allowing it to fall about her shoulders. Charlie's eyes kept track of his curious hands as he caressed a long wave between his fingers. "You look different."

She trembled. "What do you want?"

"Maybe I just want you." He let go of her hair and eyed the porch and their surroundings. "You've done well for yourself."

She kept silent and glanced down to find his hand, only moments ago caressing her hair, now resting down by his side. She remembered how vicious that hand could be. Her disappearance had its fallout, Jack's political career being one of them. Husbands were always prime suspects when wives went missing. He'd survived it, but it didn't mean she was forgiven.

He stared at her with those same bottomless steel-blue eyes she had come to hate. "You look damn good for a corpse."

"I tried death, but it wasn't all it was cracked up to be."

His hand shot out, grabbed a mass of her hair, and yanked her toward him. "The Kate I knew didn't have a smart-ass bone in her body. You want to be a tough guy?" He eyed her with contempt. "Then I'll treat you like one." He jerked her hard and up on her tiptoes, her hair pulling at her scalp.

She pinched her eyes shut and grimaced. "You're hurting me, Jack." Her eyes opened slowly.

His face twisted. "Am I? I can never recognize when you're telling me the truth." His grip lessened, and the stone porch connected with the soles of her boots. "You lied to me, Kate," he whispered. "You told me you were coming home. I believed you. And I believed the blood. I believed you were dead. I even buried you in my heart, cried for you, missed you, and it was all a grand performance."

"Why now?" Kate whispered. "Why risk coming after me, after all this time?"

He ignored her. "Who else knows about me?"

"The bastard you hired."

His brows snapped together. "You figured him out." He laughed. "Don't worry. If he'd rather put the bullet in your head, I'll accommodate him."

The backs of her eyes burned. How could she have been so foolish to think what she and Nick shared had anything to do with love. He'd screwed her and not just in Mike and Tess's bed.

"Hey." He shook her. "You trusted him—first mistake, Kate." He smirked. "You're soft."

She hauled back, ready to bust him in the mouth.

He grabbed her fist. "You want to die here?" He pushed her up against the post of the porch. "I want what belongs to me."

She pursed her lips. "I don't know what you're—"

"Maybe I can jog your memory." He tossed her something . . . a cell phone, an iPhone, the baby-blue cover and the gang from Scooby Doo, their cartoon smiles laughing at her—Bryan's cell phone. The impatient voice of Kate Reynolds played in her mind.

Did you confront him yet about the evidence? Call me.

An icy cold radiated from the center of her chest and dropped to the bottom of her stomach. She'd been right all along. He'd done it. He'd killed Bryan, and he knew all along they were working together.

He was going to kill her; it wasn't a question of if, but when.

She was his only loose end, that and the evidence Bryan had uncovered. She didn't have it. Jack thought she did, and that would be her leverage. Without it, he'd drop her where she stood and return to Maryland. She needed time, and having him believe the evidence was here in the cabin wouldn't give her that.

She'd already decided, prior to the text, where she would lead him, given the chance.

"It's not here."

"Then where the fuck is it?" Those eyes, wild with a madness only Jack understood, grabbed hold of her. His face, thinner than she remembered, grew crimson, and the bluish veins in his neck rose to the surface of his skin, pulsing.

She refused to blink or look away. "I hid it." Her legs shook, teeth chattering. She remained standing and shut her jaw. Giving him the satisfaction of knowing the fear that leached from every pore of her body would only work against her. Jack thrived on power play.

Grabbing hard on her arm, he pulled her up against him. "Are you fucking with me?"

"No." Her voice cracked slightly. "I hid it in an old abandoned mine tunnel in West Willow Creek Canyon—Last Chance Mine."

He laughed derisively, and her body turned cold. "You're funny." His eyes narrowed. "Up to your old tricks?"

She shook her head. "It's just north of here. I'll take you there, and you can have it." It. Was it the bank statement? She assumed it was. She hoped he wouldn't ask.

If she got it wrong . . .

He pulled her up even higher, then let go of her without warning. She stumbled backward and fell hard on her ass. He leaned over her, his gun pointed at her heart, the shadow of his body more menacing than she thought possible. He raised his hand as if to strike her but squeezed her forearm instead and swiftly brought her to her feet. He released her and shoved her hard down the steps. Struggling for balance, his hand once again connected with her arm, and he dragged her along until they stood in front of the driver's side door of her truck.

"You have a flashlight and shovel in the truck?"

"It's not buried in the ground."

"Flashlight, then?"

"In the backseat."

He opened the door. "Get in!"

Shaking, she stepped onto the running board, only to have his hand strike hard against her back, pushing her belly-first onto the seat. Her temple missed the cup holder by inches, but her eyes widened when she spotted it—the small silver tape recorder she used for reminders. It wouldn't save her now, but it could prove her suspicions about Jack were correct once and for all. She snagged it, turned herself around, and sat up behind the steering wheel when Jack slammed her door shut. She placed one nervous hand on the wheel as he rounded the front of the truck, still keeping his gun aimed at her head.

The thought of trekking up the mountain in his company had her trembling. Could she keep him talking? Ask the right questions? In the end, could she get him to divulge the evidence Bryan had tried to bring to the surface? It had been years since she had cross-examined someone, but she had been good at it—once.

"Keep your hands where I can see them, Kate." He startled her into sheer panic mode, his hand now on the passenger-side door.

The device small enough to fit in the palm of her hand still needed conceal-ment. Tess's jeans . . . too tight, he'd see the bulge. Her only option—Nick's shirt. Oversized, it was perfect. She tucked the small recorder up under the material around her waist just as Jack swung open the passenger door. He slid in next to her, placing the steel barrel, cold and unyielding, against her skull and nudged it for emphasis.

CHAPTER FORTY

KATE TRAVELED DOWN 149, GOING NORTH. JACK LEANED AGAINST the door, keeping the gun on her. He'd known about her whereabouts for over a month. He'd patiently waited and planned. Would he have thought to research the mines? The Last Chance Mine had been closed for over sixty years. But in recent years it had become a tourist attraction, and, thanks to her friend Quince, she knew it would be closed.

Her heart gave a little, and she frowned just as quickly. She wouldn't take him that way. She'd give anything to be saved, but not at the expense of Quince's life if he were near.

Besides, once Jack got a look at the tourist-gated entrance, he might not believe she would have had access to it. But there was the old #1 tunnel, open and away from the tourist area, she could lead him to. Kate didn't plan on getting that far. She'd get him talking early, capture his confession. She knew the area, hoped she'd find a way to escape him and, perhaps, run into Mike if he received and understood her text. She took Bachelor Loop Road, heading toward the Rio Grande National Forest, and then turned off onto the U.S. Forest Road, maneuvered her truck, and parked.

"This it?"

"Yeah." She reached back, and he grabbed her arm.

"What the—"

Her eyes blazed back at him. "Flashlight."

He nodded, and Kate reached behind, retrieving the black, metal Maglite—heavy enough that if she cracked him in the skull, it could do some serious damage.

Jack's steely grip came down on the neck of the flashlight, yanking it from her. "Got it." Her shoulders sagged, and he motioned her out with the gun and slid out the passenger side.

"It's this way." She entered the forest and shivered with the loss of early morning sunlight. He followed close behind, and they hit the trial, taking the switchbacks.

"What would have possessed you to hide it in a fucking abandoned mine?" Jack's voice was a rumble of discontent, and his breathing became more labored as they climbed the mountain.

He still had the gun trained on her back, the flashlight shoved in the back of his jeans. All she could do—keep moving, but slowly, giving Mike time to catch up. When she first came to Creede, she had read up on its history and the silver mines, particularly, the Last Chance Mine, and the map remained clear in her head. If, in the end, she was forced inside the mine, the only one who could find her alive would be Quince. She sobered. Mike and Shep weren't likely to find his camp. The mine would become her grave.

She cleared her head and concentrated on survival.

They had a good three miles to go. So far, she'd handled the climb well, accustomed to the high altitude in Colorado. She ran five miles every day, and with the heavy lifting of construction work, she was in the best shape of her life. Jack, however, struggled to breathe—one strike against him. If she really pushed him, he might just pass out.

The tape recorder rubbed against her hip bone. If she survived her ordeal, she wanted to make damn sure Jack hung himself with his own words. She only hoped the Olympus digital voice recorder lived up to its claim of 350 hours of recording time.

She glanced over her shoulder. Jack's complexion was ashen, his forehead beaded in sweat. "How you holding up back there? You don't look so good, Jack."

"I'm fine. Just keep walking." He shoved his gun forward. "How much farther?"

"About two and a half miles. I would have grabbed a bottle of water, but you rushed me before I could think of it." She peered over her shoulder again and shrugged innocently. "Do you want to take a break?"

"Don't think I don't know when you're being insincere, Kate." His voice was strained.

She turned forward and continued up the rocky trail covered in vines. "Okay, maybe it's best if I stop talking." She waited for a response, but he remained silent.

She needed to strike up a more amenable conversation with him. Arguing certainly wasn't going to get a confession out of him. Perhaps starting from the beginning . . . their relationship. If Jack became reminiscent, then perhaps he'd be willing to talk. She reached up and pretended to scratch her side and then pressed the Play button on the recorder. "Did you ever love me, Jack?" She hitched her chin over her shoulder. "Or was I just one of the dots that needed connecting on your climb to success?"

His footfalls no longer crunched behind her, and she stopped to turn around. Jack slumped against a pine tree, taking heavy breaths.

He motioned for her to stop. "I need to take a break." He waved his gun, pointing it at a large boulder. "Sit." He pushed up off the trunk and moved toward her, his expression dark and unreadable. "It started out that way." He moved closer, the gun now an extension of his hand. Her eyes followed the movement of the barrel as he placed it against her temple. He slipped the gun under her hair. "Maybe it was your blonde hair." He smiled and added, "Although, I like your new color." He slid the gun against her cheek. "Or maybe your high cheekbones." He moved the gun to her neck then down farther where he pressed it between her breasts. "You were a knockout. Still are."

He studied her for the longest time, and her body shook with the gun still resting on her breastbone. "You have a lot more power than you think, baby. I needed a wife. And I wanted you. I made sure I got you." He backed up and wiped his brow with his shirt sleeve, his breathing ragged. Keeping the gun trained on her, he leaned against a fallen pine. "Why do you think George gave you the Stolzes? Did you really believe, two years out of law school, you were seasoned enough to prosecute a death penalty case?"

She hadn't wanted the case. But George and the rest of the veteran attorneys had pawned it off on her. That had always eaten at her, and now she knew why. And now with his gun poised and one finger pull away from being a distant memory, she wanted to strangle him.

"You set me up, didn't you?" She pushed off the rock and stood. "You're so pathetic." She angled her head, her eyes wide with understanding. "You made sure the Stolzes were on a losing team. Starting with the greenest trial lawyer you could find. How'd you manipulate the Stolzes? You didn't know they'd pick Seiler and Banks for counsel."

He shrugged. "I got lucky."

Kate threw her hands up in disgust. "Great!" Clenching her jaw shut, she pulled on every ounce of willpower not to scream. If she survived her ordeal, she'd be paying her dear boss, George Seiler, a visit—the traitor.

She shuddered with the heat of his body near her, then held her breath when his sturdy arm wrapped around her waist and pulled her snug against him, the gun positioned at her neck.

"Don't take it so hard, Kate." His lips were moist, his breath hot against a thin shaft of her hair, the only buffer between his lips and her skin. "You got *me*."

Yay for me, you sick bastard!

She needed him to release her, his arm dangerously close to the tape recorder. Yes, his confession was unexpected. But confirmation that the good-old-boy network was alive and well wasn't enough.

"You know, Jack, I had no idea what little confidence you had in yourself. With all the evidence stacked against my clients, why did you need to go through so much trouble?"

He turned her around, his humor fleeting, evident by his stiff expression. "You miss the point, Kate. I didn't ask for you because of your lack of experience. Even if George Seiler defended the Stolzes, it wouldn't have changed the outcome. I asked for you, specifically, because I liked looking at you. I needed a wife, one that would compliment my ambitions. You had everything I was looking for. The public adored you—a fresh face, pretty, intelligent."

Kate could only stare at him. She'd always thought she was in control of her own destiny.

"You were building your own little empire. You never loved me." She wanted to smack his vainglorious face. Instead, she gave him her back, squeezed her hands shut, willing them at her side, and walked away.

His hand latched onto her arm and hauled her back. He stared down at her. "I didn't expect to. Like I said, you had a lot more power than you think. I fell in love with you. I would have done anything to keep you."

She wrenched her arm free of him. "Did that include murdering your best friend?"

"Bryan gave me no choice. He threatened to go to the FBI with the bank statements, show them the wire transfers."

The bank statements . . . She knew it! She had to appear unaffected, especially about the offshore bank account. But at least now she knew what she was supposed to have hidden.

If the tape recorder failed, she needed the name of the banking institution. There were so many international offshore banks—from Brazil to Europe, including the Caymans. Without it, the FBI might not find the correct one. "Did Barbosa pick the bank?"

Jack laughed derisively. "Barbosa wasn't in charge. I wasn't moving my money to Brazil."

Jack paused. Was he mulling over the question? Wondering what she was trying to glean?

Come on, Jack. Just say the name of the bank.

"You ask a lot of questions." He cocked his head, his expression thoughtful, then motioned for her to walk.

Kate reluctantly gave him her back and continued, the terrain starting to level off. She didn't think she could approach that subject again without him becoming suspicious. The switchback took a downward slope. They were getting close, maybe another mile. It wouldn't take much for Jack to snap. She needed to tread easy. At the cabin he was sarcastic and full of rage. At the moment he was even-keeled and almost pleasant. She wanted to survive. Being in this forest, the tree tops, the sky so blue, and the crisp mountain air, cleansing when she took a breath—she wanted to live.

"Jack, if I had wanted to hurt you, I would have given the FBI the bank statements." She stopped and turned to look at him, hoping he believed. Her throat went dry. Her lips rough like sandpaper, she licked them. "I wouldn't have left if I thought there was another way. I was afraid that if you knew Bryan gave me the evidence, you would kill me." Not to mention, she was the reason he came under the FBI's scrutiny to begin with. He hadn't mentioned it; she hoped he still didn't know.

He stepped closer and reached out, caressing her face. "I wanted you alive. I loved you."

Kate bit down on her bottom lip. "That night in the townhouse, I truly believed you were going to kill me. How could I trust you wouldn't hurt me?"

His face softened. "Kate, I was—"

"Drunk." Kate shook her head. "You made the decision easy."

"You'd been to the house in Tilghman."

Kate cocked her head. "You knew?"

"A housekeeper you're not. I found your shoeprint smudged right into the wood of my desk." There was no way to avoid the desk. The ladder, which had allowed her to find the bonds from its vantage point, was connected to the bookshelf.

"When?"

"It was late."

"Late? You mean you found it that night after your meeting?"

Why so vague? Wait . . . "You were with Joelle." Not that she gave a damn. Only he'd terrorized her that night before he went off for his dinner date, and, no doubt, handled his girlfriend and their so-called breakup with the utmost of self-control.

"Yes. I agreed to meet her for dinner." Jack rolled his eyes. "I did it as a favor to her father." He looked directly into her face. "I broke it off with her that night. It just took longer than expected."

Or he slept with her. *Still the consummate liar.* Kate clenched her fists.

"Once I found you had taken your passport and bonds, I knew you weren't coming back." He laughed, and his eyes crinkled at the corners, reminding her of the Jack Reynolds she had once loved. "I was on my way to being sober. You know I went back to the townhouse for you that night. I didn't know whether I wanted to strangle you or hug you. You had become my life, without you . . ." His head dipped, and he studied the gun before his eyes met hers. "But I never got a chance to do either. When I found . . . the blood . . . I cried." His expression somber, he continued, "It took a while to put it all together—the bonds, the fact you never cashed them." He wagged a finger at her. "Now that threw me."

She'd never had the chance. Before she knew it, she was on a plane and no longer Kate Reynolds.

"It wasn't until months later when Annapolis Police Department forensics confirmed the blood splatter patterns were staged that I realized I should have killed you there at the townhouse."

Kate swallowed hard. "Why didn't you?" She couldn't stop the quiver in her voice.

"Leverage."

Leverage?

"You still don't get it, do you, Kate? I couldn't kill you." He stepped closer, keeping the gun near, his fingers slipping through her hair. "But more than that." His eyes moved over her erratically. "You weren't going to mess with my political career. You'd have stayed." He laughed derisively. "Otherwise, your sister would have been next."

Her insides twisted, and Kate had the real sense of nausea hovering in her throat. Jack motioned with the gun for her to keep moving, and she did with trepidation.

They walked in silence for a while. Pine and larkspur filled the air, and an owl high in the treetops called, like a death knell, a grim reminder the mine was disquietingly near.

Kate stopped and eyed the gun in his hand. Lifting her chin, she met his gaze. She had one more question. "You seem very comfortable with that gun. Was it easy for you to kill your best friend?"

Jack's expression clouded. "I had to do it . . . for both of us. I loved you."

"That's not love, Jack. It's . . . it's sick." Her cheeks warmed with anger. "Bryan was your friend, my friend. You were wrong, Jack." Her body shivered, and she crossed her arms. "You didn't even need Barbosa's testimony—the evidence spoke for itself." She shook her head. "Why? You would have won anyway."

"I didn't bribe Barbosa." Jack's face turned scarlet, and the veins in his neck pulsed. "I didn't need to manipulate the system. I'm as good as it gets when it comes to prosecuting cases."

She had hit on something, but she was clueless as to what. "I know that," she said softly, hoping he'd calm down.

"You don't know shit, Kate." He grabbed her arm and jerked her close. The gun pressed into her flesh, stopping at her sternum. "Barbosa fucked up. Do you remember the file? The one you were looking at when I walked in and found you in my office in Tilghman? Do you know why I was so angry with you?"

She must have been holding her breath because she needed to breathe out in the worst way.

"I was angry with you because I loved you," he said, "and I didn't want you to find out what I had done. It had been five years. I thought I was done with it."

"Done with what, Jack?"

"I found out before my parents were killed that I had a sister."

"You never—"

"The documents you found were not my adoption papers. They were my sister's. My father had an affair with a barkeep in Annapolis before he was married to my mother. A month before he was killed, this woman, Rory McCarthy, contacted him. She was dying of lung cancer and wanted him to know he had a daughter."

Kate swallowed. His fingers were digging into her arm, causing jagged spokes of pain along her elbow. "Why are you so angry?"

He sneered. "You're just like my old man. He thought it was great. He had a daughter, after all these years. He couldn't wait to contact her—his firstborn. Where did that leave me?"

"You were his son, Jack. Your father and mother loved you."

"Did they? Did he? I'm not so sure. He was getting ready to contact her before their plane went down."

What was he trying to tell her? Did she even want to know? "Their plane . . . it was an accident."

"Of course it was an accident." His voice raised a notch, and she regretted her words. He tightened his grip. "Do you think I would sabotage my own parents' plane?"

She'd been thinking it. Obviously, by his demeanor, she was off base.

"The plane crash, although unexpected, was a stroke of good fortune. It made the job less convoluted. There was only one remaining loose end." Jack's gaze narrowed.

Oh God. Now the glimmer of hope that he wouldn't end her life was gone. The confession she'd hoped for had become multiple and intertwining. Her eyes widened, and her jaw went slack. He'd tangled her in with them, and there was no way she could free herself. He had ambushed her with this last one, and she couldn't disguise her emotion of stone-cold shock. "Jenna McGuinn was your sister."

He only smiled.

Damn him.

The words needed to be said. She straightened, and with deliberate calm, she spoke them, "You hired Barbosa to kill your sister because you were that hung up on the Reynolds fortune. You were afraid if she knew, she'd want half."

"Very good, counselor." He smirked and let her arm go. "Now you know."

She shook her arm and massaged her bicep, trying to regain feeling, his phantom fingerprints still penetrating her flesh.

"One more thing. Did you kill Barbosa?"

"You bet. That bastard would have bled me dry."

His confession was as good as she was going to get. If she prodded and tried to lead him, he'd catch on. Afraid the recorder would malfunction or tape over what she had already captured, she reached up and pulled on her shirt and pretended to adjust it while simultaneously hitting the Stop button. The click echoed in her ear, and she cringed.

Jack's eyes beaded in on her, and his hand shot out, clamping down on her tender bicep, causing her to whimper. "Mother fucking bitch. What's in your shirt?"

CHAPTER FORTY-ONE

J ACK SHOVED HER HARD AGAINST THE WALL OF THE MINE. SHE
stumbled and fell to her knees. This was it. He was going to kill her,
with or without the bank statements. When he wrestled her to the ground,
just inside the tree line of the forest, giving her a pat down that could rival
any police search, she dropped the recorder into the dense overgrowth.

Just because he couldn't find it didn't mean he believed her. It was then he
spied the cut of the gravel road just outside the forest's opening. She refused
to help him further. But then he rounded the gravel mound of earth, with her
in tow, and spied the opening leading to the mine. He dragged her the rest
of the way toward the tumble of jagged rocks on either side of the dark abyss.

Now, the cold steel of the barrel pressed up against her head. Her hair
hung loose, long curls cascading down her shoulders. Her eyes shut tight,
and she bit down on her bottom lip in anticipation of the bullet that would
shatter her skull.

"Step away from her, Reynolds. It's over."

Thank God, Mike.

Jack gripped her arm, yanked her up, and pulled her in front of him for a
shield, his arm a vise around her neck. The gun was pointed at the back of
her skull, its barrel painfully resting at an angle that couldn't possibly miss.

"You had your chance, Sheriff."

"Shut up, Reynolds," Mike boomed, his voice echoing through the opening of the tunnel.

An orange haze descended, making her feel muddled in the brain, like a
private joke she wasn't privy to.

"Mike?" His name seemed to linger on the stagnant air inside the opening of the mineshaft.

Mike stood just outside, the uneven terrain of the rock bed crunching
beneath his cowboy boots, when his hardened expression fell, and she knew.

"Charlie." His voice softened. Frowning, he shook his head. "It's a damn shame it's come to this. I had hoped this rabble-rouser would have stayed back East and let me handle things my way."

She glanced behind her to see the smug look on Jack's face and turned back to Mike. She couldn't put the two together. How was it possible they knew each other? And for how long?

"H-handle what, Mike?" She struggled against Jack's chest, trying to free herself by rocking her shoulders from side to side.

"Let her go." Mike's stance was hard and unwavering. His gun raised and pointed directly at them.

"Fuck you, Coulter. You knew it would come to this if you failed, so put the gun down and let's finish it."

Mike grabbed a handkerchief from his back pocket. Keeping his gun trained on both Jack and Kate, he pushed his Stetson back and wiped his brow. Tucking it into his back pocket, he whistled through his teeth, and pulled the brim of his Stetson back in place.

"Ya know, Reynolds, I'm getting too old for this shit. Let's get this over with, so I can put my quiet little Western town back on its feet and forget about the both of you."

Before she could wrap her brain around their conversation, Jack jerked Kate off her feet and dragged her several feet farther into the tunnel of the mine. She struggled against Jack's grip. With little air in the mine, it was difficult to breathe. Throw in Jack's arm pressed hard around her neck, and she was suffocating. Sweat dripped down her back, and Nick's shirt clung to her skin.

She turned her attention to Mike, his eyes unreadable. "Mike," she begged. "Tell me what's going—"

Jack slammed her back against him. "Good idea." His breath hot against her cheek made her cringe. "Go ahead, Mike. Explain to your friend Charlie, here, what's going on."

"Shut up, Reynolds. Let's just finish this. Give her to me."

"What? And miss out on all the fun?" he drawled.

"Reynolds, are you that fucking stupid? Go ahead and put your bullet in her head. I don't know where you got your gun or who it'll be traced back to, but if you want to risk it, then be my guest. In my line of work, there are accidental discharges all the time."

"No, I'll take your advice. But I think Kate's right. It's only fair she go to her grave knowing the truth."

Well, aren't you a prince.

She had prayed for Mike's intervention, but now it was apparent he was the last person she wanted to see. He had actually asked to put a bullet in her head. She didn't want to believe it was possible, but the man looking back at her couldn't hide behind the badge any longer.

Shaken, but wanting the truth, she swallowed hard and focused on the man who had become a surrogate father to her. "You need to tell me what's going on, Mike. I need to know," her voice cracked. "And now, damn it!" She gritted her teeth so tight her jaws hurt.

Mike shook his head. "It's not important, Charlie."

She looked over her shoulder at her captor and then back at the man in front of her, his gun trained on her center mass. Everything she knew about the man known as Mike Coulter was a lie. She stared straight into his eyes, eyes she had come to read, now blank and emotionless. "Fine, you stubborn old ass, if you don't have the balls to tell me, then I'll wing it. He told you who I was." She focused on Mike as she struggled to stay upright against Jack's chest. "You've known for a while . . . probably several weeks . . . which would make sense."

She pressed her head back against Jack, trying to get a glimpse of his face. "I figured that out last night. The intern you conned at the blood bank decided to tell her superior. My doctor called last night."

"Tedious work. AB negative is rare. Still, it took almost two years to track you down through your hemochromatosis bloodletting." He laughed, the sound derisive. "Always knew there was bad blood in your family."

She ignored Jack and his idiotic comment and nailed Mike with her eyes. "You broke into my home." She waited for him to deny it, but he remained stone quiet.

"You son of a bitch." She squirmed to get away so she could strangle him with her bare hands. "You bastard. I truly believed you loved me like your own daughter. I considered you my family. Well, fuck you, Mike Coulter. Fuck you and your badge." She pulled forward, gasping for air against Jack's arm. "I hope you got your money's worth."

Mike took a step closer. "Charlie, it wasn't like that," he said quietly.

"Like hell it—"

"Don't be so hard on him, Kate. Mike here was a reluctant party in this charade." Jack brought his face next to hers, the corner of his mouth curling against her cheek, and she knew he was smirking. "It seems ol' Mike here has a past. And because of his transgressions, he was an easy target."

"Target for what?" Kate kept her neck craned so she could keep Jack in her sights.

He smiled. "I found our mutual friend, here, had a secret of his own."

"That's enough, Reynolds." Mike moved in closer.

"Ah, come on, Coulter. I'm sure she would like to know why I chose you."

Mike remained quiet, his jaw tense.

"Did you know Mike isn't from around here, Kate? In fact, he lived and worked on the streets of Austin, Texas. He was a detective and a good one, until he and a few others sworn to uphold the law decided to circumvent the system." Jack gave her a quizzical look. "Are you aware how much a dime bag of coke can cost? The drug trade is much more lucrative than a cop's salary." Jack snickered. "He and his cohorts would have gone undetected, but they got greedy. Instead of every other drug bust, they began to take most of the drugs for themselves. Needless to say, a pattern formed, and they were caught red-handed."

"That's enough, Reynolds," Mike barked.

Jack's hold tightened. "Don't worry. Mike did the right thing. He turned against his cronies and offered state's evidence. He served six months and was released."

Was this just another one of Jack's ploys? "You're lying. If it's true, he'd have no chance of landing a job in law enforcement." She struggled against him, her face flushed.

"Very good, counselor, an excellent deduction. It would seem Mike, here, laid a golden egg when he came to Creede. They were in need of a sheriff, and he had all the credentials. Creede was in the process of upgrading their computer system. They weren't quite up to speed with NCIC, and Mike slipped through."

Her shoulders slumped, and she looked at Mike, his tanned complexion almost ashen, his expression one of resignation. "Is it true?"

"I've been the sheriff here for over thirty-five years. I thought I was done running from my past, until this bastard contacted me." Mike took a labored breath. "Hell, Charlie, Tess would leave me, take my kids. I'd lose my job." He swallowed hard. "You of all people can understand that. We both ran from something so big it could swallow us whole if we stayed. I needed a new start, just like you."

So those were the demons he'd mentioned the night he'd given her the lecture—*hypocrite*.

He peered over her head and gave Jack a meaningful scowl. "He made it seem simple. My job was to keep an eye on you and find those damn bank statements. Then he'd go away." He gave her a brief smile. "I never wanted to hurt you. You *are* like a daughter to me. I'm so sorry."

Mike's mission was doomed before he began. Even if she did have the evidence, Jack would never have just gone away peacefully with the bank statements and left her behind.

Mike shook his head. "I didn't want it to end this way. But I have no choice now. It's either you or me." He turned his attention toward Jack. "Let's get on with it, Reynolds. I'm sick and tired of apologizing for something I have no control over. You going to give her to me while you look for these bank statements? Or you going to continue to entertain her caterwauling?"

Jack's eyes focused on Mike. Scowling, he released her. Unprepared for the abrupt force, she landed on all fours. Her brain attempted to compartmentalize everything Mike had said. Within seconds, Mike's bull-like grip encircled her forearm, pulling her to her feet. Turning her quickly to the opening of the tunnel, he pushed her hard toward the entrance to the mine. "Run, Charlie!" His voice trumpeted through her ears.

The gunshot was deafening as it ricocheted off the opening of the cavern walls and the canyon beyond. She stopped, unable to follow through with Mike's command, and turned in what seemed like slow motion. They both remained standing. Mike's back was turned toward her, Jack's silhouette cloaked in darkness, barely discernible, several feet in front of Mike.

She took a breath, looked down, wondering if she had been hit, but found no blood. She brought her gaze up. A stain of crimson spread through the back of Mike's tan jacket and his towering frame caved. He fell to his knees, his service weapon dangled on his index finger before it dropped to the ground, rattling against rock.

"Mike!" She darted forward. It was a stupid move but an automatic response. Standing in front of him, his eyes wide open with stunned disbelief, a matching stain on the front of his once white shirt. A moan rolled up her chest. "Oh my God, Mike."

He teetered back and forth on the verge of collapse when she reached out to steady him, both of her hands on his shoulder. She gave him a hard look. "Don't you die on me, Coulter." Her voice was harsh, demanding, and angry.

"Ch-Charlie. I-I'm so sorry—" His voice was rattled, blood oozing from the corner of his mouth.

"No. This is my fault, all my fault. If I hadn't picked Creede, none of this—"

"Well, isn't this touching," Jack snapped. "But I'm on a time schedule."

Pain stabbed her when her head jerked back. Jack's hand, now entangled in a mass of her hair, yanked hard and hoisted her to her feet.

Pointing his gun at the base of her head, he shouted, "Move!"

Her body took an about-face as Jack pushed her into the darkness and handed her the flashlight.

"Turn it on," he ordered.

She clicked it on and lit a path, sidestepping the cross ties under the old rail system, running down the center of the tunnel. Mortised beams creaked, water trickling from somewhere in the mine. Kate kept trudging on; she had no choice. He had placed her out in front and to the left of him so he could see the beam of light. Even with the flashlight, it remained eerily dark and cold. Every time she faltered, he pushed hard on her back, and she stumbled.

Hot tears ran down her cheeks, the taste salty when they reached her lips. Her body rocked with grief. Mike had not betrayed her. He tried to save her, and it may have cost him his life. How could she have doubted him? She couldn't imagine her life without him and his incessant badgering. He'd been pushed into service to spy on her, but she knew deep down he was only trying to protect her, hoping he could prevent an up-close-and-personal visit with Jack.

"Is this it, Kate?" His hot breath came up on her suddenly.

"What?" His rough voice pulled her out of her reverie.

"You stopped walking. Is this it?" he asked again, more irritated, pushing the metal of his gun into her spine.

She hadn't realized she'd stopped walking. She was so very tired, tired of the pretense, tired of running. Her life in Creede had been a heaven on earth for three years. She had been free of Jack, had almost forgotten her past, only to have it smack her square in the face.

She turned slowly to look at him. "You know, Jack, this *is* it. Funny, it's taken me this long to realize it, but I'm done running. I should have faced you head-on when I had the chance. If you want to end my life, be my guest. And just so we're clear, you'll never get your hands on the—"

A beam of light shone on the two of them. Charlie couldn't see its origin.

"Kate Reynolds." Everything came at her at once—surrounded in darkness for so long, the gun pressed against her skull, the bright beam of light making her squint.

"Kate Reynolds, it's Agent Parker with the FBI."

His authoritative voice jerked her out of her murky thoughts, and she placed her hand out to shield her eyes from the intense light, fumbling her own flashlight, the metal hitting the rock floor with a crack, the fan of light gone. "A-agent Parker?"

"Yes, Kate. You're a hard woman to track down."

Jack stood to her left, pulling her by her neck, his arm like steel pressed up against her throat. The gun dug into her skin under her right jawbone at the side of her throat, the muzzle pointed upward toward her brain.

"I'll kill her, Parker, if you step any closer."

"Reynolds, it's over." The dash and scurry of footsteps came from the tunnel they'd traveled from. "We have the bank statements."

"Bullshit, your ploy isn't going to work with me. It's here in the mine."

"No, Jack," Kate said. "It was at my cabin. The FBI must have found it."

Jack's gun clicked. Her reaction split-second, she reached back with her boot and slammed her heel straight down onto the bridge of his foot, and he cried out. When he released her, she dove for the ground and rolled away from him. A gunshot ripped through the mine, echoing against solid rock, and she turned. Jack hit the tunnel wall hard and fell to the ground. Agent Parker still had his flashlight trained on both of them. Jack grabbed his shoulder, blood flowing through his fingers, and dropped his weapon. It clattered as it hit rock. She scurried over and grabbed onto the gun and kept it pointed at Jack, the gun shaking wildly in her grasp.

"Slide me the gun," Agent Parker ordered.

She laid it down and pushed it toward the intense brightness.

"Good. Last thing, Kate."

"What?" she croaked back, her eyes squinting against the bright bead of light.

"Here are my handcuffs." He turned his flashlight down toward the floor of the cave and threw the cuffs. She grabbed them and then turned toward Jack and stood. Now hunched over him, she grabbed hold of his good arm and slapped the silver cuff hard against his wrist, the teeth of the cuff snapping into place. She jerked his other arm around his back and rolled him over on his stomach.

Jack screamed in pain; he was far from dead. But he was definitely incapacitated. He'd survive and that was a good thing because she wanted him to suffer. He'd go to prison and die a little each day knowing he could never escape. That would be her justice for Jenna, Jason and Kristie Stolze, Bryan, Mike, and herself.

Taking her knee, she jammed it in his back, grabbed his other wrist and slapped the cuff against his wrist bone as hard as she could muster. He let out a cry. She hauled him up by his forearms to a kneeling position.

He turned on her and peered into her face, his once cool eyes registering a fear not unlike the one she had lived with for years. She was tempted to spit in his face.

Shards of light danced on the walls, a disorderly blast of shouts disorienting her as a rush of agents descended. A woman with her hair pulled back in a ponytail came to her. "Kathryn, I'm Agent Beth Singer. Are you all right?" Kate let go of Jack, the agent wrapping an arm around her, moving her away from him as another agent grabbed hold of Jack.

Agent Singer placed something warm around her shoulders, the lining soft—a Windbreaker. "I-I need to find my friend."

Agent Singer nodded. "Let's get you out of here."

CHAPTER FORTY-TWO

KATE COULD SEE THE LIGHT AT THE END OF THE TUNNEL, BRIGHT and bursting with warmth. Boy, was that cliché, but the truth. She'd almost run the whole way back to the entrance, taking Agent Singer's flashlight, and dragging her with her. Kate's only concern was Mike. She needed to get to him.

She kept her focus on the entrance. Her heart went cold. It was empty. She clicked off the flashlight and stepped into the sunlight. Charlie's eyes widened. "Quince?"

He stood shoulder to shoulder with Shep a few yards away next to a gurney that had been brought up by EMTs. A sheet covered Mike's body. "Oh God," she begged and threw off the jacket, sprinting toward the lifeless body, a burning sensation blazing at the back of her throat. Shep stood in front of her and wrapped his arms around her tight. The flashlight slipped through her fingers and thudded to the ground. Her heart followed suit.

"Don't, Charlie. He's gone."

"No!" Fresh tears pinched the back of her eyes and rolled down her cheeks. She buried her head in his uniform shirt, her cry muffled against his chest.

The rough hand of Quince Maynard rubbed her back. "I'm sorry, girl. Heard the shot back at the main entrance while making my rounds for Grady. Nothing I could do when I found him." Shep squeezed her and then peered over her tousled auburn hair. "Nick, thank God you found her."

Charlie's body gave an involuntary jerk. Keeping the side of her cheek resting on Shep's chest, she rotated her head back. Nick . . . holding Jack's arm. Nick . . . with Jack's gun shoved in the front of the waistband of his jeans. She straightened in Shep's arms and eyed the man who, the more she thought about it, could pass for an FBI agent. *Son of a . . .* "You bastard!"

Jack let loose with a condescending laugh. Parker jerked his arm, and Jack moaned, seeming not to mind the pain.

He was laughing at her, Charlie—Kate. Always the last to know.

She pushed away from Shep's grasp.

Parker pulled on Jack's cuffs, hard. "Shut up, Reynolds." He then motioned to a tall man dressed in jeans, a black Windbreaker, and black baseball cap with the letters FBI sewn in white coming toward him. "Powers. Take this asshole." He shoved Jack off as the tall man ran up to assist. Parker then took a step toward her.

Kate sidestepped him. Bolting up the gravel path in a full sprint, she ignored the pressure of her boots biting into her heels and slipped into the wood line, heading in the direction of the switchbacks. Her life was a lie. He was a lie. How had she not put it all together? What a complete fool she'd been. She disappeared through the dense brush, hoping to lose him.

"Kate, stop running." He came up behind her.

"Kate's dead, remember?" she yelled back. Her lungs burned, and she gulped to take a breath. She should be grateful to him for saving her. That was another thing. She called back, again, "How'd you find me?"

"GPS," he called after her.

GPS? When would he have—She stopped and turned on him. He slowed his stride and reached out, grabbing her arms to steady himself. She flung his hands off. "You sneak." Breathing hard, she continued, "My truck. You didn't need to tie your boots."

He grimaced. "I knew you'd be mad."

Hell, yeah! She gave him an irritated look and turned away, walking the area, searching. She wanted to keep running—away from him. But she needed her tape recorder. As angry and confused as she was about the situation, there was one thing that *was* crucial—Jack's confession.

She came upon the white columbine and dropped to the ground on all fours and dug wildly into the vegetation. She knew it was there, it had to be.

He came up on her and grabbed her by her arm, bringing her to her feet. Swinging her around, he pulled her hard against his chest. "I had no choice." His eyes, a turbulent blue, searched her face.

She yanked free. Bending back down, she continued to dig. "Don't take it hard. You were just an easy lay."

"Okay, I guess I deserve that. But you're lying to yourself if you think that's all it was." Crouching down, he snagged the small silver device deep in the vegetation and shoved her tape recorder under her nose. "Is this what you're looking for?"

She turned abruptly.

"What is it about this gadget that has you digging like a scavenger for lost treasure?"

She grabbed for it, but he pulled his hand away. "Answer the question, Kate."

His jaw always did that thing when he was mad, flexing, the tendon beating like an ireful heart beat.

Well, guess what, big and bad FBI man? You deserve my wrath for lying to me. But she needed to get past that. The fact he was an FBI agent meant she could finally tell someone, someone who could actually do something with it. "Jack killed her." Anxious, still breathing hard from running, she tried to catch her breath. "Correction, he had her killed. He didn't bribe Barbosa for his testimony. He paid him to kill."

He stared at her for a brief moment. "Killed her? You mean Trooper McGuinn."

"You knew?" she asked, breathing deep through her nose.

He shook his head. "I found out from Washington last night when you were in the shower—the relationship between Jack and Trooper McGuinn. I didn't know for sure he was responsible for her death. Although, I figured it was possible."

She gave him an astonished look. "Why didn't you tell me?"

"You were Charlie at the time. And you were angry with me. You probably would have beat the snot out of me, if I told you who I was."

His handsome face split into a grin, and she ignored the dip in her stomach.

"Right . . . but you had no problem making love to me as Nick Foster. Did you?"

He turned slightly on his haunches, his muscular thigh pressed up against her. His strong and capable hand squeezed her knee. "I wanted you to know who I was." Her eyes followed his movements—his thigh against her, his hand squeezing her knee. Same controlled, reassuring voice—it had all happened once before. Her life flew before her in reverse.

And she remembered.

"It was you in the cigar shop. You followed me. Y-you ran into me." She cocked her head. "Then you knew about the locker."

"The locker, yes. Not the contents." His brow shot up.

"What? You know Bryan didn't leave me the bank statements. All I had in my hand was the key."

He looked deep into her eyes. "Do I? What about what you told Jack?"

She gave him a knowing look. "What do they teach you in the FBI Academy, anyway? If I told him I didn't have it, I don't think I'd be here arguing with you."

He smiled. "Point taken. Then how did you know it existed?"

She pointed to the tape recorder in his hand. "He confessed." Kate frowned.

"But I couldn't get the name of the banking institution out of him."

His hand came down on her shoulder, his eyes connecting with hers. "Kate, we already have the bank statements."

Her eyes widened. "How?"

"Ally Wexler."

"Ally?" Her name floated on the cool Colorado mountain air. She'd missed her so much. She never really thought about Ally's reaction to finding Kate missing and presumed dead so soon after she'd lost Bryan. She'd wanted to reach out—to explain. But it would have been at a great risk. "How?"

"She found them a few months ago stashed in a humidor of her husband's in a back closet."

She shook her head. "Him and his damn cigars." Then she scowled at him, dusted the dirt from her hands, and began to stand, swatting his hand away as he stood, trying to help her up. "What the hell, Parker? Why are you here? You've got the evidence."

"Not my star witness."

She swallowed hard. "You track me down through my blood just like Jack?"

"Yes and no. It was mostly your sister."

"Bren?" She beaded in on him. "Why would—"

"She wanted you back. I promised I could make that happen if she cooperated."

"What does that mean?"

"She coordinated the search through NIH."

"How'd Jack—"

"Illegally." His body slumped just a little. "Kate." He took a breath and touched her cheek. "IrishEyes. Why didn't you tell me what was going on?"

"You figured out it was me?"

He nodded. "I was going to try to talk you into protective custody the morning of our meeting. I would have protected you from him."

She studied him for a moment. "What's the matter, Agent Parker? Couldn't that investigative mind of yours figure out why I didn't wait around for our meeting?"

"I never had that luxury. I could only mourn your passing." He raked his hand roughly through his hair. "Your little murder scene was very convincing, Kathryn."

"Bren tell you about the blood bank?"

"Nope. Figured you'd stolen it." He nodded toward her arms. "Sealed it for me when you detailed your trip to the blood bank this week." He fell back on his heels, crossing his arms. "Just curious—the blood splatter patterns—how'd you manage to fool forensics for so long?"

She shrugged. "You'd be surprised what you can learn on the Internet—a large sponge and a hammer."

He rolled his lips in, shaking his head, she assumed, sorry he'd asked.

CHAPTER FORTY-THREE

JESS HAD GIVEN INTO KATE AND WALKED THE TWENTY MINUTES down the mountain to her truck. She'd walked right over to the passenger side, bent down where the four-door cab of her truck met in the middle, and reached underneath, struggling until the magnetic tracking unit came off in her hand. He backed up when she looked like she'd bust him in the head with it before she calmly dropped it in his hand.

The rest of the ride to her cabin she refused to speak to him. Once they arrived, she opened the door, giving him her back. Jess followed her up the log staircase, down the hall, and into her bedroom. She stopped short in front of her doorway, causing him to ram into the back of her.

"What the hell, Parker?" she snapped.

"You—"

"Don't talk to me." She raised her hand to silence him. "You're a liar."

She'd made it perfectly clear on the ride to her cabin with the silent treatment—he wasn't forgiven. But at least she was talking to him now.

He leaned against the doorjamb to her bedroom. "That's an awful bold statement for a woman who's been masquerading as someone else for three years," he reminded her.

"That's different. I was forced to assume an alias," she shot back as she stepped into the room. "What's your excuse, Agent Parker?"

"Wait till I get hold of your sister," he mumbled to himself. "'She's fragile,' she said, 'you can't just yank her out of her new world,'" he mimicked Bren.

"What are you ranting about?"

He looked her in the eye. "What I'm saying is, you're anything but fragile. You're tenacious. You cuss like a sailor when you feel it's warranted. You run a construction site where, I swear, you get your rocks off by lording over the likes of Shorty and his co-workers. You'd go out of your way to protect a friend, even if it means putting yourself in harm's way." Frustrated, he struck the wall with his fist. "I should have ignored your sister's urgings and done things my way."

She turned her back on him as she took measured footsteps. Stopping in the middle of her room, she made a sharp right toward the closet and counted off several more paces. Taking her booted heel, she kicked at the floor board several times until the wood popped up like a trap door.

Jess's mouth fell open. *Son of a bitch.* He could have searched for days.

She bent down and reached inside the floor and pulled out a letter-size envelope several inches thick and handed it to him.

"What's this?"

"A debt I owe someone."

He gave a half grin. "Charlie Robertson owes a loan shark?" he asked, trying to make her smile. Even though he knew full well this was the fifty thou Bren had taken from the farm's emergency fund, unbeknownst to Rafe, to start Kate on her new life.

"Something like that." She remained stone-faced. "Agent Parker, when you see Bren, I need you to give this to her. And tell her thank you. If you're finished with me, I'd like to shower and check on Tess Coulter."

"Kate," he said. "We're scheduled to depart Denver for Baltimore in less than six hours. There's no time to see—"

"Agent Parker, I'm not going anywhere with you. Kate Reynolds is history. She doesn't exist any longer."

Jess followed her, grabbed her shoulder, and spun her around. "Kate, don't do this. You're an attorney, you know the laws—"

"*Was,* is the operative word."

"Don't use semantics with me. You know damn well what's expected."

She struggled to free herself but lost her balance and fell back against the log wall.

Jess moved in against her, his arms resting on either side of her shoulders, his head leaning up against the side of her temple. He whispered against her ear, "Don't fight me on this, Kate. You know it's my job."

She tried to escape, but he only leaned in further against her. She moaned a protest, her body stiffening. "Agent Parker, look the other way. You've got the evidence, Jack's taped confession, and all the supporting documentation you could ask for. Forget about Kate Reynolds and Charlie Robertson. I can be packed up and gone. You could say I gave you the slip."

He pulled away and looked into her pleading eyes. He'd struggled with the same issue the past few days. But he needed her testimony. She was spot-on about the taped confession. He could nail Reynolds without her. But he wanted her, and not for her testimony in court. If he let her go, she'd sprint as fast as she could away from him and, if he wasn't quick enough, she'd slip away into a world so vast he might never find her again.

He could never let her go.

He slid his arm down the wall and brought his hand around to cup the back of her neck. Pulling her close, he kissed her. She tasted so good. He teased her lips with his tongue until her lips parted. Her rigid body began to yield to his touch. He deepened the kiss. She stilled, and then pulled her mouth away, pushing against his chest.

Jess gave her some space.

She wiped her mouth with the back of her hand. "Agent Parker, I think you need to leave." She held his gaze, breathing heavy and looking so vulnerable, yet ready to battle him if he didn't heed her advice.

"For Christ's sake, Kate. Stop calling me Agent Parker. I'm Jess—not Agent Parker, not Nick Foster, but Jess." He raked his hands through his hair and searched her face. "I'm in love with you, damn it. Stop making this harder than it has to be."

A flush rode up her bronzed cheeks, and she pinned him with her eyes. "I hate you. You're the reason Mike's dead. If you hadn't been so covert, he'd still be alive." Tears streamed down her face, and her body quivered. She slid down the wall onto the floor, drew her legs up against her chest, and sobbed.

His heart broke. She accused him of exactly what he had been wrestling with since he arrived in Creede. Would things have turned out differently had he followed protocol?

She was a witness in a federal investigation. He should have treated her like any other witness. But he hadn't. He shouldn't have felt things for her. But he did. He should have come into her life dressed in a dark suit and flashing his badge. But he didn't.

Jess walked over to where she sat, her head bent down, her body shaking. She'd been battling him all morning, and now reality was slowly catching up with her. She was finally allowing herself to feel her loss.

Jess reached over and stroked her hair, his hand caressing her shoulder. He tenderly squeezed it. "Kate, I never meant to hurt you. I did what I thought was best at the time. Now, I'm realizing it wasn't enough. I'm so sorry for your loss."

She shrugged his hand off her shoulder and refused to look at him. He bent over and kissed the top of her head.

"Leave me alone," she whispered, lifting her head to expose a tear-stained face, puffy and red. "Don't you understand anything? This is all my fault. Ryan Stolze was executed because of me. He was my client—they were my clients. I let them down. I certainly can't face Kristie Stolze when this is all over. And my father . . . I never got the chance to say good-bye."

Her father . . . That would be the next subject he'd have to discuss with her. But now was definitely not the time.

Jess put his head close to Kate's. "You had no evidence. It wasn't your job to save the Stolzes. It was ours. If anyone's to blame, it's me, not you, sweetheart." Was he getting through to her? He was tempted to scoop her up into his arms and hold her there until she forgave him and herself, but a loud rap on the front door of the cabin thwarted that idea.

He reached out and touched her cheek. "Kate, I have to get the door. Agent Powers is supposed to meet me here," he said apologetically. "Please don't do anything stupid. I need you to get a shower and change clothes. We need to leave the cabin in two hours." He stopped to look down at his watch. "Around two fifteen."

Thirty minutes later, Kate's body continued to convulse. She stepped from the shower and slipped into her bathrobe. Fresh tears fell, and she pressed her palms into her eye sockets.

Mike was dead, if for no other reason than knowing her. Tess's sweet face invaded her thoughts, and Kate sobbed. Because of the jerk downstairs, it was unlikely she'd get the chance to see her friend. Although, what could she possibly say? "I'm sorry I killed your husband. Can you forgive me?" She wouldn't blame Tess if she banished her from her life altogether.

Kate managed to comb her hair and patted her puffy, blotched face with a cool washcloth. If she was going to survive this, survive Jack, she needed to get her head back in the game. Dwelling on what she couldn't change wouldn't serve her, and, in the end, Jack would win. As much as she wanted to curl into a ball and shut the world out, she was discovering the feds, including the lying, no-good bastard with the dreamy blue eyes, weren't going to allow her to skip town.

She was going home. And that did have its upside. The thought of seeing her family after three years overwhelmed her. She wasn't Kate Reynolds any longer. She had become Charlie Robertson, a blue-collar, take-no-crap general contractor—not the frightened woman she had left in Annapolis.

Except returning had its own set of hurdles. She'd be front-page news, and the headlines wouldn't be kind: Kate Reynolds Returns from the Grave After Saving Her Own Ass at the Expense of Her Clients.'

Okay, maybe that was exaggerated—but so true.

A knock came. "You decent?" She recognized the concerned male voice. Kate moved into the bedroom area. "Come in."

The door clicked, and Ben shoved his head inside. The tears started again. He moved toward her, and she threw her arms around his neck and hugged him. His I'll-never-let-you-down arms held her close.

"Mike's dead, and it's all my fault." She sighed, and new tears welled up in her eyes. "They won't let me go see Tess to tell her how sorry I am." She snuffled. "It's my fault he's—"

"It was his job."

She shook her head. Ben wouldn't know about Mike's past. It would come out eventually, but she wouldn't be the one to tarnish his name.

"You listening?" Ben shook her lightly and held her at arm's length, giving her a reproving stare. "He loved you, and he died trying to protect you. Just remember that."

She frowned. "Tess probably blames—"

"No, she doesn't. I saw her before I came over."

Kate's heart broke for Tess. Last night, they'd been enjoying the holiday. Mike had stopped by and promised to see them when he got home. Had he gotten to kiss Tess good night, tell her he loved her? Kate slumped. "Ah . . . Ben, his kids—do they know?"

He nodded.

Kate sat on the edge of the bed. "If only I had told him the truth. Then maybe—"

"Hey, sweetheart," he said, pulling her up and lifting her chin, "this is not your fault. Your husband gave you no choice."

She'd told herself that the night Rafe, Bren, and she had saturated the sponge with her blood. Striking it with a hammer, her blood splattered walls, carpet, furniture, and the floor, creating a crime scene that could rival CSI. By that point, however, she had said, "Don't want to be here, no way, no how." So she didn't object too fiercely when Rafe and Bren pushed her out the door and into a new life.

She'd made the right decision.

Although, she did regret not being able to say good-bye to her dad. Bren and Rafe would have told him once she had flown out of Baltimore. If he had wanted to stop her, it was moot.

Kate threw her arms around Ben one last time and hugged him. "I'm going to miss you. But I'm coming back after this is all over." She pulled back from Ben and sighed. "That is, if you'll have me back as your partner."

"You know there's no one else to take your place."

That's why she loved Ben—he was one of the good guys. Kate's face crumpled, and she began sobbing. "I'm so sorry, Ben, about everything. I never meant to lie to you. I wanted to tell you—" Her bottom lip quivered. Damn it. She was going to cry again.

He pulled her back into his arms. "You did what you had to do. I admire you for your grit, Charlie. I mean . . ." He pulled back to look at her. "What should I call you?"

"Whatever you want. I think I'll always be Charlie. Somehow, Kate doesn't seem to fit. And the name Reynolds is definitely going."

Ben laughed out loud. "I can't believe you were married. To think, all this time I was carrying on with a married woman." The mirth in his eyes disappeared, and he became pensive. "How did you ever end up with an asshole like Jack Reynolds?"

She shrugged. "It's a long story. One I never want to repeat as long as I live."

Ben nodded grimly before his eyes widened. "So you're a friggin' attorney? All this money I've been shelling out to Dickey James for contracts, and I had one in-house all along."

"I suggest you keep a retainer with old Dickey. I rather like my current position with Sterling. I don't plan on going back to practicing law." Her shoulders curved in. "Besides, I'm probably disbarred anyway. I guess Agent Parker filled you in on my many escapades, including faking my death and assuming a false identity."

"Oh, I see. It's Agent Parker now?"

Kate smiled ruefully. "You do know I love you, Ben Sterling, just not in that way."

"I know. You're in love with someone else."

She stepped back. "What's that supposed to mean?"

"Don't play stupid with me, Charlie Robertson. You're in love with that FBI agent downstairs, and I'm afraid he's hopelessly in love with you. I think maybe I should give him my condolences now."

"For your information, I'm not in love with anyone, especially Agent Jess Parker."

"Okay." He put up a hand. "Look, I should be going. I just didn't want you to leave without seeing you." He pulled her back into his arms. "Do whatever it is you have to do. I'll hold down the fort until you get back."

He turned to leave.

"Oh, Ben! Shelley and Gunner . . . I want them to stay here. She'll always have a home with me and Scooter." Kate turned to see her beloved cat sprawled on his back, belly exposed, lying on her bed, the noon sun picking up the brown tint to his fur. "He needs someone to take care of him. I know Shelley. She'll feel like this is a handout, but it's not. I need someone to take care of Moochie and my house. As far as the utilities—"

He pressed his finger across her lips. "Don't worry. I've got it covered." He leaned in and kissed her forehead. "All right, I've got to go. I'm going to miss you like hell." He stopped in the doorway. "You have my cell, office, and home phone. I expect a call at least once a week, and if I don't hear from you, I'm going to be pissed." He smiled. "So, if you want to keep me off your doorstep in Maryland, you better heed my advice and call me."

That made her smile. "I will, I promise."

CHAPTER FORTY-FOUR

"I'VE GOT IT." KATE ROUNDED ON JESS, HER VOICE RAISED IN THE baggage claim area of Thurgood Marshall Airport in Baltimore.

At nine in the evening, he was beat and in no mood to argue. "Fine," Jess snapped. "Have it your way." He gave her a scowl of his own and let go of the handle of her suitcase.

They covered the distance from the baggage claim area to the main terminal of the airport in silence. The glass doors slid open, and they were met by the early summer air, heavy with humidity, a stark contrast to the constant cool breeze in the Rockies.

The terminal bustled with passengers moving in all directions, baggage agents directing wayward travelers. Outside, the occasional horn blast accompanied agitated cabbies and motorists as they navigated jaywalkers and illegally parked vehicles.

Jess immediately recognized the dark sedan parked to the right, its emergency lights flashing. He motioned to Kate, who nodded, rolling her suitcase behind her as she followed him to the waiting car. Jess conversed briefly with Agent Rodriguez and then opened the rear passenger door, motioning for Kate to get in. Without a word, the trunk popped open, and Jess placed her suitcase and his duffel bag inside. After shutting the trunk tight, Jess moved to get in the back and stopped. Kate's shapely leg rested outside the rear passenger door, her face searching his.

He checked his phone and pocketed it in his suit coat. "What?" he asked.

"Why are your bags in the trunk? I thought you were handing me off to another agent."

"Move over, Kate."

"What's going on?" She leaned toward him and frowned. "You lied to me, didn't you? There's no other case. Who is Silver Fox? I want to know how it's connected to me, and I want to know now." Her hand braced against the upholstery below the window.

Raking his fingers through his hair, Jess took a deep breath, blowing it out slowly. "Kate, just move over." She had that combative look in her eyes, and her legs remained resolutely positioned outside the frame of the door.

"Make me."

Jess rolled his eyes. She was an easy read. "Ah, hell." Jess ducked inside. "Don't try my patience, Kate."

"Then tell me what's going on," she pleaded, her voice little more than a whisper.

He scooped her up against her shrieks of protest and placed her in the middle before dropping onto the seat next to her. He slammed the door and nodded toward Rodriguez. "Washington County Hospital."

Kate's mouth fell agape. "Hospital? Tell me. Please . . . Jess."

He grabbed her hand and held it firmly. She was listening to him. Her eyes were locked on his face, and she looked so frightened. He knew once he told her she would be devastated, but there was no way around it. "Kate, your father had a stroke a few days ago. The phone call I received that night at Mike's cabin after dinner was Bren."

Her face crumpled. She blinked, and tears ran down her cheeks as a small whimper sounded from her chest. He drew her to him and held her. Kate looped her arms around his neck, burrowing her face into his chest. The need to protect her overwhelmed him. "I'll take you to your dad, baby." He kissed the top of her head and whispered, "I love you, Kate. I wish I could make this all go away."

Jess felt sure Kate realized it would be wise to keep him in tow, just in case she actually needed him. But that didn't stop her from ditching him in the hospital's parking garage. One minute she stood next to him, the next she was slipping into an elevator that looked like it was ready for the scrap yard. He hesitated, like he always did, when it came to elevators.

Her eyes widened, and she gave him that what-is-your-deal look right before the elevator doors closed. Truth be told, he was afraid of them. Of course, he couldn't admit that. Five flights of stairs later, he finally made it to the fourth floor of ICU and located room 412. He found Bren and Rafe outside Daniel's room, looking on through the glass.

He grabbed Rafe's shoulder and whispered, "How's Daniel?"

Rafe gave him a sideways glance and a rough smile. "His prognosis is much better." He nodded toward the glass. "He's awake and talking to Kate."

"Come on." Bren grabbed Jess's hand. "He's been asking about you." She motioned to Rafe with a lift of her chin, and the three cleared the doorway.

Daniel's color looked good. Actually, better than the last time Jess had seen him, several weeks ago. Jess couldn't help but think that the stress of wondering and worrying if Jess would find Kate had somehow contributed to Daniel's stroke. He remained hooked to oxygen and heart and blood pressure machines, their wires running to monitors behind his hospital bed.

Daniel's blue eyes smiled at Jess. "Well, there. I hope she didn't give you much trouble, son." He winked at Kate and lifted their joined hands. "Thank you for bringing her home, me boy."

"You're welcome."

"She's a tough one. From what she tells me, she's a general contractor now."

Jess nodded. "And a damn good one from what I've seen." He smiled at Kate, but she refused to acknowledge him.

"Aye, she's a Fallon, me boy." He frowned at Kate and gave her hand a hard shake. "Now there'll be no more talk of forgiveness, do you hear?" He sighed. "You've had a long journey, now." Daniel's chin rose. "Bren, I'll leave it to you to get your sister settled, then."

Bren took a step forward. "Dad, Kate's under protective custody until the trial."

His head swiveled from Bren to Kate. "Are you telling me I won't be seeing you, Katie girl?" Daniel's voice shook with uncertainty.

Jess moved to the end of his bed. "We can set up a schedule. While you're in the hospital, I'll have the agent protecting Kate arrange to bring her by to visit. Same when you're released."

Kate leaned in and kissed her father's cheek. "Daddy, I'll see you as early as tomorrow." She gazed into Jess's eyes almost pleading. "You can arrange that, Agent Parker?"

He nodded. "Of course." He concentrated on her father. "We can make it work. The only thing I want you to think about is getting better." He looked at his watch, then Kate. "We should probably head out and get you on your way."

Kate stood and squeezed her father's hand. "You need to get some rest." She kissed his cheek and smoothed down his blankets. "We'll talk some more tomorrow, Daddy."

"We'll have a nice visit, to be sure. You can tell me about your life in Colorado, then."

"I will." She held his hand one last time. "Please, rest."

Kate passed Jess, said nothing, and gave Rafe a quick hug, and then wrapped her arms around Bren. "I missed you so much. If you need me," she said, glancing at Jess, "contact Agent Parker."

Bren laughed. "Okay . . ." She eyed Jess.

Jess shook his head and shrugged. *Still Agent Parker.*

Kate pulled away and gave one last look. "I've missed all of you. More than you'll ever know." Her eyelids fluttered with exhaustion. She turned to Jess. "Agent Parker, I'll meet you at the elevator." She moved past them and down the hall toward the bank of elevators.

Bren shot a questioning brow in Jess's directions as if to say, What's going on?

He shrugged his shoulders and gave Bren a quick smile. "She's been through a lot. She needs some time alone to decompress and come to grips with what will be expected of her at trial." Jess stepped forward and gave Rafe a rap on the back. "I'll see you." He then looked at Bren and smiled. "Stay out of trouble." He reached down and patted Daniel's leg under the blanket. "We'll do some fishing once you've been sprung."

The twinkle was back in the old man's eyes. "If you have time, mind," he said, nodding toward the hall where Kate had headed a few moments earlier. He gave a lift of his chin. "Go to her. She needs you." He winked at Jess.

Jess hesitated.

"Go on. She doesn't bite," he said with a chuckle, and then added, "hard."

Jess laughed. "Thanks for the warning."

Daniel gave him a knowing look. "An independent girl, she is. I see it plain as day, now that that horse's ass is out of her life." He winked at Jess. "She can be a hard one, did you know, Jess? If you are in love with my daughter, you need to rein her in." He put up his hand. "The right way, not like that eejit she'll soon be divorcing."

Jess turned to give Bren a meaningful glance but couldn't hold the hard stare long before smiling. "You have a big mouth." Bren had called back that night at Mike's—late. She'd pressed him during that phone conversation, and he'd admitted that a lot had happened in a very short time in Creede. He hadn't actually said, "I'm in love with your sister," but Bren seemed to have figured it out.

She tapped her head with her finger and gave her father a stern look. "Inside thoughts." Bren looked at Jess and shrugged her shoulders. "I have no idea what he's talking about."

"Yeah, right," Jess said, dubiously. He motioned to Bren. "Before I go after your sister, I need to see you for a minute."

Bren nodded and followed him a short distance down the hall. She gave him an expectant look. "What's up?"

Jess checked the hall. Rafe remained in the room with Daniel. He placed his hand inside the breast pocket of his suit jacket and pulled out the thick envelope totaling fifty thousand dollars. "You get me involved in more shit, Bren Ryan. It's a damn good thing I'm an FBI agent. Otherwise, they'd have frisked me, and I don't know how I would have explained this bankroll."

"Oh my God, Jess." She gave him a quizzical look. "How?"

"Your sister's a successful business woman in Creede—bought into a general contracting business that builds million-dollar log homes."

"You're kidding." Bren touched the envelope and then pulled her hand back. "I don't have any place to put it."

Jess eyed her outfit. Boot-cut jeans, a white shirt neatly tucked into her waistband, and a tan corduroy jacket. "Stuff it in your waistband and pull out your shirt, the jacket will conceal it. There's no way in hell I'm keeping it." He handed it to her, pulled her close for a hug, and kissed the top of her head. "I gotta go."

Jess skirted hospital staff and dodged moving stretchers and crash carts lining the hallways as he made his way toward the elevators, his mind, all the while, replaying the words of Kate's father. Daniel Fallon had gotten it right. His daughter was definitely a hard one, more like hardhead, hard-ass, hard . . .

"Oh hell," he mumbled. He turned right and jogged down the corridor to the elevators and into the direct path of the woman who was either poised to rip him a new asshole or determined to piss him off without uttering a single word.

The thought of being in this metal can any longer than he absolutely had to unnerved him. But because of her, this time, he'd hold it together.

Kate had him breaking all the rules. He had fallen in love with a federal witness, who was still married to the asshole he'd shot just over twenty-four hours ago in Colorado. He had already received an ass chewing from his commander for the seven days it took him to bring Kate Reynolds in. So what the hell, he thought as he stood next to her inside the elevator, only to have her step away, giving him her usual cool exterior. He reached over and hit the emergency button. The elevator slowed then gave a lurch before coming to a complete stop.

"Are you insane?" As endearing and vulnerable as she looked with the soft, white lacy thing under her suit jacket she had left unbuttoned, her stance was combative. He wanted to pull her into his arms, but she looked ready to strike if he came any closer.

"We need to talk."

"We have nothing to say. I'm a federal witness, and you're a federal agent assigned to get me from point A to point B." She folded her arms across her chest.

Jess took two easy strides to her, pressing her against the elevator wall with his body. Cupping her defiant chin, he tilted her head up so he could see her clearly. "You don't really believe that, Kate."

She attempted to pull away, but he kept her delicate jaw held fast in his grip.

His expression softened. "I wanted to tell you about your father. I struggled for the right moment. It just wasn't there. Once you discovered who I was, until just a few minutes ago in ICU, you've refused to talk to me. And when we did talk . . ." He paused and angled his face. "Actually, I was talking, you were yelling." He grinned. "The point is, Kate, we haven't had one moment alone since we got off that damn plane." And he meant completely alone.

He took a deep breath as he settled in against her soft body. Her once tidy hair hung like a mass of auburn silk against her shoulders. That unkempt hair had him reminiscing. She looked like that the night she'd begged him to take her—to make love to her. To love her. Well, damn it, she had gotten what she wanted. He *was* in love with her. "I get it, Kate. You're angry because I lied to you. I hated like hell deceiving you. But at the time your sister's reasoning had merit."

She narrowed her eyes into him. "Don't blame Bren—"

"I'm not. I'm only explaining my thought process and why, we . . ." He cleared his throat. "I mean, *I* chose to use an alias."

Her body relaxed a little against him.

"I appreciate your candor, Agent Parker, but—"

Maybe he was just Agent Parker to her now. But he was close enough to her that he could feel her heart beat. Not slow rhythmic ticks, but erratic beats like she had just finished a race.

He held her gaze. He could always tell by her eyes where he stood with her. What they told him now was she was lying to him and to herself.

He traced her cheek with his finger, and her eyes softened. Her heart still beat frantically against his chest. He tilted her face up to his, placing her lips in the right position so that, if he timed it correctly, after he told her what he had to say, he'd be able to quell her argument before the words ever left her lips.

"Kate," he said, his voice rough with emotion, "I'm in love with you."

As he expected, she opened her lips to rebuff his proclamation, and he was ready with his counterassault.

His lips came down hard, crushing hers beneath his. She stiffened. Who did he think he was, anyway? Yes, she was angry. He'd lied to her. But his lips were making it increasingly difficult to stay mad at him. She struggled to pull away, but his strong hand pressed against the back of her neck sent a warm sensation down her spine.

His hand now rested on her rib cage below the swell of her breast. A moan escaped her as he glided his thumb across her nipple, sending what felt like a warm lava flow from her belly to rest in the soft center between her thighs.

She pushed her hips against his, needing to feel him pressed snug to her. What she didn't expect was to find him long and hard pressed up against her. She wanted to pull away from his lovemaking and say, "You've got it all wrong, Agent Parker. Yeah, you're a man, and you're well versed in giving a woman want she wants, but that's as far as it goes—for me, anyway. So take your rugged good looks, your masterful lips, and your dick, and hit the road."

But she couldn't, because he was right. He wasn't just a federal officer to her or an easy lay like she had told him that morning on the switchbacks. She had fallen in love with him, too.

Whether his name was Agent Parker, the staunch FBI agent, or Nick Foster, the strong and capable retired Navy SEAL, at this very moment, as his lips tangled with hers, she knew who he truly was to her.

He was and would forever be Jess, the man who at present sent shock waves through her body. She couldn't deny him even if she wanted to.

CHAPTER FORTY-FIVE

Baltimore, Maryland, two months later . . .

KATE TOOK A DEEP BREATH, LEANED TOWARD THE MIRROR, AND pressed her warm hands on the white porcelain sink, its smooth surface cool against her palms. August 23, another blistering day in Charm City—Baltimore—where air conditioning wasn't a luxury but a requirement. She couldn't blame her condition on the U.S. District Court. Cool air wafted down from the ceiling vent, but it did nothing to curtail the heat rising in her face or sweat on her skin, making her feel as if she'd stuck her head into a gigantic oven.

She hadn't seen Jack since the FBI had taken him into custody outside the Last Chance Mine over two months ago. It would have been fine by her if she never had to look into those steel-blue eyes again. But she didn't have a choice, not today. Today the prosecution would be laying the groundwork for their case against Jack. Kate's testimony was the underpinning to their success.

Her tribulations with Jack Reynolds read like a Hollywood movie: Justice for a cop's murder brought them together. Jack's intimidation tactics kept them united, and cold-blooded murder tore them asunder.

Today she'd face her nemesis for the last time. Her stomach fluttered like the first dip of a rollercoaster—eager, yet uneasy.

The door to the restroom swung open, and she jerked.

"Mrs. Reynolds?" A tall brunette security officer stood in the doorway. "Court is in session."

Kate cleared the double wooden doors of the courtroom and sat next to Bren, their hands automatically intertwining with one another. Her sister looked nervous, more nervous than Kate, if that was possible. She tightened her hold on Bren's hand and gave her a quick smile. "It's going to be okay."

Bren smiled back and nudged her shoulder with hers. "I know . . . *I know,*" she added. "I just don't like the idea of him being so close to you."

Kate searched the courtroom. Jess wasn't there yet. She wouldn't let that bother her. He said he would be there, and she trusted him. And this was his case—his testimony scheduled for late in the day.

She needed to see him, Kate was discovering. She missed not having him around. And the times they had spoken by phone over the past several weeks did nothing to make the distance between them more bearable.

"He'll be here, sweetie." Bren smiled mischievously. "Agent Dependable wouldn't miss this if his pants were on fire. Trust me. He wants to see Jack get what he deserves . . . We all do."

Kate relaxed, glad that Bren had followed her instructions and chosen two inconspicuous seats on the prosecution side, several rows back—far enough away from Jack, but strategic enough so she could watch him from a distance. It wasn't until the solid-wood doors closed and the bailiff locked the door from inside that she stiffened. Her eyes did a frantic search of the room. No Jess.

The prosecution and defense teams were assembled up front. She recognized Jack's legal counsel, and right away her anxiety level shot up. Jason Devereaux, Jack's lead defense attorney, was a hotshot. His tactics for rattling the witness were well publicized. She'd made it a point to check out Jack's counsel prior to the trial and was prepared against losing her composure. She could do this, hotshot or not. The trick: Block the dapper trial lawyer and his charismatic smile from her mind, along with his slick tongue. She'd answer his questions. She *had* to answer his questions. But she wouldn't give him any slack with which to hang her. Jack Reynolds couldn't be afforded that luxury. He was going down—today.

Kate refused to revert back to her nervous habits. She placed her hands in her lap and willed herself not to touch her cuticles. He couldn't hurt her anymore. She scanned the courtroom. Thank God federal courts used U.S. marshals to guard their courtrooms.

The marshal posted up front looked too mean to toy with, his serious scowl, broad, muscular frame, and Glock 22 positioned at the ready. No, he definitely didn't resemble the sheriff deputies in the courtrooms where she practiced law.

Kate listened to the proceedings. Occasionally, she'd glance at Jack, grateful she was looking at the back of his well-groomed dark head of hair. After sixty days in jail, he still appeared physically fit. Jack always looked great in a suit.

By the time the clock hanging on the back wall read eleven forty-two, the prosecution and defense had laid the foundation for their cases. The prosecutor, Druscilla Chambers, systematically took the judge and the jury through the sequence of events that had brought Jack to the attention of the FBI. IrishEyes rolled off Druscilla's lips, followed by the true identity of the source behind the screen name, and Jack's back went rigid.

Kate's nerves tingled but didn't fray. She slid forward in her chair. Ignoring Jack's reaction, she eyed the marshal and took comfort. She could get through this.

Jess would be there soon.

"Your Honor, the prosecution would like to call Kathryn Reynolds to the stand."

Kate's stomach flipped, followed by a fleeting nausea. She inhaled, cleared her head, and pushed herself up with her hands. She moved through the row of seats and headed down the center aisle. Pushing the swing gate with one hand, she slipped into an arena that once had been comfortable to her, and she trembled slightly. Jack's penetrating stare scorched her back. She made a bead for the witness stand and stopped in front of the young female court clerk holding an ancient Bible almost four inches thick. She placed her left hand against the leather grain and raised her right hand.

"I, Kathryn Fallon Reynolds, do solemnly swear to tell the truth, the whole truth, and nothing but the truth, so help me God."

The last hose beater entered the driver's side door of the fire truck and finally moved his twenty-five-thousand-pound centipede from all four lanes of I-95. What was it about firefighters and cops? As much as they worked alongside each other—accidents, fires—there was always some underlying irritation. Now Jess knew why. They always needed to make a big production out of everything, pulling out the fire hoses and blocking traffic for hours on a major interstate leading into the one city he needed to get to by nine. And for what? He knew from the scanner in his car there was no one trapped inside. The motorist had called with smoke under his hood and had remained behind the guardrail. With traffic moving, Jess put his slate-gray agency-issued sedan in Drive and slowly inched his way up to the speed limit before burying it past eighty.

Kate's dark eyes invaded his mind several times. He hadn't seen her since he'd left her with the agent assigned to protect her. It had been hell walking away. Good thing his colleague, Agent Rick Powers, also his best friend, had been with him that day and laid it out for him. *Fuck up this investigation with your dick, pal, and you'll be under investigation for an inappropriate* relationship with a federal witness, face possible dismissal from the Bureau, and allow Reynolds to walk on a technicality. Rick's third item on his list of possibilities had Jess taking cold showers. If it guaranteed Reynolds's imprisonment, he could keep his distance from Kate.

Although they spoke on the phone often, he missed her. During last night's phone conversation, he assured her that his supervisor had given him permission to see her before court got underway. Jess had cleared his calendar for the morning; nothing would stop him from being there—on time. The last thing he promised her before hanging up—*I won't be late.* He peered at his dashboard clock and cursed. He'd make it in time for his testimony set for the afternoon, but he'd already missed his eight forty-five rendezvous with Kate and Bren. Anger burned deep. It wasn't his fault. Kate would understand, once he explained, but right now he had no way of notifying her. He had both Kate's and Bren's cell numbers, but neither picked up, not surprising since they were in court. He would have thought, at least, Bren would have checked her cell phone when he didn't show up—at the very least respond to his text. Kate was probably on the stand.

Jess parked the car, traveled the three blocks to the courthouse, and took his usual mode of transportation to the third floor—the stairs—and turned down the hall, heading toward the doors of courtroom 3C. He pulled the handle. It didn't budge. "Shit, locked." With all the added security, he should have counted on that, the little red eye of the security pad a maddening beacon of irritation. He scanned the area to find a potbellied security guard heading in his direction, his belt of keys, mace, and handcuffs swaying on his wide hips.

"Court's in session. You'll have to wait until recess."

Jess examined his nameplate, Wendell Wadell. *They got the waddle right.* This day was going to shit. First, the firemen and the traffic they'd caused with their need for drama. And now Wendell Wadell was going to flex his muscle. Jess reached into his breast pocket.

"Whoa there, fella. Put your hand out to your side. You just can't go reaching into your pockets like that." He gave Jess a wry look. "Did you go through the magnetometer?"

Jess moaned and placed his arms out. "Look, I'm Special Agent Parker with the FBI. My ID is in my pocket. Either let me retrieve it, or reach in and get it yourself."

Wendell nodded. "That's okay." He reached behind him and swung out his own personally issued mini-magnetometer. "I'll just check you myself."

Was he even listening?

Wendell raised the wand and waved it around Jess's body.

What a moron.

Jess stood there, his jaw flexing. In a minute, he was going to pump twenty-one into the stupid son of a bitch and steal his passcode key.

Little red lights started going off, accompanied with a siren when Wendell hit on Jess's right hip. Jess rolled his eyes.

I guess dumb-ass didn't expect an FBI agent to be carrying a gun.

Wendell's eyes lit up, and he yelled, "Gun!" Before Jess could grasp the situation, he was surrounded by Wendell look-alikes, every one of them drawing down on him and looking as if they were going to puke. That was all he needed, to be shot because some rent-a-cop freaked.

Jess raised his hands above his head. "Wendell," he said in a firm voice. "I told you, I'm a federal agent. My ID is in my pocket, and the gun is my service weapon." Jess waved his right hand. "I'm going to get my ID. *Don't shoot me.*" Jess's words, a serrated edge, brought the guard's eyes into focus.

He nodded. "Okay, but no funny stuff."

Right.

Jess reached into his suit jacket and pulled out his ID and let it hang open for Wendell and the rest of his colleagues.

Wendell sighed and looked around to the misfits in badges. "He's FBI."

No shit.

Wendell wiped the sweat from his brow and reholstered his weapon, waving to everyone. "It's okay. Put your guns away."

Jess replaced his ID and wondered how the hell these slovenly, out-of-shape guards had been cleared to carry firearms. "Okay, Wendell, open the door."

"No sir." Wendell shook his head.

What the hell?

CHAPTER FORTY-SIX

KATE'S LEGS BEGAN TO CRAMP. SHE CHECKED HER WATCH. SHE'D been on the stand for over an hour. The questions from the prosecution went smoothly—she had expected that. The defense attorney would be a totally different story. Devereaux's cross-examination made her wish she had magical powers. Being invisible would be a nice one.

She wasn't on trial, but the seasoned defense attorney was masterful at manipulating evidence, placing innuendo, or creating doubt, reducing the most credible witnesses to babbling fools. She didn't want to be one of them.

Jason Devereaux stepped up to the podium. The man oozed elegance right down to his Louis Vuitton charcoal suit. He shot his cuffs and leaned over the podium.

Devereaux smiled at her and then fixed the jury with a decisive stare. "Testimony is only as good as the witness. Integrity is crucial in proving or disproving actual events."

"Objection, Your Honor." Drusilla Chambers remained seated, her back rigid, shoulders squared. "Right out of the gate, defense counsel is testifying instead of asking the witness a question."

"Sustained." Judge Masters's gaze shifted toward the defense table. "Counsel, this is your warning. You know better."

Devereaux, not seeming to be fazed, cast a reproachful gaze in Kate's direction. "Mrs. Reynolds, isn't it correct that three years ago, on January 6, you visited NIH's blood bank for your scheduled phlebotomy under the pretense of stealing your own blood?"

A wave of gasps erupted in the gallery and prepared to crash down on Kate, which was why Charlie Robertson had wanted to stay in Creede. Kate Reynolds was not innocent. She had been forced to break the law, and the bastard with his self-satisfied smile and designer gold-rimmed glasses beading in on her knew it.

But she wasn't on trial, so where the hell was the prosecution's bloody object—

"Objection."

Thank you.

Drusilla Chambers flushed with an indignation that matched her cranberry suit, stood with her hands on her hips. Devereaux glanced back, dismissing her as nothing more than a bug that he was getting ready to squash.

He smirked and turned back to Kate. "A real Thelma and Louise, you and your sis—"

The gavel came down, and her ears smarted when it connected with the sound block. It didn't matter. Devereaux got his point across. She would have used the same ploy under the circumstances.

Kate stole a look at the defense table, embarrassment flooding her cheeks. Jack sat back in his chair with a tight smile, silently laughing at her discomfort.

She gave Devereaux her full attention. She knew he was going to shove everything she did to escape Jack down her throat. He had to know he was going to lose. But that didn't mean he wasn't going to take a potshot or two on his way down.

"Isn't it a fact, Mrs. Reynolds, you and Bryan Wexler were extremely close?"

"We were friends. His wife and I best—"

"Isn't it correct that when Bryan Wexler lay dying from a strong-armed robbery, he asked for you specifically, not his wife?"

Robbery, my ass. Of course, not proven—yet.

"He was killed by—"

"The question, Mrs. Reynolds."

Stoked with his innuendo, Kate's insides fired up. She and Bryan did have a special relationship—close friends, nothing more. She didn't want his memory tarnished because this asshole in his meticulously tailored suit loved drama. She glared at Jack. He was every bit responsible for the questions that sprang from Devereaux's mouth. Bryan didn't deserve this. And where the hell was prosecution's objection?

"Objection. Irrelevant. Kate Reynolds is not on trial here, Your Honor." Drusilla Chambers stood at attention.

Way to go, Dru . . . only a little too late.

Judge Masters slammed the gavel and tossed it onto his desk. He leaned over and slid his wire-rimmed glasses down his patrician nose, his eyes tiny pinpricks zeroing in on Devereaux. "You're that close to contempt of court, counselor." He looked at the prosecution's table. "Sustained."

Devereaux nodded. Kate scanned the courtroom again, but still no Jess. She ignored the pinch of anxiety along the base of her neck. The courtroom, full to capacity, made it difficult to pick anyone out. When she finally locked in on her sister, there was no need for words. Bren knew her concerns and shrugged. She, too, didn't know what to make of Jess's absence.

Kate took a sip of her water and swallowed. Devereaux's hand rested negligently across the podium, his Harvard Law School ring glistening under the recessed lights of the courtroom.

He cocked his head in reflection. "We live in an age of advanced technology. Digital cameras and digital recorders, great gadgets. I have one of each myself." Kate's slim Olympus tape recorder still lay flat against the podium, next to Devereaux's elbow, where the prosecution had left it. Excerpts had been played for the benefit of the jury. Jack's voice unmistakable. "But the authenticity of a recording can be challenged. This recorder here," he said holding it up for the jury, "runs about $29.99 in Walmart. Makes you question its reliability."

Why was she not surprised? Kate grabbed hold of the edge of the oak chair she sat in. She wanted to wrap her fingers around Devereaux's neck. She waited for prosecution to herald an objection. Nothing.

"This particular model allows you to hook in to your PC. There are several software packages that allow you to dub recordings." Devereaux paused.

Kate didn't want to alienate Judge Masters. Disobeying his unwritten rules in court could get you slapped with contempt. Best to remain silent until Devereaux asked her another question. Her answer would be respectful. She couldn't afford to engage in a heated volley. Although, Drusilla Chambers didn't need any help from Kate. *Not.* For all the wind with her at pretrial, she had been reduced to a light breeze.

"Mrs. Reynolds, isn't it true that the day the recording was captured, this tape recorder—" Again he displayed it like he was taking orders for it on QVC. "—was dropped and left for several hours in moist vegetation, in the high altitudes of the San Juan Mountains, subject to the elements?"

This was insane. Kate's eyes pierced the prosecution table. Drusilla sat stoically, picking a piece of lint off her nicely pressed cranberry suit. Unbelievable. Couldn't she see the objection in Devereaux's line of questioning? No more nice. If the prosecution couldn't do its job and keep her away from the saber teeth of the defense, she would.

Kate took a breath. She hadn't argued a case in over three years. Other than her verbal sparring with Ben, she'd had no need to plead a case. But this was personal. The evidence was sound, she knew. But sometimes Goliath, even though his defeat was inevitable, needed to know she wouldn't be bullied.

"Yes. I dropped it. Jack had a—"

"Thank you, Mrs. Reynolds."

Kate eyed the judge, then the prosecution. "Mr. Devereaux, don't interrupt me. You asked a question, and you're going to let me finish it. I dropped the tape recorder to avoid being shot point-blank by my husband. And in regard to your insinuation about authenticity, I never doctored the tape. As you well know, recordings are classified as 'writings' in the California Evidence Code Section 250, which means they must be authenticated before they can be admitted into evidence, that's California Evidence Code Section 1401(a), *People v. Mayfield*, California, 1997. In regard to whether the voice heard on the tape is Jack Reynolds, as you well know, a recording may also be authenticated by circumstantial evidence. For example, it may be reasonable to infer that the voice on the recording is Jack's voice."

She glanced at Jack, his chair cut to the side of the defense table, the four fingers of his left hand curled around his gold ballpoint pen. His thumb slid back and forth along the gold filigree stem, looking like he could snap the metal in half. She turned her attention back to Devereaux.

"It could only be his because he spoke of matters that were unlikely to have been known by anyone other than him. I know you're thorough, Mr. Devereaux, but if you need to refresh your memory, try *People v. Fonville*, California, 1973." She took a sip of water and continued. "Jack was the only one who knew the FBI was on the wrong trail. He didn't bribe Renato Barbosa for his testimony. He hired him. Jack was the only living legal—"

"Objection." Devereaux's arm flew up, and he took a step closer.

Judge Masters shot a fulminating look at Devereaux. "Counsel, you asked the question. You may not like the answer, but Mrs. Reynolds may finish her response." He nodded for Kate to continue.

Kate cleared her throat. "Jack was the only living legal heir that anyone knew about to the Reynolds shipping fortune, worth, at the time, seventy-five million. He was greedy, Mr. Devereaux. He wasn't about to share his fortune with his illegitimate sister. The wire transfer for ten thousand, prior to Jenna McGuinn's death, is proof of payment, which he admitted on tape—his words, his voice. There's your beyond a reasonable doubt, counselor."

The gallery grew silent, the judge exercising extreme calm. Devereaux, for once, looked out of sorts, flipping through a stack of files.

Kate glanced at Jack, whose complexion was flushed. He looked ready to tear across the defense table, but the U.S. marshal had zeroed in on him, his hand resting on his steel baton.

Jack had caused all of this. And she'd be damned if she would shrink from his penetrating gaze. "Jenna McGuinn didn't know Jack and his millions existed. She didn't know her biological father was worth millions or that he had finally decided to reach out to her prior to his death—but Jack did. He couldn't stand the thought of sharing his fortune with her. Or with anyone." Kate turned to Jack. His eyes, sharp and cutting, met her stare and held. "The sad thing is, Jack never met Jenna McGuinn personally. He never spoke with her on the phone. He didn't even know if she, in some way, resembled him or his father. All he cared about was getting rid of the threat, and he wasn't above cold-blooded murder to accomplish that." Kate shrugged. "And, who's to say Jenna would have wanted her share? Maybe she would have been content to know she had a brother. From all accounts by her employer, friends, neighbors, and family, Jenna McGuinn seemed content with her life the way it was."

A loud scuff sounded as Jack stood abruptly, his face taut and red and twisted. He opened his mouth. "It was none of your damn business, Kate. None of this had to happen. Barbosa should have nev—" Jack's voice broke off when the marshal pressed him hard on the shoulder, shoving him down in his seat.

As pitiful as he looked, Kate wouldn't feel sorry for Jack Reynolds. He was responsible for the demise of too many people. The ones remaining, the families of the victims, had their world shattered forever because Jack had to have it all.

"You're right, Jack. I realize now the murder of Trooper McGuinn was supposed to go unsolved. You'd done your homework, opened an untraceable bank account offshore, and hired your very own assassin." Kate laughed derisively. "Too bad for you, your hired assassin lacked discipline. He just couldn't help himself when he read the trooper's brass nameplate—McGuinn. Must have glistened under the highway lights like a pot of gold, his victim only inches away. The 125K payoff that much closer. There's that lack of discipline I talked about. He shot her with Ryan and Kristie Stolze present and connected you to the crime when you were named the prosecutor for the case. You scrambled then, paid Barbosa an additional 125K to keep his mouth shut and testify in court."

"Bitch." Jack lurched forward. Devereaux, Jack's height and build, grabbed Jack's arm, keeping him glued to the floor. The marshal grabbed his handcuffs, prepared to make an arrest.

Judge Masters slammed the gavel down. "Order!" He stared at Devereaux. "Control your client."

Kate reconnected with the man she shared a last name with. He sat slumped over the defense table, his face buried in his hands. She clenched her teeth. His display of emotion was not from remorse—she felt sure. As with everything connected with Jack, it was all about him. For once his actions had caught up with him, and, judging by his demeanor, he knew it. That gave her some consolation.

"I'm calling for a recess." Judge Masters eyed the defense counsel. "All counsel, my chambers—now!"

Finally. She had been on the witness stand for over two hours. She needed to find Jess. It wasn't like him not to show up. Something must have happened. The bailiff gave her the all clear. She kept her eyes trained on Jack, when she stepped down from the witness stand, refusing to look away. She wasn't the Kate he remembered. She'd survived him, but, even better, she had thrived and would continue to do so.

That would eat at him for the rest of his life.

She looked away then. She was done with his bullshit.

Kate cleared the center stage of the courtroom and reached out to the swinging gate, relieved to take a break. She glanced out of the corner of her eye, and Jack jumped to his feet. She turned toward the commotion. Jack's chair clattered to the floor. He rammed the marshal, causing him to lose his balance, and Jack grabbed for his gun. Her heart lurched. The marshal and Jack struggled with his gun. A gunshot rang out, and the marshal dropped to the floor. Kate pressed back desperately against the wooden gate, only to have Jack snag her by her right arm.

He yanked her back and whispered hard into her ear, "No one leaves me, Kate." His head swung wildly from side to side, his voice a low growl. "I'll kill her if you don't back off!" He wiped his brow against her head, the gun digging into her side.

The two guards remained at the entrance, dumbstruck. Kate struggled to escape, but he snaked his arm around her waist and jerked her in reverse. Her back slammed into his chest. His arm, a vise holding her in place, took the fight out of her.

Kate whispered to him, "Jack, they'll kill you. Once you shoot me, they'll kill you. Do you understand?"

He was breathing hard. "It doesn't matter anymore, Kate. Don't you see? They're going to fry my ass." He pulled her snug and rubbed his head against hers. "I loved you. It wasn't supposed to end this way. Renato fucked up. He should have never killed her at the traffic stop."

"Jack, it's okay," she said softly. "Just let me go. You don't know the verdict, but you'll definitely die if you shoot me."

"Then we'll go together."

Jess pushed agitated fingers through his short-cropped hair. His white dress shirt, wrinkled from the ride in the car, remained damp with perspiration from anxiety over Kate and frustration with Wendell. Disheveled, out of sorts, he'd been arguing with this *jackass* for the past twenty minutes, using every ounce of patience not to shoot him.

"Wendell, open the goddamn—"

The gunshot exploded in Jess's brain. Instinctively, he pulled his gun. He turned toward the guards. "Get away from the door." He sent a menacing glance toward Wendell. "You either open the door, or I'll blow a hole in it."

Wendell reached for his back pocket and found the passkey. Fingers shaking, he slid the card through the electronic lock, and a light buzz sounded before the door lock clicked. He stepped back. Wendell wasn't only an asshole, he was a yellow bastard. Jess put his hand on the knob and opened it slowly. He had a direct view up the center aisle, and his whole life—Kate—became razor sharp.

Jess slipped inside the courtroom and caught a glimpse of Bren, who had crouched down at the end of the row of chairs.

"Where the hell have you been?" she whispered fiercely. "Do something before he kills her!"

Jess let his training take over. Jack held Kate tight against his chest. Dragging her backward, he jammed the gun under her chin, snapping her neck back. Jack's head swiveled from side to side searching for an avenue of escape—there was none. The arm in which he held the gun hard and fast against Kate's throat trembled, and Jess ignored the sick sensation spreading through his gut.

He'd never trained to be a sharpshooter. His Glock 22 wasn't equipped with a scope. But his entire life stood forty paces away. If he missed, he could kill Kate. Sweat began to pool between Jess's shoulder blades. Jack hadn't seen him yet, too involved with Kate to notice. Jess pushed past spectators spilling into the aisle as they fell and tripped over one another, surging toward the only exit. Wendell and the other security guards scrambled in behind him, adding to the pandemonium. He sent up a silent prayer that none of them decided to fire their weapons. He crept low, the herd thinning as he slid between them, identifying himself as FBI and ordering them to move to the rear.

A hand touched his left shoulder, and Jess glanced to the side. His buddy Rick was beside him, crouched down, motioning he was going to the left.

Jess nodded and whispered, "I'm going to take the shot. If I miss . . ." His words floated, and he couldn't finish his thought.

Rick nodded. "You won't."

Still crouched approximately ten feet away, Jess verified his backstops. This wasn't like shooting at the range. But if he missed, Kate would be dead, and it didn't matter what happened to him then.

Okay, Parker, just aim and shoot.

He struggled. Maybe he'd be better off calling Jack's name and then shoot. Throw the sick bastard off. He decided on that plan, stood, and took aim. "Reynolds, drop the gun."

Jack stopped, stared in Jess's direction, and smirked. With no hesitation, Jess pulled the trigger. Pure hell, he could only describe the millisecond between when he pulled the trigger and when the dark, grisly hole appeared on Jack Reynolds's forehead. Kate stumbled forward, caught by Jason Devereaux, her expression one of surprise and relief. Jess headed in her direction but found himself sandwiched between those still remaining in the courtroom. When he had finally cleared a path, she was gone.

The bailiff, with the judge's orders, rushed Kate back to his chambers. He spoke with her briefly, offered to stay, but she declined. She needed to be alone. Trembling, she paced the paisley carpet. She couldn't stop shaking.

Jack was dead. The bullet had come within inches of her own head. She'd never been more frightened in that moment—frightened for Jess. She'd put him in an extremely difficult situation.

A knock came and Kate tensed.

"Kate." She recognized the rasp, along with the stress in his voice.

She wanted desperately to see him.

He knocked again but harder. "Kate, open the door. I know you're in there. This is ridiculous." Jess kept up the pounding on the thick wooden door of Judge Masters's chambers.

Why was he making this so hard on her? She loved him so much that she was willing to let him go. Didn't he understand? Jess had killed for her. She had made him kill. Jack had it coming; she just wished it wasn't Jess who had been forced to pull the trigger.

"Come on, sweetheart, just open—"

Kate unlocked the door and swung it open. Jess was dressed in a dark-blue suit and a familiar powder-blue dress shirt and burgundy tie—so handsome the way his athletic body filled out his suit. He stood there with his hand on the door frame. His blue eyes serious, the tendon in his jaw flexed.

He wasn't happy.

Kate leaned into the doorframe and rested her head against it. "You need to stop." If hurting him now would save him from a life of trouble with her, then she'd play hardball. "Jess, it's over. In fact, it never really began. I want to forget this . . . this courtroom . . . Jack." She couldn't stop from trembling. "My life isn't here in Maryland anymore. Your career—"

"Kate." He stepped forward. His rugged hand caressed her cheek. "Baby, don't do this. I know you're hurting. I know you want to forget all the bad stuff, but don't forget us." He pulled her away from the door and brought her into his arms. "You need to talk about what happened. You need to talk to *me*."

His eyes crinkled in the corners against his tanned, handsome face, and she saw his pain. Pain she had caused. Jess Parker never took a case to bed—poor choice of words. She would have laughed if she wasn't so damned heartbroken. The sad thing was, she'd never once said, "I love you." And she so very much did—love Jess with all her heart. Now those words could never leave her lips. She was going to protect him from herself.

She'd connected with him long ago as IrishEyes. Although she'd only known him as Jess Parker in the flesh for a total of three days since he'd admitted his true identity—once on the plane coming back to Maryland. The night they spent at his condo—totally against FBI protocol. And the last, when she locked into his eyes as he concentrated on her and the shot that meant everything.

It was at that moment when she realized the position she had put him in and the turmoil she created in his perfectly organized life. And it was now, as he held her so close she could hear his heart thrumming against her own, the warmth of his hands tender, yet completely capable, caressing her waist, that she would set him free.

"I don't love you." She pulled away. "Go home, Agent Parker."

CHAPTER FORTY-SEVEN

Creede, Colorado, autumn, two months later . . .

K ATE FOLLOWED THE RISING DIRT ROAD TO THE UPPER MESA WEST of Creede, her truck soon clearing the timber supports on either side of the weathered wooden sign above, etched with the words CREEDE CEMETERY. The land here remained untouched by time, a meadow of clumpy grass and wildflowers growing untamed over crumbling tombstones.

She passed several family crypts, safeguarded behind timeworn wrought-iron fences, parked several yards up, and got out. She searched the graves, a mix of tree trunks carved into monuments, white wooden crosses, simple wooden markers, some flanked by battered fences, and the one she sought made of granite. Her chest tightened.

It has to be here.

She kept walking and studied each grave, her heart giving a little when she came to it. Kate knelt down, her hand coming to rest on the granite stone—MICHAEL JARED COULTER, LAWMAN, HUSBAND, AND BELOVED FATHER. He'd asked for forgiveness . . . There was none to give. Sheriff Mike Coulter, her friend, died saving her. Had she never chosen Creede for her new life, Mike would still be alive.

Jack had taken a lot of things away from her. Her self-esteem and her freedom had suffered devastating blows. But it was the people he had taken away that pained her the most. She thought of them often and refused to let their memory fade with time.

Kate regretted every day she spent away from her family, but it was her father she missed the most. She'd never had the opportunity to kiss him good-bye before she'd disappeared. Older and wiser, he'd have nixed their plans from the beginning had they confided in him. He learned it from Bren, after the fact. She didn't want to think about his pained expression or the hurt she'd caused him over the past three years.

Even now that he recovered from his stroke, which she was sure she'd help caused, he never brought up those events or the time they'd lost.

He loved her that much.

And, finally, Kristie Stolze had been given back her life with her young son—less eight years and her loving husband, Ryan.

Now that was one footnote that would forever be left dangling on the page for Kate. She'd never forgive herself for protecting her own ass and ignoring her conscience. A man had died because of her inaction. The law professionals could explain it away and had, but for Kate.

A shadow formed above her, and she jumped.

"Kate?"

She turned around and pulled her Stetson down to protect her eyes from the sun. "Tess." Kate swallowed and stood. "I'm sorry. I should have asked your permission to visit his grave."

Tess reached over and scooped Kate into her arms. Kate stiffened and then wrapped her arms around Tess. Her tears burned, and she let herself mourn for her friend. "I'm so sorry, Tess. Mike never would have—"

Tess pulled on Kate's braid and stepped back. "Don't make me mad, Kate." She pointed a manicured finger in Kate's direction. "This was not your fault. Mike made the wrong choice. He should have told me about his past and told your husband to go to hell." Her serious face softened. "He loved you. Whether you were Charlie or Kate, he loved you so much, sweetheart. Don't ruin it by blaming yourself."

Kate smiled. She'd remain in Creede and live with the good memories of the past. She'd remember Mike, a loving soul who did his best to protect her from her past, and she'd move on from here. Life slowed but never stopped, and there was too much to experience and not enough time to dwell on sadness.

Looping her arms around Tess, she pulled her close. "If you and the kids need anything, you call."

Tess gave her a tight squeeze and drew back. "I will." She kissed Kate's cheek. "You settling back in?"

"I just got back yesterday." She cocked her head. "Any idea why Shelley and Gunner moved out?"

"Ask Ben, honey." She clasped Kate's hand. "Have lunch with me at Tommyknocker's when you're settled."

"I will. I'll see you later." Kate turned to walk away.

Kate hopped in her truck, silent tears rolling down her face as Tess knelt in front of Mike's grave. She allowed herself a moment to collect herself and started the engine, pulling out. She cut out of the cemetery and headed toward the highway and downtown Creede. Colorado in fall, the aspens in full color, a mix of gorgeous oranges and yellows, welcomed her back, and she smiled.

She pulled left onto Main Street, anxious, yet relieved to be back as she slid into an open parking space in front of Sterling Log Homes. She wanted to surprise Ben. She hadn't given him a specific date for her return. She only hoped he didn't make good on his promise to give her job away. He was joking, of course. She didn't think he wanted to deal with a hellion if and when he ever tried to sever their partnership.

Kate took off her Stetson, cleared the front office, and opened his door. "Hey, the 'Prodigal Partner' has returned."

Ben looked up from his desk and grinned. "Hey, yourself." He stood and stepped around his desk. Ben wrapped her up into his all-encompassing arms. "You look great." He pulled her back and gazed into her eyes. "I'm sorry about . . . you know."

Kate shrugged. "It's okay. Jack deserved everything he got."

Ben cocked his head. "Where's your FBI agent?"

Kate nervously twirled her Stetson in her hand. "I thought it best to end our relationship." She shook her head. "Too many emotional memories."

"Huh." Ben leaned his butt against the desk. "I thought you loved him?"

Kate dropped into the chair and stared up at Ben and ignored his question. "This has been a long day." She gave him a half smile. "Sorry, I'm feeling more tired these days."

Ben arched an eyebrow. "You sick?"

Kate shook her head. "No."

"Sure? I could get Shelley to make you some homemade soup."

Kate shot him a sideways glance. "You could, could you? Since when does Shelley have time to make homemade soup with waitressing at Tommyknocker's?"

Ben held up his left hand, revealing a gold band.

"Ben, you devil." Kate sprang to her feet. "Why didn't you tell me the two of you got married?"

Ben shrugged. "I don't know. It didn't really seem appropriate under the circumstances, especially with what you were going through."

Kate drew him into her own bear hug. "I'm so happy for you two."

"Me too." Ben sat on the edge of the desk and crossed his arms. "Are you back to work?"

She smiled. "Yes sir."

"Good. Are you too tired to talk to a prospective client today?"

"No. I'm fine." She didn't want to admit that a nap would be more appealing. After all, she was back, and she had duties to fulfill. "Who's the client?"

"The new sheriff. He was hired about a week ago by the town council. I've never met him, and I'm embarrassed to say, I don't even know his name. Tom Davenport from the board of county commissioners asked me to stop by and pay him a visit this afternoon. He's staying at the Coulter cabin until we build him a home."

Kate leaned in and gave Ben a kiss on the cheek. "I'll go now. Do you think I should call first?"

Ben smiled. "No. He's expecting me." He laughed. "Just make sure you explain you're my partner. We don't want him to get any wrong ideas about your status around here."

"I see you haven't lost your sense of humor."

"Nope." Ben turned around, grabbed a Sterling Log Homes pencil, notebook, and a tape measure. "I don't know what your truck looks like, but just in case you can't find what you need."

Kate laughed. "Thanks." She took the items of a general contractor from Ben and turned to leave, then swung back. "I'll call you once I have this guy pinned down."

"I'm counting on it." Ben gave her a wide smile.

Jeez, I didn't know his lips could stretch that far. Weird. Too happy for Ben Sterling. She shrugged it off and headed out the door.

Kate headed toward Love Lake and Mike's cabin—funny, it would always be Mike's cabin to her. She lowered the window, the mountain air helping to settle her stomach. She turned down the winding gravel road toward the cabin, and a twinge of sadness pinched the back of her eyes. Stepping from her truck, she grabbed the small notebook and pencil and headed toward the steps.

The past flowed through her, standing on Mike's front porch, Love Lake glistening behind her. Kate shook her head with the irony. The last time she was in this very spot she was running away from . . . nothing. She put the memory away and knocked on the door. No response. She looked behind her. There was a black pickup parked off to the right. She knocked again, still nothing. And then she tried the door, and the knob turned in her hand. *Well, damn.* Ben said he was expecting him.

Curious who the new sheriff was, she slipped inside. She surveyed the room and found the bedroom door cracked with light spilling though the slit of the door. He must be in the bathroom. This was awkward. Thinking better of it, she turned and then stopped. She heard the familiar creak of the door, and her shoulder slinked upwards.

Crap! He's going to catch me.

The heat crept into her face. How embarrassing—she had interrupted the guy washing up. While his face was hidden beneath a white terry cloth towel, Kate contemplated taking off before he found her standing in what he considered to be his home. He spoke, but his voice was muffled. She got the gist. He was explaining why he hadn't heard her knock and began to remove the towel and then repeated his earlier statement, "Hey, I heard the . . ."

They both stood, and the weight of their stares collided and held. And then she got angry. "Who put you up to this?" She held up a hand. "Don't bother. This has Ben Sterling written all over it."

Jess took a step toward her. "You put me up to this. If you wouldn't have been so bullheaded in Baltimore, I wouldn't have had to call Ben."

"Ben?"

"The man knows you inside and out. He told me the sheriff position hadn't been filled and suggested I consider it."

She shook her head and bit down on her bottom lip. "You quit the Bureau?"

"Early retirement."

"You love your job."

"Not anymore."

"Why would you quit the Bureau for a small, uneventful, Western town like Creede?"

Jess gave her a knowing look. She guessed that was a stupid question. For months, Creede had been splashed over the national news, CNN, FOX. A real den of intrigue. But "eventful" was in the past, and Creede had reverted back to a sleepy Western town. Jess wasn't here because he was looking for a slow-paced way of life, and she didn't know how she felt about that.

"Go on." Jess's prodding brought her out of her stupor.

"Okay, was uneventful . . . you know what I mean. Jess, you'll get bored."

"I doubt it."

She needed to be hard on him. He *would* grow bored of Creede. She didn't want him, someday, to look at her and regret his decision. He needed to go back. If he stayed, he'd find out about her secret, and then he'd really feel duty bound to stay. No, Special Agent Jess Parker was going home.

Kate squared her shoulders and lied. "I don't want you here. You don't belong here." She wanted to run into his arms and never let go. Instead, she reached down deep and threw daggers. "Creede's my home, not yours, so take your federal ass back to D.C. and leave me alone." Kate turned on her heels, headed out the door, and down the wooden steps.

The curse words flew out of his mouth, his bare feet slapping the hardwood floor after her. Realizing she had left her keys in the cabin, she passed her truck, tossed her notebook and pencil along with her Stetson into the bed, and headed for the dock—which was stupid. It was October. She certainly couldn't swim away from him, but there was Mike's boat. She could paddle away from him. She didn't think past that, just kept running. Her boots trampled across the uneven boards of the small pier, and she jumped into the johnboat and began awkwardly untying it from its moorings. She glanced up. He was coming up on her fast, and he looked pissed. She couldn't stifle a small laugh. He was bare-chested and barefoot, cursing across the gravel driveway and looking too sexy for his own good.

She struggled with the ropes. With one untied, she worked on the other when he hit the dock at a dead run. The second rope slipped off the cleat of the dock, and the small fishing boat began to float away. Jess growled, let loose with several more choice words, and then jumped. The boat rocked furiously. His body slammed into hers, sending both of them to the floor of the boat. She struggled against him, and he held her tight. "You're going to listen to me. I'm not leaving."

His full weight was on her for an instant before she thrashed wildly. "Jess, get off me. You're too heavy. You could hurt the baby."

Jess pushed off of her. "Baby?" He gave her a quizzical look. "My baby?"

Kate shook her head and smiled sheepishly.

Jess sat his rump down in the boat and carefully pulled her up on his lap, gathering her to his chest. He placed his strong fingers beneath her chin and gently brought her face up to meet his.

"Kate, I ought to throttle you," he said in a most serious tone, although his eyes were dancing with mischief. "You know you have to marry me. Once Daniel Fallon finds out I knocked up his daughter, he'll demand I do the right thing."

"Oh, I see. You need to own up to your culpability."

"Absolutely, I have a duty to marry you now."

Kate struggled. Exactly, duty-bound Jess. "I don't need your pity, *Parker*."

"Hey, you say that name like it's a bad word. You better be careful, Kate. It's going to be your name in the not too distant future."

She wanted this man in the worst way. She loved him. She wanted to be with him for the rest of her life. When she found out she was pregnant, she'd wanted to brain him. She had slept with him only twice, without protection either time. Something told her it was the first time they made love that their baby was conceived.

"Jess, I'm not holding your feet to the fire on this. You don't have to marry me because of the baby."

Jess's chest rumbled with laughter. "Kate, I wanted to marry you before the baby. I love you, sweetheart." He gently rubbed her belly. "The baby's a bonus." Before she could respond, he pressed his lips up against hers, gentle and tender. She kissed him back, and his kiss deepened. A tidal wave of emotions came over her, and the tears escaped through her lashes. Jess pulled away. "Kate, why are you crying?" The corners of his eyes crinkled with concern.

She shrugged her shoulders and sniffed. "I've never really felt completely settled. The farm . . . I loved the horses, my family, but I never felt content. When I got married to Jack, I truly believed he loved me, but I was only a requirement." Kate wiped her face with the back of her hand. "Oh, Jess, I'm such an idiot. I love you so much, I thought . . ."

"Kate, that's the problem."

She looked at him. "What is?"

A boyish grin crossed his lips. "You think too much."

His lips covered hers, and she sank into him. His strong arms cradled her, and she was safe. Finally, she was in a good place where true, unselfish love triumphed over everything.

I'm home.

Impressions

Mineral County has had its share of outlaws. They call it Americana, now. It amazed him that complete lawlessness could be romanticized in our history books. But it had. His town of Creede had been no exception; in fact, it could be said Creede was the epicenter of wickedness when men would sell a piece of their very soul for a fortune in gold or silver.

Of course, that had been watered down, too—the historians who lived around town preferred a colorful past. He guessed "colorful" had its place. Colorful language maybe, but he'd go for the word "unforgettable." Hell, there was even a museum no more than a couple blocks from his office that said just that.

They say at the height of the mining boom, Creede had swollen to a population of ten thousand, a might big burden on a town that had sprung up overnight and lay sandwiched between the cliffs of the San Juan Mountains.

He had heard their names as a child—the ones that gave cause for the term "Wild West." Sheriff Bat Masterson, Soapy Smith, Calamity Jane, and the infamous Bob Ford—the man solely responsible for killing Jesse James—had all been holed up in Creede at one time or another.

He and his friends had often taken the outlaws' names for their own when they were re-creating shoot-outs and saloon brawls in his backyard in Killeen, Texas.

He preferred the part of lawman over villain.

They were just spirits now. Most died from years of hard livin.'

The town of Creede he knew, his town, had been transformed overnight when the price of silver had plummeted in 1893 and the final ounce of silver was extracted. Creede had rolled up its wooden boardwalks, shut down its saloons and brothels, and moved on.

He chuckled to himself—*his town*—but that's how he felt. It was presumptuous of him to think he owned a town, especially since he was not from around these parts originally.

Plenty before him had made the same claim. Although their claims had been more tangible than his.

He took a long draw on his thin cigar and blew out several circles of smoke as he watched them get larger and then lose their tight shapes before frittering away to nothin.'

He supposed he'd end out his days in Creede and be buried in its only graveyard like the rest of the characters who had stood on the streets of Creede when it was just dust and dirt.

Creede in its current form was a mere pinprick on the Colorado state map, with a population of five hundred, give or take. Nothing much happened in Creede, nowadays.

Sheriff Mike Coulter liked it that way.

He sat immersed in his thoughts as he gazed out on Creede's main thoroughfare, his cowboy boots polished to a high luster, one stacked on top of the other as they rested on his desk.

People respected him, now.

That's how he intended to keep it.

He hadn't thought about the Austin Police Department in years—usually referred to as the APD. *That* man didn't exist. He was a stranger now—thank Jesus for that.

After thirty-five years of service with the Mineral County Sheriff's Department he'd be damned if, at sixty-two and nearing retirement, that past life was going to bubble up like some friggin' oil well that had been dry for years and stain his reputation, in *his town*.

The Town of Creede

While researching the perfect safe haven for my character Kate, I gazed westward. I wanted a close-knit community with small-town charm—a town Charlie Robertson could thrive in and one her husband and the FBI wouldn't think to look in.

I found it in Colorado, also known as the "Centennial State"—named for having received its statehood in 1876, a hundred years after the signing of our nation's Declaration of Independence. I searched many towns in Colorado, all equally beautiful with emerald valleys and majestic mountain ranges. But Creede, with its historic Main Street once carved out from the sweat of dreamers and wooden boardwalks built to bear the footsteps of both lawmen and villains, tugged at my curiosity.

As a child I'd seen movies depicting the discovery of gold and silver and the tent cities that soon followed—*Paint Your Wagon*, starring Clint Eastwood and Lee Marvin, comes to mind. I loved the movie and its premise and couldn't wait to create my own modern-day tale set in this town so steeped in American history.

Although notorious during the silver mining boom of the late 1800s, Creede quietly slipped back into a quaint western town tucked between the cliffs of the San Juan Mountains. Today, with a population of five hundred, give or take, it was perfectly suited as the backdrop for a woman named Charlie Robertson, looking for a fresh start.

A secret little gem not widely known, the town hosts summer vacationers seeking picturesque mountains to bike or hike in, the shimmer and wayward route of the Rio Grande, ideal for fly fishing, and a chance to step back in time and visit Creede's claim to fame—the silver mines, including the Last Chance Mine. Rightly named, I couldn't help but be drawn to this particular mine for my heroine and her plight in *Defiant*.

Most of the historic buildings on Creede's Main Street still stand today and host a multitude of shops and restaurants. Charlie's hangout, Tommyknocker Tavern, really does exist. Recently established in 1997, it is making a name for itself and, just as portrayed in the book, has become the town's present-day watering hole.

But the warm folks from Creede, who never tired of answering my questions and the friendships made, I will treasure most.

They say once you've discovered Creede with its abundance of outdoor activities, adventure, art and theatre, and its colorful past, you'll keep coming back.

Last Chance Mine in Creede, Colorado.

Creede & Mineral County
it is the place to be...

Late May	Taste of Creede Arts Festival · Nat'l Small Print Show Opens Quick Draw & Silver Chef Competitions · Art Auction
Mid-June	Father's Day Rodeo & ATV Poker Run
July 3-4	Creede's Annual July 4th Street Festival Fireworks · Colorado State Mining Championship Days of '92 Mining Events · Elks Lodge Annual Dance
Mid-July	Creede Woodcarvers Rendezvous
August	Rock & Mineral Show
September	Labor Day Weekend · Salsa Fiesta · Balloon Festival Creede Mountain Run · Gravity Derby · ATV Rodeo
September	Cruisin' the Canyon Car Show Silver Threads Quilt Guild Quilt Show
November	Chocolate Festival · Scoop Chase

904 S. Main St · (800) 327-2102   www.creede.com

Keep reading for an excerpt from P. J. O'Dwyer's next novel

FORSAKEN

The third and final book in the

FALLON SISTERS TRILOGY

Available from Black Siren Books in July 2013

FORSAKEN

CHAPTER ONE

Laughter filtered through Devlin's Tavern on the outskirts of Rosslare, Ireland. A local pub, it catered to the villagers living and working near Rosslare Harbour and the tourists who found their way to the seaside village Dani Flynn called home. Tonight, it was brimming with business, and many a tip to be had, except she wouldn't be afforded the extra quid to line her pockets.

There was more to be made along the docks.

She reached into the pocket of her apron and touched the crisp one hundred dollar bill a handsome Yank had shoved in it when she passed by his table. Even the unexpected tip would be no match for the income she would earn tonight.

Dani filled her last pint of Guinness, leaned over the bar, the dark harp sloshing onto her fingers. She grimaced and wiped them on her apron. "That's the last you'll get from me, Rogan."

Rogan Gillis's blue eyes twinkled. "And where might you be running off to?"

He'd sized her up long ago—called her a fairy, no less, hair the color of moon-kissed sable. He'd once wrapped his finger through it, tugging a long strand as she passed by him on her way to the bar. She'd eyed him, her blue eyes sharp and questioning. He only laughed, his hand falling away.

She'd hurt him, and she was sorry for it. She'd known him most her life. A few years her senior, tall, blond, and a prize of a husband he'd be, had she taken him up on his many proposals of matrimony. But at twenty-seven, she'd make no promise to a man unless her heart followed, and sadly, it didn't for Rogan.

He kept his eye on her still, smiling, and nodded toward Patrick Malone. Close to sixty, still holding onto his dark youthful locks with just a touch of gray at the temples, he was busy belting out a tune while his daughter Darcy, a beautiful redhead, accompanied him on the fiddle.

"You'll not get me in trouble with the boss this day, Rogan." She slapped the top of his large hand and smiled. His fingertips, callused from working his farm, reached out, curving around her hand. But she pulled it away just as quickly. "I've already got preapproval from the barkeep himself." She gave a lift of her chin toward her employer. "I'll see you tomorrow, then, Pat."

Patrick Malone's tall frame spun around. He stretched the last line of "Danny Boy," his eyes black onyx, glimmering with purpose, fully aware the emotion he drew from the soft, sad tenor of his voice.

"Aye, tomorrow night it is." He waved a hand. "And take your supper. Rachel gathered it up for you and something to drink, mind."

"I'll do that, and thank her for her kindness, you will."

"Aye, I will indeed." His broad smile thinned. "And, Dani, I'll thank you to remind Kara she's walking a jagged cliff." Gone was the laughter in his voice, and with the added lift of his brow, he didn't need to say more.

"To be sure, you've got my word." She nodded and headed toward the kitchen. Kara Gilroy was not a subject she wanted to belabor with Pat. He'd long gone round the bend from her excuses for showing up late for work or not at all—tonight being one of them.

After clocking out, she took the brown sack with her name on it and a bottled water from the fridge. The Malones took care of her, and she loved them both for it. She unzipped her backpack and placed her supper inside, grabbed her sweatshirt as well, and slipped out the rear door.

She'd see Kara soon enough. It was Kara's message on her mobile earlier that had her begging an hour's leave at the end of her shift. She hadn't held out much hope, since Kara's absence had put them one shy a server tonight. But Pat had granted it just the same. She'd thank her staunch work ethic for that. In the nine years since her employ as a part-time server and now barmaid, she'd not missed her scheduled shift or arrived late.

She couldn't afford the luxury.

On her own since the loss of her dear mum at the age of sixteen, she didn't fall under the responsibility of the child protective services—which was just as well. Being a ward of County Wexford didn't appeal to Dani. As far as her da, she only knew of him, and it'd be a cold day in Hades before she'd reach out to him. Besides, she'd been earning a decent wage since finagling a job at Carrigan's Racehorse Stables where her mum had been employed till she'd . . .

A familiar pinch hit the back of her eyes, and she let the memory fade. She'd accepted her loss long ago—and the pity of Joseph Carrigan.

Grooming racehorses wasn't a chore. She had a knack for it, and taking care to bathe and see to their health each day was more reward. She loved them. Her wage could afford her space in a boarding house in Rosslare Village and the bus fare from Rosslare to the O'Hanrahan Station, where it was only a short walk to the stables. And the pub, which she worked at night, gave her a bit of cushion each month.

The night air blew cold across her bare arms. Dani shivered and drew her dark-blue sweatshirt on. Her pocket jingled, and she slung her backpack onto her shoulder and reached for her mobile, only to find she'd missed Kara's call. The dock was eight kilometers east. Squinting against the small screen, she frowned: ten forty-three. She'd be lucky to make it to the docks by eleven. There was no time to change or fancy her face with the makeup Tommy Duggan required that she and Kara wear to meet his clients whenever their ship pulled into the harbor.

His clients . . .

She'd just as soon forget their faces and do what she was paid to do. She only hoped that Tommy made good on their arrangement. The standard five hundred euros would help ease the burden this month. She still owed the garage for the repair to her scooter. *It's historic*, she smiled to herself. Or, as Pat would say, "More relic and undependable is more like it."

"Let him crack jokes," she muttered when she reached the bike rack and her 1980 yellow Honda scooter, complete with rusty fenders. So it wasn't a shiny Fiat or some fancy Renault 5. It didn't matter. She didn't have a driver's license—didn't need to have one for a scooter under 55cc's.

She wouldn't let her position in life or her education dampen her spirits. She'd never had the privilege of finishing school. She could read, but she wasn't much for figures and memorization. Even if she had the means to afford a car, she'd never put her head to passing a driver's test.

Dani fumbled inside the small pocket of her backpack for her keys, freed the scooter, and tucked the stiff, coiling lock in with her clothes. She automatically reached for her wallet. Her fingertips skimmed the soft leather grain and the teeth of a closed zipper holding her most important papers, and she relaxed.

The boarding house was affordable, yes. But many a thing went missing. Her valuables she kept with her: an old business card, a photo of her mum, and a worn legal document that confirmed who Dani Flynn belonged to— even if *he* never wanted her.

Her fingers tightened on the strap of her backpack. He wasn't her business. It'd be best to remember that and put the ridiculous notion of finding him out of her head. With the weight of her belongings firmly against her shoulders, she hopped on and started the engine. Tying her hair up and trapping a dark, wayward wisp behind her ear, she grabbed for her helmet attached to the back and started out.

The stone pub with its thatched roof and chimney disappeared behind a hill, leaving only a curl of smoke from the turf fire to blow against a blackened sky. With no moon to brighten the gloom, she took the road running along the jagged coast and headed toward Rosslare Harbour. The air was damp and cool against her hands. Summer on Ireland's east coast could never be described as balmy—more windswept and temperamental, like a woman, giving way to bursts of sun and rain on a minute's notice.

Dani took the curve and followed the rise of the road. To her left the Atlantic smacked the rugged cliffs, churning the water into an angry mix of waves and foam. On her right, the soft grass of the meadow swayed against a gentle sea wind.

It would be calming, if it weren't for the constant hum of her phone tucked away in the front of her sweatshirt. Dani had a fair idea it would be Kara's name backlit on her mobile. She wouldn't be fiddling with it just yet. Or she'd find herself in the hedges, to be sure.

A chain-link fence snaked along the harbor, guarding cold, industrial buildings. Large containers littered the shipyard, with the merest hint of a pilothouse cresting the warehouse she would be entering. Turning left, her bike bobbled over train tracks. She pulled through where the gate had been left open and angled her bike next to Kara's battered lorry. With a quick turn of the key, the engine coughed and sputtered into silence. Lifting her helmet off, she hooked it over the handlebar and got off.

The docks at a quarter past eleven were dark, particularly so without the moon, and quiet. The eeriness shook her to her marrow, and she yanked her phone from her pocket and dialed Kara.

"You're a bold one, leaving me to the mercy of Patrick Malone to explain your absence. I still need to get dressed, and I don't suppose you have a mirror to—"

"Shh. You jabber so, Dani Flynn."

Dani frowned into her mobile. Still keeping it against her ear, she crossed the parking lot. She glanced back to account for the number of cars. "Where's Tommy, then? I don't see his— "

"He's not here."

"Why not?"

"There's no ship tonight. I've something to show you." Kara's usual calm voice shook.

A trickle of unease entered Dani's bloodstream, and she hesitated, just a fraction, before entering the warehouse and shutting the door. "Where are you, then?"

She squinted into the darkness and took a tentative step. There were rows of towering shelves filled to capacity with storage units, leaving her sandwiched between walls of metal. At five foot two, she couldn't begin to see above the first row.

"At the end, on the right."

She moved further down. A hand shot out, pulling her around an enormous shelf, and she stumbled and fell.

Dani fought through the pitch black. Silky, long hair clutched between her fingers, the color, she knew it to be blonde. "Have you lost your freakin' head?" Her heart beat as though she'd climbed the highest hill in all of Ireland.

"Shut your gob, Dani," Kara hissed and slapped her hand hard against Dani's mouth, her eyes wide and staring down at her. "We're in a load of shite, and I need you to keep your wits about you. Can you do that?"

Dani shook her head, her own eyes growing rounder.

Kara removed her hand. "Did anyone follow you? You didn't see Tommy's black Spider?"

"No." Dani gave her a hard look and rubbed her lips.

"Shh."

"No," Dani whispered it this time. Straightening away from Kara, she sat up, the concrete cold against her bum. "What is it?"

Kara crawled over toward the edge of the shelf.

Dani pulled the straps of her backpack onto her shoulders and remained seated, blinking into the gray murk. They were in a corner of the warehouse closest to the pier, the thick metal walls making it difficult to hear anything but their heavy breathing.

Kara kept a steady watch toward the single door Dani had come through. "I went by Tommy's to get my bob. He carried on, complaining he didn't have it. He left me standing outside his apartment, the bollocks, too stupid to realize while he was laughing in my face and heading out with his man O'Shea, he'd forgot to lock the door." She turned and reached into her jean pocket and handed Dani a wad of euros.

Dani hesitated. The last thing she needed was Tommy Duggan angry with her. She could have waited until he paid her. Kara was impatient and stupid. Tommy was a businessman, aware of how much bob he had down to the last schilling. He'd miss the money, and he would know who took it.

"I don't want it." Dani pushed the euros back and tried to stand.

Kara's mouth twisted. "Do you never take risks, then, Dani?" Kara yanked her down beside her. "Well I do. I wanted the money same as you, only I took the risk. He owed it to us. Calling us last minute to hand-hold his so-called clients—at midnight, no less. Did you ever wonder who they are?" Their eyes met. Kara's usual light blue ones were dark and boring into her.

Of all the things to say.

Heat pinched Dani's cheeks. She had, on more than one occasion, spoke it aloud, her misgivings. Only to be—

"So you're going to ignore me, then. 'Tis fine. But you're here now, so live with it."

The purr of an expensive motorcar brought their attention around.

"Did you hear that?" Dani whispered, a shiver shooting down her spine.

Kara's grip tightened. "It's Tommy." The words fell from her lips in hushed warning.

Dani's heart jumped in her chest. He knew they were in the warehouse. She could explain she had nothing to do with it—the money. He might believe her, but then he'd beat it out of Kara until she came out with it. She couldn't let him hurt her. Tall, blonde, and at the moment incredibly without a brain wasn't reason enough to leave her to him and O'Shea.

"Let's go." She pulled Kara up with her. "We're only asking to get caught." Dani for one wasn't taking a hand to her face. "There's a back door. We double around while they're in the warehouse. If we're quick, we can escape them and put the money back."

"It's not the money he's looking for."

Dani stopped, her fingers digging deep into Kara's jacket.

"Ow. Let go of me arm."

Dani released her hold. "What did you do, Kara?"

"He lied to us. The people are not as he would have us believe."

"Then who are they?"

The doorknob rattled and creaked open. Thick-soled shoes clicked on the concrete floor.

"We're lost if we don't move." Kara grabbed her hand. "Don't make a sound."

They ran along the back wall toward a single door that opened to the pier. Dani's runners squeaked against the slick concrete floor, and she winced.

"Shite." Kara turned as they moved down the back row, her brows snapping together. "You're going to give us up."

"I'm—"

"Is that you, Kara?" Tommy's deep voice filled the warehouse. "Come out, luv, and we'll talk about a few euros and a certain thumb drive, then."

Dani swallowed and held tight to Kara's hand, still moving with her until they reached the door. Kara grabbed for the knob.

The male whispers behind them and the thump of heavy footsteps gave every indication O'Shea was with him. She didn't like O'Shea. He was stocky and thick with muscle to the point he looked as if he'd burst. His blunt, wide features made him look angry, even the few times he smiled.

They needed to get out. The door? Would it be—

The knob turned in Kara's hand, thankfully, and they moved through the door without a sound, Dani shutting it behind them.

"Run," Kara whispered back, and her grip on Dani's hand was gone. Kara headed left toward the shipping containers.

Dani caught up with her and cursed the pack on her back. They weaved between the painted containers, rusty and scarred, their height equal to that of a first floor apartment.

Dani stopped, grabbed Kara's arm, and held her in place. Both breathing heavy, Dani raised her chin, her eyes an accusing Celtic blue. "You don't own a bloody computer. I know what a thumb drive is. What the devil are you doing with it?"

Kara pulled out from her grasp and kept going. She shifted her head back, her blonde hair whipping around her face. "I'll tell you." She gasped for air. "I promise. But move your arse before they catch us."

Dani's senses sharpened. The usual sounds along the dock became a little more disturbing. The wind had strengthened, whirling her hair about her eyes. The sea that had been calm earlier slapped the bulkhead with a ferocity only the Atlantic could deliver. She clenched her hands, moist from a combination of the damp sea air and her own nervous sweat.

She followed Kara, legs pumping, looking for an escape. And to where, she thought? They might outrun him tonight, but depending upon Kara's confession, she might never rest her head down in peace.

All her life she'd worked hard to survive on a ration of income. She didn't require much, a dry roof and a warm bed. But she wanted more and chose unwisely. For what, mind you? So his clients could relax a bit after being locked up in tight quarters for a week or more at sea. And *her* ridiculously dressed in high heels, slim skirt, and blouse like a professional bitta fluff from Dublin.

How incredibly stupid, Dani.

Tonight she certainly wouldn't be afforded a moment's leisure under a blackened sky with the threat of rain.

Dani ran even with Kara. "They're going to catch us."

Kara slowed and eyed their surroundings. "To the left. We hop the fence and hide on the freighter."

The freighter loomed above several stories high, with containers stacked like children's building blocks. It was the one thing she could see. But unlike the blocks of a child, they offered no delight—only a desperate attempt to hide.

Kara darted around the last container in the row closest to the fence. Dani came behind her. They grabbed onto it and hoisted themselves up. The metal shook in Dani's hands and gave with hers and Kara's weight, leaving it to bulge out, making it awkward to climb.

Cursing the added weight of her backpack, she grabbed the fence above her and climbed higher, refusing to free herself of her belongings. No matter what it took, she'd scale the fence. Whatever Kara had taken, merely giving it back wouldn't suffice.

"He's going to kill us, you know. Whether you opened the files or not, he'll be a fool to assume you haven't." She kept climbing.

"Is that all you can do is complain and worry?" Kara breathed hard. "Next time I'll take me own bob and forget about yours."

Dani gave Kara a sideways glance. "Like I asked you to put me in the middle and make me to run for my life. I don't mind hard work, Kara. I've done it most my life."

Angry, and with good reason, she'd been blathering on, climbing without a care for its difficulty and had left Kara to struggle below. Above her remained only a few handfuls of chain before she reached the top.

Razor wire, gnarled and glistening sharp, ran the length of the fence. *Shite.* They'd both be bloodied and shredded once they crested the top.

"Kara," Dani whispered down, her voice harsh with insistence. "Hurry—"

A door flew open and slammed, metal to metal.

"They're on the dock." Dani couldn't control the tremor of her voice.

Footsteps echoed in the distance. The height of the containers left Dani to wonder how close they were getting.

"The docks," Tommy's voice burst low with demand and impatience, and Dani froze unable to move.

I'm going to die.

Kara's blonde hair, a mass of tangles, spanned her shoulders and back. Her face tilted up, and she frowned. "I'm stuck. It's my jacket. It's freakin' hung up on the fence. Go it without me. I'll catch up." Kara continued to go at it like a snared rabbit ready to chew off its foot.

Leave her to Tommy and O'Shea? No. She couldn't do it.

Dani moved down. "Where are you stuck, then?" She angled her head to get a look.

"It's caught. The zipper." Kara tugged on the jacket, cursing.

"Leave it be. I'll get it." Dani grabbed for the corner of the jacket and pulled, trying to free it. The full weight of her body and the backpack made it a burden to hold onto the thin metal of the fence. It dug into her palm and fingers. "It won't budge. You'll have to take it off."

Kara shimmied out of the left sleeve, and Dani helped with the right.

The footsteps came first—hollow, metallic, and much closer than before. Dani glanced over her shoulder, and her body grew incredibly cold.

A Message from Black Siren Books

In an effort to support horse rescue organizations and their mission of rescue, rehabilitation, and education, P.J. O'Dwyer and Black Siren Books will donate a portion of all Fallon Sisters Trilogy book sales, and all future literary works purchased through **www.pjodwyer.com** or the publishing house of Black Siren Books, to horse rescues around the world.

ABOUT THE AUTHOR

Born in Washington, D.C., and the oldest of five children, P. J. O'Dwyer was labeled the storyteller of the family and often accused of embellishing the truth. Her excuse? It made for a more interesting story. The proof was the laughter she received following her version of events.

After graduating from high school in the suburbs of Maryland, the faint urgings of her imaginative voice that said "you should write" were ignored. She opted to travel the world instead. Landing a job in the affluent business district of Bethesda, Maryland, as a travel counselor, she traveled frequently to such places as Hawaii, the Bahamas, Paris, New Orleans, the Alaskan Inland Passage, and the Caribbean Islands.

Today, P. J. lives in western Howard County, Maryland, with her husband Mark, teenage daughter Katie, and their cat Scoot and German Shepherd FeFe in a farmhouse they built in 1998.

P. J. is learning that it takes a village to create a writer and relieved to know she's not in this alone. She's an active member of Romance Writers of America. She also participates in a critique group, which has been an invaluable experience with many friendships made and an abundance of helpful praise, and, yes, criticism. But it's all good. Improving her craft is an ongoing process.

Writing is a passion that runs a close second to her family. When she's not writing, she enjoys spending time with family and friends, fits in her daily run with her husband, and tries heroically to keep up with her daughter Katie's social life. Who knew how demanding the life of a teenager could be, especially for Mom?

When asked where she gets her ideas for her stories, she laughs ruefully and says, "It helps being married to a cop." Actually, she admits, "Every day I find a wealth of possible stories and plots in the most unsuspecting place—my daily life."